The

NICHAN

SMILE

The
NICHAN
SMILE

C.J. MERWILD

THE NICHAN SMILE
C.J. Merwild

Edited by Meredith Spears, Enchanted Ink Publishing
Coralie Jubénot aka C.J. Merwild asserts the moral right to be identified as the author of this work.

ISBN Hardback: 979-10-699-5779-4
ISBN Paperback: 978-2-9574532-0-7
ISBN Ebook: 978-2-9574532-1-4

Legal deposit: February 2021

FOR BENJAMIN

The

NICHAN

SMILE

TULEEN
SEA

ARAO

ZATO

SURHOK

KAERMAT

SIRLHA

SARUAN

PAPEMA

VHULAT

KEPAM

TANMA

CHILSA

NOKTCHEN

VISHA

BERAAKAN
SEA

ZIRU

MEISHUA

MAPPING OF THE ARAO BASED ON THE KAIBALAR ARCHIVES

FOR RISKAN MAKOUN. THIRD UNAAN OF THE RISKAN CLAN

RIGHT ARM OF THE ARAO

OSSKA LAKES REGION. SOUTH TORBATT. Y 181 aGE
COROMAN CONTINENT

PART ONE

LOST CHILDREN

I

THREE NICHAN BOYS HID IN THE THICKETS.

The oldest, Mora, served as a defense between his younger brothers and the potential danger he'd accidentally led them into. The one in the middle, Beïka, pulled on his eldest brother's tunic. Caught in the cold of early winter, he shook and sweated all the water out of his body at the same time. To his right, the youngest of the boys breathed with the same discretion as boiling water. As mist filled his sight, he covered his mouth to stop condensation from betraying their presence.

This one was called Domino. And what he saw over his brothers' clenched shoulders and the dark foliage was as ordinary as it was frightening.

Humans. Two men.

They weren't the first humans the three nichans had met. Kaermat, the coast village where they'd grown up and just left in a hurry, was home to more than one representative of this species. Domino had been around them near and far since his birth. However, these two individuals were different. Their tight-fitting garments, cut from many pieces of gray fabric pleated here and there, were not Torb. Domino had never seen such clothes. They seemed foreign; from the north, perhaps. Or the east. And although their attitudes didn't display any form of threat, the sabers they wore at their waists didn't send the same message.

One of the men got up. He was tall for a human and wore his dark hair cut short under a dirty sheet hat with worn, leather-rimmed edges. His pale, sunken face was speckled with red around his eyes, mouth, and nostrils. He coughed, rummaged the walls of his throat, and belched deeply before spitting a blood clot into the campfire—it hissed as it died on the flames. His companion, sitting by the heat, didn't flinch, although the projectile passed close by his ear.

"Fuck it," grunted the spitter, lifting his hat to scratch his head. "I'm done. Get the rope ready. Let's get it over with."

"Where are you going?" asked the other when the first one retreated from the camp.

Stepping over the tall grass, the human untied the belt holding his thick pants on his hips. "I'm gonna take a shit. Wanna help?"

"Don't get lost like last time. I won't come looking for you."

The first man marched in silence, didn't even make any sign to indicate that he had heard this statement. Before disappearing between the trees, the man threw his hat back with the same exhaustion that weighed on his every move. The hat flew through the camp and fell back to the child who rested by a haversack, eyes closed, face down.

A child.

Not two, but three humans.

The youngest of the three nichans stretched his neck to get a better look at him. This little human was a pale, tiny, scrawny thing. His crown of blond hair stuck to his forehead by a thin layer of grime. His arms were like twigs, so frail a simple gust of wind could have twisted them. He kept them wrapped around scratched knees bent against his chest. He wore thin, stained nightclothes and boots on his feet.

Is he sleeping? Domino wondered.

He moved up a bit to try to discern the little human not through but over the blackish leaves this time. Before he had a chance, the man by the fire sneezed his lungs out, frightening the birds perched in the branches and almost snatching a stupefied cry from Domino. The child tucked his neck in, made himself as small as possible while the sound of sputum disturbed the camp. When the man took his hands away from his face, his palms were stained with blood. Like his friend who'd left to relieve himself, his skin was studded with red dots, his bloodshot eyes darkened with deep circles.

"Faces, witness me." The man slid his palms down his pants, painting streaks on the fabric. "You're not worth a damn." Silence.

Even Domino held his breath, his pulse still running too fast in his veins.

"All this trouble for a kid," the man added, wiping his nose on his sleeve before angrily pulling at his collar. "Look at that costume. Why am I going through all this shit? For what, huh? Five hundred myrts. You Sirlhains don't know how to estimate a man's life. Mine's worth more than five hundred fucking myrts. Whereas yours—hey! You listening, or . . . "

A deep frown showed behind the myriad of red dots puncturing his skin. On the other side of the camp, the child had still not reacted, as if asleep or too weak to open his eyes.

"Oh yes, I forgot," the man said with a bitter sneer. Then he spoke words unfamiliar to Domino.

This time the little human raised his head and opened his eyes. And what eyes! Amber, like fire, and black extending from edge to edge. His heart hammering against his ribs, Domino stretched his neck out to look at them.

Even at six, he knew humans looked no different than his brothers and him. "We are bigger and stronger than them, but our camouflage is good," Ako, his mother, told him one day. "The Gods did a good job."

This child looked human, but his eyes, not so much. Was the reflection of the campfire to blame for this illusion? But Domino couldn't guarantee his own eyes were failing him. Night was never far, even in the middle of the day.

"That's what I thought," the man continued. "You're not only an abomination, you're also a bit of an idiot. Don't worry, it won't last. I'm done too."

He left the rolled-up blanket he was sitting on—each movement evoked those of a man responsible for carrying the weight of the world in addition to his own—and rummaged through the bag next to the child. The boy tensed as the man approached, closing his trembling arms around his knees. From his bag, the man pulled a rope and a flask. He hesitated, then unscrewed the cap and drank a good shot of whatever it contained. He coughed even more, enough to startle the little thing curled up at his feet, eyes wide open behind the hair that hid half his face. When the man handed the bottle to him, the child retreated into himself, eyelids fluttering fast as if a slap had been close to meet his face.

"You're right," the man said. "You don't start fires without fuel."

He poured the rest of a brownish liquid all over the boy. On his clothes, his hair, his white hands. With such a small body, a single flask was enough to soak him. Beyond the bushes, Domino clenched his fists. He looked at his older brothers. From them came no reaction, no movement, no sound. To remain undetected was essential. Domino couldn't grasp how they'd come to be this close to these humans. Hunger, exhaustion, or both? But he'd understood for some time that he, Mora, and Beïka would stay under cover until the danger had passed. There was no telling what reaction these two humans would have if the brothers were discovered.

But more and more, a cold, suffocating presentiment swelled in Domino's chest. It warmed him to the point of discomfort and pressed on his bladder. He understood what that feeling was when the man in the camp grabbed and unrolled the rope hanging from his arm, prepared a simple knot, briefly tested its strength, and then passed the noose around the child's neck, like a thread in the eye of a needle.

The child jumped again when the man grabbed him and set him on his feet.

Domino froze. A small, flesh-colored wing with a thin, translucent membrane darkened from the middle to the tip, and another, much larger, opened and closed and stretched in frantic motions behind the child's back.

Wings! A little boy with wings.

A worried look in his eyes, his frail body trembling, probably cold to the bone, the human boy swayed on his legs. The man tightened the knot around the child's throat, as unfazed as a man trimming his nails. Then he knelt down to take the boy's shoes off. It was too much for the child, who shouted in a broken voice and pushed the man away with force, as if pain came from revealing his toes.

With one hand the man captured the child's bony wrists. "Don't be a pain, not now," he said without interrupting his work. "We've been this far. Just let go." The first boot fell on the side, then the next one opened under clumsy fingers.

The little human struggled all the same. His naked foot struck the man, missed him, and the child collapsed when big hands laid him flat against the wet earth and anthracite grass. Keeping the child down seemed to be a trivial concern as the second boot was quickly removed. The child screamed again. It was the cry of a trapped animal, mad and heart-wrenching.

"Shit!" Mora swore as the child fell backwards, his unnatural wings disappearing under his body.

The curse was spat in a breath. Domino snuck a quick glance at his brother, whose dark olive complexion had lost its color. When he turned his attention to the child still resisting his captor, feet kicking like those of an upturned beetle, the second man was walking back to the camp, feet sinking deep in the ground, finishing tying his trousers.

He looked up at the ashen sky, darkened here and there by the inky stains of the Corruption, and pointed to a branch. His companion nodded, grabbed the end of the rope snaking on the ground, and threw it over the branch. The other yawned as he pulled the rope. The little boy's body was soon dragged along by the traction. Pulled by the neck, the child was yanked up, and up, and up until his feet were several inches off the ground.

Beïka gasped. Mora reached back to silence his brother.

Behind them, tears covered Domino's cheeks.

The little human struggled, his feet shaking in the air. On his back, his most developed wing flapped in the wind as if to fly away. The other hung lifeless, useless. The child tried to grab and loosen the rope holding his throat. Impossible. Those skinny arms were far too weak. Beneath the dirt, his white face turned scarlet. He was no longer screaming.

A deadly silence choked the air.

Domino panted in the same erratic rhythm as the child's legs, this icy feeling exploding in his chest. It was what he had sensed without being able to name it. He had known things would turn badly. He had felt death coming. His breathing quickened. He ignored the mute warning Beïka sent him through a black glance. Nothing mattered more than that suffocating child; nothing mattered more than the echo of the screams he had uttered before . . .

That damn rope.

It was going to kill him.

Those men were killing him.

A scream shook the forest, betraying its peace for good.

Everyone looked in Domino's direction when he stood, screaming, full of rage and sorrow, his dirty face streaked with tears. There was nothing his brothers could do to stop him. Too late for that. Domino was already jumping over the bushes, charging at the two men who were putting the little boy to death.

It all happened in a handful of heartbeats, like in a waking dream. One man drew his blade. Mora and Beïka rushed after their little brother. The other man shouted something, let go of the rope, and put his hand on the hilt of his saber.

The little human crashed to the ground. Without thinking, Domino threw himself on top of him, covering him with his barely taller frame. But it was enough to shield the other boy.

Domino shifted his eyes to his brothers. With grins stretching from ear to ear, both of them had pulled out their long fangs. Their claws stretched out. Their skin was now as dark as night, like smooth leather, their eyes completely black.

They were already fighting. The hangman fell first in a hissing gasp, his mouth lacerated and spitting waves of striking red blood. Ruby flesh slapped the earth nearby. The tongue had been cut clean.

At only seventeen, Mora was already taller and more vigorous than the remaining human. The latter held his weapon in both hands, trembling but his eyes bright with resolve. Mora and Beïka circled around him. With agility, they avoided the edge of the blade, which passed within a hair's breadth of their tensed muscles. The miserable man lost his balance, the weight of his weapon—or his own exhausted body—dragging him.

It offered a perfect opportunity for the nichans to attack.

Mora grabbed the man's arm hard enough to force his hand open, his sharp claws biting into the flesh. He squeezed harder. The man screamed as his skin and muscle parted from his bone. The blade fell to the ground. With a desperate growl, the human tried in vain to claw the nichan in the face with his free hand. It soon got stuck in the vise of Beïka's jaws.

The man was left with only his voice to scream some more. Blood colored the scene, from his shoulders to the crackling fire. Domino turned away his ever-watery eyes. Ignoring the screaming and the humid sound of crushing bone, he stared at the child he protected. Still alive. The stench of alcohol and filth burned his nostrils. Then he discovered the boy's luminous eyes up close. Black and amber, fringed with short blond eyelashes. These eyes gave him back his gaze. The little human then coughed, his wheezing breath pathetic at best.

Hurrying, the young nichan freed the boy from the rope encircling his neck and pressed a hand to his shoulder.

"Breathe," Domino said, his face wet, snot running from his nose to his lips. "You breathe, okay?"

The human was still shaking. He pushed away the hand Domino had put on him and rolled to his side. He squirmed on the floor, as if in pain.

No, Domino thought. *He's trying to run away from me.*

A red, wrinkled, bloody burn marked the delicate skin of the child's throat. His squirming was that of a suffocating fish on the bank. His irregular breathing seemed too shallow to fulfill its goal. Yet not for a moment did he stop slowly crawling away.

A rough hand grabbed Domino's arm. The child thought the end was coming for him. In his shock, it took him a full second to recognize his brother Beïka standing next to him, his mouth dripping with human blood, his eyes filled with anger.

"You fucking moron! What is wrong with you?"

A resounding slap collided with Domino's cheek and the child cried again, trying to push his brother away as much as free his arm of his grip. "Let me go!"

"You want to get us killed, huh?"

"No!"

"Then what's your problem? Are you a hero? You're not a hero. You're just an idiot." Beïka hit his brother in the face again.

Domino screamed, defended himself with his fists, then showed his teeth.

Before the enamel met the flesh, their elder brother approached and shoved them apart. In the icy air laden with black dust, Mora gauged the other two nichans from his full height, holding each of them by an elbow. When he freed them at last, leaving bloody imprints on their brown skin, Domino stepped back and returned to crouch beside the human still crawling away.

Mora stared at the two children and for a moment opened his lips, the vague shape of a word modeling their curve. Whatever he wanted to say never came out. Instead he turned to the two bodies lying in the middle of the camp.

Domino dared to look in their direction. There was blood everywhere, more than he had ever seen or thought two humans could contain. Only human blood. A severed arm lay a couple steps away. The tongue had not moved, like a dead worm lying in the grass. In the small camp, the atmosphere had darkened, slowing down the shy light of day. Black particles, thicker than smoke but thinner than ash, drifted all around them, following the current of the wind. But the thick mass they formed came down like snow toward the corpses.

The Corruption. It loved death and embraced it. Soon it would cling to the surface of the two bodies, wrapping them in its black veil, making its way through every orifice. It would attract spirits.

"They must be buried," Mora said.

He searched the camp, messier than it had been minutes ago. He quickly put his hand on the shovel the humans had brought with them. Another token of death. One never left a human or nichan corpse out in the open, for no one wished to share this world with spirits. Even a child as young as Domino knew this fundamental rule.

"We're not leaving?" Beïka asked as he scanned the surroundings loaded with death, as if new assailants were about to attack them.

Domino mirrored the reaction, the nape of his neck stiff with cold and shock, his cheek burning with pain. He instinctively leaned over the little human boy, ready to shield him again if any other fool charged them to seek revenge.

The shovel sank into the rocky ground. Once, twice. Then Mora stood up, spotted a second shovel, and pointed at it. "First the dead," he reminded his younger brother. "Help me."

Beïka sighed. "We should just leave. Who cares about them?"

"Right now, Beïka. The sooner we get it done, the sooner we'll leave."

An infallible answer.

They dug a hole and threw the first man in. They did the same for the second dead man, throwing arm and tongue with their respective owner. Wet earth covered both graves, blocking the black dust's path. The Corruption dissipated, drifting away with the wind.

Then silence, and as the area cleared, a bird called in the distance.

Domino's brothers knelt down, side by side. The young boy didn't miss a single step of the ritual that followed.

Hands raised to the sky, Mora recited a few words. "This is your bed for the days to come and for all eternity. Find rest and forgiveness, for we have forgiven you. May you reach the realm of the Gods. Faces above, bring us the Light. Let it shine on the way."

It was over.

Mora approached the travelers' haversacks and searched them, soon to be followed by Beïka. They found leather flasks filled with water, but for some reason, Mora disposed of them. In the end, they set aside matches, a cloth bag filled with flatbread and dried meat, and a square satchel rattling with the sound of clashing coins. The same bag snatched a smile from Beïka before Mora took it from his hands.

Then came the turn of the human child.

"Domino, come here," Mora called, but the little nichan refused, pressing himself by reflex against the child who had finally given up running away. Domino knew Mora wouldn't beat him—he never had. Yet he feared the punishment he would have to face as well as the disappointment in his brother's eyes. "By the Faces, Domino!"

Mora walked through the camp, cleared now that the dead were out of the Corruption's reach. He stopped near the two children and lifted his little brother's chin. No surprise or annoyance appeared on his face when he discovered new tears in the youngest child's eyes.

"Why did you save him?" the teenager asked.

The answer was obvious to Domino, but under his brother's insistent gaze, he answered anyway. "He's very small and he was in pain." His sobbing resumed. Air was pain in his lungs, and he took a deep shaky breath.

"You could have been killed. That child . . . You saw his wings? He's no ordinary human; he's a Vestige. Do you know what that is?"

The word was familiar, but Domino shook his head nonetheless. Adults said so many things, gave so many orders, then added more words as to make everything confusing. How could he remember everything?

"Mom told you about it, Domino. Everyone in the village talks about it. Vestiges can be dangerous."

"No, not him," Domino said, shaking his disheveled head. "He's very small. He can't hurt. The others wanted to hurt him, but we don't hurt children, do we? We don't put ropes around their necks. We . . . we can't . . . we can't . . ."

Breathing turned into a beloved memory as emotions grew inside him, filling all the available space. It was no longer a question of finding his words but rather of freeing himself from the crushing weight resting on his chest and thoughts.

Mora applied a tender hand to the little boy's tousled hair. "I know, calm down. Breathe, Domino."

"We . . . He comes with us, right? He's hurt." Domino swallowed a boulder-heavy sob, raising his eyes to his brother's face.

Mora thought for a moment, watching the surroundings, then looked down at the small figure lying in the vegetation. "We can take him with us, but . . . No, no, no. Don't be too happy. Domino, if the clan doesn't want him, there's nothing I can do about it. It's not up to me. Do you understand what that means?"

"He's . . . nice," Domino said to defend his cause, sniffling between words.

"Do you understand, Domino?"

"You want to take it with us?" Beïka asked. He swayed from right to left behind them, his patience about to fail. "You said it was dangerous."

"I said he could be."

"That's enough for me. I say we leave it here. Mama wouldn't want that thing with us."

He's not a thing.

"He's coming with us," said Mora. "It's too dangerous for him out there. He won't survive on his own."

"So what?"

"We didn't take all these risks to leave him behind. Now shut up! He's coming with us."

A smile appeared all over Domino's face, and he turned to the blond child. Having squirmed in all directions, the young human had pushed back the hair previously stuck to his face. On his dirty skin was a fresh burn, pink and swollen in places. It covered the left cheekbone and part of the child's forehead. Domino failed to suppress a gasp. When his hand reached out in spite of himself, the human turned away, burying his face in the plants on which he lay.

"It's all right," Domino told him. "We'll be there soon."

"I don't think he speaks our language, Domino," Mora said.

Mora carefully grabbed the human who, once again, struggled. The teenager didn't seem to mind this reaction, for a nichan would always be stronger than a human. After a while, the little boy resigned himself, letting Mora carry him, his thin arms hanging along his body.

Walking beside his older brother, Domino grabbed the tiny, pale hand swinging in the air and squeezed it once. When the human boy lowered his strange eyes toward him, Domino offered him a bright smile. As if touched by a flame, the human snatched his hand back.

II

THE FOUR BOYS HADN'T SLOWED OR STOPPED SINCE THE morning.

"I need to pee."

Everyone finally halted at Beïka's pressing demand.

The sky was at its highest pitch of light when it came time to rest and drink from the stream running swiftly beside their feet.

Not a fish in sight, yet the water was clear, every single pebble coating its bed visible through the undulating swirl. Mora collected some in the palm of his hands and brought them up to his little brother's mouth. Domino drank, water dripping down his round chin. Several sips in, his attention veered back to the human who, curled up against an old stump, hadn't made a sound since they'd rescued him two days and two nights earlier.

Mora sighed. "Domino, drink some more."

"I have," said the little boy, his black eyes searching for answers in the prostrated posture of the other child.

Who was he? Where had he come from? Was he in pain? That upset pout on the lines of his mouth most definitely meant pain.

The human didn't speak, barely drank, only let himself be approached when it was time to get back on the road. Whenever his orange eyes landed on Domino, they were cold as ice—like the rest of his person—and hard as steel. His body vibrated without interruption, even when he lay close to the campfire Mora had lit for the night, making a good use of their newly acquired matches.

"Humans are more sensitive to the cold than we are," Mora had explained as he'd led the way, the child half asleep in his arms, jumping intermittently, hiding his face behind his hands.

Originally from the northern territories, nichans, whose lively blood was infused with the Gods' Lights, proved to be more resistant than humans during the winter. And their thick skin protected them from many other threats.

"We have to drink more than that," Mora insisted, forcing his little brother to face him with an inflexible, wet hand. "Hey, are you listening?"

Food was running out. Apart from the supplies collected from the belongings of the men they'd killed, the four boys had nothing to eat. There wasn't a beast around, and hunting required time and celerity. Moving forward and reaching their destination would be quicker. They had to save food and strength and fill their bellies in any way possible. Drinking was the key. Without it, they would quickly weaken, and Mora didn't have the strength to carry his brothers in addition to the human, he said. They had to hold on.

Domino bowed over the stream and sucked up small sips, his lips and nose grazing the wavy surface of the water. Not far away, having finished urinating against a tree, Beïka turned around and laid his eyes on the human. Domino immediately recognized disgust in his brother's expression.

He stood up, his face wet. "Stop."

The human was as still as the stump supporting his back, eyes lowered, his blond eyelashes brushing against his cheeks. Beïka approached anyway, wiping his tacky hands against his pants.

Domino leaped to his feet. "Stop!" he shouted again in a high-pitched voice.

Beïka only obeyed when their older brother ordered him to leave their protégé alone.

After several minutes of tense rest, they set off again. Domino kept casting suspicious glances at Beïka.

The human's face remained concealed behind his hands.

Blood lined the road leading to their destination.

Mora stopped as he discovered their route—and the surrounding half-naked trees—splashed with dark trails carrying a stench of carrion.

Beïka stepped closer to the stains, sniffed the air, mouth partly open to taste every note of the smell on his tongue. "That's blood? Look, it won't stop."

"Where do you think you're going?" Mora caught him by his collar with the hand not busy holding the human.

"What? It's not that way? You said to follow the water."

"You stay close to me," Mora ordered. "Domino, be careful. Don't step in the blood."

The tracks were thick and bright on the surface of the flattened grass. They stretched on and on, their density diminishing little by little, even though the stench remained.

Following his brother closely, Domino kept watchful eyes on the ground, mouth dry. Concentrating on his every step, darkness casting a shadow over the forest, he ran into Mora. The teenager had just stopped.

Before them, the stream continued straight on and disappeared under a high bamboo wall. The group came to a halt. Voices came to them along sounds of a nearby presence. Many heartbeats vibrated against Domino's eardrums. The little boy sniffed the air. All he could detect was a faint smell of smoke and burnt fat, similar to the one coming from the lamps they used at home.

"I think it's there," Mora said.

Following the blood as if this path had been left for them, they found themselves face-to-face with a massive double door decorated with grease lanterns swinging in the nocturnal breeze with a slight squeaking noise. The sound of metal against wood reached them from the other side of the ramparts. Domino was far too small to see what was beyond. He looked down and clutched his brother's tunic. The hemorrhagic thing that had left its stench for miles had passed through the gate they now faced.

In Mora's arms, the little human also stared at the dark, impenetrable walls. Biting his lip, Mora laid him down on the ground—Domino jumped at the occasion to approach the child, who rolled into a ball, his expression fierce—and took a step toward the door.

There was no soul in sight, only the flickering glow of the lamps through the veil of dusk.

"Hey! Anybody there? Hey, is that the Ueto Clan?" called Mora, standing before the door nearly twice his height.

No answer except the distant cry of a bird, for only birds dared to live near nichans.

Mora cupped his hands. "Please! We need help. Hey!"

Several seconds passed during which Domino doubted having found the right place, fearing the silence would become eternal.

"Maybe they're dead," Beïka said, his eyes still on the blood trail.

Mora ignored him.

A head appeared over the wall. In the darkness, it was impossible to discern its features.

"Hey! Ohay, is this the Ueto Clan?" Mora cried.

Voices rose up on the other side of the bamboo, unintelligible.

Above the wall, the slightly disheveled figure turned around and said, "Kids. Four of them."

"We are Ako's sons. My brothers are with me," Mora added.

He avoided talking about the human they brought with them. He'd told Domino that he was a Vestige, who were rumored to be dangerous. Would this reason deny them entry? They couldn't hide the boy's wings for very long, or even his eyes, unless he closed them.

A creaking shook the group, and Mora stepped to his left to stand before his brothers. The doors opened, revealing more lamps hanging along a path that had no end in sight. One massive individual appeared in the opening, shirtless, bearded, and bald. He was covered in blood, the same color that stained the road.

From the ramparts, the other silhouette disappeared.

Domino grabbed the human's hand and squeezed it, and, as two days earlier, the human moved away, keeping his hands out of reach. Domino agreed not to touch him again when the newcomer stood in front of Mora, close enough to study his face.

"Ako is your mother? Are you Mora?" the man said in a deep voice. The blood had dried on his muscular hands, arms and chest, cracked where the skin was solicited, like a network of roots.

Mora let a long second pass before answering. "Yes."

"By the Faces!" the man said with calm. "You look just like your mother."

"So I've heard."

"It's me. Ero. You might not remember me," the man said, and Mora remained quiet for a handful of seconds. "The last time we saw each other I was probably in a cleaner state."

"Yes, I remember, of course."

Domino couldn't tell if his brother was a good liar or not.

"Mom left the clan when I was three. I was too young to

remember Ero," Mora had said a few days after being separated from their mother.

"She doesn't like him," Beïka had recalled. "We shouldn't go there."

But they were here now, because Mora had made it clear: "She wouldn't send us to Uncle Ero's if it was dangerous. Now stop it. You'll scare Domino."

Which Domino had been quick to deny.

Now that he had his uncle in front of him, the young boy repeated the same words to himself. *I'm not afraid, I'm not afraid.* Lying ran in the family tonight.

Even stuck in his human form, like all nichans had been since the dawn of the Corruption, Ero was an impressive beast. His broad shoulders were all muscles, just like his neck; the curves of his thick thighs were evident through the linen fabric of his pants. He was more than a head taller than Mora. His bald head and part of his face were marbled with long, deep scars, as if someone —or some creature—had tried to split his skull in slices.

Beïka, eyes wide open, was stunned.

Except for his black eyes and brown skin, their uncle didn't look like their mother at all. Ako was of a smaller build—enough to pass as human—like Mora, and thin despite her powerful limbs.

But above all, she wasn't there. Domino couldn't resist looking back, as if his mother was about to emerge from the dark forest to finally join them, as she had promised.

"Where is your mother?" Ero asked, his eyes still on his nephew's face.

Mora released a trembling breath and shook his head. "I don't know. She sent us here. There were . . . problems at home."

"Problems."

"The Blessers' partisans."

Their uncle's expression adjusted to the news, casting deep

shadows over his eyes. Mentioning the Blessers' followers often had that effect on people's faces. For Ako and her sons, the presence of the supporters of the eastern cult in the vicinity of their village had marked the beginning of an ongoing separation.

Ero nodded and placed one of his huge, bloody hands on Mora's shoulder before withdrawing it, probably remembering that even dried blood was messy. "Your mother was right to send you here."

He monitored the rest of the group. Ero's gaze lingered a little longer on the human child, briefly deepening his frown. The child didn't react, unlike Domino, who came closer to his pale body folded in on itself.

Ero was still a stranger to them, so it would have been difficult for Domino to judge him on this first impression. On the other hand, he'd heard bits of conversations between his mother and brothers about the man. One thing was certain: their mother had left her clan because of her complicated relationship with her older brother.

"He disappointed me. I don't know if I'll ever be ready to forgive him," Domino had heard during a meal, paying only half attention to the conversation keeping their small house lively.

Forgive what? He didn't know, but it was enough to instill caution in him about his uncle.

Another man came out of the village gates and stood next to Ero. He was much younger, perhaps Mora's age, and his face was peppered with freckles and curiosity.

"Need help?" the newcomer asked. His enthusiasm dissipated as soon as he discovered the Vestige. "What's it doing here?"

Ero turned to the newcomer. "Javik, go back and tell your mother about our guests. Have someone get them something to eat. Something warm."

But the teenager remained camped on his feet, unresponsive to orders. The human then noticed the attention that had just turned to him. He lowered his chin. In his back, one of his wings unfolded to wrap itself around his right shoulder, protecting him like a shell.

"Papa . . ." Javik turned pale, his black eyes ranging from Ero to the human.

"Don't make me repeat myself, Javik."

The man and his son stared at each other and words passed between them without the need to utter a single one. With his jaw clenched, the teenager finally obeyed Ero and returned to the village.

An owl hissed in the distance. By reflex, Domino had placed himself in front of the human.

"Come in," their uncle said, once the uneasiness was partly over. "We've just come back from hunting, so don't mind the mess. You're going to eat and rest. I'll pass by the baths. That's no way to welcome family."

"Thank you," Mora said.

Inside, the village paved with stone slabs here and wooden planks there consisted of bamboo huts on stilts. They were black —flames kept vermin and humidity at bay—and their roofs were rounded, vaguely resembling the shell of a walnut. Unlike Kaemat, the village facing the sea in which the three brothers had grown up, Surhok was built around a small central square in the middle of which stood a large bronze bell suspended from a barked trunk carved with spirals. The enormous tooth of a beast hung under the skirt of the bell. At the end of the square, away from the houses, was a building with a pointed roof overlooking all the others. This building had no windows. Like the rest of the houses in the village, this huge structure rising to the sky had been burned black.

Surhok Sanctuary, Domino guessed. Most towns and villages where nichans lived had one.

Even at this late hour, the village was still bustling with life.

Through the evening mist, many eyes cast curious glances at the numb and exhausted children arriving from the Gods only knew where. Most of them quickly noticed the small blond head carried by Mora, with his strange eyes and asymmetrical wings. But no one acted beyond those intrigued glances, as if Uncle Ero— Unaan of the Ueto Clan—at the head of the group was enough to legitimate their presence.

The newcomers understood moments after entering the village, where the blood trails they'd followed for so many leagues came from. In the central square, a group of men and women expertly peeled and dismembered a nohl. From up close, the giant centipede beetle reeked of iron and excrement. One of the women had her arm buried up to her elbow in the insect's entrails. With a sharp jerk, she freed herself, her brown skin beaded with clotted blood. At the end of her arm hung a viscous sac streaked with green veins, of a yellowish color recalling a pus-soaked abscess.

Fat. Nohls used it to keep their newly killed food fresh in their nests. Nichans burned it for light.

Domino had never seen one of such size; at least sixteen feet. More than twice the height of an adult nichan. A thousand questions bubbling in his mind, he moved away from the specimen, whose scattered guts glowed under the lamps and torches.

Ero left his nephews there, abandoning them to the mercy of curious looks and the strong smell of blood. He returned a few minutes later, washed and dressed in a warm beige tunic. He invited the three brothers and their protégé into the village sanctuary.

They entered a large room filled with long tables and benches. It was lit by grease lamps placed everywhere or hung from hooks, projecting a dim light that struggled to reach the high, dark ceilings. A few nichans ate and chatted at one of the tables as they entered, but their attention quickly faded from the children.

Food was served to them. Mora sat down with Ero at a different table from his brothers. They were close enough for Domino to hear their conversation, though he already knew what his older brother soon told their uncle.

They'd left their mother at dawn about three weeks ago. Domino and Beïka had helped their brother count the days. What was meant to be a distraction had later turned into a source of worry. Their mother had promised that she'd eventually follow them, that if all went well, she'd even be able to catch up to them within a few days. Domino now assumed that nothing had gone well. After more than two weeks, Beïka had asked not to count the days anymore, getting angry when Mora insisted on him continuing.

"Do you know why she decided to leave you?" Ero asked.

"She said there were Blessers inland, close to our village. Or partisans, she wasn't sure. Apparently they'd captured several nichans and humans. She'd heard they were closing in on us. She told us to leave, that she and other people in the area would try something to fend them off."

At the other table, Domino looked down at his full plate. He dreamed of digging into the steaming, spicy meat and tasting the turnips that came with it. His stomach grumbled, hollow. But he didn't like to eat without everyone at the table, so he didn't touch anything. To his right, Beïka coughed and grabbed his clay cup to help swallow the food he choked on. He always ate too fast. To Domino's left, the human stared at the grease lamps burning on the table.

He's waiting for Mora to eat too, Domino thought.

"Know that your mother will be welcome when she arrives," Ero said to Mora. "However, you are my responsibility for the moment. Do you understand?"

"Yes, I understand."

"You'll have to swear an oath to me. Only nichans who do so may stay. A matter of precaution. Do you know what it is?"

"The oath? Yes."

"You boys don't have a chief, do you?"

"No."

"No, of course you don't. No need to worry about that. It won't be a blood oath; you and your brothers are just passing through. Your vows will suffice for now. As I said, nothing to worry about. We'll see about that when the time comes."

Mora nodded and thanked Ero before getting up.

"One more thing." His uncle stopped him, and Mora turned to him, tense from head to toe as Ero stared at the little human with a glance sharp enough to cut through flesh. "Can you explain that to me?"

That? Domino frowned, upset. This human child was no object or beast, even if his behavior . . . He was a person, not *that*.

Mora looked over his shoulder at the human and took some time to consider before answering. "About two days ago, we came across some humans. They were going to kill him. Purify him."

The deep burn imprinted by the rope on the child's throat was as noticeable as his inhuman eyes.

"So you saved him?" Ero asked, and tension moved from one body to the next, leaving Domino stiff on his bench.

How would he be punished when his uncle learned that he'd endangered his brothers by attacking these two humans? Beïka had slapped him that day. The punishment to come would probably leave a more noticeable mark.

"It just happened," Mora said. "We didn't think." Even Beïka stopped eating at these words and gave his little brother an unpleasant look. "I know he's a Vestige but . . . he's just a child. I thought he might have a better chance of surviving if I took him. The Blessers have no hearts. We do."

"You have a point," Ero confirmed. "But humans aren't meant

to grow with nichans. Least of all Vestiges. We're not in Netnin here. This isn't a freakshow."

"I know."

"Anything strange happened since he's been with you?"

"No. No, nothing at all. He doesn't talk. He's a bit of a wild thing. They had time to hang him," he whispered. "I don't think he speaks our language, though. We found this on the men we killed."

Mora held out the leather satchel, which chimed as it landed in Ero's palm. The man opened it and chuckled. Mora hadn't let them look inside, but he'd told his brothers that the money in that purse could have bought their house ten times over, if not more.

"Sirlhain myrts," Ero said. "Did you count them?"

"Two hundred silver heads and change. I don't know much about Sirlhain money, but one of the humans mentioned five hundred myrts."

"You understood what they're saying?"

"They had an accent, but I'm pretty sure they were Torbs. I have the feeling someone hired them to kill the child."

"Paying them in Sirlhain currency," Ero whispered as he looked down at the Vestige. "The Sirlhain Blessers kill the Vestiges, and nichans they capture themselves. They have no reason to hire foreigners to do their dirty work. Somebody went through a lot of trouble to get rid of this kid."

Mora cleared his throat. "You can keep the money."

Ero smiled slightly, as if amused by this generosity. His expression seemed to say, *You bet your ass I'm going to keep it.*

"If the Vestige is Sirlhain, we have someone here who can talk to it," Ero announced, awakening Domino's attention. "I'll send her when I have time. Maybe she'll be able to find out exactly where it came from, and if it's wise to keep it here."

III

THE HUMAN'S NAME WAS MARISSIN. MEANINGLESS. HE'D WIPE it out of his brain if he possessed such power. If someone called him that again, he'd feign ignorance. No one would know the truth. He'd never say anything.

Never.

Hidden in the shadows, he curled up and hugged his legs. Through the many pounding footsteps coming from all sides, he knew safety no longer stood, that he'd be caught eventually. He blocked his breathing, tucked his neck in.

Go away, you don't want to find me. Just leave me alone.

A mute and useless prayer. He'd begged anyone willing to listen to be left in peace since those men had come for him. No one listened. The Gods had not answered a single prayer for nearly two centuries. They'd disappeared. Their beautiful faces no longer brightened the sky. It was the first thing ever taught to Marissin.

Leave me alone . . .

These people, so tall, with their dark eyes, wouldn't respond to his plea. Only unknown, incomprehensible words came out of

27

their mouths. Even if his prayer turned into a scream, the only result would be a sore throat.

Long, bare feet passed his hiding place. The child followed their progression.

Go away!

Then the same feet retraced their steps. When they stopped in front of him, Marissin straightened up like the rope that had been passed around his neck. Instinctively, his hand covered the aching wound circling his throat. If they captured him, would they put another rope around his neck? It had felt as if they'd tried to separate his head from the rest of his body. He . . .

No, not now. It was that memory, that feeling that no words could convey, that threatened to surrender the rest of his strength. He couldn't afford to think about it.

After his escape, he hadn't gone far—it was no wonder he'd been found so easily—yet a glimmer of hope had turned him into a fool. A fool who could not run, who could not go back home. No one could be trusted, he was certain of that. Not a single soul, not when even Mother had left him . . . No! This memory had to be suppressed as well.

A shadowy face appeared in front of the corner sheltering the child. The newcomer sighed before saying something in his unknown language. Then he extended his hand toward the human, who reacted by reflex. A faint squeak escaped his lips as he bent down to grab this outstretched hand with his teeth. His jaw snapped in the air. It didn't stop a second attempt, and another. Each missed its target. The person facing him yielded and growled something. It was an expletive, Marissin was sure of it.

The table above his head suddenly shook and then rose with a loud grinding sound. Light invaded the child's hiding place, and he unfolded his legs to flee. But where could he run? A fool, through and through.

So the tallest of the boys grabbed him in his arms and shattered his hopes.

DOMINO SHOULD HAVE BEEN in the water by now. The fumes rose up behind his back, their comforting warmth inviting him to forget about everything else and immerse himself completely. He'd gotten rid of his wet, cold clothes, exposing his skin to the soft clamminess of the baths, and then turned to the human. Mora had found the blond child in no time at all. It had to be said: the winged boy reeked of sweat, piss, and filth. Any nichan could have tracked him down with eyes closed.

"Go wash yourself, Domino." Mora had repeated himself more than once, but his little brother still didn't obey.

Domino wanted to wait for the human. In his condition, the child would probably need his help to clean himself. On the other side of the long room, Beïka was vigorously rubbing his belly and arms with soap. There were no such places in Kaermat. Soap, a bucket of water, and a sponge had always been enough. Here the instructions were different: they would wash from top to bottom in front of a fountain that could be activated with a pump. Then they would rinse themselves under the same fountain before going to the stone basin flooded with hot water to warm up and loosen their muscles. To bathe in cold water, one had to turn to an identical basin on the other side of the room.

A pile of clean cloths and towels had been placed at the baths' entrance.

When Domino turned his attention to the human, Mora undressed. Wordlessly, the teenager sniffed his tunic and rippled his soft face in a deep grimace. Then he grabbed the braid of black hair resting on his shoulder and repeated the same process.

Each gesture was studied to serve his purpose: it was time to wash.

It didn't have the desired effect. The little human pressed himself harder against the wall.

"He doesn't understand," Domino said, noting that his brother's impatience was beginning to wane.

"Of course he understands. He's just scared."

"Why? We're nice, aren't we?"

Mora sighed and rose to his feet, unraveling his long braid. "The door is locked. He's not going anywhere."

"But he must wash himself. I can help him."

"Forget it."

How? Domino looked down at the human and wondered if he could ignore his presence. His wings, his fascinating eyes, his hair that must have been golden underneath the dirt. After a brief reflection, he decided that it wasn't possible.

"This is the last time I'm telling you this—go wash yourself, Domino." Mora walked away, took the rest of his clothes off, and sat on a low stool in front of one of the faucets. When the water began to pour, Domino was still studying the human's curled up body.

There had to be a solution. That stench, that filth, not to mention the boy's blood-crusted nails and skin—Domino could stand neither the sight nor the smell of it. They awoke discomfort in his belly while reviving the memory of the man pulling the rope. The child probably ignored how badly he needed a bath.

He was scared. That was why Domino had to help him.

It would be impossible to carry the child to one of the fountains and clean him, yet Domino couldn't stop marveling at the thought. He'd saved this boy's life. Bathing him would probably be child's play. Mora had done this dozens of times with his brothers when their mother was busy. Domino still lacked strength, but he could do it. He had to, otherwise who else would take care of this little one?

He walked to one of the fountains and pressed it down several times. Water sprinkled on his legs and feet; it was hot. A glance over his shoulder reassured him. The human had not moved an inch. Domino took the brown soap from a small wooden dish and one of the cloths hanging on a hook and passed them under the water. His fingers disappeared under the lather, and a strong, musky scent mixed with the surrounding sweat.

Now ready, he returned to the boy, whose wide eyes promised danger ahead.

"Just to be clean." And Domino crouched down in front of him, gently bringing the wet cloth to the child's pale face. The child moved backwards, his gaze going from Domino's to the cloth carefully wiping the corner of his chin.

The dirt gradually faded away, and Domino continued his cleaning, gaining confidence with each passing swipe over the jaw, the cheeks, the brow. He avoided the sensitive burned part on the boy's temple and forehead.

Before him, the little boy was as still as a rock, but the tension in his body was thickening the hot air into paste. The thunderous beating of his heart reached Domino's ears. The nichan slowed his movements. A small voice whispered to him that he was taking a risk.

Yet the human was letting it happen.

This was permission enough for Domino. "The rest we must clean up too," he announced.

He reached out and grabbed the hem of the human's tunic. Before he realized his mistake, Domino was shoved by two small hands. He collapsed backward, right onto his ass.

"Domino, get away from him," Mora ordered.

Domino froze, staring at the child, who now rubbed his filthy hands all over his face. The shock of seeing his help and efforts rejected was more painful than the hard stones against his cheeks. What was the reason for this? What had he done wrong? Domino only wanted to help him. If the human let him, he would see that Domino meant him no harm. Until he was older and big enough to fight, this was the only place where he could prove himself useful. Maybe he had to try harder.

Yes, harder.

As he stood and walked forward again to take over the human's ablution, a hand gripped Domino and shoved him away. Breathlessly, the child dropped his cloth and soap.

"Leave him alone," Mora said, frowning, the spitting image of their mother at that moment. "Go and wash. Now."

At last Domino obeyed.

———

THE DARKNESS WAS a poor attempt at familiarity, although Marissin was used to it. He'd spent most of his life lying on or sitting in its cold embrace. It seemed to him that all sorts of things could, like him, lurk in the dark—things with no faces, waiting for him, preparing to hurt him.

The darkness had always been there. Then Mother came, the sound of her footsteps gradually approaching. The door opened, and she joined him in the back of the room only lit by a white crystal lamp that sizzled continuously. In the distance, the man in black waited. He didn't move, didn't utter a word. He always stayed too far away for Marissin to discern his features.

Mother watched, judged, then talked. "I can see you didn't sleep, Marissin. You don't have to wait. I'll be back when I'm back." She opened the Artean, the Book of Blessings, placed it on her lap, asked Marissin to sit up straight and listen with all the attention the Gods had given him. The little boy listened, as concentrated on the words Mother recited as on the movements of her thin lips, of her white fingers on the worn pages. However, no matter how much attention she forced him to devote to the teaching, he always ended up looking toward the door.

Leaning against the frame, the man watched them with his arms crossed.

Mother would finish reciting her verses, finally feed her son, then get up to leave, sometimes allowing herself a caress on Marissin's hair. Every time he looked up at her, she would remove her hand and step back, clenching her jaw.

"Don't look," she'd say, raising her voice. "Eyes like yours must stay on the ground. Do you hear me? I told you that a million times. Don't look at me."

So he lowered his gaze, tears gathering at the edge of his eyelids. Then she left the room, only to return hours later. The man would disappear with her on the other side of the door. And Marissin couldn't sleep.

It was unlikely the man would come back tonight. Marissin had not seen him since the two strangers had taken him away. Neither him nor Mother.

Now sitting in the corner of the dark room, he fought to keep his eyes open. Since the three boys had found him, he'd barely slept. He wouldn't close his eyes. Behind his eyelids was a rope and two men to pull it hard enough for Marissin's body to fly and hurt. Sometimes he didn't even need to see it to feel the burn on his skin and the air leaving his mouth in a mute cry. But it was getting harder and harder to stay awake.

The others lay on a mattress settled on the rough, woven floor, eyes closed, breathing peacefully.

They'd been brought here after their bath.

The bath. Torture. The two tallest ones had washed Marissin without giving him a choice while the smaller one looked across the foggy room. The human had struggled. His chest swelled with fury that he was too weak to fully express. He'd screamed and cried. He didn't want to cry—tears were the statements of the weak, Mother used to say—but this treatment had overcome his resolve. He didn't like their hands on him. He hated the imposed nudity just as much. It didn't matter what their intentions were, or that the human was covered with dirt so thick it ran down his legs to the slabs on the ground in dark nets. No one was to touch him. The Book of Blessings said so.

Mother had said so. "People . . . people like you taint the air. They make the milk curdle, and they darken the sky. The Corruption is such that anyone who touches you will see their soul blackened, stained by the Corruption as well. O Marissin," she moaned as she took his hand, letting it go immediately. "Giving birth to you has already damned me. As Blessers, it is our duty to erase this defilement. It's the only way to return their Light to the Gods, to bring them back. I . . . I didn't think it would be this hard." Tears had filled her blue eyes, and she'd left, refusing to be one of the weak.

He rubbed his face and shook his head, as much to chase away this memory and the voice that echoed through it as to keep himself awake.

What was the point of all this? She'd read the Artean day after day, had dictated a course of action to him—what he could do, what he could say, what actions would cost him punishment. But outside the dark room where he'd lived, the world was absolute nonsense. Everything was brighter, blinding sometimes, and at the same time so much more frightening. She hadn't prepared him for what was on the other side of the door. It wasn't fair to him to have botched such a teaching.

Marissin was doing his best. When someone spoke to him, he looked down. But these men had hurt him. He'd let himself be beaten despite the rage bubbling inside him. Then he'd fallen into the flames . . .

"The way of an abomination is submission. Don't look. Don't answer. Don't fight."

He'd disobeyed Mother. He'd fought and watched. Now that he'd tasted the forbidden, its sweet flavor had become addictive. He couldn't help himself. He wanted to look and see what would happen. It gave him . . . strength. But it went against his faith.

Without Mother to guide him, what could he do? He missed her. He resented her. He wanted to see her. He hated her. Every emotion almost suffocated him. Truth be told, it was easier to hate her than to mourn her presence. If he learned to hate her hard enough, would he stop hurting? Could he even achieve that?

As sole answer to his thoughts, his stomach growled. He pressed his hands against his belly as one of the boys stirred on the bed. It was the smallest one. Lit by the lamp hanging by the front door, he sat up as he rubbed his eyes, his wavy short hair pointing in all directions. Marissin pressed harder on his stomach, but there was only one way to hush it.

He couldn't see the boy's eyes but knew they were watching him. For a moment, the room and its inhabitants remained still.

Leave me alone. Don't look at me.

Marissin wanted to lower his eyes, as he'd been taught, mainly to divert attention from himself.

Another fool move. The moment he looked away, someone would catch him. Who would catch him? Anyone. There was always someone to trap him as soon as he let his guard down, and there was nothing he could do against the powerful hold of their arms.

The black-haired boy tilted his head to the side. *"Korono ʃhi otta?"*

It was only a whisper, other words whose meaning passed beyond Marissin's comprehension. On the mattress, the little boy looked around. He got up, and Marissin suppressed a sob. The other child turned to the window and tiptoed up. He turned his back to Marissin, hiding his actions. Water splashed on the black-haired boy's feet, but the wriggling of his toes was his only reaction. There was a loud scraping sound, and one of the other boys rolled and grumbled on the mattress — though no waking up on the horizon.

When the younger boy turned around, he held something in his hands. After a few steps sprinkled with a little water, the child stopped and that something he held appeared before Marissin's eyes: a cup filled with water. The boy didn't come any closer. Marissin had used all his strength to push him away in the baths, and he would do it again if necessary.

Without making any sudden movements, the black-haired boy squatted down and put the cup on the floor. He tried his luck and pushed it with his fingertips a few inches toward Marissin, who stood motionless, stunned. Then the other one left him in peace, going back to lie down on his mattress.

Silence returned.

Marissin stared at the cup with his swollen eyes. The flame of the lamp was reflected on the water. He'd never seen a flame before the men took him away, only the white crystal that lit up Mother's pale face and red hair and crackled endlessly.

"Fire will make you pure, my son." A promise.

He missed the white crystal.

He missed Mother.

He was hungry.

He threw himself on the water and drank it as his stomach growled again. And in spite of himself, he fell asleep a few minutes later, his face pressed against the wooden wall.

I V

AFTER THE NEWCOMERS WERE ALLOCATED A SMALL HUT, THEY were offered a place in the large dining room of the sanctuary. They settled there the following day, as quiet as rocks, sitting at one end of an empty table. After a moment, Mora motioned to stand up. All around them, other nichans brought food from what must have been the kitchen.

Before Mora was up, the young man called Javik approached them. He carried a steaming dish of vegetables. Behind him, a little girl followed, dressed in the same plain, blue tunic that all the kids wore in the village. Her arms were charged with plates and dishes. She must have been a little younger than Beïka, wore her long hair parted in two braids, and had mismatched eyes — one black, the other water green.

They lay their burdens down in front of the boys.

"This is Memek, my sister," Javik said.

Nodding in their direction, the little girl greeted them, then, with a movement so simultaneous that it seemed rehearsed, she and her brother focused their gaze on the human.

No clothing was adapted to the child's unnatural morphology.

So they'd found clothes too big for him whose seams and aging weave threatened to tear with every move. On the back, two slits had been roughly cut to accommodate his wings.

Next to him, Domino bent forward to set up the flatware, hoping to divert the attention of their visitors with a little hustle and bustle.

Mora got up. "So we're cousins," he said, helping his little brother arrange the pewter and clay plates.

Javik and Memek didn't seem to be leaving, but they'd only brought four plates. They didn't intend to share the meal with them and had come only to offer their own to Mora and his brothers.

Unlike his little sister, Javik looked away from the Vestige and forced a smile. "You don't remember me either, do you?" he said to Mora.

"Actually, I do. I remember a little boy running naked through the village on rainy days."

Javik laughed more sincerely than he smiled. "All the kids do that."

"They don't all do it carrying a hen over their heads and hoping to fly away."

Domino had no idea what the two boys were talking about. He would have gladly asked, but he kept his eyes on Memek. She stared at the little human, head tilted to the side, an enigmatic smile on her lips.

She noticed Domino's worried look and immediately turned her attention to Beïka. Children always did that. Their eyes never stayed on Domino for too long.

"Can your Vestige speak?" Memek asked.

A plate in his hands, Domino opened his mouth to answer. Beïka went ahead of him, generously helping himself to the sweet reed shoots and turnips. "We found it in the woods. It was screaming like a pig being butchered."

Domino shuddered. On the bench, knees bent over his frail chest, the human peeped at the vegetables.

"But it talks, yes or no?" insisted their cousin, and her brother and Mora turned to her. "Just make it talk."

"I can't. It's half wild," said Beïka. His plate was filled at a glance.

Mora took the spoon out of his hands. "Who told you to eat everything before anyone else?"

"I'm hungry."

"Does it have the gift?" Memek continued.

Next to her, Javik pursed his lips, studying the child with unblinking eyes. Where Memek seemed fascinated about a rare specimen, her brother showed more circumspection.

"Of course it doesn't. It's dumb," Beïka said.

"He's scared. Leave him alone," Domino cried, seeing the center of attention hiding his face between his knees. Wrapped in his right wing, the little boy breathed hard but slowly. His shoulders shuddered with each passage of air through his lungs. Surrounded by all those nichans, he was tiny and yet unmistakable due to his light skin and hair. Domino's chest tightened. "And he's not dumb. He's nice."

No one paid any attention to him. Memek asked again if the child could speak, and Beïka received a slap to the back of the head when his words became too coarse for a twelve-year-old.

After that, their cousins took their leave. Unlike them, they said, they ate either in their hut or at the big table near the brazier, with the clan chief and his partner, their parents.

But before leaving, Javik dipped his hand into his trouser pocket and placed a handful of sparkling silver coins on the table. The young man smiled at Mora, responding to his surprised look. "The booty of a hunter. Twenty heads. I'm sorry not to bring you the rest of it. My father is a hard man to bargain with."

Most nichans followed this same ritual, sharing the fruits of hunting and crops in their own hut, or in the sanctuary. Since meal times depended on each individual—and their habits and chores—the main sanctuary room was always half empty when the boys came to eat.

However, on the third day after their arrival, the hall filled up entirely in minutes. The wooden benches scraped the floor in a continuous cacophony (the human sitting between Domino and Beïka cowered, pressing his hands over his ears), and nichans sat right next to them, some waving at them, sharing names, others smiling in a friendly manner, staring out of the corners of their eyes at the winged intruder, who followed the three brothers everywhere. Everyone feasted in a din of conversation, laughter, metal banging metal, liquor constantly filling empty cups.

Uncle Ero ate with his partner and children at the other end of the room. He gave his nephews but a brief glance that day.

Something was missing.

First of all, their mother. Days went by, and no one showed up at the gates of Surhok. Mora asked his brothers to be patient, which was neither of their fortes. Domino often woke up at night and wondered where he was. When he remembered that their mother wasn't around, his heart became overwhelmed, and new tears stung his eyes.

Just like him, his mother hadn't been sleeping very well. When he struggled to find rest, Domino would turn to the lamp burning on the other side of the bed, huddle up against Ako, and follow the movements of her nimble fingers as they patched his worn-out tunics—until he was old enough to do it himself, like his brothers—sometimes until dawn returned. Then they would get up together and go out to fetch water from the well, listening to the waves rolling and crashing on the shore. Domino insisted on carrying the bucket no matter its weight. Then he would help his mother prepare breakfast, recognizing the signs of her good mood in her offering to cover his cassava with a drizzle of honey.

Besides her alarming delay, there was an almost total absence of activity. Everyone in the clan lived at a steady pace. Chores were everyone's lot, and days were short. When they still lived with their mother, the three boys took care of their responsibilities throughout the day. Cleaning, cooking, clearing traps outside the village or the nets in the sea, picking up fruits from the trees in the area, clearing the vegetable garden. Things were no different here, yet no one asked for their help. Every day, their meals were brought to them without anyone expecting them to reciprocate, despite Mora's repeated offers to do so. Someone would always come to collect their laundry and bring it back the next day.

There was a simple reason for this: they hadn't yet sworn an oath to Ero, the chief of the Ueto Clan, and without this oath, Domino and his brothers were there as guests. Guests who were taken care of, but with limited liberties. They were no Uetos, and since their mother was supposed to join them here, they didn't have to be.

"We shouldn't take the oath," Beïka mumbled during lunch on the seventh day.

Mora looked up from his plate and peered around the room. Even though nichans' senses were highly developed, the words remained between them.

"What are you talking about?" Mora asked, relaxing.

"I don't want to take the oath."

"Why not?"

"Mama will be here soon, and we'll leave. Right? If we take the oath, it means she won't come back. He'll force us to stay."

This distracted Domino from his food. Next to him, the human had turned away from them to munch on a piece of meat, the juice of which ran down his wrists. Mora had stopped complaining about the boy's manners within a short time. As long as the little one ate without making any noise, it suited him, he'd said.

41

"Are you talking about Ero?" Mora asked.

Beïka raised his eyebrows as if the answer was obvious. "Who else?"

"Do you think he's forcing us to stay?"

"Maybe."

"And what's in it for him? Can you tell me? No, don't answer now. Think before you speak."

Beïka darkened and hit the bottom of his plate with his spoon again and again. Unlike his brothers, he'd already finished his lunch.

Mora finally answered. "Tell me, Beïka. The food you're eating right now—do you think it falls from the sky, sent by the Gods? We are mouths to feed. It's Uncle Ero who feeds us. These vegetables come from his gardens. It's he and his hunters who go out to brave the world so we don't starve."

Beïka turned pale, and Domino looked up, his lips forming an O. Ero approached them, close enough to have heard Mora's words. Their uncle smiled.

A woman was at his side. Domino knew at once that she was human. Much smaller than Ero, her skin was black and her frizzy hair as dark as Domino's. She was dressed in the Torbatt fashion like all adults there, wearing a dark blue tunic cinched at the waist with a shawl partly thrown over her shoulder. But what caught Domino's attention was the woman's left eye. It was entirely blue—a pale, pearly blue—with no pupils or irises. Like a small blackbird egg, or a round, polished crystal. The other eye wasn't as disarming, of a deep brown color.

Strangely, it was difficult to determine this woman's age.

Ero and she stopped at their table.

"What kind of a person lets his nichan brothers and sisters starve to death?" their uncle said.

Mora stood up. "Good morning, Uncle Ero."

The man turned his attention to Beïka, then Domino, who

nodded to him. When the man lowered his eyes to the human, every trace of his smile vanished. The child returned the look, a wing spread around his shoulder, chewing his piece of meat ever so slowly.

Domino had noticed that the human had been chewing carefully since the first meal he'd agreed to share with them. That day he'd left a tooth behind. A baby tooth, fortunately, but the blood covering it proved that it hadn't been meant to fall out yet. Domino had retrieved the tooth that lay on the corner of the table, thinking that the child didn't possess anything, and here he was, falling into pieces before his eyes.

Beïka had taken the tooth from Domino's hands and thrown it into the village woods once out of the sanctuary. "It's fucking gross! Why are you doing that?" the boy had scolded, and Domino had frowned.

"Why not?"

"Because it's gross. I just told you."

Ero motioned to the woman to his left. Her detailing of the human child lasted longer than the Unaan's.

"Matta will take care of the Vestige," Ero said. "She speaks Sirlhain and Tuleear. The rest of you, come with me. You will finish your meal later."

Domino froze for a moment as Beïka stood up and followed Mora and Ero. Leaving the human alone with this stranger? The woman probably didn't know that getting close to the child came at a risk. She wouldn't get anything but screams from him. If he didn't warn her, she'd lose her fingers. As Domino was about to open his mouth, the one called Matta grabbed the human's arm above the elbow and pulled him off the bench. He shouted, mouth still full, and clung to the table, trying to flee in the opposite direction. But nothing seemed to mar the calm and solemn expression of the woman, who carried the child out of the room without the slightest effort.

"Domino, hurry up!"

The young nichan had watched the scene in horror, not knowing whether to react or not. On the other side of the building, Mora called him again, and Domino found no reason to not join him. He took one last look at the spot where the human and Matta had disappeared, wondering if he had abandoned the other boy to a terrible fate.

Ero led the three brothers to the center of the great hall near the brazier, whose flames warmed Domino's face. If half of the sanctuary's occupants had ignored them before, they all turned toward them now, forsaking their lunch, when Ero stopped by the fire and announced loud and clear, "These children are going to take the oath."

Within seconds, all the nichans present rose to their feet, and a small portion of them left the sanctuary in great strides.

Domino's apprehension won him over. Unlike his brothers, the oath remained a mystery to him. When he'd asked Beïka about the subject, his big brother had replied that with this oath they agreed to belong to their uncle—but Domino had learned to question his brother's words. Mora, on the other hand, had said, "We'll be part of the clan. We will have a leader who will protect us and whom we'll obey. That's all right. We'll do that. You have nothing to worry about, Domino."

But the young nichan was worried, for if his older brother refused to reveal more, it was a cause for concern.

As if to confirm his thoughts, Mora put a firm hand on his brother's head and smiled when their eyes met. Mora and their mother were so much alike that it was disconcerting. They had the same square face, protruding cheekbones and large, tired black eyes. According to their mother, Domino and Beïka took after their respective fathers. Pity. Domino would have liked to look more like his mother, if only to feel as brave as Mora did today.

Soon, the sanctuary filled, and in less than five minutes, it swarmed with all the nichans of the clan. Everyone would witness this moment. For the sake of his own dignity, Domino hoped this oath wouldn't be painful.

"Mora," Ero called, and the teenager raised his chin and approached his uncle. "Are you ready to begin?"

"Yes," he breathed before getting himself together. "Yes." The second time, his voice echoed throughout the room, reaching the high ceilings, slipping between the thick wooden columns.

"Kneel."

Mora did as he was told and knelt two steps away from his uncle, who shortened the distance between them to an arm's length. Then the man looked for something in his belt and, finding nothing, sighed.

"Does anyone have a blade for me?" he asked.

Mora's shoulders tightened. So did Domino's. It wasn't what Ero had announced a few days ago. A blade to cut. To draw blood. When had Ero changed his mind? They were only passing through, he'd said.

A woman stepped to Ero's right and offered him a small, curved dagger, whose sharp edge shimmered in the light of the lamps.

"It better be clean," the man said with a slight smile.

Many nichans laughed at his words, and the woman shook her head in amusement, waving the thick jewels that stretched her earlobes.

"Don't keep them waiting," she said before returning to mingle with the crowd.

Ero smiled affectionately at her, then his attention was on Mora again. He requested the teenager's arm, who held it out to him after a moment of hesitation. Domino couldn't distract his eye from the short but shiny blade as it kissed brown skin. When blood ran down Mora's arm, the little nichan clenched his fists. They were going to do this to him. Cut his skin off.

Mora closed his fist in turn. There was a lot of blood, oily, rusty red, translucent and heterogeneous. Domino didn't hear his brother's and uncle's words. His whole mind revolved around the wound and the blood dripping on the slabs.

He didn't want the same thing done to him.

Then Ero put his thumb on the line of the blade and, once cut open, placed that same thumb against the gash crossing Mora's skin. The two wounds remained in contact for a few moments. Then the man sucked the blood from his fingertip.

If only Domino had stayed by the table. As he ducked away, taking a step backwards in search of a better place to be, Beïka caught him by the arm.

No! I don't want to. But there was no turning back. They would all go through this.

Suddenly a thunder of cheers and hammering heels shook the sanctuary from its foundations to its pointy rooftop. Mora got up, and his uncle patted him on the back. Someone brought a strip of cloth and tied it around Mora's forearm. The fabric swallowed the blood from the teenager's wound. He smiled forcibly. He sent Beïka to his uncle and stood near Domino, whose body mirrored the tremor of the flickering flames.

The blade ran this time along Beïka's arm.

"You'll be strong and brave, okay?" Mora said in Domino's ear, who once again stared at the blood flowing from the newly opened wound. "It hurts a little. Just a little. You can cry if you need to." Domino's panting breath subsided slightly. "It's okay to cry, but don't take your hand away. Do you understand?" Domino nodded. "Good. You will be strong and brave."

But Beïka's words from earlier suddenly came back to the boy's mind.

"Does this mean Mama's not coming to get us?" Domino asked.

Mora put back his hand on his little brother's head. "It's possible. I'm sorry."

Unease grew in Domino's throat. Could he start crying now?

New cheers rose all around them. Unlike Mora, Beïka's smile was colored with pride. His arm was wrapped in a bandage and an uncontrolled roar escaped him. A triumphant cry. He, who'd never gone a day without reclaiming the warmth of his mother's arms, with which she embraced him every morning, seemed to have suddenly changed his mind about the oath.

All eyes turned to Domino.

"Come here," Ero said.

For lack of other choice, Domino obeyed. Silence fell as his knees hit the stone. He looked up at his uncle. His dark figure was cut out in the golden light of the brazier on his back. He was so tall and looked so strong—a monolith rising from the earth. With the blade he held in his hand he could easily slice off Domino's arm.

"Give me your hand."

You'll be strong and brave, okay? Mora's words echoed in Domino's head, and his arm stretched out in front of him, trembling from the shoulder down. His uncle then bent and knelt on the ground to reduce the gap in height that prevented him from taking his nephew's hand. Ero's fingers were thick, warm, and calloused. They closed tightly around Domino's tiny wrist. Then the blade approached, inspiring retreat. It opened the skin widthwise in the middle of his arm. The lips of the wound spread instantly, accompanied by a burning pain that went up to Domino's neck. His tears flowed like his blood. In silence.

"My protection comes at a price," Ero said. "Swear to obey me, swear to follow me, swear to respect me, and it is yours."

All this?

Obey, follow, respect. Would their mother approve? Mora and Beïka had agreed. If Domino refused, would they throw him out? He would have no one left.

He nodded.

"Swear to obey me, swear to follow me, swear to respect me, and it is yours," Ero repeated. "Swear, my boy."

"I swear."

Ero sighed. "What do you swear?"

"I swear to obey you. I . . . and to follow you, and to respect you."

Ero's grip grew fiercer with each passing second; Domino could have sworn that too.

"I swear," he promised to end his torment.

He was sincere. He wouldn't let anyone separate him from his family.

As with his brothers, his blood was mixed with his uncle's.

He was loudly congratulated, and Ero rose to his full height before wiping the knife against his sleeve and returning it to its owner.

Domino suddenly felt nauseous, but he pushed on his legs to get up. Blood dripped to the ground, and his uncle frowned. The blood didn't pour from the cut on his arm. It was flowing from his nose. Domino raised his hand to his face, but all his strength abandoned him before his fingers reached his nostrils.

He collapsed backwards, and Mora's intervention was all he could trust to prevent his head from smashing on the ground. "Hey, are you all right? Domino, can you hear me?"

He could hear, but his answer didn't come.

Mora's arms tightened around him, shaking him slightly—or rocking him? The sensation was the same as the tide rolling against his body. "Domino, answer me!"

Domino was certain that if he spoke he'd throw up his lunch on Mora's lap. He couldn't tell his brother that, either.

"Domino! By the Faces! What's going on? What's happening to him?"

"He's young. That's a lot to take at his age," Ero said.

Domino closed his eyes. Around him the ceiling and its crisscrossing beams had started to twirl.

"Is it bad?"

"Probably not. It should pass."

"You don't know?"

"Take him to lie down. Go."

"All right."

"You, stay here. You'll clear your brothers' lunches."

"All right."

And as everyone moved around them, leaving the room, returning to their unfinished meal, Domino clutched his aching arm against him.

No one had remembered to bandage his wound.

V

WITHOUT EVER LOOSENING HER IRON FIST, THE WOMAN dragged Marissin through the great hall. She pushed open a door, pulling him into darkness, and the heat of a large oven breathed at their faces and took the boy by surprise. For a moment, he stopped fighting back, his eyes drawn to the gaping and burning mouth of the hearth where embers glowed a fierce red, before struggling once again. His feet, shod in worn leather savates, skidded on the stone, offering no resistance.

The woman tightened her grip on his arm. "Faces, witness me! This is difficult behavior."

What did she . . .

For the first time in days, words made sense, as much the plea to the Gods as the complaint.

Marissin was caught off guard and stumbled before getting his act together.

They progressed across the room. Another door was opened, and the outside light blinded the little boy. His heart drummed in his ears, and only now did he notice the slippery piece of meat between his greasy fingers. He wanted to let it go, but his fist refused to unfold.

In the next few seconds, woman and child struggled through the village, crossing the central square, its paving stones still stained with the blood of the huge nohl. The people present outside all seemed to be heading towards the large building. He and the woman entered the hut where Marissin and the three boys spent their nights.

The woman put him in a corner—the one where he settled at night—and finally freed him. "Don't move. Stay right here."

How good and strange it was to hear that woman speak words he understood. The men who had taken him away from Mother had spoken his language too. Not as well as this woman, though. Her accent was the same as he remembered, with subtly pressed consonants and a hint of unquestionable truth. It was almost reassuring, but not enough for him to lower his guard.

The woman scratched something against the wall and lit the lamp near the door, coloring the dark hut in a golden hue. She retrieved the stool on which the chamber pot rested and sat down in front of the child, staring at him with her luminous blue eye.

He wondered if she was like him, if she carried the same difference inside her.

The words of the Book of Blessings emerged in his mind. The usurpers' offspring should never be worshipped.

Her left eye . . .

Only one eye, either blue or red, or as dark as night. He'd forgotten the other shades. It didn't matter. The Matrons of Sirlha —mere giant crystal deposits whose claim to godhood was denied by the Book—had been destroyed. And the remaining ones would soon meet the same fate. At least, that was what Mother had said.

"The Matrons are an insult to our creators, Marissin. Usurpers! That's what they are. Other statements are lies. The prayers sung in their name are blasphemy. They turn men—good men, Marissin—away from our legitimate Gods. Faces above! These stones are even more dangerous than you. It's a good thing two of them were blown to bits. And their offspring . . . These men and women carry lies and our damnation in their wake," she'd said, fist over her heart, the other hand gradually erasing by dint of caresses the characters inked on the paper.

But what had she called them, these offspring, these apostates serving false goddesses? San . . . Santi . . . No, he couldn't remember. Yet, he'd listened to every word written in the Artean.

He didn't need to remember them. He knew this woman was one of the Matrons' progeny. An evil born after the coming of the Corruption. As was he.

"What's your name, young man?" the woman asked. Nothing but the creaking of the wood under her stool. "My name is Matta, daughter of Hope. Will you give me yours now?'

Still nothing.

The way she spoke. It had nothing to do with Mother's voice after all. Where was the shivering of lips, the confidence always on the verge of breaking, or the heavy swallowing of restrained sobs?

Marissin held his tongue. Matta had touched him, too, creating a bond between them. *It is wrong,* Mother's voice hissed in his head.

"You have a name, don't you? Everyone has a name."

The boy shook his head to avoid having to open his mouth.

Marissin.

No! No name. That child no longer existed. He'd stayed down there in the basement, waiting for Mother to return. Whoever stood here now, with his wings to the wall and his hands sore from the cold, wasn't sure of anything anymore.

"No?" Matta said, still standing upright on her stool. "Very well. We'll have to find you one, in this case. Start thinking about it. Now, where do you come from?"

Did he know? Saying that he came from a dark room didn't sound right. He came from Mother's womb; this he knew for having been repeated so many times. However, in light of the recent events, it didn't seem relevant to him anymore. He was alone now. The place he came from no longer existed, like his name.

"Where are your parents?" the woman continued, raising an eyebrow above her brown eye.

"Dead."

This answer eluded him in spite of himself. He hadn't thought about it until then, hadn't expected to be questioned about it. Was someone's infinite absence considered death?

When the door had opened that day there had been no Mother on the other side, just the man's shadow, then two other men. Mother hadn't protected him when one of them had covered him with a woolen blanket and lifted him up like a sack of grain. She hadn't saved her son from being thrown into the bottom of a cart. Neither had she stopped those men from looking at him, touching him, shaking him around. It was through her infinite absence that one of them had brought Marissin's face close to the campfire to get a better look at him in the dark. The teeth of the flames feasting on the meat of his temple forced him out of his sleep at night. His face was still painful today. He could see nothing out of his left eye—for as far as he could remember it had always been blind—but the pain in his eyelid was as unforgiving as the rope.

He'd been abandoned. He had no one. Dead. A word that somehow, deep down, meant *I'm alone*.

"I see," Matta said. "At least you're capable of speech. Do you know what you are?"

He hesitated, searching her words for a trap he could slip into. She'd already touched him. The link between him and the woman was made. Whatever the consequences, he would live with it. He could.

"Abomination," he said for the first time, an air of defiance passing through his eyes.

An abomination.

Soulless.

A thief of Light, the Light of the vanished Gods whose faces no longer colored the skies.

A Light tainted by the Corruption.

He could have replied that he was human, nothing but a boy, for that was true as well. But he wasn't going to pretend to be naive. He knew what others saw when they looked down on him.

Matta eyed him from head to toe and tilted her head to the side. Her scrutinizing gaze went right through him, as if every hidden truth about him could be collected with enough intention. That blue eye . . .

"What an awful word! How dare they? People here use the word 'Vestige.' Far more accurate and respectful, if you ask me. What I'd like to know is if you know what it means."

"Dead," the boy repeated.

She looked at the puckered wound circling the left side of his neck. He resisted the urge to hide it. So he let her watch. Everyone was watching. He had to show them it didn't affect him.

"You look very much alive to me."

"Soon dead."

"Nonsense. It doesn't have to be so. The nichans of this clan have no reasons to hurt you. People here aren't —"

Nichans.

The little boy's eyes widened, and his heart swelled in his chest, threatening to rip it open. Those people were nichans.

"Nichans," he said, shooting a look at the door.

"Yes, nichans," the woman confirmed.

"No."

"No what?"

He glanced up at her. She was so calm, as if unaware of the danger.

Nichans. Mother had talked about them. They'd been there since before the Corruption. "Beasts, they are beasts," she had said. She called them monsters, killers, repeated that only their presence prevented the Blessers from crossing the border to save the world from the usurpers still waiting for their sentence in the rest of the world. She said that they were cunning, that they'd learned to take human form, claiming it to be a gift from the Gods. "They're not human, they're animals. Before the Great Evil, nothing was worse than them. No, don't touch the Book!"

Beasts. The little one, hanging around him, with his tousled black hair, his grin, and his sad face. The tall one with his long braid and soft voice. The other one, whose disgusted expression felt like dirty hands on Marissin's body. All of them; they were all nichans. They'd all touched Marissin at some point.

The child rubbed his arms. He spread on his oversized tunic the fat from the meat he'd finally dropped, now lying on the ground.

"What kind of behavior is this?" Matta asked. "May I know what's gotten into you?"

Nichans.

The child remained silent and froze.

The truth was he didn't know how he was supposed to react. Every new piece of information triggered a memory in his mind. Mother knew everything, always had a truth to share about the world. This world, Marissin was finally discovering. The gray sky above him. The trees with their black leaves. White or pink worms swarming in the freshly turned earth. The wind, the sound of the wind, the caress of the wind, the bite of the wind. People, as tall as the man in the doorway, sometimes much taller, like all the people in this place.

Others, almost as small as him. Children . . . like him. He'd heard of them, never seen one before.

On the day Mother left him, the world had revealed itself in a series of colors, smells, and sounds that seeped into him to leave burning prints.

It was too much.

He lowered his head, pressed his forehead to his knees, and closed his eyes.

The darkness was short-lived. Matta lifted his chin and forced him to face her. "Always look at the person you're talking to during a conversation. Do not look down when I speak to you. It's impolite."

Don't look down.

Don't look up.

"There is no need to be afraid of me," the woman said without dropping his chin.

Marissin's stomach was in a knot. Several hiccups started through his chest. Enough of this! He fought for the control of his reactions and raised his head. He clenched his teeth and stared into Matta's eyes, as requested.

"Very well." The woman lowered her hand. "I see you've heard about nichans." The child's heart failed, but the digging of his nails in his fist gave him focus. "You have no reason to panic like you just did. Do I need to remind you that those children saved your life? They have no intention of hurting you for their own amusement, or at all. Unless you give them a motive." A pause. "People, humans or nichans, often have some concerns about Vestiges. The country you come from shows no mercy to your kind, that's a fact. Some people in Torbatt could be just as inflexible. However, the precepts of the Blessers have not been adopted by all Torbs. They—I can see by your expression that . . . Do you understand what I'm saying, young man?"

He said nothing. Matta spoke too much. He had a headache

on top of everything else.

She filled her lungs, joined her hands on her lap, and wet her lips. "I'll make it simple. Some people hate Vestiges. Others distrust them. Others are willing to live beside them. That is the case of my order. The nichans in this clan are suspicious, but they have no intention of hurting you. You seem harmless. Human Vestiges are rarely dangerous. Beliefs and superstitions have fueled hatred." She paused, then resumed her flow of speech, leaving Marissin both annoyed and calmer than he'd been in a long time. She had a soft voice and kept it low. Her full lips moved slowly, at a soothing pace. She was making great gestures with her hands, taking a few seconds here and there to silence, squinting her eyes, searching for her words. A never-ending pile of words.

When she finished her diatribe, she smiled slightly. "But you —you are able to control yourself. You are neither a plant nor an animal, am I right?"

"Yes," the child ventured.

Matta nodded and then leaned her head to the side again, looking at the child with the same disturbing look. Marissin couldn't help imitating her. He cocked his head, wondering if this movement would have the same effect on her, if it had a chance to reveal all her secrets.

She straightened. "It seems to amuse you."

He spoke no words, staying in that position. His heart had calmed, and he was able to swallow and breathe normally now.

Matta sighed through her nose. "I don't know if you have any talents due to the Light that touched you—you might not know of this yourself. That's what scares people, wrongly. Legends and rumors have emerged about Vestiges terrorizing people with the gift. Nothing but lies. It's extremely rare for a human Vestige to develop the gift. The vast majority of you is simply bothered by deformities beyond our knowledge. I wouldn't call your eyes or your wings deformities, but it is obvious that these attributes are out of the ordinary. Your wings don't seem to bother you."

He resisted the need to hug his body with his right wing. He often forgot that two of them were attached to his back. Out of the ordinary, yes, but a part of him.

Abomination, whispered a voice in his mind.

Matta went on. "People you'll meet in the course of your life will not much care whether this holy Light came here on its own, or whether you stole it. They'll always find a reason to hurt you as long as they'll ignore reality and live in fear. This could be forever, I'm afraid. For this clan and anyone outside these walls, you are a risk."

She leaned over to him. The urge to retreat overcame the child but he battled it to victory. He would no longer be intimidated, which she was obviously trying to do by cornering him like that. He looked her straight in the eye—the brown one, not the blue—measuring his breath so as not to blink.

"Did one of them hurt you?" she asked quietly.

"No."

"Good. For now, their hostility toward you is at its lowest level. But there's no guarantee that it will last. Nichans don't like humans very much. Those of the Ueto Clan don't shine through their tolerance . . . or education. I live among them only at the cost of much effort. My help is invaluable to them. If it wasn't, I could only watch these walls from the outside. If a human doesn't serve their interests, that human has no place in their home. For this reason," she concluded, "the clan leader has decided that once you've recovered from your wounds and are able to survive on your own, you will have to leave."

Marissin's heart began to race again, but the boy remained motionless.

Leave. They were going to throw him out, another way to put it. Would other men come and get him? Would they bring him back to Mother? No, after he came in contact with nichans, she'd never accept him again.

"No," he said in a breath.

Matta raised her eyebrows. "No?"

"No, I won't."

"Are you certain?"

"Yes."

"It won't be easy to convince them to keep you. You can trust my experience on this. If you want to stay —"

"I'm staying."

None of her warnings would make him budge. She seemed to come to terms with it and righted herself to take a better look at him. "In that case, there's work to be done. The Uetos won't accept feeding a dead weight forever. Forgive my harsh words, but you are that dead weight."

He wasn't sure he understood, but he let it go on without losing his determined expression.

Outside, muffled by the distance, a wave of shouting rose. Matta was oblivious to the sound. "The three boys who brought you here, help them. From now on they'll be active members of this clan. Since you're under their protection, you're their responsibility. If someone came to ask their opinion, they could speak on your behalf, defend your rights. You must do everything you can to make their lives easy. Do you understand what I'm saying?"

Yes, most of it, but not all of it. He didn't admit it. The way she addressed him annoyed him to no end. Who did she think she was?

She took his silence for what it was: ignorance.

"Help them with their chores. Obey their orders if they give you any. If the youngest one scratches his knees, at least show compassion. That sort of thing. In any case, make yourself useful without being noticed. No more screaming, no more hitting.

You're not a brainless beast; you just proved it to me. So enough of this nonsense. Learn to be grateful too. Those three brothers could have left you where they found you. They were under no obligation to save your life."

Brothers. What was that? He kept that question to himself even though it burned his tongue.

"Another thing," Matta said. "You're going to have to learn Torb, the language of Torbatt." He frowned. "Torbatt is the country in which we are living right now, on the Coroman Continent. Does it sound familiar? No? Well that is one thing you've learned today. Listen carefully to the nichans when they speak. Try to recognize the words. Some of them are close to those of our language. Torb is, of course, different from Sirlhain, but it's quite a logical language. You are a quick-witted boy; you should learn fast. I'm very busy, so I don't intend to be an interpreter. If you put your mind to it, you'll do just fine." She bit her lip and paused for several seconds. "I'll try to find time to give you . . . regular lessons, but the effort will have to come from you. A child unresponsive to orders and education is easily made a fool of. You're not a fool, so don't let them think so."

Silence returned to the room and a new, not-so-distant hubbub came over them through the thin window panes. The child dared to look in that direction, but quickly restrained himself. If the woman continued to observe him, he had to do the same.

Apart from a few words here and there, the meaning of which escaped him, he understood what she was getting at.

"You will have to make a great effort, and it isn't certain that it'll be enough. Are you willing to try?"

"I'm staying."

"Stubborn, I see. Now, do you have questions?"

Before he could even think about it, the bedroom door flew open.

DOMINO HAD ONLY OPENED his eyes once between the moment he'd collapsed in his brother's arms and his arrival in their little hut. He'd immediately regretted his choice. He hadn't had time to recognize the ink clouds in the sky as Mora carried him. As soon as his eyelids had lifted, a myriad of black and moving spots had appeared, tightening the knot around his stomach. His skull had seemed so heavy that darkness had been preferable to daylight. So all he made out of the situation was his brother's foot pushing against the wood, the squeaking of the door spread apart, then Mora taking a few more steps before laying Domino on the mattress.

"What is happening to him?" A woman's voice that Domino didn't recognize.

Mora wiped his brother's bloody nose with his sleeve. "My uncle says it's nothing serious. Domino felt sick after taking the oath. He'll be all right now."

Yet, despite the rigor he imposed on himself in front of his brother, Mora was sweating anxiety. The back of his hand rested on Domino's forehead. "You have no fever. Speak to me, Domino. Say something."

Nausea still fussed in his gut, but Domino couldn't resist the anguish in his brother's tone. He kept his eyes closed but forced himself to pronounce a few words. "I am . . . thirsty."

His lunch stayed where it was, which was a good sign. He perceived his brother's movements around him, the lapping of water, then the rough cup around which his fingers closed. He sat up on one elbow and took a sip. Just one. The upright position was a bad idea. The world tossed under his body, and Domino let himself fall heavily against his straw mattress.

"Just lie still for now. Ero said it will pass."

This name unleashed a surge of fear in Domino; not an urge to vomit, but something more painful, located in his chest and the back of his skull. "I don't—I don't want him to do that again."

"What are you talking about?"

"No more oath."

And new tears burned under his shut eyelids. As they rolled down Domino's temple, Mora wiped them with his fingertips with a tenderness more reassuring to the little boy than any spoken word.

"Of course. Only once. That's all," Mora said. "It's done now."

"You promise?"

"Yes. And you did very well, as I expected. I'm proud of you, little brother."

Domino's chest swelled with relief, and he smiled despite his sobbing. Would their mother be proud too? His heart tightened as he remembered that he might never find out.

"I'm done with this boy," the woman said across the room. "Do your best to talk to him slowly and clearly. It would be good for him to learn Torb."

"I will. Does he have a name?" Mora asked.

Domino's attention shifted to the woman, for he'd just realized it was Matta and that the human child was probably here too. If only Domino could smell him or hear his heart. Nausea reduced all his senses to crooked tools.

"He says he doesn't remember it," Matta said. "He'll have to find a new one—"

"I'll do it!" Domino cried out.

"What are you, his mom?" Mora said.

"I can do it."

"Why don't you get some rest instead, huh? Thank you for your help, madam."

"No 'madam.' Matta should be enough. Thank you for taking care of this boy. I'll drop by again sometime to check on his progress."

"All right." The woman's footsteps echoed across the room before the door slammed behind her. "Can I leave you now, Domino?"

"You're leaving?"

"We left Beïka alone to do the chores. I'll go help him."

"You're leaving me alone?"

"You're not alone. The little boy's here too, in his corner."

Domino half opened his eyes again and confirmed his brother's words. The child, as silent and motionless as a piece of furniture, was almost part of the scenery. He'd said he had no name, which meant he had spoken to the woman. Domino was sad to have missed this. Apart from the shouting, he wondered what the human's voice sounded like.

And then he didn't have to close his eyes anymore. His discomfort hadn't gone away, but the dizziness was manageable.

"I'll bring you a bandage for your arm," Mora said.

Domino dared to look at the wound. As he held it against him, he'd smeared blood on his arm and on the front of his tunic.

"It's not so bad," Mora said. "You're not bleeding anymore."

"It hurts."

"I know." Mora brandished his bandaged forearm as if to remind Domino that he was no stranger to the experience. "Try to get some rest. The cup next to you is full if you're thirsty. I'll be back as soon as I can."

With that, he got up and left the room after taking one last look over his shoulder. Then Domino and the human found themselves alone, plunged into silence and gloom.

Long minutes passed during which neither of them moved; at least, that was what Domino's senses told him, for he'd closed his eyes again. He was used to the other child staying in his corner. Having refused to join the boys on the large straw mattress, he always slept either sitting in the corner, his head pressed against the wooden wall, or simply lying on the braided reed floor. He wasn't nichan, and he offered little to no resistance to the cold sneaking under his skin at night. However, it was impossible to get close to him to offer a blanket. So the said blanket lay not far from where the little boy was now curled up, ready to fulfill its purpose.

With this in mind, Domino dozed.

He perceived words spoken in a distant but familiar voice. His mother's. His name came up regularly, sometimes his brothers'. The rest was but an echo of his own musing, of powerful feet hammering the ground, sending tremors into the marrow of his bones. Then the next moment, he forgot that he'd begun to dream. His attention was elsewhere, without trying to focus on anything in particular. Something approached. He felt its jerky, somewhat wheezy breath. That something radiated heat, a heart pulsing in its core.

Without even thinking about it, he reached out and grasped that something. There was a gasp of surprise, and Domino opened his eyes. Crouched by his mattress was the human. It was his slender wrist Domino had just intercepted. The young nichan relaxed and released the other child.

Domino expected the other boy to run away, but he didn't. The boy remained still, however, keeping his hand suspended above the nichan, seemingly struggling inside not to withdraw it, his eyes wide open.

Domino contemplated the other boy for a while. He didn't care that the little human had approached him, something he'd carefully avoided since the day they'd met. At that moment Domino had only one thought in his mind: the human was beautiful.

Domino liked his light blond hair, so different from that of the people in his family. He liked this difference that reminded him how big and how full of mysteries and secrets the world was. Unlike him, he had thin lips whose curves reminded Domino of the graininess of wood. And then there was his pale, delicate skin that revealed the bluish veins under his eyes, on his wrists, and his bruised throat. That scar. It was reminiscent of the typical twist of a rope. Was Domino perceiving it because he'd witnessed this disgusting act, or was the print as clear as he saw it? It didn't matter. What mattered was that despite all his scars, the one on his neck and the one on the upper corner of his face, the human was beautiful.

Domino decided to tell him. "Your eyes are pretty."

Then he remembered that the child couldn't understand him. He sighed softly, keeping silent, not looking away, wanting to make this moment last.

The child had come closer to him. He approached closer still, his left hand outstretched. He held his breath as his fingers found Domino's forearm. Domino lay perfectly still. This little hand was frozen against his skin, but also very gentle. He looked down. The child's fingers grazed along his still open wound. He didn't touch it, otherwise Domino would have hissed at the pain. His gaze swaying from the human face to the hand resting on his arm, Domino smiled in spite of himself.

That is when he perceived a change. First a numbness, then a slightly uncomfortable pull, or a swelling of his blood vessels. Like . . . a cramp. Next to him, the child stared at him. Domino then noticed for the first time that the human's eyes were different from each other. Both were black and amber, but the left one was almost entirely black, as if the pupil was fully dilated, showing only a thin orange outline.

As if the child had felt the change in Domino's scrutiny, he closed his eyes and his breath quickened. The muscles of Domino's arm stiffened.

The cramp then disappeared, and Domino examined his wound again. His heart leaped. The cut wasn't one anymore. It was now but a thin, pinkish scar. Amazed, he raised his arm to eye level to examine it more closely. With his thumb, he stroked the slight bump trailing along his flesh. No pain. Apart from the crystallized blood on his skin, there was no evidence that the cut had been inflicted less than an hour ago.

Grinning, Domino turned to the other child, who had pulled back to sit on the floor, panting.

He just did that! He has the gift!

Domino sat up and laughed, glancing at his arm. "You're nice. Thank you."

Lips clasped together, the human took a breath as if this act, this gift he'd just used, had exhausted him. Then he jumped when the door opened on the other side of the small room. Mora was already back, a piece of bread in one hand, a bandage wrapped on itself in the other. He stopped on the threshold, noticing how close to his brother the other child was.

He shut the door behind him, frowning. "Is everything all right in here?"

Domino displayed his arm for all to see. In an instant, he'd forgotten his earlier discomfort. "Look!" he said. "Look what he did."

Mora took a few steps and sat down next to his brother. His expression metamorphosed at the sight of the scar. He raised his eyes to the human, who watched them as if attentive to Mora's reaction to his work.

"It's he who—"

"Yes!" Domino cut him off, bouncing on the bed. "He put his hand there, and it was all strange inside my arm, and then I got better. He made the cut go away."

The corner of Mora's lips curled in a faint smile. He contemplated the closed wound one last time, then turned to the human. *"Bietche."*

Domino ticked and finally diverted his attention from his arm. "What's that?"

"It means 'thank you' in Sirlhain."

"You speak Sirlhain?"

This impressed Domino who turned to face the human. This one wore a brand-new expression Domino had never seen before. Confusion too, but still suspicion. But something had changed.

"No," Mora said. "The woman, Matta, taught me to say 'thank you' in Sirlhain. She was in the sanctuary when I returned. You should thank him too, Domino."

"I did, but he doesn't understand."

"Well, tell him *bietche*."

"*Bietche?*"

Mora nodded. Domino turned and articulated the word as distinctly as he could. The human's hands relaxed around his knees, and Domino repeated the word again, enjoying the way it sounded in his own mouth. It was the first foreign word he learned. He repeated it again and again.

"I think he got it, Domino." Mora stopped him, forcing his brother to face him. "Are you feeling better?"

So much better. "Yes."

"No dizziness?"

"I'm fine."

"I brought you some bread to get your strength back, but if you're feeling better, we'll save it for dinner."

Domino looked at the piece of flat bread his brother was holding and pouted. "Can I have it anyway?"

Mora giggled and offered the food to his brother, who froze as his mouth opened wide to take a bite. Domino had just thought of something.

"Do we have to tell Uncle Ero?"

Mora shook his head. "Not yet."

"Why not?"

"The kid's still scared of everyone. He jumps at the slightest noise. He can't even take a bath by himself. If we tell Ero, he'll ask him to treat people or . . . We don't want to scare him, do we? We don't even know what he can do with the gift." Domino stuck his arm out in front of his elder brother to refresh his memory. "I know, I saw it. But your cut wasn't that deep. Maybe there's nothing he can do about a more serious wound. He's very small, you said so yourself. Can you imagine how he'd feel if we showed him a very serious wound?"

"Like the arm of the human you killed?"

He lowered his eyes to his piece of bread, and his appetite died as the memory of the two men his brothers had fought to protect him returned, of that arm that had been savagely torn off, as only a huge nichan's mouth could do. The nichan smile, as their people called it, all in sharp points. The proud smile of a suffering people, his mother used to say.

"Exactly like that, yes," Mora said, ruffling his little brother's hair.

He was right. If the human found himself in that kind of situation, exposed to mutilated bodies, he would run away, and this time no one would ever find him again. Domino refused to put him through such an ordeal.

The usual pensive pout froze Mora's face as he studied the human from the corner of his eye. "And you know, Vestiges with the gift are . . . unpredictable. We don't always know what they're capable of. People are sometimes afraid of them. Domino, look at me. He has the gift. Now we know he could be dangerous."

"He's my friend," Domino said, words he knew woven of lies and hopes warming his innards. "I'm not afraid."

"I'm not, either. But if anyone finds out, if Ero finds out, we can't predict what will happen."

"We don't tell people."

"No. We don't tell anyone." They exchanged a long look of connivance. "I'm going to put a bandage on your arm. No one will know it's healed. Domino, listen to me." And the young nichan looked up at Mora's unexpectedly serious face. "Not a word to Beïka about it."

Further explanation was unnecessary. Domino nodded. Something in Mora's eyes spoke a reality both brothers were already aware of.

"Where is Beïka?" Domino asked.

Mora sighed. "He found himself some playmates."

Immediately Domino's mood darkened. He'd succeeded; Beïka had made friends only a few days after his arrival at the Ueto Clan. By what kind of miracle was that possible? When Domino approached the other children, they looked away and left for no reason. Why? Domino tried to talk to them. He wanted to get to know them and have fun with them. None of them ever answered, as if his breath were poison.

Bread crumbs fell on his legs as he scratched the crust, lost in his thoughts.

Mora swept them away with one hand. "Why are you sad?"

"I'm not."

"Domino . . . "

"You know why."

"You found yourself a friend too, Domino," Mora said, cocking his head to the human.

"It's not true. He's afraid of me." This fact broke his heart.

"You think so?"

Domino nodded, not daring to look at the other child.

"I don't agree. Look at your arm. Look. Nobody forced him to do that. I think he wanted to be nice to you. He's afraid of everyone, but he made a huge effort to heal you."

Filled with new hope, Domino looked for any trace of lies in his brother's eyes. There were none.

Mora resumed. "Give him time, all right? Perhaps he too needs a friend. Besides, true friendship is something you have to earn."

"So I don't deserve it?"

"Domino, do you remember what Mama told you? How you were born?" The little nichan nodded. "We thought you were gone for good. The healer who came to help give birth to you couldn't feel you move. We couldn't hear your heartbeat anymore. It had just stopped. And then, after long minutes, it came back, louder than ever, so strong Mama smiled like I'd never seen her smile before. And the healer said something to Mama. Do you remember what she said?"

Domino didn't have to dig into his memory. He loved that story about his birth, told by his mother as much as by Mora.

"She said, 'He'll be strong and brave, so he needs to get out and breathe.' "

"Strong and brave," Mora repeated, stroking his brother's hair. "That's what you are, Domino. Of course you deserve his friendship, but he doesn't know it yet."

After that, Mora cleaned the blood that had dried on Domino's arm, put the bandage on to create the illusion, then gave him a change of shirt. Not having received much clothing on their arrival, they had until then been asked for their laundry to clean it regularly. Now that they were part of the clan, it was up to them to take care of the task.

So Domino got up, recovered from his emotions, gathered up the dirty laundry, and followed his brother to the door. He turned around as it opened to see if the blond boy followed them. To his astonishment, the child had gotten up, still in his corner, a half-eaten piece of meat at his feet.

"Come," Domino encouraged him, waving.

The human hesitated for a second, two, three. At last he made his decision. He took one step, another, and then followed them outside.

Domino was delighted.

V I

"And Nida? Nida? Or Gus? I like the word 'Gus.' "

Domino's hands weren't focused on his task anymore. Bent over his washboard, he'd stopped taking care of the dirty laundry the moment his excitement got the upper hand.

Marissin refused to engage in this conversation. The sky was getting darker—heavy tarnished clouds raced in their direction from the bamboo forest—and he wanted to finish his chores before dinner. Someone during lunch had predicted rain for the evening. Marissin didn't wish to be outside when it fell.

He rubbed harder against the washboard, up and down, his legs numb from crouching by the river. His fingers were freezing, barely holding the cloth, forcing him to press against the soapy board with his palms.

Amidst the lapping of the clear water, Domino's voice resounded again. " 'Gus' is not a name, but I like it. Don't you know it? My mother used to say that 'Gus' is the word we use to talk about that moment when we're cold— No, it's when we wake up, but we think we're still dreaming. Yeah, that's it. It's special, isn't it? Gus. Gus? Gus?"

He repeated the word several times, sometimes opening his mouth without letting the slightest sound come out.

He worked the movements of his tongue against his palate, teeth, and lips. A piece of advice Matta had offered Marissin to improve his use of the main dialect of Torbatt, one Domino loved to put in practice with his own language.

Matta was a woman of words. She had come back to see Marissin as promised, first once every ten days or so, then more often. During those lessons, she sat with him and spoke mainly in Sirlhain. Domino had insisted on attending these lessons. For the first month he'd come only occasionally, appearing just before the end of the lecture, a moment before Matta judged it was time for her to return to her duties. Then Domino had gone to great lengths to be part of all these sessions, shirking Mora's supervision—which seemed to suit the young man quite well, as he had recently been spending more and more time with a young woman named Belma.

Sitting at a table in the sanctuary with the two children, Matta had laid in front of her a sheet of paper drawn from the folds of her tunic, writing down as she went along with a charcoal stick to illustrate her words. The signs she drew on the crudely pressed sheet were gibberish that resembled the footprints left in the wake of the village chickens. It had been a surprise to find out that those signs bore a meaning, just like the ones from the Artean.

Sitting high on his heels near Marissin, Domino smiled. It was obvious Matta's mouth only talked nonsense to him. Yet he rejoiced. When she'd begun to use Torb during the lessons, Domino's excitement had been snuffed out before resurfacing, as lively as boiling water overflowing from a cauldron. He then interrupted Matta once, twice, and ended up sitting in the corner of the room, forced into silence or else he would be sent outside.

After two months, the woman had decided to teach the two

boys how to write, and Domino never found himself in the corner again. The Uetos didn't write; the vast majority of them couldn't even read, Matta had told Marissin in Sirlhain. Domino would be an exception.

The intonations, the rhythm, the pressure of the tongue against the teeth, against the palate. The list of instructions grew longer every day, and Marissin found in each new addition the limits of his patience. Matta then made it clear that it was urgent for him to learn to hunt as well, for nature would be merciless once he was thrown out of Surhok. Each of her distributions reminded the boy of his resolutions. He went back to his studies. He was smarter than she thought.

They wouldn't kick him out. He'd made up his mind.

After several weeks, Marissin recognized most of the words he heard around him. He still spoke very few of them himself, but he was now able to say "yes," "no," and "thank you" from time to time.

Matta strongly encouraged him to formulate complete sentences and reprimanded him if he stuck to his overused "yes" and "no."

If speaking the Torbatt's language had felt like a silly game, after five months of intense work, his mind had turned Torb.

Nothing was more satisfying than to hear and understand. Marissin knew everyone had uttered a lot of horrors and rudeness about him. He was a Vestige, and his young age made him neither stupid nor naive. He now no longer had to wonder whether or not he was the subject of conversation or taunting, or if someone was insulting him. He knew that at best he was invisible; at worst, he was "it."

Even the language switched in his dreams. But the men rarely talked before squeezing the rope around his neck. They didn't talk much, either, when they pulled on the end of the rope . . .

The rag slipped from Marissin's grasp. A hand flew in front of him, catching the wet cloth before it got lost in the water.

"Here," Domino said, putting the cloth back in the other boy's pale hands. "It's fine if you don't like 'Gus.' 'Nadi' is good too. 'Nadi' means 'cold wind,' you know. My name, Domino, means 'day of night.'"

The other child knew that but refrained from making any comment. Answering to Domino usually led to more talking, and the current amount was more than enough.

"Mora says my name is like that because I was born one day when it was all dark. A day of—"

"Faces above, your voice makes me want to cut your tongue!" A voice cut in that startled both Domino and Marissin.

Beïka walked down the path leading to the river, lacing the front of his pants. His cheeks were red, matching the color of his ears on each side of his shaved head. "What if you tried to shut the fuck up, for once? We can hear you through the walls."

Beïka kicked his little brother's ass, and Domino turned, baring his teeth once again, hands full of clothes dripping water in the dust. Mora had gone hunting with several of the clan's other nichans, including Ero. Therefore, Beïka feared no reprisals.

Marissin knew all too well what Domino's brother was up to when he wandered into the village in the company of his friends. The human and Domino had caught them smoking long, dark, acrid-smelling cigars in the back of the village. Domino had narrowly avoided the glowing stalk that Beïka had brought close to his face to threaten him, defying his little brother to tell Mora everything.

And then there had been, the day before, that repeated sucking sound almost masked by Beïka's high-pitched groans. As they approached, wrongly worried, the little boys had only had time to see a girl kneeling in front of the teenager, her face and mouth pressed against his crotch. Then Beïka had asked his friend to swallow something, grabbing the length of her short black hair. Cheeks red, eyes low, Domino had hurried away, forcing Marissin to follow.

The human couldn't get the thought out of his mind. What had exactly happened inside their hut? He wouldn't ask Domino about it. Not to initiate conversation was also to avoid conflict.

Beïka gave his brother another push in the butt, harder, as if to test his patience.

"Stop," Domino said.

Beïka's smirk was brighter than daylight. The next second, he bent down, picked up a handful of dirt, and threw it into the basket of freshly laundered clothes waiting to be laid out.

Domino shouted and pushed his brother with both hands. A vain gesture, for Beïka was faster, stronger, taller, and a jerk craving a good fight, even with a seven-year-old.

He grabbed his little brother's wrist as it flew by. "Why do you bother trying to find it a name?" Beïka said as he pulled Domino up in the air, shaking him like a hare brought from the hunt. The little boy kicked and punched. "It's fucking useless, so shut up. And remember that shit is supposed to get out of your ass, not your mouth!"

"Let go of me!"

Marissin clenched the dishcloth. It wasn't the first time he'd witnessed such a brawl between the two brothers. The last time, there had been a crack, and Domino had squealed. After that, he'd massaged his swollen shoulder for days, trying not to strain his right arm. When the Vestige had attempted to heal him, Domino had refused, fear in his eyes. Once alone, he'd explained that Beïka mustn't know about Marissin's abilities. His gift was a secret.

The crunch would come, the human was certain of it. He

didn't want to hear that crackling, or the scream that would burst out of the young nichan's mouth. He still preferred Domino's babbling to the moaning his older brother exhorted from him with repeated assaults.

Heat rose to his face, and Marissin fixed his orange eyes on the taller of the two nichans.

"It's pointless, I said," Beïka added, smiling, shaking Domino by the arm. "The kid's retarded."

"It's not true!" Domino shouted. "You're an asshole!"

At the same moment, Marissin stood. He couldn't take it anymore, dreading more than ever the pain that would come when Domino's shoulder would snap.

But even before he stood upright, Beïka, taller than him by at least three heads, sent his foot forward. The braided leather savate reached the little boy's hip. He toppled over, unable to resist the force of the impact that sent him into the air. Wind whistled in his ears, his heart flipped in his chest, and he hit a wall of cold water. His first reflex was to take a deep breath. Water rushed into his mouth and nose. The child stirred like a madman. His foot knocked the rocky bottom of the river. In the current, he spun around. His wing twisted, its membrane stretched by water pressure, and in an urge to call for help, the child opened his mouth wide again.

A flurry of bubbles burst out of his chest.

The swirling of the river became stronger, and something pulled him out into the open air. Marissin coughed. His nose and eyes burned. His senses overwhelmed, belching large volumes of water mixed with saliva, he slipped, the current doing its best to carry him away. At the price of vigorous paddling, he controlled his balance.

Also, someone held him by the arm and waist.

Between two coughing fits, the human opened his eyes and

raised them to a dark, wet, and worried face. Domino. His brother had probably thrown him into the water too.

The river wasn't deep, but without Domino's intervention, Marissin's chance to get back to the surface was thin. Apart from the village baths—whose water level only reached his waist—he had never been completely submerged into water. Here, it reached his clavicle.

As Domino yelled in Beïka's direction, Marissin pushed back the blond locks falling over his eyes. The washboards and laundry were several feet uphill the river. The current had carried the child away as he struggled. Head spinning, he felt weak at the thought.

He couldn't swim. Beïka could have killed him. From the top of the bank, still as entertained as ever, the teenager waved to them, displayed his bare ass with hilarity, then left.

"You're all right?" Domino asked, for the human was still throwing up half the river.

He was also trembling and could hardly breathe, his chest contracted by the cough. Domino pulled him close. "We're going to get out of here. I'm going to help you out of the water. Come. It's too high up there. Come on, I'll—"

"Let go of me!" The words escaped Marissin's mouth, as sour as bile. He continued, spitting his anger for the first time in months. "It your fault! You talk too much. I not want a name. I want you leave me alone!"

Despite his imperfect Torb, the meaning of his words was unequivocal. Domino, whose face closed abruptly, stepped back. His hand loosened around Marissin's arms, who caught up with the earth and stone on the bank, heckled by the current. Facing him, the young nichan lowered his eyes.

Around them, the world had darkened. Night had fallen without warning, as if the last minutes had lasted hours.

But Marissin stared at Domino in the dark. He'd never seen

such an expression on the other boy's face. An unpleasant sensation swelled in the human's belly, tying his guts on themselves.

In the distance, a bell rang, hammered incessantly. The bell in the village square.

The children reacted too slowly. The shock of the fall and the words just exchanged nailed them to the spot.

Domino flinched. Then he jumped again and brought his hand to his shoulder. The bell stopped ringing. Marissin cried out. Something had just fallen on him, burning his skin. Then the same pain on the other shoulder, and again and again, and on the top of his head and his wings.

Was it raining? Marissin looked up at the ink sky.

"*No!*" Domino cried. "Don't look up!"

He grabbed the blond boy's arm underwater and pulled him across the stream. Marissin had no choice but to follow through the cool waves, confused, his shoulders and head burned by the drops that fell harder now. They struggled against the floods that pushed them aside and reached a cavity dug in the earth. As the water brushed against his chin, the Vestige settled against the river wall near Domino.

It was raining, but it wasn't just any rain. Marissin had to squint. The water gradually took on a dark hue. The drops coming from the sky were black and formed small puddles that didn't mix with water but stagnated on the surface of the river. And the current dragged the black, acidic puddles toward the two children.

"Don't touch them." Domino let go of Marissin's hand and pushed away the dark pools that kept getting wider and wider, stretching out in their direction like tentacles.

Four hands were better than two. Marissin reached out and pushed. He was too small to divert the puddles out of their trajectory. One of them covered his hand and forearm like a tight glove, and he winced when a burning pain nibbled at his skin.

"Keep your hands in the water!" Domino ordered, pushing the other boy's hand below the surface, quickly silencing most of the burn. Then he resumed his task, creating ripples powerful enough to keep the threat at bay. "It's the Corruption Rain. Corruption shit, they say, the grownups. It doesn't mix with water. If it touches you, you wash it in the water. Okay?"

And even without an answer, he never stopped fighting the stain that thickened as the rain got heavier. Several times he grimaced, his skin blackened with the Corruption. But nothing stopped him. In front of Marissin's eyes, Domino protected them until the rain passed.

Minutes, hours, an eternity. Hard to measure time in the dark.

The current washed away most of the slimy flanges. The bank was black with them. Above the boys, the substance slowly dripped down from the foliage in heavy, stretchy drops.

Then the sky brightened to its usual gray and light returned.

The two boys stayed under cover. Marissin didn't want to come out of it for fear that another Corruption shit would catch them off guard, punishing them for escaping it the first time. Near him, Domino stretched his neck take a look at the sky from time to time. He didn't speak anymore. Now that the danger had passed, the words Marissin had yelled in his face were probably coming back to his mind.

He shouldn't have said those words. He regretted them now. Since his arrival at Surhok, and even before, Domino had always been good to him. He always smiled at him, talked to him as if with both pairs of their hands, they could remake the world. Sometimes it was too much for Marissin. Mother had not taught him to smile like that. Neither Mother nor anyone else, for that matter. What reason did he have to smile? His priority was to stay here, to survive. He had no energy to waste in words and smiles.

But Domino smiled, day after day.

And he looked at Marissin the way he looked at Mora, the way he stared at the sky sometimes.

"You think the sun is really yellow? If it lights yellow, why is everything gray? The others say it's the Corruption. Me, I'd like to see the sun. Yellow and round, like an egg, all shiny," Domino had said while watching the dark clouds that concealed the skies, and he had smiled. As he lowered his eyes to the human, his grin had remained, as had the glow in his black irises.

No one else in the village looked at Marissin that way. It unsettled him. Sometimes he felt a warmth rising in his chest, and the hope invading him ached enough for him to shy away.

He thought of the hand Domino had used to repel the waves of black oil flowing toward them. Under the turmoil, his hand appeared reddened. A few blisters swarmed over his swollen skin. Marissin reached out to make the necessary contact to heal the other boy. He could do this, the gesture would only take a few seconds. Domino had enjoyed every time he'd treated him before.

When their fingers brushed against each other, Domino jumped up and stepped aside. They exchanged but a brief glance before the nichan turned away, wedging his burned hand against his heart, taking a series of shivering breaths.

A nichan approached the river some time later. The woman appeared above them, pushing a solid, lumpy pile of filth with a rake. As it fell into the water, it splashed on the children, who shouted in unison. The woman noticed their presence, and her face turned pale.

Domino and Marissin were helped out of the water. Their laundry, left unprotected in the rain, was ruined. They were taken through the village, which the nichans scraped meticulously to clear the remains of the black rain. Then the idea of burning the houses and the sanctuary's facade didn't seem stupid anymore. In spite of the rain, all the buildings remained unaltered.

"The first Corruption shit in two years," someone said.

"I hope the hunters found shelter in time," said another.

Then the children were taken to the baths. The path to the bathhouse had already been cleared.

Neither boy spoke as they cleaned themselves.

When they went to bed that night, exhausted, shoulders flecked with superficial burns, they'd still not broken the silence.

VII

THE SAVING RAIN, THE ONE THAT HAD BEEN FORETOLD, succeeded the black rain in the middle of the night and didn't cease until the next day's first light. Everywhere in the village, although still having the tint of the Corruption, mud replaced the stains. But the roofs were rinsed off, and the river washed and carried away most of the disaster.

What better way to celebrate the Gods' merciful rain than a glass of potato alcohol shared on everyone's porch? The enthusiasm seized every soul, from the eldest to the youngest nichan.

The children gathered in the central square to play a game they had named, "The Flight of the Chickens." The slippery cobblestones and the usually dry earth of the village were now a pool of sticky, slate-colored mud. Not a single child would come out of this in their original colors. But with one-fifth of the clan hunting and gathering supplies at the nearest human village, and half of the adults cradled in the sugary heat of alcohol, the younger ones felt audacious.

The children took place all around the square. Half the

players offered the curve of their back to another child. Facing one another, the porters were no longer children. They were brave hens taking their eggs back to the coop, the egg being the child each was carrying. Two children, chosen more or less at random, played the role of birds of prey. Their goal, to make an omelet of those eggs and ruffle some feathers, if possible. Simple enough, in theory. The raptors suffered no limits—death was not even an option in these kids' minds. Reaching the henhouse was sometimes quite a feat. But none of these young nichans were shy. To win the Flight of the Chickens made you a better hunter, they said.

Birds inspired freedom and courage. Just like the Gods, the animals had never seen enemies in nichans. They never flinched, never fled. If this wasn't a sign of exceptional power, then what was?

Two lines formed. The children climbed on their friends' backs. Beïka, one of the biggest, wore the hungry grin of a raptor today.

Domino held his breath, waiting for the start. A bird cried out in the distance, and the children took off.

Mud splashed everywhere, staining their legs, soaking their pants. The birds of prey threw themselves on the hens with dazzling speed and ruthless strength. Shouts of encouragement rained from the eggs. Less than three seconds after the start, several children collapsed in the mud.

Sitting on the steps of a nearby house, Domino didn't know where to look. The children screamed, fell, slid, charged to reach their goal by brute force. In the middle of the fiery muck, a merciless war raged. And neither Domino nor the human boy was welcome on the battlefield.

Especially not the Vestige, the other children had said. He was going to turn the mud into quicksand, replied a boy named Jaro, a pest who spent too much time in Beïka's shadows.

"That's bullshit," Domino had said, unable to restrain himself.

If Mora hadn't left with the hunting party, Domino would never have used such language. Moreover, the human had told him the previous day that he spoke too much, so perhaps the best would have been to keep quiet.

Beïka hadn't defended them. He often did that, pretended Domino wasn't his brother, that he had nothing to do with the little boy. When Memek, their cousin, had complained that the game should have started by now, all the children had turned their backs on them to have fun.

Now, Domino imagined himself in the middle of the tumult, the human perched on his back, his wings flapping in the wind as Domino made his way through the crowd of other chickens and birds of prey. He dreamed that at least once they would let him and Gus play.

Gus, Gus . . .

Domino couldn't get the name out of his head, but he had to. The child had said he didn't want a name.

Next to him, the human's face bore the same mask of boredom and indifference. Nothing in this display of force seemed to move him. Unlike Domino, he hadn't asked to play. As usual, the little blond boy was content to wait in the distance, his eyes wary.

Maybe it wasn't a bad thing not to be on the field with the others. With his small build, the human would get trampled if he found himself on the ground.

Beïka shouted a rather convincing imitation of a hawk and then hurled himself at the other children. At thirteen, he was far too old and big for this game. He didn't give the kids around him a chance. But the friends he'd made were all younger than him, enough to offer him a place among the players.

He gave a violent shoulder blow to a girl that sent her and her little brother face-first in wet dirt. His entire body freckled in black mud dots, Beïka yelled another victorious cry.

Domino looked away. That his brother was allowed a single second of fun after what he'd done to the human revolted him. If Domino had not freed his arms from Beïka's fist, Gus might have drowned . . .

The village gates opened below.

Several nichans entered, faces grim. They'd only been gone for three days. What was the meaning for this premature return?

Very few of them brought back meat or provisions. A hare or two hung from their belts. Not enough to feed everyone.

Then Ero walked through the gates, and the air in the village filled with fear. Excitement gave way to trouble, and the children stopped playing. The fallen got up, black with mud, bruises on their knees. And they watched the nichans coming in one by one in a silent procession.

Then they appeared. Two nichans each held the end of a rope, one in front, the other behind. In the middle was a small man.

Human.

He was bare from his muddy feet to his sticky hair, dirty, bruised, and bleeding from his nose and mouth. What seemed to be dried vomit coated his chest. He was restrained. The hands behind his back had been tied tightly hard, painting the palms and fingers a nauseating purple. The man looked young and exhausted under all that blood. Terrified too.

The nichans dragged him through the village, then Mora came in, strands of hair escaping his long braid. He spotted Domino and the human immediately and ran to them.

For once, Beïka joined them without being asked. "What's going on?"

Before he could answer, Belma, Mora's friend, joined them in a hurry and examined the teenager from head to toe.

She had a round face devoid of angle and was a little taller than Mora. Her forearms were tattooed with long intertwined lines. She had arrived in Surhok a few years before the three brothers, accompanied by her great-grandmother, both survivors of an incident in which part of their family had lost their lives. When his brothers asked him about it, Mora remained vague; out of respect for his friend, he said.

"Are you all right?" she asked, and Mora nodded. "I heard . . . Is it true?"

"Yes."

Belma cursed in a whisper.

Domino glanced between them as the last nichans entered the village, shielding everyone in as the doors closed. "True what?"

"Everyone in the square!"

The powerful call, as deep as a chasm, came from the other side of the village, from Ero. Standing on the highest step at the entrance of the sanctuary, his eyes searched the crowd before going down to the prisoner who had just been forced to kneel on the muddy cobblestones. Even twenty yards away, the dried blood staining their uncle's clenched fists was unmistakable.

"What's going on?" Beïka repeated as he moved towards the square, reacting to Ero's call as if it were an order.

Mora held him by the arm, looking dark. "No, you stay here with Domino. You go back to the hut."

"Why?"

Mora pulled him toward him and brought his face closer to his cadet's. Despite the age gap between them, the two brothers were the same height. "They're going to execute someone. It is no sight for children."

Beïka's eyes widened, and Domino recognized the same excitement his brother had displayed during the game. "I definitely want to see that!"

The little square was filling up. Parents sent their children back to the houses before gathering around Ero. The Unaan came down the steps, his bald skull protruding in the sea of brown heads.

Beïka tried to free himself from his brother's grip. Mora lost patience and pushed them all, Beïka, Domino, and the human, between the houses, away from the commotion. "I said no! You stay here and look after the little ones."

"Mora . . ." Belma backed away slowly, worry in her eyes, following the tide of the crowd.

Mora took one last look at his brother, then let go of him to follow his friend. Seconds later, ignoring Mora's orders, Beïka slipped between the huts, out of sight.

Domino stayed put before turning to Gus. *No, to the human*, he remembered. Normally, Domino would have asked him if he wanted to follow them. But he talked too much, didn't he? So he held his tongue and turned his back on the human. Then he mirrored his brothers' footsteps.

He reached the crowded square and stopped at a wall of fully grown nichans. They all held their breath, waiting.

Everyone except Ero. Domino could recognize his deep tone through his heavy breathing. After a long moment during which Beïka, a little farther on, tried to see something over the shoulders of his fellow villagers, the clan chief spoke.

"My son is dead. Javik . . . My boy is gone."

Domino let out a sharp breath at this announcement. A groan of pain rose from the crowd. It was a woman's voice.

Ero had many children. Five daughters and two sons. As in the case of Domino and his brothers, most of these children had been conceived without love; an agreement between two adults offering a woman the opportunity to be a mother. A common practice among nichans. Domino ignored his uncle's other children. The man was no father to them, only a genitor. Memek and Javik, however, were the children Ero had had with his life partner, Orsa. Children recognized and raised by both parents.

And now Javik was no more. He'd been seventeen, Mora's age.

Domino hadn't taken the time to get to know him. Javik was a stranger. And yet his heart tightened, as if a frozen current had washed through his bones. Another member of his family had just died.

Mama should be here, Domino thought. After more than five months, he and his brothers had come to terms. Ako wouldn't come.

To his right, in the shadow of the huts, Beïka pulled out a wooden box, climbed on it, and no longer needed to stretch his neck to witness the event. Domino searched for something to raise his position. He turned around and froze. The human had followed him after all, and waited a few steps behind. He made no movement. With his striking gaze, he just stared at Domino.

He's not here for me. He just wants to see.

He placed his hand on a barrel, ignoring the other child's presence, and was soon as tall as the others.

In the middle of the square, in the exact spot where the nichans had skinned the nohl the night they'd arrived in Surhok, were Ero and Orsa. She was as tall as the clan's Unaan, her figure long and muscular. The lower half of her hair fell down her back in an endless cascade, the rest gathered in a braid at the top of her head. Like most Uetos, her earlobes were distended by thick wooden jewelry.

Domino had always found Orsa intimidating. Today, she was nothing but a bundle of unrestrained tears.

Ero held her tightly in his arms. She clutched him with the strength of despair, each squeeze of his hugging sending tears down her cheeks, like a sponge. Ero was crying, too, but while Orsa's eyes stared at the marred sky, he kept his own on the prisoner.

And as soon as Domino spotted him, he couldn't look away from him.

The man was on his knees, shaken with untimely tremors.

Though nudity was a natural state for nichans, Domino knew humans kept it to the privacy of their home. Was stripping this man bare part of the punishment? There was no doubt this human was somehow responsible for Javik's premature death.

Ero embraced Orsa for a moment. She later broke away from him to try to catch her breath through her heartbreaking sobs.

"This human killed my son," Ero said as he stood before the man who dared raise his head to challenge the Unaan's gaze. "Look down!"

Ero's fist crushed the man's jaw. A crackling sound echoed throughout the village and dark blood blended with saliva flowed from the man's swollen and cleft lips. The prisoner collapsed backwards, as limp as a boneless fish, but was kept upright by powerful hands. Head dangling sideways, his jaw hanging off its axis, the prisoner choked on the fluids filling his mouth. Several teeth slipped out of his parted lips and got lost in the mud on the ground. The blow had been restrained, for even in his human form Ero could have torn the human's jaw off. All his strength hadn't yet been released.

Voices approved in the crowd, and the shadows of several transformations stretched here and there, like a wave spreading over the surface of the water. These nichans—no doubt those who had gone hunting with Ero and who therefore knew the details of the affair, as well as his closest friends—craved revenge.

The Unaan passed a hand over his face and beard to wipe away his tears. "My son should have lived," he said, grabbing the man by the hair. The prisoner's small body shivered like a leaf in the wind. Ero made eye contact and his fingers snaked around the human's throat. "He would have become a man, a powerful nichan. He shouldn't be resting in the dirt away from his clan."

A new groan from Orsa. A smaller woman with bloodshot eyes approached and hugged the Unaan's partner from behind.

Orsa screamed at the sky and the arms encircling her waist held her with more comforting force.

The rules regarding the dead were as strict for nichans as they were for humans. A body had to be buried immediately after death. Always. The person was then given a decent burial to appease their soul and allow them to rejoin the Gods, wherever they were now. Without this, the Corruption would grow around the corpse and a spirit would emerge on the scene, calling for justice and peace. No one had yet learned how to communicate with the spirits to understand their heart, so it was necessary to appease the dead to keep the Corruption at bay. For this reason, Javik's body hadn't been brought back to Surhok. His father had been forced to bury him within minutes of his death, probably near where he'd been murdered.

Away from home.

Tears came to Domino's eyes, and for the first time he felt a surge of compassion for his uncle and his partner. And his cousin Memek, was she aware of the news? Domino took his eyes off the prisoner to seek her out. In the midst of this dark and compact crowd, Memek was nowhere to be seen.

Still bending over, Ero brought his face closer to the prisoner's. "You, motherfucker, will have to endure shame and oblivion. No one will hear your last words, no one will ever find your grave. Say goodbye to your hands. There's no way I'm letting you reach the Gods' faces." The human hiccuped, blood flowing onto his broken jaw, and tears washed parts of his face. "For what you've done to my son, you will not be forgiven, no matter the words spoken on your grave."

Ero's face changed. His brown skin turned to raven black, his mouth widened into a grin of several rows of fangs, remodeling the limits of his human bones. Ero's muscles swelled and tightened, protruding all around his broad neck, through his clothes. The hand holding the prisoner's hair lengthened, and claws as long as Domino's forearm lacerated the human's scalp. Blood ran between his sweat-soaked locks, along his forehead and into his mouth.

Like a chant, the nichans growled and praised their Unaan's transformation.

Domino felt this common hatred all around him, making the air denser in his lungs. All over the square, the nichans transformed. They abandoned their human camouflage, favoring their original form.

As Domino had already seen in his brothers, many shouted or moaned in frustration, for this was only a fragment of the transformation they were seeking to accomplish. In the old days, nichans were majestic four-legged beasts. Their strength had once been unmatched. Only then. Today, as every day since the Gods disappeared from the sky, they should all be content with what their essence altered by the Corruption would allow them to do: only a semblance of transformation.

A shiver crawled up Domino's spine as the nichans plunged into the shadows, revealing their murderous shape. He turned to Beïka. He, too, had shifted. Domino was still too young to do the same but something in him called for action.

Gus . . .

Behind Domino, the young human had retreated several steps to stick himself against a hut. The surge of rage that now saturated the place could reach him as well. Domino wanted to join him, but Orsa's voice brought him back to the execution.

"Let me do it. Ero, let me . . . Let me bleed this animal."

She walked over to Ero and placed a trembling hand on his shoulder. When he agreed to her request, she had already transformed.

The human's hands were released, and the two nichans guarding him forced the man to reach forward, like an offering of his own flesh. He tried to fight back, but to no avail. No human could resist such strength. Panting, he opened his eyes in terror when the rope that held him seconds ago was wrapped around his neck.

From his perch, Domino's reflex was to cover his own throat.

Orsa took her husband's place. She lowered her bottomless black eyes to the man who had killed her son. He looked so small and harmless compared to her, like an animal in a trap. How had such a weak creature managed to kill Javik?

Orsa didn't need an answer to that question. Her son had been taken from her. She would care later about how.

With a powerful blow, her claws pierced the man's right hand. A moan followed, then a deafening scream. With a sharp jerk, she spread her arm, tearing the tortured man's hand to shreds. Domino squeezed his hands to his chest, perceiving in the man's screams all the suffering he could no longer hide. Orsa repeated the process with the second hand, this time starting at the wrist. Blood and fragments of bone spurted across the square and onto the stone and mud. The nichans grunted their approval.

Then Domino almost choked on his breath. Ero threw the end of the rope wrapped around the human's neck over the scaffolding from which the village bell hung. As in a nightmare Domino had already experienced, the man's body rose, up and up in sharp jerks under the acclamation.

Shredded flesh hung limp from his bloody arms. The naked body, stripped of all modesty or respect, shook with jolts. The head hung purplish on the other side of the rope. This was what everyone witnessed.

Everyone.

Including the Vestige behind Domino.

Endless seconds passed before Domino escaped his daze to react. He jumped down from his barrel and threw himself in front of the little human, using his own body to block the view. He wrapped his arms around the human, who froze for a moment, gasping for air.

"Don't look," Domino said.

In response, the human jostled him and broke free from his embrace. As pale as death, he ran out of the square, sneaking between houses. After a moment of paralyzing torpor, Domino followed him. Nearly panicking, he passed a hut and looked around. Gus had vanished. The child had probably returned to the hut he shared with Domino and his brothers. It was the first place to search.

The little nichan went in this direction but stopped in his tracks. Belma and Mora had left the square as well and were walking his way. Domino jumped behind the corner of the closest hut and ducked.

Mora seemed to be in a state of shock. His complexion had paled, and Belma held his hand, urging him to move away from the din animating the village center. The two stopped in the shade of a house.

"I've seen death before," Mora mumbled. "I guess I forgot . . . "

"I know. I've already . . . It's hard."

"Belma. I'm so sorry."

The girl pursed her lips and shook her head. "That's not the same. It's the memories that hurt. It almost makes me feel good, what they just did to that man."

"Because of . . . what happened to your parents?"

"This human is like the ones who took everything from me. He deserved it."

Mora nodded his head, not taking his eyes off his friend. "I—I saw Javik's body . . . after that man killed him."

"How?" Belma asked after a hesitation. The bones of her round jaw hardened.

"Javik had—" said Mora, searching for his words, running a

hand over his forehead. "His face was shredded. The human, he used one of those explosive weapons. I was outside Zato, in the woods, but I heard the sound it made. It was worse than thunder. Those weapons are faster than us."

"It's a Blessers thing, huh? Only they could invent weapons like this and put them in Torbs' hands."

Mora swallowed heavily and sighed a trembling breath. Belma's hand went up his arm and captured the teenager's face. The girl then bent down and placed her lips on Mora's. She lingered there for several seconds. When she moved back, Mora held her close to him, eyes veiled, mouth half-open as if to savor her scent. From his hiding place, Domino dismissed the perfect opportunity to escape. He was fascinated.

Mora had regained some color. The corners of his mouth shivered, heralding a smile to come. "You . . . Isn't it a little strange to do this now? After that, I mean."

Belma shrugged, playing with the braid hanging on Mora's shoulder. "I don't know. I want to. I need to. Would you like me to stop?"

This time, it was Mora who approached to kiss the girl. She allowed him to do so, pressing herself against the teenager's body, cheeks rosy. Her lips parted and the pink of wet tongues flashed between their open mouths.

The kiss dragged on, and Domino finally took advantage of the diversion to slip away in silence and join their hut.

The human sat in the farthest corner of the room. It had been months since the child had cowered there. Knees bent against him, his head leaning against the wall, he was still panting. He looked in Domino's direction but avoided his gaze the next second. Like Mora, the shock had swallowed the colors of his face.

No, it was far worse than that. A man had been hanged before his eyes with a savagery Domino was still unable to process. The man's torn hands, his face swollen and covered in blood. And the rope tightly wrapped around his neck. Ero hadn't wasted his time preparing a noose, as if his son's murderer wasn't worth the trouble. All of it was now carved in Domino's mind. But in the end, the result remained the same. The human child had just experienced through another the torment he himself had survived.

Domino hesitated to come closer. He knew the boy, his way of closing in on himself when fear ruled his mind, when he was angry, his way of pushing him away if Domino tried to offer him help, like the day before. He wanted to comfort the human, to tell him that he understood. Did he, though? It wasn't around his neck that a rope had been tied.

Then he thought of Mora. He remembered his brother, his trembling hands, his troubled breath and Belma, whose support — that kiss — had worked miracles. Their mother used to do that too. A kiss on the cheek or on the forehead to soothe them, to send their fears away. It hadn't always worked, and he figured the answer was there, outside. The cheek or the forehead. Belma had kissed Mora on the lips.

Could he do that, too? Would the other boy feel better? A kiss to ease his heart and fears.

The little nichan stepped into the room. The other child stayed still. Domino was still too far away to read it as a good sign. So he went one step further.

Without warning, shouting voices rose from the other side of the door, along heavy and alarming footsteps. The house door slammed open, carrying a vague metallic scent. Ero stood there, human blood smeared on his chest, face closed, eyes red. He lowered them first on Domino who backed away by reflex, assaulted by his Unaan's anger. Then they landed on the human. The child straightened, his chest swelling with the frenetic rhythm of his breathing.

Without a word, Ero walked up to the human, grabbed him by the arm, and dragged him outside.

"No!" Domino cried.

He shouted again and again but his uncle wouldn't listen. Ero kept dragging behind him the human whose legs were too short to follow his long strides.

"Ero, please!" Mora called as he followed the movement. "I beg you!"

What was going on? Why was Ero going after Gus? What was he going to do to him?

The rope.

The man they'd hanged under the bell.

No!

Domino ran to catch his uncle, who cut through the village. At the end of his arm, Gus—the human struggled. He was trying to unfold Ero's fingers. Did he know that each of his fingers was more powerful than all the strength the child possessed? It was a lost cause.

The main square was now empty. As he reached its center, Domino grabbed his uncle's tunic. He had to hold him back. Ero pushed Domino away, and the boy crashed into the crimson mud. He got up immediately and charged towards his leader. In the village, the now-scattered nichans followed the scene without a hint of emotion.

Mora was still begging Ero, palms up. "Please stop!"

"Get out of my way."

"Ero, he's just a child. Don't throw him out."

Out? He was going to expel Gus, leave him outside, to the wild animals? And there were worse than animals outside these walls. He would die out there.

"No! No!" Domino yelled, grabbing Gus's other hand to hold him down.

He wasn't just a human. It was his friend; he was Gus.

So Domino held tight. The result was the same: insignificant.

Gus screamed, torn between the two forces pulling him in opposite directions. But Domino had to save him. He couldn't let his friend go. He couldn't bear it. Gus couldn't die.

The doors of Surhok were opened, and Ero dragged the two children after him, not caring who would get stuck outside the rampart.

But he stopped when Mora spoke again, in a voice as clear as desperate. "He has the gift! The child has the gift. He can heal wounds. He can save lives. Ero, I beg you!"

Without freeing Gus, Ero slowly turned to his nephew. Hands clasped, eyes round, Mora looked as if he was about to fall to his knees before his Unaan. Ero approached him, forming a chain with the two little boys still clinging to his arm.

The man's black eyed gaze plunged into Mora's. "Say that again."

"He has the gift. He knows how to close wounds with the gift."

"You'd be willing to lie to me to save his miserable life?"

"Don't say it!" Domino cried, horrified to hear Mora confess this truth, but his brother ignored him, responding only to his master's words.

"I've seen it with my own eye. He did it. On Domino."

"How long have you known about this?" Ero asked.

"Several months."

All the sorrow that had marked Ero's face gave way to an icy rage that made Mora suddenly retreat. The young man slipped on the dirty cobblestones and lost his balance.

"Very well," said Ero. "Let's make sure of it."

He overtook Mora, returning to the village center, taking Gus and Domino in his wake.

"Wha—what?" Mora followed them. "Where are you taking him?"

"To the infirmary. One of our people will get hurt eventually. He'll stay there until we need his gift. Under guard."

"He's only a child — "

Too fast for Domino to catch the move, his uncle spun around and reached out. The next second, Mora's collar was trapped in the man's grasp. Domino let go of Gus's hand and gripped his brother's instead. He pulled him back, but Mora didn't move an inch.

Couldn't he do anything? "Leave him alone," Domino cried, noticing his own tears only now.

Again, no answer. Ero didn't even seem to see him. "Several months," he said between his teeth, so close to Mora's face that his forehead brushed against the teenager's. "Fucking months of keeping this to yourself. You think this is a game? You think you're above the law?"

"No," Mora promised in a gasp, shaking his head.

"You wanted to challenge me? For fun? To see what it would feel like to lie to my face day after day?"

"No."

"My son . . . Javik could have — " His hand squeezed Mora's collar tighter, limiting the space for air to reach the young man's lungs. "It took you all this time to tell me this. So we'll wait. The Vestige will stay as long as it takes in this hut."

"No!" Domino cried.

And his entrails froze when Ero's eyes met his. It was brief, a fragment of a second. The next moment, his uncle released Mora.

"You know what?" he said. "I don't have time for this bullshit. Let's get it over with now."

Ero's hand disappeared behind his back. This time he found a knife.

Mora, startled, opened his mouth.

Domino had no time to react. Ero waved his hand in front of

him, as if to show him the edge of the blade. A searing pain wrenched a scream out of the boy.

Domino raised his hands to his face. The pain was all the worse.

"*No!*" Mora choked.

Without knowing how, Domino found himself on the ground, crying his eyes out. A warm liquid ran down his cheek and neck. It filled his right eye.

His brother leaned over him. "Let me see it. Domino, let me see."

"It hurts!" the child cried, refusing to take his hands away.

The flesh seemed to move beneath his palm, as if it were no longer attached to the bone of his skull. But Mora insisted on looking, removing one by one the hands Domino was pressing against his face.

A shrill scream escaped the little boy.

VIII

Marissin's blood froze, every nerve in his body paralyzed by this heart-wrenching scream. In an instant, he stopped resisting the bone-crushing grip on his forearm.

Under Domino's left eye dangled a small piece of pink, bloody flesh. At the bottom of this deep wound, one could see the flashy white of the bone. Nausea rose in Marissin's gut. Had Ero even hesitated before stabbing Domino? A flick of his wrist, face devoid of emotion, and blood had spilled everywhere, unstoppable.

The little nichan brought his shaky palms back to his bloody face.

Mora stopped him. "Don't touch it! It's all right. It's all right, Domino." Then his eyes were on the other child. "Hey. Come on, help him."

All that blood, and Domino shouting at the top of his lungs.

With disdain, Ero threw the human to the ground next to the two brothers, as if he weighed no more than a rag. The child tasted the cold water of the mud and stood there on all fours, staring at the triangle-shaped hole carved in Domino's cheekbone.

"Please." Mora reached out his hand to him, a begging mask plastered on his face. "Come. Come closer."

It took a long time for Marissin to move and get up again. He didn't want to look into this wound. He wanted to touch it even less. And the smell of blood . . . But most of all, he couldn't stand to hear Domino cry anymore. The sounds fused inside his head, rubbing against his skull like a metallic claw. It had to stop.

He stepped on his trembling limbs and waded through the mud. He knelt down beside the young nichan, who didn't even seem to notice his presence. With his hands forced away from his face by Mora, Domino groaned between sobs and cries, cheeks dripping with tears and oily, rust-colored blood.

Marissin raised one hand. A rush of blood overflowed from the wound. As if touched by a flame, the child backed away.

"Hey," Mora said. His voice was soft behind its tremor. "You can do this. Listen to me. It's going to be all right. After this, it will be over. You hear me? You can do it."

The child had never doubted anything more in his entire life. He'd never treated anything like this before. It'd been easy to take care of Domino's arm several months earlier, or of the few cuts that had followed. He knew how to do that. He'd done it before. Mother had cut the palm of her hand once—an eternity ago. Without thinking, he'd closed it up with a caress and healed the abrasion before Mother had the reflex to reprimand him. Yes, nothing more than a scratch. That hole that reached into the bone of Domino's skull was no scratch. An inch higher and . . .

Marissin battled the surge of images invading his mind. Not fast enough. A vision of the boy's eyeball planted at the end of Ero's blade flashed before his eyes and flipped his heart upside down.

Ero. Was mutilation a nichan tradition? The three boys had come here to escape danger, to find shelter and family.

Family. Did that even mean anything?

"Hey!" Mora repeated, shaking his arm, and Marissin looked up at him. "He's in pain. Please. Hurry."

Summoning all the courage he had left, the little boy raised his fingers to the level of Domino's face. He had to touch the skin, not necessarily the wound, but for sure, he had to get as close as possible to the tissue in need of healing. So he placed his fingers along Domino's cheekbone. The nichan trembled in his brother's arms, reducing his lips to a thin line to keep the screaming at bay. Marissin closed his eyes, and the sensations submerged him.

At first nothing but Domino's quivering skin against his. Silence swallowed his surroundings, then his entire person.

He saw them now, like thousands of diverted streams, overflowing out of their beds. Muscles, blood vessels, severed nerves. They formed a devastated landscape. The wound on Domino's arm had been but a furrow dug in fresh earth. One hand had been enough to smooth it out. This time, it would take more than one stroke to restore the skin to its original condition. *You can do it*, he repeated to himself, an echo of Mora's voice. He could do it. It wouldn't be perfect, he knew that. It never was.

He concentrated, and the work began. He attached one by one the disconnected nerves and veins. There were so many more than he had ever seen before. A sudden rush of blood splashed the surface of his mind. He struggled through it and held on to keep going. He plunged into its tide to tie the flesh together, emerged to catch his breath, and then dived once more as another thick wave surged at him. Exhaustion quickly overtook him, and he drew the necessary energy from Domino. He found plenty, so much of it his own body seemed too small to contain its overwhelming volume. He needed it; he couldn't do it all by himself.

He felt resistance under his busy aching hands. With a thrust, he overcame it and narrowed the gap, closing the wound's lips. Beside his fingers, the skin gradually closed. He didn't slacken his efforts, not until blood stopped flowing. The skin was the hardest part to repair. It was a complex, irregular mesh, all the more fragile in a child. To be sure to close it, each knot had to be strong. Respecting the original pattern didn't matter. If Marissin attempted to do so, he would lose his health to the monumental task. He followed the line of the wound, rewove the thick and tender tissue. In his wake, the scar formed. In one last effort, he reached the limit of the opening.

He was done.

His eyes opened. He barely had time to appreciate Domino's peaceful face before he fell backwards. His butt hit the wet ground, soaking him to the skin. He was out of energy, out of breath, starving. But he had made it. He raised his chin and admired his work. As he had expected, Domino's cheek—on which he had left two muddy fingerprints—was marked with a curved, hollow, pale scar. He had given his all; it would hold.

Returning his gaze, the young nichan raised his hand to his blood-covered face. Without hesitation, he delicately tested the flesh, rolling it under the pulp of his fingers. Relief overcame him, and he sat upright. He wasn't yet seated before a hand grabbed Marissin's wrist and put him back on his feet.

"Perfect," Ero said between his teeth, and he forced the child to walk to the houses on their right.

"Ero . . . Ero, he succeeded," Mora called without leaving his brother restlessly fighting in his arms.

After one last glance, the human looked straight ahead. To look at the two brothers' faces would be his undoing. He couldn't let them see the tears rimming his amber eyes. Tears were for the weak, but he wasn't weak if he called them back before anyone could see.

"I want a word with you," Ero told Marissin.

Without further ado, he led him with a firm hand down an alleyway that separated two houses, walked to a hut, and opened the door. Inside there was no light except that of dusk filtering through the windows. There was no furniture, either. A scent of freshly cut wood and wet stone. The grates and the cast-iron basin of the brazier in the center of the room were clean; it'd never been used before. No one lived here, or maybe no one had ever lived here.

Ero pushed him inside and closed the door behind him. When the little boy turned around, he was alone. He watched his surroundings, his body stretched out like a clothesline. His eyes refused to adjust to the darkness.

Where had the clan leader gone? Why bring him here? He'd said he wanted to talk to him. So he should talk. Listening to Ero wouldn't hurt. Where was he?

The child didn't dare move. He could have opened the door and fled, but what was the point? He was in enough trouble already.

A minute passed. Then another. Impossible to catch his breath. His heart pounded, threatening to go up his throat.

Through the walls, the familiar sound of footsteps grew louder. The boy stepped back as the door opened on Ero. The man was almost twice his size. Draped in shadows, his silhouette wore a familiar essence. No, not the silhouette—Marissin had never met anyone so imposing. It was rather his presence, cold and inflexible. Like a constant threat.

His throat tightened, his intestines became animated, his healthy wing folded against his back.

Fear.

He couldn't flinch. He had to be stronger than that. He gathered all his courage again to hold his head high.

Ero entered the room, forcing Marissin to retreat. After a few steps, the man walked around the child and explored the area. Ero's hand ventured here and there. The unlit brazier was offered a caress. The man then walked to one of the two small windows and leaned against the wall. A bit of light revealed the square features of his scarred, bearded face. His eyes were still bloodshot.

He sniffed and stared at Marissin indecipherably.

"This is where my son should have lived. His mother and I built this house for him. He was so excited, like a child going on his first hunt. He was waiting for his first night by the fire, his first meal. He'd never entered it." He fell silent, gently shaking his head, as if facing once again the same inescapable reality. "No one will ever live here. All because a human decided that nichans had to die." Another pause filled only by Marissin's deafening heartbeat. "What you've just done outside is impressive. Javik had wounds on his face too. His neck. His chest . . . He was shot in the face. I wonder if there's anything you could have done about it. Maybe you could have saved his life. Or maybe not. The answer rests with the Gods now."

He ran a hand over his beard, rubbing its black, bushy curls, and took a deep breath. Something was pinched between Ero's fingers. It was small and blue. Marissin couldn't see well, and the twilight thickened as the nichan spoke. "I heard you want to stay with my clan. The last human who claimed this honor had to prove that she was essential to my people. I believe you are too. So you may stay. There are conditions to this privilege.

"You'll do what it takes to heal the wounded. You're not allowed to leave the village. For now you're too slow, but when we deem it necessary, you'll follow us on the hunt. This gift in you, no one knows its limits. Or even its tricks."

He raised his hand and showed the child what he held between his thumb and forefinger. "Do you know what it is?" He continued without waiting for an answer. "It's an Op crystal. A crystal named after a God. Op. It's not easy to get your hands on one. It's very rare. They say it only appears on the burials of certain dead people. Why? Go figure. A fragment like this is worth a small fortune. It was around the neck of the man who butchered my son. Apparently, he had a problem with Vestiges too, not just nichans."

Marissin didn't understand anything anymore. An Op crystal. He'd never heard of it, it wasn't in Mother's book. It didn't matter. He just wanted to get out of here.

"I've never seen its effects," Ero said as he scanned the blue pebble between his fingers, then the child's face.

The man brought his hand to the narrow window sill and dropped the crystal.

A scream sprang from Marissin's throat. He collapsed, unable to breathe. To think. The pain, it was everywhere. His blood boiled in his veins while a million thorns pierced his flesh. His bladder emptied, his bowels followed.

Mother! Mother!

The pain subsided and disappeared in an instant, as if it had never been real. Lying on the ground, his arms hugging his thin body, the boy opened his eyes. The piss and shit in which he lay was real, as was the blood escaping his nostrils, flavoring his mouth.

With the energy of desperation, he crawled backwards until the wall put an end to his retreat. On the other side of the room, Ero again held the crystal in his hand. He nodded, raising an eyebrow, and approached Marissin. Once close to him, he crouched down and showed him the rough blue stone up close. The child wanted to scream but his throat didn't respond. Only his legs did, shoving his small silhouette against the wall. This time, nothing could hold back the fear that had replaced the pain throughout his body. If Ero dropped that crystal again, Marissin would die — his sole certainty in his life.

"It's a warning," Ero said. "As long as you don't hurt anyone, as long as you behave yourself, you'll never see the color of this stone again. You can make yourself useful as much as you want, but don't forget one thing: in spite of your usefulness, you remain a Vestige. An inconvenience. Try not to remind me of it."

With that, he closed his hand on the crystal and left the place.

It took much longer for the child to gather his strength and spirit and flee the hut to hide.

As THE MINUTES WENT BY, Domino became more and more afraid of never finding the human again. Something bad had happened. No proof needed; he felt it in his heart. Ero had reappeared an hour earlier, alone, on his way to his house where his grieving partner and daughter waited for him. But Gus remained absent. (Domino no longer made the effort to rectify the name in his mind. He was far too preoccupied.) Even more alarming, the human boy's scent had vanished. Outside their hut, Domino couldn't identify it among the others, as if it had been erased. It was dark now, and the days of late winter preceded increasingly cooler nights.

Mora refused to leave Domino. After what had happened, it seemed beyond his strength. As they searched the village, his hand remained pressed against his little brother's shoulder. Domino appreciated the gesture, however. The blood on his clothes was only beginning to crystallize, making the stained collar and front of his tunic as rigid as frost.

He raised his hand to his cheekbone and played with the newly repaired flesh. Beneath the scar, the muscle consistency had hardened. The pain had been excruciating, spreading in his skull in burning thrusts. Now it was but a phantom sensation at the edge of his right eye. It was hard to accept that Gus had fixed everything in less than a minute. And though he was now calm, Domino was still in shock, his body tense but tired. Something had drained his strength while the other boy took care of his cheek.

He stopped at the edge of the village, facing one of the high bamboo walls, and inhaled the air, filling his chest. A faint smell of excrement came up his nose. It wasn't Gus's scent, or the scent of his skin or hair, yet Domino clung to invisible tendrils of the stench. Something was wrong.

"Why does it smell like poo here?" Domino asked as he followed this trail.

"The waste pit is on the other side of the village," Mora noted.

Before he could come to any conclusions, Domino heard it through the soft whistle of the wind. A muffled moan. Forgetting the tiredness numbing his muscles, he raced in that direction. He jumped over a fence that led to the clan's chicken coop and barely caught up when his foot got stuck in the bamboo.

"Domino, watch out!"

But the child ignored the warning. He crossed the farmyard, waking up the shady hens brooding in their aviaries, and found him there, hidden between two rows of pens. His face couldn't be seen, for Gus had buried it between his trembling knees. He was slumped against one of the cages, as if asleep or in lack of strength to sit by himself. Domino walked to him and noticed the filth on the human's pants. The closer he got, the more disgusting the smell of the droppings became. But even another Corruption Rain would have failed to stop Domino.

"Gus." His whisper triggered no reaction.

Of course it wouldn't. Gus wasn't his name. Domino had said it without thinking.

Behind him, Mora discovered the child's condition and spoke in a low voice. "Damn it. What has he done to him?"

Without further ado, Domino approached the human and sat down beside him. The space between the pens was narrow, yet Mora found a way to squeeze through as well. Still moaning, his hands flat against the wet soil, the child's breath quickened upon the two brothers' arrival.

"Gus," Domino repeated. "Are you sick?"

The human's breathing grew sharper, shivering, and Domino's fingers found the other child's hand. This one, frozen and in slight spasms, didn't avoid the touch. For the first time, Gus accepted what little comfort the young nichan offered him. The next moment, he did more than accept it. He leaned over to Domino, rubbing his shoulder and the corner of his head against the wooden pen, and let himself go against the young nichan.

Taken by surprise, Domino froze. Gus had never done this before. His behavior had been a succession of hot and cold responses. And for the first time, Gus was huddled up against him. How frightened and hurt was the human to willingly seek affection?

Recognizing the value of this gesture, Domino wrapped his arms around Gus's feverish body. The shoulders, the back, the wings, even the terrible smell; he hugged it all in a protective embrace. Immediately, the human burst into tears. Domino's arms held him tighter, amplifying the other child's weeping. Tears burned Domino's eyes, but he managed to swallow them. He had to be strong for Gus. He found his brother's gaze on them, taken aback. Mora was as shocked as he was.

What had Ero done? Domino was certain Gus wouldn't tell him. All he knew was that his friend needed him, and he would be there.

His friend, yes. Domino would be his friend, if only for as long as the other boy would need one.

With exhaustion, Gus's tears dried up after a few minutes. All the while, he remained leaning against Domino. The tension in him diminished. His breathing slowed, more regular now.

Domino didn't loosen his embrace when Mora broke the silence. "Let's bring him back home. Clean him up. A nice bath.

Something to eat. Let's get him warm. Gus, can you hear me?" He called him Gus, imitating his youngest brother. A few seconds passed, then the child nodded against Domino's shoulder. Mora sighed. "Good. We'll take care of you. Don't worry. Can you get up?"

This time, the child answered in the negative.

"I'll take care of it," said Mora, rising despite the lack of space.

With his face still hidden under his hair, Gus sighed. A small voice came out of his mouth, hoarse with exhaustion. "Am dirty."

"It's all right," Mora promised. "We all need a bath tonight."

With that, he gently captured the child in his arms, stealing him from Domino's, and they left the barnyard.

Domino pulled the blanket up over Marissin's shoulder and lay down in front of him. He smelled of soap and his thick black hair was curling, still wet. Behind him, Beïka, who had reappeared after the children's bath, was sleeping. Mora kept watch.

Beneath the thick layer of braided wool, Domino's hand found the human's. Their fingers remained together for a while, intertwined, one absorbing the other's heat.

Marissin refused to close his eyes. There were so many more chances for bad dreams to haunt him tonight. As long as he saw Domino's face, then his dreams couldn't reach him. He would eventually fail, but he wanted to stay in control of himself for as long as he could.

"Don't you want to sleep?" Domino whispered.

He, too, seemed to struggle to keep his eyes open. He had never needed much sleep; he always spent half the night ruminating and fidgeting in bed, finding reasons to get up before dawn. But tonight he would pass on. The dark circles under his eyes confirmed that it was time for this day to end. That was a lot. Too much.

Marissin didn't answer.

No. Not Marissin. He'd stopped answering that name months ago. "Gus," he said.

It was a shallow breath in his mouth that he could barely hear himself. But Domino shook his hand under the blanket. "Yes," the nichan said.

"Gus is my name."

Domino nodded, a slight smile on his lips. It was good to see him smile again, even if it stretched the deep scar under his eye. "I can tell you a story . . . A story about the sea. Or about the birds who came to . . . "

But Gus lost his fight and didn't hear what happened next even though Domino's voice soothed him for a while longer. His lids fell over his eyes, and he fell asleep.

That night it wasn't a rope that startled him out of sleep, but the dark blue of an Op crystal.

PART TWO

TRUE NATURE

IX

THE YOUNG NICHAN'S SKIN TURNED BLACK AND A SMILE stretched his mouth, wetting his dark, leathery lips with spit. He was young, no more than nine years old, and a whistle passed between his long sharp teeth. Nothing but bluster, but this child, if he wasn't careful, could do a lot of damage.

Facing him, taller by at least three heads, Domino readjusted the rosary of dead hares on his shoulder, feigning indifference. It happened like this every time. Peace had become a luxury.

Domino squinted and took a quick look at the boy from head to toe. "You know it's forbidden, right?" he said to the child.

The boy's expression shifted, but with the nichan smile splitting his face in two, it was impossible to read it.

"My mother says you're a failure," the child spat.

The words, almost incomprehensible, were deformed by the rows of teeth that altered the movements of his tongue. But the meaning was easy to grasp. It wasn't the first time a kid insulted him. Domino was far too hot to argue or to take offense at the words of a child just out of the egg who barely knew anything about life.

He sighed. "Yes, great. It's still forbidden."

"I do what I want."

More words half eaten by his beastly mouth. Like most children who were still learning to transform, it would take a few years for the child to express himself clearly. A quick observation on Domino's part. All the kids in hunting training shared the same issue.

"Do you, now?" Domino asked.

"I'll transform if I want to."

"A nichan has no right to attack a nichan from his own clan. The transformation means death, you stupid slug. If anyone sees you doing that, you'll be whipped. Personally, I don't give a shit. I'm just reminding you of your options."

The child seemed to hesitate. "You're lying."

"You want to check?"

"You're lying! You're just jealous. And I can even attack you if I want because my mom says you're not truly a nichan."

Domino had stopped counting the number of times a kid decided to throw those words to his face. The little one in front of him wanted to play big because he had recently gained access to a power far beyond anything he'd ever experienced before. Mora said that he'd felt invincible during this period of his life, before being quickly brought back to reality by their mother. As for Beïka, nineteen, he still hadn't returned to reality.

Domino smiled. He didn't know how he would feel when he finally managed to transform himself. In any case, a disrespectful offspring wouldn't get the best of him.

He grabbed the rope that bound the five hares he had just pulled out of the traps set in the land around the village and threw the limp animals into the dust. "If you want to, go ahead. Attack! But hurry, I have better things to do today than kick your ass."

Once again, the child hesitated and his smile seemed to fade.

Domino knew the risks. With his young, thick fangs, his claws still supple but deadly sharp, this kid had the ability to inflict serious injuries. And even though the gossip about his tardiness was somewhat true, Domino didn't want to be gutted to prove his point. He was offended, although he didn't let the child see it. At thirteen, Domino should have been able to transform himself long ago. He should have participated in a real hunt, not in the simulations reserved for younger children and supervised by a member of the council. He worked every day on his transformation, even when Mora didn't have time to help him. He could do it; he refused to doubt it. But the Corruption had robbed nichans of some of their abilities. How could they be sure that Domino wasn't the next stage in the evolution of this taint?

He stood on his feet and waited for the child to act or give up. Part of him hoped for the latter.

The young nichan growled. "You're trying to trick me."

"Of course I am." Domino laughed.

A stream of spittle spattered between the kid's fangs and fell into the rocky dust. Domino had had enough of this. He was thirsty, had already emptied the bottle hanging at his waist, and fresh water waited for him in the village.

Let's get it over with.

"Go back to the village with your tail between your legs and tell your mother how you quit," Domino said, his senses alert.

A good reflex, for the child charged immediately. Still a novice, he kept his arms back where any older nichan would have wielded those sharp appendages while jumping up and down to destabilize their prey. Domino bent and raised his hand. He then closed his fist on the child's bowl-cut hair, stopping him dead in his tracks. As he expected, the child tried to free his hair from Domino's grip. As his clawed hands rose to attack Domino's fist, passing a hair from the teenager's face, Domino bent his legs and mowed down the child's.

In a brown cloud of dry earth, the boy collapsed to the ground with a dull sound. The shock disturbed his concentration. He barely understood what had happened to him that he had already returned to his human form.

"I'm going to kill you, asshole!" he roared as he got up in a hurry.

"Numo!" called someone a little farther away.

The child was startled and turned his eyes at the sound of his name. A woman approached. Omak. She watched the children today and carried on her back a half-asleep little boy whose ankle had doubled in size. She was small for a nichan, thin and muscular, with round cheeks permanently hollowed out by deep dimples, and skin as dark as Domino's. She was in her thirties, and her annoyed expression marked the closing end of this long day.

With heavy steps, she approached, not as furious as she should have been. "What are you doing, Numo?"

The young nichan held her gaze, but he couldn't hide his shame. "Nothing," he lied.

"Nothing? Then what are you doing here? We called the retreat. Why are you hanging around?" He opened his mouth to defend himself but was denied the chance to do so. "We're leaving. Now."

The boy took his time, and Omak kicked him in the butt without shaking the child she was carrying on her back. Grimacing in his sleep, the child seemed not to notice what was going on around him.

Domino was picking up his hares when Omak turned to him, eyeing him up and down. "You know kids don't like you," she said as if reminding him of the time. "Why don't you stay away?"

Domino bit his tongue and smiled, raising his eyebrows in a falsely innocent manner. "They're adorable, don't you think? Why stay away?"

"You're too old for this."

"Well, let's just pretend I'm here to watch them, yes?"

"Oh really? Then maybe you should stick with me during the training. I'd probably have a thing or two to teach you. Who knows?" She licked her lips, eyes on Domino's bare chest, then abdomen.

She was bathed in sweat. The hair cut short around her face stuck to her smooth skin. And as Domino turned to her, she pushed open the neckline of her tunic, revealing the inner curve of a breast. Then she smiled at him.

Her glance and posture seemed to wait for an answer. On her back, the boy she held stirred, assaulted in his sleep by a feisty fly.

Something pressed at the back of Domino's skull, and he shook his head. "I'm fine."

It was Omak's turn to sigh. "Whatever. If you ever change your mind . . ." He wouldn't. "Come on, keep moving. I want to get home before the storm hits."

Domino overtook the woman. Once his back was to her, his smile faded.

FOR TWO MONTHS, the heat climbed, reaching new heights, making the nichans' toil unbearable. The riverbed of the village dried up, as it did every summer, leaving the source running deep under Surhok as the only access to fresh water. No one in the clan had ever endured such heat. It weighed and slowed down every gesture, kept everyone awake at night, soaked each individual in their own juice. And it brought in its wake a pungent and volatile dust that triggered coughing fits in the most fragile ones.

Only children still had the energy to run around and act as if this season hadn't turned into an inescapable torment.

The cries of those same children returning from "the hunt" caught Gus's attention. He raised his nose from the mulberry leaves he was spreading in various iron boxes and tiptoed up to look out the open window. (He may have grown up, but nichans always placed their windows above the level of his eyes.) Under a steel-gray sky, a group of children crossed the limit of Surhok. After the first wave, a second flowed into the village. Domino was among it.

"Are you done cleaning up? I can see you snooping around," said Muran, the herbalist, across the room.

Gus ignored her. Outside, Domino smiled and stood up straight as an "I" despite the heaviness of the air and the sweat covering his half-unclothed body. Despite his playful and optimistic nature, the nichan's grin right now was forced. Gus knew something had happened.

"Damn it, aren't you done daydreaming yet?"

Muran seemed overwhelmed by the heat. Her voice was barely a whisper, with no vigor at all. A brutal cough squeezed her chest, and she hurriedly searched her things. Under the table on which she prepared her mixtures, the older woman found a terra cotta jar closed with a cork. She swallowed several sips and coughed a little more — a cough of a whole other nature. However, the alcohol in the jar had the desired effect, and the woman spilled the liquid one last time into her greedy mouth.

When she turned her attention back to Gus, he sighed his displeasure. He'd missed his chance. There was something in the infirmary he'd promised to get his hands on.

"Won't you share a sip with a poor, thirsty boy?" Gus asked in an equal tone.

Muran sighed and the jar went back to her belongings. "You're almost done. You'll go quench your thirst somewhere else. Water is scarce this time of year."

Did she truly believe she was fooling anyone? The woman's penchant for the bottle was nothing new. And she dared give into that habit in a place meant for medical care.

Two knocks rang out against the door of the infirmary. The woman dragged herself to the entrance with a limp gait. On the other side of the door, Domino appeared. His smile widened as he saw Muran—another forced grin—but his gaze softened as it fell on Gus. Gus relaxed and winked at his friend. With a slight wave of his chin, he pointed to the location of the object he was to take and then pointed his finger at his own chest. Domino's expression remained unchanged. He knew what to do.

"Muran, one of the kids sprained his ankle," Domino announced, leaning against the door frame before wiping sweat from his shiny forehead.

"Where is he?" the woman asked. "Why didn't you carry him here?"

Domino had the herbalist's full attention. Gus seized the opportunity to act before it passed.

"Omak's the caretaker," Domino said, shrugging. "She'll be here soon. I'm just the messenger."

"That's all you are? If Omak's already planning to come here, what good are you?"

As false distress and scruples danced across his face, Domino shook his head. "You're right. What is wrong with me? I'm really useless. I thought you were going to close the infirmary. I didn't want you to have to come back. Please forgive my unfortunate behavior. What a fool I can be—"

"All right, shut up."

Sighing, her voice still broken from the cough, Muran took one step to turn around. But Gus wasn't finished. Domino's voice echoed from the threshold.

"Wait."

"What now?"

Gus replaced the boxes he'd just moved and signaled to Domino that the coast was clear.

"Do you have something to drink for me? My waterskin is

hopelessly empty," the boy said, waving his flat-skinned flask as proof.

As he closed and put away the jars Muran had entrusted to him to justify his presence in the infirmary, Gus smiled. On the other side of the room, Domino was innocence incarnate, a gentle smile curling his lips.

But the herbalist had had enough. "Get the taint out of here, both of you, and drink somewhere else. Yeah, that goes for you too, Vestige. Get out and close the door. You're bringing dust in."

With his fist clenched on his booty, Gus obeyed. When the door slammed behind their backs, Domino frowned and wiped his face again.

"If I hear her call you Vestige again . . ." he said as they put distance between the herbalist and themselves.

"With all that alcohol in her belly it's a miracle she remembers her own name," Gus eluded, refusing to let Muran's attitude cloud their mood.

Domino probably understood his intention, for he moaned like a dying man, raising his arms and face to the vanished Gods. "I'm fucking thirsty!"

The nearest fountain was close. The water they spurted out was warm, but Domino shot toward it without hesitation and then placed his head right under the bronze faucet. "It's decided. I'm staying here until the end of summer," he said as he pressed on the pump again and again, water trickling faintly from the back of his head to his forehead and cheeks.

"I'm thirsty," Gus said, and his friend immediately gave him room. "Hold this for me." He handed Domino a small dark cigar as a reward for their day's work. Domino caught it between two wet fingers as water dripped from his black curling hair to his shoulders.

Water was a miracle in Gus's throat. He rinsed his hands and face before throwing water on his wings over his shoulders. He straightened up as Domino was about to turn his heels.

"Wait," Gus said, raising his hand high—Domino was at least a head taller than him—and capturing the nichan's chin. "You're bleeding."

The wound was small and shallow, but brown dust was sticking to the blood crystals.

Domino let Gus wipe the wound with his wet thumb, smiling slyly. But a slight blur had time to harden his features. "The war wounds of a nichan returning from hunting," Domino joked. "I escaped death, you know. It was a merciless struggle between the beast and me."

Gus smiled, but the tirade—though of the purest intentions— couldn't hide the nichan's discomfort.

The wound is so clean. Who did this to him?

Domino had never transformed. A shameful reality from which he'd escaped with varying degrees of success. Domino spent an hour every night repeating the concentration exercises Mora had advised him to practice. To no avail.

"If I really can't do it, I could still become Orator," he had once joked.

Domino, to become a man of the Gods, renouncing his beastly form for good? Never in a million years.

Gus didn't have to close his eyes or focus. It was nothing but a scratch. He ran his thumb three times over the wound that cut through the corner of his friend's chin. After the third pass, it was gone. Not even a scar.

Gus lowered his hand. "That's it."

"Thank you." Domino smiled and beckoned his friend to the sanctuary for dinner.

NATSO, Mora's son, came into the world during the following suffocating and stormy night. As everyone dreamed of it, the storm thundered in the distance. Under a sky darker than the bottom of a grave, nichans gathered among the vegetable plants in the stepped gardens to watch the lightning illuminate the clouds through which the Corruption's spasms recalled the beating of a heart. Barely refreshed by fans crafted out of water lily leaves, everyone waited for the storm that had been announced that morning, but the wind was playing hard to get and nothing was pushing the rain towards Surhok. Not yet.

Domino collapsed onto the dry earth sown with sunroofs and rutabagas, lengthened his long legs, and contemplated the nothingness stretched above their heads. It was said that before the Gods had disappeared, the night sky had been freckled with stars, like the ones dancing before his eyes when he ran out of breath. The stories of the Orator and the elders of the clan hinted at a bright and colorful past.

The veiled skies. Yet another effect of the Corruption.

Near Domino, sitting cross-legged, eyes in a haze, Gus blew a cloud of smoke. The taste of kesek reminded him of morning breath. Like shit, plain and simple. If the dried leaves hadn't had the gift of relaxing muscles and mind, the two boys wouldn't have pilfered the cigar from Muran's belongings. The woman wouldn't notice anyway. Only the disappearance of one of her precious jars of liquor would scratch her attention.

Gus swallowed another puff of kesek, kept it for a while in the warmth of his lungs, then shared his little cigar with Domino.

Half-naked, they sat at a fair distance from the others. Most of the men and women of the clan were bare in the gardens. Nichans didn't care about their nudity; it was a natural state, the state in which all were born, and in which they would join the Gods after death. Once the chores were done, nothing relieved them more than getting rid of the clothes they wore for the sake of convenience. Summers became more and more uncomfortable as the skies darkened and the nights grew longer. At some point, undressing wouldn't be enough anymore to survive the heat.

Gus was startled. A finger had just landed in the hollow of his back to divert the fall of a drop of sweat rolling off his fair skin. The teenager looked over his shoulder.

Cigar wedged in the corner of his lips, hand under his disheveled head, Domino raised his gaze burdened with heavy eyelids to Gus. "You're melting," he said, his voice sluggish.

"Stop it," Gus sighed, pushing his friend's hand away.

But Domino's finger remained on his back, bouncing against the flesh. "You're not ticklish."

"You know I'm not."

"What about now?"

"No."

"No?" His fingertip poked out right under Gus's ribs. "And here?"

The outline of a smile appeared on Gus's thin lips, lit by the torches framing the gardens. Tiny dimples hollowed out his cheeks. "You're going to lose a finger if you keep this up."

"I'll risk it," Domino said.

The next moment he burst out laughing when Gus's hand found his, bending it, forcing it away from his side. Then Gus lay flat on his stomach in the dry earth (dust immediately got stuck against his skin) and retrieved the cigar from Domino's mouth before carrying it to his own.

This was his seventh summer in the service of the Ueto Clan.

Seven years since he had been given a new name. Gus. Time flew by.

Next to him Domino was still smiling. His black hair stuck to his temples, his shiny chest rising at a gentle pace in this furnace. Gus unfolded his wing and waved it up and down. A slight gust of wind passed over Domino's extended body.

The boy groaned with relief. "Again," he begged as Gus stopped, bothered by the amount of effort necessary to raise the limb.

Yet he flapped his wing again, closing his eyes, enjoying the momentary effects of kesek in his veins.

Soon, the wind picked up and thunder rumbled through the valley below. In the vegetable garden, the excitement mounted in the shape of singing and heavy laughter.

Thunder responded in the distance, still too far away.

Then the labor began. The baby was coming, but no one in the gardens heard the news. Until they called for Gus. While the child had not yet come out, Belma had started to lose a lot of blood. He went up to the baths, the only decent place for a birth.

Mora had been born here. Twenty-five years later, his child would carry on the tradition.

Men were only allowed in the baths during childbirth with the mother-to-be's consent. Mora waited outside. Gus was inside. Despite the extensive medical care he had administered over the years, he'd never attended a delivery before. He'd never seen the details of a woman's genitals, either. He discovered both the same night in a vision disturbed by the flickering flames of grease lamps and the groans of pain Belma tried to suppress behind her shut lips.

Face burning but unreadable, not allowing the sight of her naked body and exposed sex intimidate him, Gus knelt in front of the woman's wide-open thighs.

Apart from Belma and the herbalist, there was an old nichan woman tattooed from clavicle to ankle sitting near the hot water basin. She rested her ink-blackened hands on her knobby knees. She kept her eyes closed and mumbled into her moustache. It was Belma's great-grandmother, Dadou. Gus ignored her and went to work.

He put both hands on the woman's hard, swollen belly and

closed his eyes. The rest was done instinctively, without the need to think about it. Since his arrival at Surhok, he had treated hundreds of wounds. He cared for this one as he had for the many others: with attention.

But he'd barely begun before he was interrupted to let Belma push. With controlled breathing, she wiped her forehead and continued the task she had begun before Gus's arrival. She pushed, again and again, her hands flat on her belly, without anyone's help, master of her own body.

"I'm waiting for you," she panted toward her child, the top of whose head finally appeared between her stretched out flesh. "I will take care of you. I will never leave you alone . . ."

As a tear rolled down her face, Dadou placed a bony hand on her great-granddaughter's round belly.

More efforts, more tears. Then the child arrived. Muran picked up the baby and turned him over before slapping him firmly on the bottom. As if in a trance, Gus rested his palms on the mother's belly once more. He had spotted the damage inside her, the lesion lost between the flesh and the mucous membranes. He had to complete his healing for the blood to remain where it belonged.

As thunder roared louder over the village, as rain finally poured down on the vegetable gardens and on more than relieved nichans, the baby gave his first cry in Muran's hands. Gus came back to his senses. He opened his eyes and noticed his fingers partly inserted into Belma's burning private parts. Delicately but without delay, he pulled them out before retreating to the back of the room. He hadn't felt his hand move while he was giving his care. He'd probably needed to get as close to the wound as possible.

But Belma didn't mind, for she only had eyes for her son, who was still connected to her by the whitish, deformed cord coming out of her womb. She seemed to have forgotten Gus's—or anyone else's—presence and gave into tears as she kissed the infant's forehead.

It was over.

Gus took a deep breath to get rid of the dizziness that plagued him. As always, his discomfort lasted a while. Drenched with sweat, he closed his eyes. He could feel it; there wasn't just blood on his hands. The smell, heat, and fatigue made his heart pound.

Air. He needed it.

With a flick of his shoulder, the door slammed open in front of him. A powerful thunderbolt tore the sky and clouds. Gus took a few steps and found himself standing in the rain. Behind him, the baby's cries defied the din of the storm.

In between, Belma called out to her partner. "Come and meet your son, Mora."

The man's eyes opened wide. Domino embraced his brother before grabbing his shoulders and shaking him affectionately, his face brightened by a grin. Soaking wet, Mora ran a hand across his face. Anguish had given way to a contagious relief. A wave of friendly pats slapped the new father's back. Laying a grateful hand on Gus's shoulder as he passed by, Mora disappeared into the baths.

Domino stood in the rain, his skin glistening, intermittently lit by the lightning flashing across the sky. "Is she all right?"

"Yes," Gus said. "I think so."

"And you?"

"Never better."

"You want to sit down?" An even brighter smile appeared on Domino's lips and he walked to Gus, who shook his head to refuse. "In that case, don't get mad," Domino said.

Before Gus could grasp the meaning of the words, his friend lifted him up in the air, shouting with joy, laughing like a madman, arms wrapped under Gus's ass. Gus was caught unawares and tried as hard as he could not to touch Domino with his blood-covered hands. He failed and caught the nichan's shoulders. The world whirled, with laughter, fresh rain, and the smell of wet grass and dirt.

"Put me down before you scare the storm," Gus ordered, struggling to hold his own laughter.

Domino complied and took his friend's face in his hands before pressing a smashing kiss on his wet forehead. As he stepped back, Gus sighed and looked up at the nichan's black eyes. The last time Domino had seemed so happy was when he and Gus had first played their own version of the Flight of the Chickens in the hen house when they were little. Domino had screamed with joy, unable to take his smile off his face, out of breath with incessant laughter. And just like last time, the teenager blushed and his tears mingled with the rain streaming down his cheeks.

"Mora is a dad," he said and cried. "Damn it! I'm an uncle."

"Looks like it," Gus confirmed without breaking eye contact, batting his eyelashes to chase away the drops clumping together.

Mora had waited many years before daring to become a father. Raising his brothers and a human child had never been part of his plans. Domino had always encouraged his brother to pursue his own happiness. It was now a done deal.

Nothing was worth the expression on Domino's face. That smile, that look, that joy of breathtaking sincerity. Gus suppressed his desire to take Domino in his arms and tilted his head back, sighing deeply as rain finally cooled him down. In front of him, Domino did the same.

X

Domino's smile had never disappeared this fast.

"What? Why?" He got up, the movement unintentionally menacing.

Facing him, Mora sighed through his nose, long and firm. In the adjacent room, only separated by a wooden screen decorated with dried plants, the baby had finally calmed down after several exhausting hours of relentless shouting.

Mora's eyes almost begged Domino to lower his voice. "Hey, not so loud. Do you want Natso to scream again? Belma needs her rest."

But Domino was somewhere else. "Why?" he repeated, lower this time.

"They're the clan's Stones. He was never allowed to go up there. This occasion isn't reason enough to change the rules."

Tomorrow morning would be the baptism of Mora's son. The family would go to the Prayer Stones to introduce Natso to the Gods and receive their favor. Domino had never attended such an event and excitement had been building up in him for days like a bubble charging toward the surface of the water. He'd thought that at last Gus would be allowed to climb up to the Prayer Stones, that the two friends would contemplate the view of the village and the whole hunting territory together. The subject had been recurrent over the years. Domino had convinced himself that one day Gus would see it with his own eyes.

Of course he wouldn't. It didn't matter that Gus was family. Only one man had a say when it came to their sacred place, or anything related to the clan, in fact.

"Did Ero say that?" Domino guessed as Mora gestured for silence again. "Of course it's him. It's always him. It's not just a Calling; it's your son's baptism. It won't happen twice. It's not the rules, it's a punishment. Ero knows that."

Domino refrained from spitting his uncle's name.

"Believe me, I insisted, Domino," Mora said. "You know the man's nature."

"I'll talk to him," he said, bypassing his elder brother.

Gus wouldn't be left out. Even after all these years, many nichans still refused to treat the boy as one of their own, or even to call him by his name. Gus did all his chores, took care of the gardens, the laundry, the village, and its people. He did as much as anyone else here. In the end, all his efforts were only meant to keep him within these walls, not to give him the respect he fully deserved. This injustice boiled in Domino's chest.

With a firm hand, Mora stopped his brother and forced him to face him. "What are you gonna do about it, eh?"

"Reason with him. I will—"

"Reason with him? Since when did this become an option? Do you think it's a good idea to talk to him like this? You just go for it like you always do. That's not an approach you can take with Ero, unless you're looking for shit. We both know how he works."

They exchanged glances and a phantom pain tugged at Domino's cheekbone, where only a hollow scar remained today. Yes, he knew perfectly well how Ero worked, taking it out on the first person within reach, preferably the weakest one. Even though Ero had been in mourning at the time he had mutilated his nephew, Domino had never been able to forgive him. Nothing had ever been the same between the two brothers and their uncle. As for Beïka, it was another story.

Domino thought of Gus again, and his anger turned into sadness. Domino had been rambling about the baptism for days, repeating that his brothers had attended his own in the days following his birth. Anyone who attended the ceremony became an active part of the child's life. Gus deserved to be there.

"So it doesn't matter that he saved Belma?" Domino said. "This baby still has his mother because of him."

"Tell me something I don't already know. I don't even want to imagine what would've happened if Gus hadn't been there. I could never thank him enough for what he did."

"That's not the only life he saved!"

He was talking for himself now because he understood that nothing and no one would come to his aid. The problem was that Mora—everyone—didn't understand what it cost Gus to use his gift. Domino had promised his friend to keep this to himself, not to reveal that Gus was exhausted and suffering when taking care of patients.

"It's like being squeezed on all sides," Gus had tried to explain a few months earlier. "As if . . . as if I have to disappear or become insignificant so that all that remains is my will and the wound. Sometimes, when it goes on too long, I feel like I've gone out of my body, like I've gone too far. When I come back, my body feels alien. It's stupid, when you put it that way. Does it make sense?"

Domino couldn't stand that his friend had to go through this, that he talked about it as a side effect and not as a pain he'd been enduring for years.

"I'm not going. I'm not going to the Stones. Not without him."

Disappointment marked Mora's features. "He is your nephew,

Domino. You just said it—it won't happen twice. You . . . you have to be there for Natso. There's nothing to even discuss."

"That's easy for you to say. Gus is my best friend. He's—" He paused, trying then failing to describe the bond he'd formed over the years with Gus. "I can't turn my back on him and agree to Ero's stupid rules."

Mora passed a hand over his forehead, and Domino felt his brother's frustration grow. He knew words sometimes went beyond his thoughts. On one side there was Mora. On the other was Gus. Torn between the two of them, Domino lost track of what was right and what was foolish. Sometimes he felt so stupid, as if tangled up in his own mind. But he had to express himself before his nerves suppressed his ability to think for good.

As whenever he felt on the edge, his hands tickled and invisible stings crept under his skin. He clenched his fists to chase the sensation.

"For what it's worth, I don't think Gus expects to be invited," Mora said. "He's been at peace with that for a long time."

Domino clenched his fists harder. "That's not the point!"

On the other side of the screen, the baby began to cry.

Domino took a step back. He'd screamed. Almost transformed.

Almost.

Not that he knew how to do it. He'd never been able to. But in that moment, he'd wanted to. He apologized immediately. It was forbidden for a nichan to use his bestial form to attack a nichan of his own clan. Domino had just narrowly avoided a disaster, but for a moment he'd stood on the edge of a precipice, ready to jump, driven by his anger and constant frustration. Even though the odds were close to nil, something had shifted in him, a purpose that he had been cultivating for almost three years in hope of transforming himself, like any other teenager his age could do.

He ran a hand over his sweaty face, as if to check that the

nichan smile wasn't splitting his face in two. If there was a nichan Domino refused to threaten, it was indeed Mora.

"I don't know what . . . I . . ." he stammered.

Mora's hands rested on his shoulders and he led Domino to the low bench behind him. Then the man knelt in front of his little brother, his tender touch on the top of Domino's head. "Breathe. Calm down."

"I'm sorry."

"You did nothing. You just shouted. It's fine. Just breathe. Breathe."

Domino did so as a soft, tired voice soothed Natso on the other side of the hut. The soft humming of Belma's voice reached even the teenager's heart.

It wasn't uncommon for the younger ones to have poor control of their transformation. Unable to transform, Domino reinforced this well-known rule. However, poor control of emotions was a problem that only he seemed to face.

"Look, that's just the way it is, like it or not," Mora said. "Gus is a big boy, he'll understand."

"That's the problem. We shouldn't have to keep asking him to understand why we're shutting him out. I hate to hurt him," Domino whispered, still mastering the comings and goings of the air in his lungs. "You know what it's like when he shuts down."

Silence, not a look, a tense posture, and a cold expression. This was what Domino feared, for then he felt unable to help his friend. As soon as Gus closed up to him, it was like stepping back in time, to the days when the human's behavior was closer to that of a frightened beast struggling in a snare than an ordinary child. But there was nothing ordinary about Gus. Domino knew this better than anyone.

"It's only a morning," Mora said in a soft voice. "We must be at the Stones before daylight. Tell him he can sleep longer. We know he's dreaming about it."

But the joke fell flat.

"Do you want me to tell him?" Mora suggested, though he probably knew the answer.

His brother shook his head and stood to leave.

GUS WAS ALONE when he woke up the next morning. A sweltering heat bathed him in his own sweat. He turned on his wings—a somewhat uncomfortable position—and gazed at the wooden frame and the rudimentary insulation of woven bamboo.

The hut officially belonged to Domino. He himself had built this modest dwelling when Mora had decided to move in with Belma and Dadou, long before the young woman's pregnancy was announced. Even though Mora and Gus had helped him, most of the work was Domino's doing.

"Not too bad for an offspring. Look at the roof; it's still standing," Domino joked sometimes.

He'd only been eleven at the time, taking part in his first hunting trainings around the village with the other children, learning to live with a body that suddenly demanded the change all nichans went through.

And on his first night in this hut, Domino had offered Gus to share it with him.

The hut that the three brothers and Gus had occupied until now was reserved for visitors. It had no fire to warm them on winter nights and no water supply. Now that the three nichans had freed it, only the Gods knew where Gus would find rest at night. He had hesitated to accept his friend's proposal even though it made sense. Domino's hospitality knew no limits when it came to Gus, which reminded the human how much his well-being within the clan depended on their friendship.

"This is your home," Gus had said in a detached tone, devoid of sadness, as if sleeping on a pile of dead leaves was not bothersome.

"You're right." Domino had smiled as he slumped down on his bed, which had made a creaking sound, stealing a grimace, then a laugh from him. "So, if it's my home, I'll invite whoever I want, right? So consider that my home is your home."

The two boys had been sleeping side by side for years. They used to lie down and talk, to discover the stories Domino was making up, interrupted most often by Mora or Beïka, who ordered them to shut up and sleep. Gus had had no desire for this to change.

He had moved toward the bed, leaning forward, palms flat against the mattress, and pretended to test its solidity. Domino had grown so much that it wouldn't be long for his feet to stick beyond the bed frame. He'd looked at Gus with a smile on his face. Then Gus had laid down beside him.

Yes, he liked it here.

Gus sat up on the straw mattress and stretched out his arms and wing. Then he remembered Domino had gotten up long before dawn to follow his family to the Prayer Stones. He wouldn't be back until lunch. Gus got up in turn.

The heat slowed his every move as he took care of his responsibilities. Washing the bandages and sheets of the infirmary. Sweeping the sanctuary. Collecting nuts that had fallen from the trees inside the village. He stuffed half of them in his mouth for breakfast and then settled under the foliage, crushed by an irresistible languor.

That was when she appeared. She walked with a determined step, her frizzy hair gathered along her skull in fine braids, a bucket of burning fat hanging from her arm.

Gus hadn't seen or spoken to Matta since . . . Shame rose to his face. He couldn't say exactly how long, but for sure more than two years had passed since their last lesson. Maybe even three.

The last lesson hadn't really been one. Domino and Gus were running out of attention. The nichans had just returned from a hunt and had brought back the fresh corpse of a huge saurian, or what was left of its carcass. It was time for the kids to know what these creatures could look like, not to study. They'd run away without heeding the woman's firm warnings. Upon their return, Matta was gone. She'd then ended their weekly sessions for good.

· Gus followed the woman's procession along the edge of the woods. She went to the nearest lamp and filled it with several ladles of solid fat.

He missed their lessons. He'd learned so much from Matta. Unlike most of the Uetos, Gus and Domino could read and write. Knowledge they had no use for within these walls, but whatever. It was something that would never be taken from them.

Matta was a Santig'Nell. In the end, Gus didn't have to remember the word; she'd told him herself. A Santig'Nell, a human chosen by the Matrons to serve the peoples of the world.

"The Matrons?" had asked an eight-year-old Domino before uttering words that had earned him punishment later that day. "Are those the giant rocks everyone's talking about?"

"They are our guides, our protectors in these difficult times," Matta had said once her anger had passed. "They are not rocks, but magnificent crystals of great purity, thousands of years old, witnesses of our world's creation, entities whose understanding of life and history far surpasses that of beings of flesh and blood. The world was brutally wounded when the Gods were taken from us. From the height of their wisdom and greatness, the Matrons watch over us, like mothers. We Santig'Nells share their word and watch over the Gods' creatures, as they have instructed us to do."

"Can I be a Santig'Nell too?"

"We're not; we become."

"Oh. Can I become one, then?"

"No, Domino. To be eligible for such an ascension, one must be a host devoid of all Light. In the blood of nichans already flows the Gods' Light. You all call it Essence, right? What makes your transformation possible. A wonderful gift. The Eye offered by the Matrons requires room, plenty of room, to develop its full potential."

"Plenty of . . . room. A larger body? But I, too, will become very large."

Matta had smiled. "That is not the point. Only humans are chosen by the Matrons and raised by the Worth of the Santig'Nell to prevent wars, to protect the peoples, to — "

"Stop the Blessers?" Gus had interrupted. The title of Usurpers hadn't been erased from his vocabulary yet.

Without his knowing why, Matta had then ended their lesson.

A simple thought occurred to him. Gus wasn't the only member of the clan forbidden to climb to the Prayer Stones. Matta was the other one. Two humans, he a Vestige, she a Santig'Nell, living among nichans.

Gus lost sight of the woman and left the cover of the trees. He didn't know what to say to her, but he still wished to trade words, if only to let her know he hadn't completely forgotten her. Before he'd even decided what he'd say, he was bent over the hen houses, looking for eggs that had already been collected before he woke up. A few steps away, Matta continued her task by another lamp, and then another, gradually getting closer to Gus. Then she stopped and noticed him.

Innocently, he looked up at her.

"Good morning," she said, her forehead covered with sweat under the leaden sky.

He bent down to search the straw under the belly of a hen. Nothing, of course.

"Long time, no see," he said.

"Well, I'm not to blame. You know very well where to find me. In fact, I don't remember you asking me for lessons lately."

"Lessons? Do you still have anything valuable to teach me?"

He felt foolish from the moment those words came out of his mouth. He showed no sign of it and went to the next pen, kicking away with a light push the poultry lurking around him, on the lookout.

"I sure do," Matta said, walking to the next lamp a few feet away. "You'll understand one day that we creatures of flesh and bone and limited intelligence never cease to learn. And I have the feeling a number of my lessons have already vanished from your memory."

"Have they, now?"

"Of course. My methods are not infallible, I must admit, and you and Domino were not always attentive students. A lesson in first-rate conduct: your peers will always appreciate a proper greeting."

Gus continued to search the cages, stood, and at last turned his eyes to her. "Hello," he said, and she giggled briefly.

"I forgot you reached this point."

"This point?"

"Yes, this point. This difficult age for all humans and nichans. Even we Santig'Nells have to bear the burden of this change. Always showing a bit of insolence, playing with orders and adult advice, pretending to know more than they do, challenging them to find out where their limits stand. Like a game. Let's hope it passes too soon rather than too late."

"Gods forbid, I already can't leave this village. Without it, I would be quite bored."

Realizing that he was feeling sorry for himself—which he loathed above anything else—Gus looked away. His eyes landed on the vegetable peelings stored nearby, and he threw several stiff handfuls of them at his feet. The hens rejoiced.

Just as he feared, Matta took pity on him. "You know where to find me if you need lessons . . . or company."

"I'd rather remain insolent," he said, cutting short the conversation.

He turned away from her and cursed himself for not paying more attention to his own tongue. Good thing Domino wasn't around. His reaction would have pissed off Gus even more.

He didn't want anyone's pity, not now, not ever. He'd survived until today because he'd fought, not because he was pitied, he thought. He would survive no matter what happened, here or even outside the village. His coexistence with the Uetos was his doing—yes, it was his decision.

He repeated this to himself a second time as he returned to the sanctuary to complete his morning chores.

XI

When Domino returned that midday, his smile heralded great plans.

Sitting in the sanctuary, determined to enjoy the meal he deserved after all his efforts, Gus watched his friend sit across from him, his eyes shining. His smile kept getting bigger and bigger, mischievous. Domino was preparing something, which he hadn't done in a long time.

Gus liked the possibility, although he remained impassive. He was still trying to suppress the remnants of his bad mood after his conversation with Matta. "That's a big smile."

"Do you want to go out?" Domino said offhandedly.

"Out? In the village?"

"I feel like going for a swim. It's way too hot today. Don't you want to go out?"

He was talking in a low voice, even though no one was within earshot, according to Gus. His senses weren't as developed as a nichan's.

Gus put down his spoon and tilted his head to the side. "You bet I want. We're roasting outside. In here, we're stewing. Do I look like a piglet?"

Domino shook his head hilariously, without taking his eyes off him.

"What's on your mind?" Gus finally asked him, lowering his voice, leaning forward, immediately imitated by the nichan, who spread out flatter on his stomach on top of the table.

"Everyone's busy, half stunned by the heat. I like this torpor in them. I could spend all day snoring, and it would go way over their heads. And that's good; I don't feel like working today."

"This part was clear already. You said you wanted to swim. Where?"

Domino looked around. At the end of the adjoining table, Ero and his daughter had just joined Orsa, who was already eating. Beïka sat farther away with other nichans, laughing, his mouth full of wild pig and carrots. No one cared about the two friends. Not even when Domino jumped from his seat.

"Are you ready to be blown away?"

For an answer, Gus followed him.

THE VILLAGE RIVER WAS SHALLOW, as wide as a man's height, and the Uetos used it to irrigate the gardens and wash their clothes. In early summer, before its bed dried up, children would play in its flow from early in the morning until late after nightfall. It was not in its water that Domino wanted to bathe today, and Gus had already figured that out.

His suspicions were all the more confirmed when Domino led him to the far end of the village, far from the houses, their two silhouettes hidden from the world by the wild bushes and the dense black foliage. Once they reached Surhok's limits, the nichan squatted and hit the high wall once with his palm.

And again. Each time the impact vibrated through the muscles of his arm. Then he looked up and peered around. They were alone. His palm knocked several times again, harder. The blows were powerful but absorbed by the hollow bamboo.

Standing next to him, Gus smiled as the bamboo trunks pivoted at last. The wall was breached. "Faces above . . . You did this?"

Domino's face lit up with a new and irrepressible pride. He wiped the sweat from his face and neck and put back in place the dark wooden studs stretching his earlobes. "We can still wait for Ero to give you permission to go out, if you feel like it, but I'm sick of asking for permission."

Gus smiled back, absorbing his friend's excitement. "You won, I'm blown away," he said, which added to Domino's joy. Gus, however, considered the consequences he had no desire to think about right now—but someone had to. "We'll be in trouble if anyone finds out."

"No offense, but I can't hear a single word you say," Domino said, busy stooping to the opening. "So we should go before someone actually finds out."

If someone realized what they were about to do, they would be beaten. They were used to the beatings, but the pain and humiliation had never snuffed out their enthusiasm—nothing could, really. Domino would cover for them to lighten their punishment. He'd always done it until now, for consequences were nothing but an inconvenience. Fun was always worth it. And even without the healing gift of his best friend, the burns left by the whip always healed in no time at all.

"I have an outer crust," Domino used to say.

Gus's smile stretched. He didn't care, either. He wanted to get out; he wanted to follow Domino and see what was on the other side of the walls. Neither Ero nor anyone else would stop him.

Freedom sometimes required one to look life in the eye and say, "I'm coming for you."

The two boys bent down, sneaking between the bamboo trunks, and found themselves outside the village walls. Domino bit his lip. He'd probably planned his move before today. He put the trunks back in place, leaving a gap wide enough to slip his hand through on their return, then faced Gus, who was waiting, frozen on his feet, hesitant.

He hadn't seen the outside world since he arrived at Surhok. He'd stayed indoors like an obedient pet, as Ero had ordered him to do years before, sometimes ogling the view of the forest as the village gates opened. Not today.

The blue stone was always here in his mind. The Op crystal. His chest tightened.

That's what he wants. Ero wants me to be afraid. He can kiss my ass. I'm not afraid . . .

Gus looked up at the trees that stretched as far as the eye could see and listened to the lively chant of the wilds, recognizing here and there the cheery song of a bird, the creaking of a branch, the fall and crash of a fruit. Even the hot breeze caressing his chest and slipping in his nostrils smelled different.

He was ready. "Shall we?"

Domino nodded vigorously, jumping from one foot to the other, excited.

They raced under the trees, following each other. They quickly reached a dirt path Domino obviously knew. As he trotted behind Domino, Gus scanned the surroundings. The lack of walls in his way was both intimidating and a thrill. He could have swerved off the path and explored the dark woods and its environs without anyone to hold him back and force him to stay still. Once far enough away from the village, he could scream to frighten the birds, or for the sole delight of breaking his voice. Just because he could. At that moment, as Domino turned around regularly to make sure Gus didn't lose his stride, all he could think of was the infinite distance he could potentially travel without encountering an obstacle. He forgot the heat and the tingling in his burning feet, forgot that his white skin wouldn't last long under the gray, yet merciless summer sky.

He accelerated, imploring the Gods to make this moment last.

After long minutes of running, the lapping of the water reached his ears. The two boys came closer, and it grew stronger, livelier. The flicker passed between the trees, and Gus pushed on his legs, frustrated not to be there already.

In front of him, a pool of clear water splashed against pink granite rocks. From the towering heights that stood blocking their way, a waterfall broke along a cliff, before becoming one with the pond.

Gus was speechless. He gazed at the view and then the delicate scent of moss and wet rock filled his lungs.

Without warning, two powerful arms lifted him into the air. His happiness having reached its climax, it was time for Domino to enjoy himself. Gus knew at once what he had in mind.

"Don't you think about it," Gus said, laughing as his friend approached the edge of the pond. "Domino!"

The next second, Gus flew through the air, propelled by the nichan's force. He sank into the water, which enveloped him in freshness from head to toe. He touched the bottom with the tips of his toes, stretched out his legs, pushed, and rose to the surface. As his head emerged, a mass of arms and legs smashed against the water. Domino reappeared moments later, snorting and howling, scaring all the birds out of the area. In front of him, Gus pushed back the blond hair falling in front of his eyes, unable to stop smiling.

"One of these days you'll have to learn to be subtle," he mocked, struggling to get rid of the sleeveless tunic that water was sticking to his skin.

In response, Domino undressed and threw his wet pants in his friend's face. "Never!" He laughed.

Gus sent the pants and his own clothes to the nearest rock — they would drain and dry in no time — and then dived under again.

Having grown by the sea, Domino had taught Gus to swim years earlier. A few weeks after the drowning that could have cost him his life, Gus had headed for the village river and dove down, not allowing himself to be afraid, determined to save himself. He'd regretted his boldness until Domino joined him, pulling him out of the water yet again.

Gus was a quick learner. Soon fear left him for good. He and Domino would always stay in the water until their skin crumpled, their teeth chattered, or until Mora dragged them out.

As Domino grew up, it had become impossible for him to dive into the river without pounding the bottom hard. A few years later, Gus had encountered the same problem, and their love of water had been curbed.

Here, nothing could stop them.

They fought, splashed, and challenged each other. In the midst of swarms of bubbles and dead leaves, repressed instincts regained their rights. If this had been possible, they would have abandoned the earth and the waves to take over the sky. This moment and the world were theirs entirely. Beautiful and infinite.

Face blushed as much from the physical exercise as from the invisible sun burning them even through the thick clouds, Gus put his palms on Domino's shoulders, wedged his foot in the palm of his friend's hands, and prepared to jump. Facing him, Domino had his hair all over, his eyes bloodshot from hitting the water with his whole body again and again for over an hour. Yet nothing on his face expressed any tiredness. He tightened the muscles in his arms and back and pushed.

The jump was underwhelming. Gus's foot had slipped. He

dove down and returned to Domino in a few fathoms for another try.

He'd never had so much fun. When his hands landed on Domino's shoulders, he squeezed them against the wet skin, as much to hold himself as to make sure it wasn't all a figment of his imagination.

"Give it your all this time," he told Domino. "I want to believe my wings can fly."

He spread the one he could control. Water ran along the diaphanous membrane. The other wing, which had stopped growing when he was a toddler, hung on his back, dripping, lifeless.

Domino uncovered his teeth in a grin. And he pushed once more, shouting.

───────

LYING on his stomach against a rock, the lower half of his body still submerged, Gus opened his eyes. The light had changed in the sky, turning sandy through the puffs of black clouds. The heat continued to warm his neck, his back, his arms, his wings. He was lying down like this, one arm under his cheek. Next to him, their clothes were dry.

Domino, who had left the water a few minutes earlier, hadn't bothered to put his pants on. It was far too hot to get dressed, and they still had time before they had to return to Surhok. He approached Gus, back from a lonely jaunt in the area, and sat down on the rock with his legs crossed. A bunch of small items rolled out of his hands—a fruitful picking.

"I found some nam nuts." Domino put them on the cloth to prevent the fruits from rolling and getting lost in the water. "I saw an Oné tree over there. It's full of fruits, but I couldn't reach them."

"Well maybe I can," Gus said after a silence.

A few minutes later, Domino helped him climb the tree he'd spotted. After several attempts—which almost went wrong without Gus giving a damn—he came back down, his tunic rolled up into a ball loaded with gold- and translucent-skinned Onés. Fruits like these were far too rare not to be enjoyed. Where the heat peaks seemed to suffocate and kill everything else, Onés would gorge themselves on it, reaching maturity when the temperature became unbearable for other living things.

It was also the only fruit in the region to retain its original color after the Corruption had dyed the great majority of the world black and gray. A miracle in a world sorely lacking in them. The Uetos therefore attributed great power to this fruit, whose oval shape was reminiscent of a human heart. They believed sharing Onés with loved ones brought strength and luck. The only Oné tree in the village had died a few years earlier, its trunk gnawed away from the inside by larvae. A bad omen, the clan's Orator had announced.

"I've never really liked this fruit," Gus admitted before spitting a seed on the opposite bank. "Mine's a little floury. It's too ripe."

Domino looked up at him in surprise. "Why did you climb that tree if you don't like it?"

"You looked disappointed. And they bring luck, don't they? Besides, I'd never climbed a tree this big."

Domino smiled. "You went from human to monkey today."

"To what?"

"A monkey. I heard there are some in Meishua."

"What's that?"

"The country, Meishua."

"No, I'm talking about the monkey thing."

"It's an animal. Never seen one. Dadou talked about it this morning on the way home."

Domino stopped chewing and fell silent, leaving a heavy blankness stand between them, like an impenetrable wall. As if nothing had happened, Gus placed his half-eaten Oné on the stone and grabbed a nam nut Domino had cracked. He wasn't upset anymore about the restrictions. No Prayer Stones for him. So what? By now Gus had given up the idea of seeing these monoliths with his own eyes. He and Domino could have gone there now without anyone knowing about it, defying the prohibitions imposed by Ero, but it took more than an hour to reach the site from the village. Neither boy wanted to waste so much time when this pond was so close, full of possibilities. The Stones were not meant for fun, and they wanted to have fun, not to contemplate a circle of rocks under which nichans prayed every month during the Calling.

Sitting in front of him, Domino pursed his lips as if to trap the words, and then gobbled up what was left of his snack with a pensive look. He gave the impression of walking on eggshells, as if he'd committed treason by mentioning Natso's baptism. Gus didn't want that discomfort. Not here, not when he was feeling happier than ever.

Happy.

It was time to break the taboo. "How was it? The baptism, I mean."

After a hesitation, pulp sliding down his chin, Domino spoke. "Long and not very fun." He seemed to think for a second, and a furtive smile passed over his lips. "Until the creature came. Yes, you heard me. I saw her, like I'm seeing you right now. Huge legs, multicolored rows of giant scales, a mouth wide enough to swallow the whole village with a single bite. The Meishua Calamity appeared out of nowhere, tearing the sky open."

"Oh really?" A light smile curled Gus's lips. He appreciated the trouble Domino went to in order to warm up the atmosphere.

"Yes. True and true. That was quite amazing. I think Beïka

shit his pants. Before she attacked, Ero knelt before her. 'Have mercy, mighty beauty of the south, O greatness of the past! Do not attack me. I am an Unaan, so please spare me and devour my family instead!' But the Calamity looked at him, with her beady eyes, like this, and said, 'Then I will just kill you, for I don't want your filthy flesh, you disgusting, pudgy thing.' "

"What a perceptive beast."

Domino nodded, breaking the shell of another nam nut in the hollow of his fist. "You have no idea. I knew that the moment I looked at her. She's got a knack for spotting assholes." A slight grimace twisted Domino's face but he chased it away and continued. "Ero then asked, 'What should I do? I'll do whatever you want. Ask and I'll oblige.' And do you know what she answered?"

"I'm all ears."

Domino bit the inside of his cheek and looked down, as if uncertain. "She floated to Ero, her nostrils steaming. There was a scorching smell in the air. I thought she was going to spit acid in his face. But she didn't. What a missed opportunity. But no. Instead she said, 'Kiss me.' "

Domino looked up, his obsidian eyes shining like pearls.

Facing him, Gus swallowed hard, confused and not quite sure why. "And in reality, what actually happened?"

"In reality, we stayed up there praying for hours, longer than during a Calling. Natso started crying as soon as Belma put him on the altar."

"Not a very comfortable crib for a baby."

"Yeah. That, and the fact that he'd crapped himself."

Domino laughed, and Gus smiled.

After birth, a nichan infant would remain in almost constant contact with their mother's or father's skin—or anyone's willing to give a hand—for up to two months after birth. To take the child away from this primordial comfort to be laid on hard stone under the gaze of Gods who had been gone for nearly two centuries seemed like a form of mistreatment, according to Gus.

"It was hilarious," Domino said. "Belma felt he needed to be changed. Ero told her to wait. He used his big voice: 'These are the sacred Stones; the Gods are watching us.' You see what I mean, as if the Gods mattered to him. I'm not even sure Belma would have taken the Orator seriously if he'd been there. She didn't wait. She said she didn't want her son to be introduced to the Gods with a change full of shit, and she cleaned Natso, just like that, on the baptismal altar. Beïka was shocked. The clan chief's good little dog. What a dick. And Mora and I were laughing. Even Memek was having a hard time holding back. Only Dadou kept on praying, as if nothing happened."

His laughter subsided. He put one hand on his chin to wipe it off and noticed Gus's insistent look. After a few seconds, Domino admitted, "Okay, even the reality was a bit funny."

"That's good."

And he smiled. Domino smiled back, a warm grin that turned his already generously colored cheeks red. Then he dropped his Oné and rummaged through the pile of nuts in front of him. Something shone through his fingers. Amber and transparent, smaller than the nuts, and of an anarchic shape. Domino raised the small object to Gus's eye level and presented it to him. Dried sap, it seemed.

"I found it farther away," Domino said, both shy and satisfied, biting his lip. "I should be able to tie a string to it and wear it around my neck."

Ueto jewelry was the craft of the children of the clan. The little ones, developing their dexterity and attention to detail, would spend long hours kneading clay, tinting it with cheap pigment or gold, and shaping beads that would then be worn as necklaces by their parents. Domino and Gus had no parents.

Since he'd raised them, Mora wore the necklaces the two children had crafted back then.

"That's nice," replied Gus, confused by his friend's somewhat embarrassed reaction.

A few seconds later, after silence had slipped between them, his eyes still focused on his piece of sap, Domino confessed, "I like this color. A lot. It reminds me of your eyes."

Gus's heart boomed in his chest. He hadn't expected that. Was that a compliment?

Mouth half-open, he studied his friend's face before looking down, his own face flushing like hot charcoal as his eyes fell on Domino's naked body. A body he'd seen so many times. Yet his gaze veered up, focusing on the black curls framing the nichan's face.

My eyes . . .

The peculiarities of his appearance. Gus was embarrassed to be reminded that he wasn't an ordinary human being, and that it showed at first glance. He'd never liked his eyes. That bright orange lost in black, all hemmed in with pale eyelashes. Most days he was able to forget what they looked like, what the woman in the basement had vehemently showed him in the mirror.

"I remember telling you that you had beautiful eyes," Domino continued, not daring to cross Gus's gaze, his fingers playing with his loot. "We were very young. You didn't speak Torb yet. You'd never been so close to me before. On purpose, I mean. It was right before you healed me for the first time, after I took the oath. I forgot I had a sore arm, that I felt sick, and I said, 'Your eyes are pretty.' "

Gus's heart kept pounding against his ribs. He remembered that moment, the result of his new resolutions. Matta had asked him to be nice, to help the three brothers who had saved his life. So Gus had. If he'd grasped Domino's words at the time, he would have changed his mind. He would have been scared and wouldn't have healed the wound on the boy's arm. But today, he was able to resist the urge to run away. To tell the truth, he wanted to hear Domino utter those words again.

"Why?" Gus said in a controlled voice, feeling a new warmth rising to the hollow of his belly. "Why did you say that?"

Domino finally looked up at him. "Because it's true." A pause, a flurry of heartbeats, and Domino added, "Not just your eyes. You're beautiful."

It was furtive, so fast Gus thought he had imagined it, but he could have sworn Domino had looked at his lips before directing them back to his piece of sap, taking a deep breath. As if this sight had awakened something in him, Gus glanced at his friend's mouth, at his round lips slightly ajar. Domino wet the pulp of them with a slow course of his tongue. A hot flush grew in Gus's chest, spreading further down, and he looked away once again.

Farther on, a dark shape dragging itself moved and disappeared behind the waterfall's wall, attracting his attention.

Ignoring the pulse drumming in his ears, Gus stretched out his neck. They were not alone. "There's something over there."

XII

Hurled out of his thoughts, Domino looked over his shoulder. Nothing except the curtain of water and the sound of the waves pouring into the basin.

"What is it?" he asked as he surveyed the surroundings.

"I don't know. It was moving fast. It disappeared behind the waterfall."

Gus's eyesight was quite weak, so it could have been anything. A human, an animal, the movement of the trees shaken by the wind. Domino stood and squinted. Immediately he spotted a trail of blood in the distance. It stretched across the surface of the rocks before venturing out of his sight.

"You want to take a look?" Gus asked, putting on his pants, already decided.

Domino wasn't reassured. "There's blood over there. Did it look like a wounded animal?"

"I didn't get a chance to see."

Domino hesitated. If he got closer, he would recognize the smell of blood. Animal, human, or otherwise.

"Do you want to go see?" Gus repeated, rushing for it.

It was early. There was still time before they had to return home. If it was just a wild beast that had come here to die in peace, they had no reason to leave. The thing hadn't attacked them, hadn't even come close. It was probably a wounded animal. Might as well know for sure.

Domino pulled himself together and nodded. "All right."

So he put his clothes back on. He gave Gus his piece of sap for safekeeping (his own pants didn't have pockets), abandoned the fruits he'd picked, and jumped from one stone to another for about thirty feet to get closer to the waterfall. Even before reaching it, he recognized the smell of animal blood. Each creature, according to its species, sex, age, and build, had a distinct scent. His experience was still to be made, so Domino was unable to accurately identify the animal.

Closely followed by Gus, he walked around the waterfall and scanned the area. A narrow cavity cutting through the rock provided access to a passageway. Domino walked along the wet wall to the entrance. Natural daylight illuminated a slightly wider path covered with sand, pebbles and dead leaves. The trail of blood—mixed with water—continued from there.

"It's an animal, it might still be alive," Domino said loud enough to cover the sound of the splashes without shouting.

"You want to finish it off?"

Yes and no. Domino felt something else besides the animal. Something he couldn't identify, odorless. It was more of a hunch than an alert of his senses. He opened his mouth to speak when a yelp resounded against the rock and reached them from an out-of-sight area of the cavity.

Domino didn't need a weapon to kill this beast and end its ordeal. At thirteen, he already had enough strength to break the neck of a deer with his bare hands, even without transforming. He knew this from experience. All nichan children were at one time or another entrusted with the fate of an animal caught during a hunt. And death was the only acceptable fate for the animal involved. A kid unable to accomplish such a basic task would be nothing but a burden during a hunt. The clan's survival allowed no weakness. Domino still remembered the terrified deer lying on its side, bound by its legs, that had been thrown at his feet. The gesture, though reluctant, had come naturally to him. The twisting of muscle and bone had put an end to the beast's life. Domino had been ten years old at the time.

The moaning he'd just heard sounded very much like that of an animal of this species. So he entered the cave without a sound so as not to signal his presence to its resident, Gus on his heels, just as discreet as he was. Domino took the first turn, following the noise of a regular rustle impossible to identify, avoiding walking in the blood with his bare feet. The light was faint here, the smell of rock cold and musty.

Something then moved in the rocky corridor, and the nichan stopped. It was but a ripple in the air, then a reflection of translucent, moiré colors a few steps away from him. The shape was close to the ground, as if kneeling. Behind Domino, Gus leaned over to peer at it.

The more Domino stared at the thing, the more its composition stood out in the darkness, as if the entity emitted a faint light shining in its core, reflecting off the surface of its body. The thing seemed to scratch the ground with a small hand or a paw. But nothing happened; the hand had no effect on the sand and dust. The thing then raised its eyes, two bright spots without eyelids, and Domino knew what it was.

A spirit.

Its vaporous silhouette didn't look human but rather like an animal taking itself for a biped. No one knew where spirits came from. Like many other changes in this world, they had appeared after the Great Evil. Spirits were born from the unburied dead, whose corpses attracted the Corruption in black flakes as light as ash. A lone spirit was harmless. The more they grew in number, the greater the danger grew with them . . .

Domino tried to calm his heartbeat. One spirit. That must have been what he'd felt at the cave's entrance. If that spirit was there, it meant a human or a nichan had died somewhere close. Being attached to the deceased, the spirit couldn't leave the cave. Judging by its behavior, however, it was calm.

Another yelp resounded in the distance, even attracting the spirit's interest. It turned its strangely curved head in that direction, straightened up, and rushed toward the sound. Its substance faded like colored smoke with every step. After half a dozen steps, it was gone.

Domino glanced at Gus. His expression was serene, but something made his amber eyes shine. His breathing was tense.

"It won't do anything to us," Domino whispered.

"I know," Gus said through his sugar-flavored breath.

"We can leave, if you want."

Like all nichan children, Domino had finished off more than one struggling hare or wildcat with its paw caught in a trap. Death was a part of the circle of life, of survival. The Gods had allowed it. Domino was used to it by now. But Gus was foreign to the experience. He'd never followed the clan on a hunt before.

Yet what was in the cave didn't seem to frighten him. And if it did, he probably wouldn't show it.

"Go ahead," Gus said, with a slight chin twitch.

Domino nodded.

A cave opened before them, lit by a shaft of light piercing through the rock far above their heads. No spirit in sight.

Domino came to a sudden halt, his heart at the edge of his lips.

There was an animal lying on its side in the middle of the cave. A deer. Its jaw was hanging down, as was its long, rosy tongue.

The flesh and skin covered with brown hair was torn from the muzzle to the base of the skull, where an ear was missing.

The deer was now dead. Bile rose in Domino's throat. Instinctively, holding his breath, he hid Gus behind him.

The deer hadn't arrived here on its own. A huge creature, black in places, grayish in others, was moving over the animal's body, thrusting against it. It had three arms, one of them protruding from the side of its abdomen. From the ends of the arms emerged numerous filaments. They bent and unfolded with disordered movements similar to those of a pile of caterpillars assaulting a leaf. It was as if they were moving and twisting according to their own will.

The creature's face, on the sides of which hung dark pieces of flaccid skin, had no nose or eyes, or maybe they were closed. In any case, the thing had a gaping mouth, and the soft, boneless flesh of its jaw rocked with each start.

In a slower movement, tilting its skull to the side—a skull covered with long, heavy, dirty strands of hair—the creature readjusted its position. Retreating, its deformed, bloody phallus pulled itself out of the exposed entrails of the deer. With a squeaky rattle, the creature sank back into the dead animal, clinging to the broken jaw and antlers to keep its balance and resume a pace suited to its needs.

Domino held his breath. He didn't dare move, and he hoped with all his heart Gus would mirror his behavior and that he couldn't see any of the monster's actions.

That's—that's a dohor.

The thing couldn't be mistaken for anything else. Nothing in this world had been more tainted by the Corruption than this creature. Once a great and powerful species, once as clever as nichans and humans, this was all that was left of their descendants today: brainless monsters, driven by the basest instincts. And that dohor was seeking its pleasure in the still warm belly of a dead deer.

The two teenagers had to leave. At once. Dohors were huge, as fast as nichans, and almost equal in strength. When one of them spotted prey, it didn't let go.

A few steps from the dohor lay human bones.

Heart pounding, Domino searched for Gus's hand behind him. He didn't dare divert his full attention from the creature. He found his friend's fingers and squeezed them. Gus's hand was ice in spite of the heat. Shifting his eyes away from the creature for a moment, Domino discovered Gus's horrified expression. He was petrified, paler than ever, eyes wide open.

It's more than time to go.

Without further ado, Domino tiptoed away from the cave, pulling his friend in his wake, not letting go of his grip on his hand. Slowly, they retreated until the creature left their field of sight. But before they reached the exit, a shrill scream echoed against the rock and pierced their eardrums.

They had been spotted.

They ran for their lives, leaving the winding corridor of the cave, jumping from one rock to another, nearly slipping into the basin whose crystalline reflections had lost all their appeal. Another cry rose, close by. Too close for Domino's liking. Looking over his shoulder as they finally reached the edge of the trees, he spotted the dohor emerging from the cave. Still excited, its cock dripping with blood, its back arched, its milky white eyes finally open, the creature stopped. Its head shifted in their direction, making its loose jaw swing from side to side. It had located them. With breathtaking speed, the dohor bent on its bandy legs then leaped over the pond in one jump.

"Fuck!" Domino swore.

He didn't want to see this thing up close or know what would happen if it caught up with them. He didn't want him and Gus to end up like that deer, leaving as the only trace of their time in this world little spirits that would never rest in peace.

Without thinking, letting his survival instincts take over, Domino bent over and pulled his friend toward him.

"My back. Get on my back!"

Gus obeyed. Domino was stronger and much faster, even with a load on his shoulders. So Gus wrapped his trembling arms around the nichan's neck, jumped up, and closed his legs around his waist. Despite its too long and deformed limbs, the dohor sprang towards them at a terrifying speed. Domino ran away and never looked back.

He drew all his energy and ran like the wind, not caring that his muscles would snap under the effort, that his breath would run out. Fear had swept through him, but his instinct now guided him. Domino yielded everything to it. His body, his every reaction, his thoughts. The trees around him turned into gray, fuzzy shapes. The earth beneath his feet propelled him forward. So he ran and ran and ran and never slowed, holding Gus firmly against him.

Several disembodied cries echoed through the woods for the next few minutes. They only pushed Domino further on.

The village walls emerged between branches and trunks. In a last effort, he accelerated and then skidded to a halt. Without searching very long, the two boys found the hidden passage leading to safety. Domino put Gus down and pushed him into the opening. Once on the other side, a few seconds later, Domino collapsed into the ferns.

The adrenaline deserted his body. His lungs ached as if he were drowning, his limbs felt nailed to the ground. He barely saw Gus pushing the bamboo with all his might to put it back into place. Domino ran one hand over his face and fought to at least remain seated. He couldn't stand. His legs shook, the air burned his chest, the world spun like a tornado.

Gus was close by, out of breath. He placed one hand on Domino's shoulder. The other was pressed firmly against the nichan's mouth.

"Hey, breathe through your nose," Gus panted. "Slowly."

Domino nearly choked but complied. Breathe in. Breathe out. The stratagem proved its worth, and soon his breath stabilized. Gus withdrew his hand, looking apologetic. The nichan, lips moist with saliva, closed his eyes. He didn't know where Gus had learned this, but at least air seemed to find its way to his lungs now.

"Give me . . . give me a moment." Domino nodded, clinging to the hand his friend held out to him. "We . . . we have to warn the others."

Gus agreed, his cheeks red, sweat sticking his golden hair to his face. He took a deep breath to restrain his own emotions. Domino did the same, or at least he tried to contain his exhaustion. He couldn't let go now. As long as this thing was running around their territory, he had no right to let his guard down.

"It's my fault," he said between gasps. "I'm the one who lured this thing here."

"Keep this to yourself," Gus said.

"They'll know we went outside."

"We'll be punished. I don't give a shit. We're alive. You don't need to tell them how far we've gone. We just went out to have fun. That's when we saw the dohor, and it followed us when we fled."

He was right. They'd both get punished, no matter what. All that mattered now was getting rid of this thing, not worrying about less pressing issues.

"All right," Domino said, bending his legs to get up. "All right, let's do that."

"All right."

ERO WAS IN THE SANCTUARY. Surrounded by several nichans, including Orsa, Memek, and Beïka, he was organizing the division of labor for the next hunt. Focused and sweaty, like the others, Ero had no idea that the next hunt was imminent.

Domino clenched his fists and, followed by Gus, stopped near his uncle, who he hadn't even spoken to this morning during Natso's baptism.

"We've got a problem," said the teenager with more fear in his stomach than he would have liked.

Why was it still so hard to talk to the man? He should have asked for Mora's help first. Mora would have found the right words to announce such news. No, in truth, it was best not to involve Mora in the matter. The dohor was roaming around because of Domino, because he'd failed to interpret the bloodstains and the signs, because he hadn't been discreet enough to get out of that cave without being noticed. So it was up to him to face the damn consequences he'd decided to ignore.

His uncle looked up at him briefly and then turned his attention back to his partner. "Not now."

Yes, now. There was only one thing left to do.

"There's a dohor near the village walls."

All the faces around the table turned to Domino. Ero's expression shifted from boredom to shock.

Beïka sighed heavily. "Damn it, Domino! What the fuck have you done?" he barked in a sham of authority that left his little brother unmoved.

"Say that again," Ero asked, his brow furrowed around the dot tattooed on his forehead, a tiny part of the honorary marks—most of it covering his broad shoulders and chest—that had darkened his body since his son's death.

"There's a dohor near the village walls," Domino repeated,

obeying his Unaan's order. "I . . . I wanted to get out of the village. I wanted to . . . "

Ero leaped to his feet, rising to his full height. Domino had prepared himself for it, but at that moment he felt like an insect his uncle could crush under his foot. He looked down then, forced himself to hold the gaze of the clan's Unaan, remembering that the man wouldn't forgive such cowardice.

"You better talk. You say there is a dohor. How did it get there?"

"I left the village to look for a place to bathe. It was in the woods. When I ran away, it saw me."

"You're fucking stupid, Domino," Beïka spat, like so many times before that day.

This time, Ero silenced Beïka with a gesture without turning away from Domino. "Was it still there when you went over the wall?"

"I'm not sure. I couldn't hear it anymore. It didn't have a nose, so I doubt it could follow my scent—"

"Dohors don't rely on the same senses we do, you idiot," Orsa cut him as she stood up, face and shoulders tattooed, as intimidating as the clan chief. "Their bodies are covered with glands that feel the slightest movement, the slightest heartbeat. They don't need their eyes or nose to find you."

"Fetch the rest of our best hunters and warn the sentries," Ero ordered his partner, who complied immediately.

Around the table, all the nichans got up and left the room. Ero's daughter followed suit. The man gently grabbed her wrist, catching her attention. Like her parents, Memek had been tattooed a few days after Javik's death, when she'd been eight. Now, the teenage girl's forehead, chin, and hands were dotted with ink. All the patterns, although different from those marking her parents' skin, were perfectly symmetrical.

"You stay here," Ero told his daughter, who opened her mouth to reply. "Your mother and I are going on a hunt. One of the three of us must always stay in the village."

"I can run faster than you," Memek said before eyeing her cousin. "I run faster than him."

"It's not a race, Memek. This thing has to die."

Ero didn't have to repeat himself. He turned his attention to Domino and then to the blond head sticking out behind him.

"I'm sorry," Domino said to attract Ero's bottomless eyes to him instead of Gus.

"You'll be sorry when you see what you'll get for getting out of the village. Do you get hard for every rule you break?" Domino refrained from answering. "In the meantime, you're coming with us."

Domino widened his eyes. "What?"

"You're the only one who knows exactly what path you took. And since this thing has been chasing you, it will consider you its prey until one of you dies."

"You're using him as bait," Gus guessed, and Domino moved to his right to come between his friend and uncle.

But it was too late. Ero's eyes cursed the human as if he'd been a flea jumping around in his clean sheets. Gus spoke again before Ero had time to get more infuriated. "Do you need me to come?"

No! Domino thought. In addition to not being able to keep up, Gus would be in danger. He too was one of the dohor's targets. Ero didn't know it yet, but if he found out, maybe he'd consider using a different bait.

"You have something to do with this?" the Unaan asked him.

"I was referring to treating the possible wounded." Gus's voice was calm and composed, as if Ero didn't impress him in the least.

"I don't want you in our way," Ero said, and he guided Domino to the exit and then to the central square.

Many nichans had come out of their houses, attracted by the

hunters' gathering. Mora was among the curious ones. As soon as he spotted his brothers, he left the porch of his hut to join the group preparing to leave.

Domino gritted his teeth. In the end, he couldn't stop Mora from getting mixed up in his antics.

"Hey, where are you going like that? No, no, no. Why are you following them?" Mora asked, forcing his little brother to face him. Apparently, the situation had gone around the clan in a matter of minutes without the need to ring the village bell.

It was Ero who answered. "There's no need to worry. I will keep an eye on him."

"Yeah, me too," Beïka said, stopping near his brothers, looking sour.

Domino saw on Mora's face the moment he made his decision. Mora had no trust in his younger brother. And contrary to Beïka's opinion of himself, Ako's second son wasn't a particularly reliable hunter. Everyone knew that.

Domino didn't wish for his brothers to get into this, responsible for this mess or not. But just as he couldn't stop the monster from following him here, he couldn't do anything to keep Mora in Surhok, either.

"I am coming with you," Mora said.

"You're not a hunter, Mora," reminded Ero.

"I'll let you deal with the dohor. I'll deal with this one."

He pointed to Domino, who searched in his fear for the words that would change his brother's mind. But when everyone began to march under the clan chief's leadership, he was at a loss for words.

As he walked out of the village, following the group, Domino was only able to look back. Gus stood at the entrance of the infirmary, about thirty paces away, anxiety piercing through his usual calm.

UNDER A STORMY SKY casting a yellowish hue over the forest, the hunters split into two groups. One, led by Orsa, headed northeast. The other, led by Ero, searched the woods in the other direction, drawing a large circle around the village. Domino pointed in the direction in which he'd entered Surhok a few minutes earlier. Mora never let him out of his sight. The nichans progressed silently, most of them already transformed, ready to eliminate the threat to whatever end. Slowly, step by step, the group dispersed to cover more ground while remaining within earshot of one another. Only Ero, Domino, and Mora advanced in line.

For more than an hour, as the darkness deepened, they searched the woods, smelling the air, looking for any traces the creature might have left.

"Silence," Ero whispered.

Domino listened. Not a rustle, not a song from the treetops. All the birds had deserted the area, yet birds, from the smallest hummingbird to the largest vulture, weren't afraid of nichans. The dohor had driven them away. If none of the birds had returned since Domino and Gus had fled . . .

Without making the slightest sound, Ero transformed himself, soon to be imitated by Mora. Domino felt that the slightest disturbance in the air would lead the dohor back to him. So he purposely walked in Ero's footsteps, followed by his brother.

A scream broke the silence. From the south. The three nichans stood still. Another scream, just as inhuman, this time from the north. Domino's heart missed a beat, icy sweat cutting between his shoulder blades. A call crept through the vegetation, the voice of a nichan. Another. Then another. The calls came from all sides. A means to distract the creature.

Creatures, Domino recalled.

Being, as Ero had said, one of the dohors' prey, his own group had to remain silent and undetected.

If only Domino could master his transformation. He would have grown stronger, faster. But as the dohor's cries continued to echo through the forest, he couldn't even remember his brother's instructions on how to proceed. Returning to their original form was no longer natural for nichans. Even though everyone knew how to metamorphose, this change required practice, both to invoke the nichan essence that coursed through their veins, and to endure the crushing frustration once the transformation refused to reach completion.

But nothing. Domino could think of nothing but this monster defiling the corpse of this deer, banging the animal's lifeless skull as it sought to pleasure itself.

A knot circled his stomach. He was running out of air. If he was breathing too hard, would that thing find him faster?

Mora's clawed hand rested on Domino's shoulder. If this was meant to calm Domino, it failed miserably.

At the same moment, the scream tore the sky apart.

The creature came out of nowhere amidst the distant cries of the nichans. As Ero stood in its way, protecting his nephews, Mora pushed his brother behind him. The Unaan charged and his claws sliced gray and black flesh repeatedly. On reflex, the dohor retreated, a huge mass of skeletal limbs. Even Ero looked small compared to this creature's elongated figure. But the Unaan was fast and well trained. Unlike a traditional hunt in which the clan chief would have given a wild dog or a saurian time to lose blood and weaken, Ero didn't waste a moment. The hunt could sometimes turn into a game. This was an execution.

He charged at the monster, slashing diagonally, again and again, driving it away from Domino and Mora. The dohor's whitish blood and flesh sprayed the trees, the ferns. But the creature didn't give in. As if indifferent to the pain, it leaped in the air and caught up to the branches with its two arms.

Domino took his eyes off the fight taking place in front of him. The dohor that had chased him, the dohor from the cave, had three arms. This dohor had marked him as a target, not the one Ero was now dealing with.

"No . . . " Domino sucked on a breath as he searched through the lines of trees for the second creature.

Ero pulled with all his strength on the monster's legs, and it let go of the branch and collapsed gracelessly. The nichan seized his chance. He knelt over the dohor, pinned it to the ground with his claws and knees, bent his head and ripped out its throat with his long teeth. Its flesh stretched in elastic strands, then snapped. More blood as filthy as pus gushed from the shredded throat of the dohor. After endless seconds, the creature's bowed and splayed legs stopped shaking. Ero got up as Beïka and two other older nichans arrived on the scene. They immediately noticed the corpse at Ero's feet. The Unaan generously spat out the blood staining his immense smile.

"You got him," Beïka congratulated him with a smile.

His joy was short-lived.

"There's another one," Mora said.

"Domino, was it the one stalking you?" Ero asked through his fangs as he turned to him, but no answer came.

Domino looked around and felt his brother's hand—this time human—close on his wrist. "Domino, pull yourself together."

A new cry made them jump and transform. Domino spun around, bathed in sweat. His breathing stopped abruptly.

A three-armed dohor. It charged at him. At Mora.

No!

Domino's pulse came to a stop.

People shouted his name over and over again.

Someone pushed him.

Then Domino's vision blurred as a figure stood before him.

He shivered from head to toe. His fingers, his feet and then the rest of his body burned. When the change in him occurred, nothing made sense. Not the sky, not the world. Even his name faded away.

As if his body was breaking in two, Domino screamed.

Then nothing.

XIII

WHISPERS ON THE RIGHT. THREE—NO FOUR HEARTBEATS. Domino's head hurt, heavier than ever. A hot, constant twinge in the left side of his skull. And a familiar numbness in the side of his right calf. For a moment he kept his eyes closed. He felt the blanket wrapped around his body, the softness of the mattress under his weight. He also recognized the smell of old wood and herbs from the infirmary.

He decided to wake up completely.

Two lamps were burning without a sound on either side of the headboard. Above Domino hung garlic cloves and juniper berries. With a painful but surmountable effort, he raised his head to look around. Gus was there, on his left, leaning against the enormous table of herbal preparations, staring at him with both dark and bright intensity.

"He's awake," said a woman.

In the opposite corner of the room were Ero, Orsa, and the clan herbalist, Muran. They all stood a good distance from the bed, looking cautious. Even Gus.

"Can you hear me?" Ero asked in a softer voice than Domino was used to from his uncle.

What a strange question. "Of course."

"Good. How are you feeling?"

"I'm fine. My head—" Running a hand over his cheek and jaw, he noticed the loose flesh of his earlobes. The large wooden jewels that stretched his skin were no longer there. Passing his index finger through this now empty hole, Domino lay still and tried to think. "Where are—"

"Domino?"

He gathered himself. "Did I faint?"

Unintelligible voices came through the small window of the infirmary. One of them seemed to be sobbing. Ero sent Gus to close the window with a forceful glance. The boy obeyed without a word, every gesture tense.

"Domino, are you all right?" Ero insisted once Gus settled in his original spot.

Why was he asking again? Domino felt somewhat muddy, and his skull probably wore a nice bump or a cut—even though he couldn't tell what was to blame for it. Apart from that, he was fairly fine. He'd been through worse. He repeated this to Ero, avoiding the innuendoes that would reproach his uncle of having once marked his face with a blade. It wasn't the right time for this, for Domino sensed that something was wrong.

He could see a shadow mask on the faces around him. "What's wrong? I'm fine."

"Good," Ero said.

The Unaan approached Domino. Behind him, Orsa stirred and came closer as well.

While Domino tried to put his memories in order, his uncle continued his interrogation. "Do you remember what happened during the hunt?"

Immediately, the gravity of the situation resurfaced, and

Domino straightened up on one elbow. He was taken by vertigo, his vision clouded for a moment, but he remained in that position.

"Tell me it's dead. Tell me you killed the other dohor."

It didn't matter that his requests sounded more like orders than pleas. In his condition, Domino barely felt the tug that accompanied a nichan's insubordination toward his leader. He needed to know.

Even Ero made no bones about it. "It's dead," the man said. "But it was you who killed the second one."

"What?"

"You killed it."

The teenager let out a breath full of stupor. He'd killed a dohor. It was hardly believable.

"I did? Me?" Would his uncle lie about a point of such importance? "I don't remember that. How did I—"

"You transformed," Ero cut him off before pausing, as if to measure his words. "You've achieved a complete transformation."

"I . . . You . . . "

"You turned into a *real* nichan, the shape of our ancestors, right before our eyes. A pure blood."

Domino barely caught up with the useless question hanging from the tip of his tongue. By the Faces! He had done it. A complete transformation, from his human camouflage to his beastly form, the one that no nichan had managed to reach since the disappearance of the Gods. Not a single one of their kind—as far as they knew—in nearly two centuries had succeeded.

Domino swallowed heavily and passed a hand over his face.

He had succeeded. He had it in him.

How could one believe in this transformation? He had no memory of it. He grabbed the blanket wrapped around his waist and lifted it up. No clothes. Had they been destroyed during his transformation? At that moment all of this seemed plausible.

"I . . . I can't believe it." As he inspected his bare legs under the blanket, the twisted line of a scar on his calf attracted his attention.

A scar . . .

This one is new. This feel in my leg . . . Gus healed me.

"You really don't remember anything?" Ero insisted, forcing Domino out of his musing one more time.

"I felt strange when the dohor jumped on us. I—Mora? The dohor didn't touch him, right?"

Behind his thick beard, Ero pursed his lips and breathed in and out slower than necessary. "First of all, you should know—" he began before his partner interrupted him.

She handed him something. In the dark room, Domino recognized the twisted shape of a rope. With a shake of his head, Ero dismissed Orsa's silent suggestion. On the other side of the infirmary, Gus stood imperceptibly. His pulse was now frantic.

"Domino," Ero said, "you should know that we saw the whole thing. Beïka, Anon, Garik, and me. It was an accident."

Domino's heart took a turn for the worse. He wanted to sit up but was afraid he might fall out of bed. The room was spinning around him, and a burst of adrenaline rushed to his chest, tongue, and lips.

"I don't get it," he said.

"You saw the dohor, you transformed, and attacked it. But . . . your movements were messy. You could barely stand on your feet, as if you'd never learned to walk, like a child."

This time Domino sat up. He didn't care where he'd throw up or which side of the bed he'd fall on if he lost his balance. He didn't like this conversation at all. "Where's Mora?"

Silence. This one was heavier than the one in the forest just before the attack.

Ero opened his mouth. "He's dead."

Those words made no sense.

"Where is he?"

"I'm sorry, Domino. I told you. It was an accident. You deserve the truth. Beïka is devastated, and . . . I had to tell you before he did. His words wouldn't have been so kind."

Still no sense.

Domino turned to Gus. Gus wouldn't lie to him. Gus would tell him it was all a lie. But his friend's eyes suddenly expressed nothing but bottomless sorrow. He wasn't crying, but his body, his stiffened muscles, his staggering breath, his hands clinging to the table he was leaning against . . . His whole being confirmed Ero's revelations.

"Where is Mora?" Domino asked him nonetheless, unable to pronounce any other words.

Gus shook his head, jaw shut tight.

That was too much. No one here was saying anything clear to him. No one was telling him what he needed to hear. Domino wanted to be told that Mora was fine, that he'd gone home after the hunt to tell Belma what had happened and to take care of his son.

Belma.

Natso.

Mora.

Domino left the infirmary bed and pushed his uncle's hand away when the man tried to dissuade him. Domino was called repeatedly. He ignored the voices each time. Even his best friend's. He'd apologize later. For now, he needed to talk to his brother. He needed to see Mora, desperately.

He walked through the village square which, despite the late hour, was crowded with nichans. He ignored them too and ran to his brother's house, holding the blanket that concealed his heavy legs in one hand. Mora had taught him to behave well, to thank people, to ask forgiveness, and also to knock on doors before entering someone's house. Domino forgot all these rules, sliced through the crowd without worrying about the nichans he pushed, or those who suddenly retreated and jumped out of his path.

Breathless, a dull rhythm constantly banging against his eardrums and bruised skull, Domino opened the door that blocked his way.

Belma knelt in the middle of the dark room. The baby was asleep against her skin, in the folds of her tunic. Next to them, her great-grandmother prayed, also on her knees. In front of the two women were burning herbs and spices in the blaze, as well as candles whose pale wax would soon run out of their wicks.

Candles reserved for the wake of the dead.

Where is Mora? The words stuck in Domino's throat.

Belma turned to face the intruder. Her eyes were swollen, bloodshot. A strange emotion burdened her face as she recognized her partner's brother. Without saying anything, Belma entrusted Natso to Dadou's care and slowly got up. Unable to breathe, Domino looked for his lost words. Even before the shadow of a syllable came to his numb mind, a bitter slap crashed on his cheek. And another. And another.

"You fucker! *Fucker!*"

Belma screamed as she hit him, each slap more powerful than the last. Domino backed away step by step. Then, at the end of her tattooed forearm, Belma's hand formed a fist. It met the teenager's jaw, and he staggered and fell backwards, hitting the cobblestones, dropping his blanket. As he waited for the next blow to reach him, several nichans subdued the woman, but not the flow of insults.

"You fucking monster! Fucker! You killed him! Why did you do that? Don't you ever come near my son! Do you hear me? If you go near him, I'll kill you. I'll kill you! You're dead, Domino!"

She burst into tears, and they took her home.

Sprawled on the ground, Domino tried to get up. His legs

didn't respond to him anymore; his lungs filled and emptied at an alarming pace.

Nichans surrounded him but remained out of reach.

Mora.

A sob came out of his throat. He no longer recognized the faces around him.

Mora was dead.

He was asked to calm down. He could no longer breathe. He grabbed his throat with both hands and squeezed to dislodge the pain festering under his skin

He had killed Mora. He had —

A mass hit the back of his skull. His vision swirled, turning the world upside down, then darkened.

***

GUS SAW THE WHOLE THING. Belma's blows, Domino's skin turning black, the shape of his back undulating, spreading the span of his shoulders, then Ero slamming his fist on the back of his nephew's neck to knock him out. Everyone witnessed it. Once the teenager was unconscious, the clan chief picked up Domino, threw him on his shoulder like a sack of vegetables, and ordered his nichans to go home, stating that the situation was under control.

This time Ero accepted the rope his partner offered him. Domino was laid in the infirmary and the tying began. Gus, who followed them closely, felt bile burning his stomach and a dull anger awakening in him.

"No!" he cried, placing himself between the clan leader — mass of unshakeable muscles — and his unconscious friend.

"Get out of my way," Ero warned him.

The sight of the rope in the nichan's hands brought back memories Gus had been pushing away day after day for the past few years. He trembled from head to toe, as much in anger as in horror. Yet he kept his breath under control and didn't look down. No way was he going to let Ero tie Domino up as he'd done with the human they'd massacred in the village square. Domino was one of them. He was a victim of circumstances the clan had never experienced before. He wasn't to be treated as a threat, or worse, as a criminal.

"If he wakes up tied, he's going to panic," Gus said.

He knew Domino better than anyone. This was a desperate situation. No one could have predicted how the boy would react to his most extreme emotions. He'd accidentally killed his brother, an act of such violence it had instantly put an end to Mora's life. If Domino transformed again, would he be in full control of his strength? If not, who would be hurt? Who would be killed? No one could answer this question until it was too late. But one thing was certain: Domino needed to be reassured. He too was in mourning. To avoid another accident, it was necessary to calm his emotions, not exacerbate them. That rope would only make things worse.

"Get the fuck out of my way," Ero repeated, his face slowly turning grim. He seemed to have already come to the limits of his patience.

But Gus pushed him to the other side, cold and inflexible to this man who had more than one means of pressure on him. He would defend his friend no matter what. "No."

Ero's hand closed violently around Gus's neck. He pushed the teenager against the wall. His wings and back slammed against the wood with a bang. Iron pots and jars full of plants fell from the shelves to Gus's left.

He couldn't breathe. Ero was barely holding his strength.

"You piece of shit!" The man bared his teeth, pressing the boy against the wall. "Do I need to remind you what you risk by challenging me?"

Suffocating, his hands trying in vain to open the powerful fingers compressing his windpipe, Gus heard a familiar voice nearby.

"Unaan Ero, I'll take him out. He has no business being here."

Matta was here.

Relief washed over Gus as air charged into his lungs in dry waves. The pressure around his throat dropped. He caught hold of what he could as his legs gave way under his weight. He felt a thick sheet between his fingers, then his right kneecap hit the floor, his wing rubbing against the wall as he lost his balance. Despite all this, despite the pain throbbing in his neck muscles, his anger was as strong as ever and his determination intact.

His vision was sparse with black spots. Through the dancing dots, Ero stared at him, his eyes fully darkened. Gus's blood froze as he discovered the Unaan's condition. Ero had come very close to transforming. Even though Gus was human, even though he wasn't a proper member of the clan, he was no threat. Ero had no right to attack him.

Yet he'd done so in the past. Who would stop him?

The memory of a blue stone flashed, accompanied by a rush of adrenaline.

I am not a Ueto. He can do what he wants with me.

Gus resisted the urge to run away, to go back to hiding in the shadows as he'd done so many times. With tremendous efforts, he held Ero's gaze and stood up again. Then Matta entered his field of vision, occupying it entirely. She grabbed him by the shoulder and pushed him toward the exit.

"No! No!" Gus repeated in a broken voice, triggering a violent coughing fit. "I must—"

"Enough!" Matta said, pushing him more firmly, revealing the strength that was hers and which he couldn't oppose.

Gus, however, resisted, cursing Ero with his eyes, almost challenging the man to lose control again, to strike him full force.

But before he was thrown out, Domino caught his eye. The tears on his brown face hadn't yet dried. The cheek that had been slapped by Belma continued to redden. His lower lip was split.

This was unnatural. Gus's place was here, with Domino. He had no right to leave him at a time like this.

Yet the door closed as Ero tied the rope around one of his nephew's wrists.

GUS SHOVED Matta's hand away. "Let go of me!"

He spat on the wooden slabs on the floor. A little blood mingled with his saliva. He massaged his neck and pushed back with all the strength of his will the tears that threatened to flow. No more tears; he'd forbidden himself long ago.

"Will you calm down?" Matta said. "Breathe, my boy."

"Don't tell me what to do!" Each word hurt his sore throat.

"Oh, but that's exactly what I am going to do, and if you value your life, I advise you to listen with the utmost care."

He spat again on the floor, raising his chin, his gaze going frantically from the woman to the glow of the lamps filtering through the infirmary's window. He was soaked in sweat, as much from the heat as from his nerves about to snap. He wanted to scream, to break something.

"What is happening today, right here, is beyond your comprehension," Matta said, pointing at the infirmary. "These nichans are facing a tragedy and a miracle, one having caused the other."

"It was an accident!"

"I'm not done talking! You think you have a place in this matter?"

"I do!"

"You're wrong. None of them need your opinion, Gus. Right now you're a nuisance, a mosquito buzzing in their ears. If you keep bothering them like you're doing now, one of them will finish you off."

"Fuck them!" Gus hissed between his teeth, pointing at the infirmary with a trembling finger. "He's tying Domino up like an animal."

"There are nearly two hundred souls in this village. It is Ero's duty to protect them."

"That's not how he—You can . . . Look. Look inside. Look what's happening in the infirmary. You can do that with your Eye, right? You can do it! Just do it!"

Spy. It was for this reason alone that Ero had accepted Matta into the village. Everyone in Surhok knew that by now. The crystal set in her eye socket apparently had prodigious abilities. Matta had always chosen discretion in this regard—even though Gus and Domino had gleaned some information over the years, such as the Santig'Nell's great age, or her unfailing memory.

But it didn't matter to Gus. Only Domino mattered. She had to help him.

The woman scowled at the young man's command. "I will do no such thing."

"I've got to know what they're doing to him!"

"This is none of your business."

Had he understood right? Did she know how absurd her words sounded? If someone was messing with Domino, then it was Gus's business.

"It's a nichan affair that has to be settled by nichans," Matta added calmly. "Domino is as much a hope for his clan, for his entire species, as he is a threat. What the Corruption has inflicted on nichans is still to this day a gaping wound. The change in their bodies, the loss of a part of the essence that makes them who they are . . . It's not up to us to intervene. We can't even understand how they feel. You know Domino's heart, his fears, his sorrows, his joys. But you ignore everything of his true nature. Despite your appearance, you are more human than he will ever be. Whatever your feelings, whatever friendship you have with Domino, you must stay out of this."

Matta's pale blue eye pierced Gus, trying to make him absorb this speech. He pushed away every single truth it contained in its entirety.

"No," he said.

It had to be clear. It was about Domino. Domino, who had faced men twice his size while Gus had been hanged from a tree. Domino, who'd fought to stop Ero from throwing Gus out of the village. Domino, who'd given him his first smile, his first laugh . . .

Domino.

Gus turned and kicked a pewter bucket that lay by a hut. The metal racket reverberated throughout the village as the bucket waltzed between two houses. The teenager held his head in his hands and leaned against the nearest wall. He was at the end of his rope, his body pulled down by exhaustion, but every muscle was tense, ready to be unleashed.

Once again, he tried to master the breath that slipped from his grasp. When that didn't work, he began to count. *One, two, three, four.* He breathed in. *One, two, three, four.* He spat out air more than he blew it out. The technique Mora had taught Domino didn't seem to work. Yet he insisted.

"You have the right to let go." Matta's voice was now soft, her flow slower, as if she was afraid to rush him. "You have the right to cry."

Nichans cried. Domino cried. Of pain, of joy. He never held back and wore his emotions with pride. Gus didn't cry. No one needed to know how he felt, so why display it?

He let go of his head and leaned it against the wall behind him. "I don't want to cry."

"I know exactly what you want. You have to control yourself.

Don't add to your situation. I know fighting is easier than facing your pain."

"What pain?"

"You lost someone you cared about today."

Mora.

They'd buried him in the woods just after his death, away from his family. When the nichans returned from hunting, Ero carried Domino in his arms. The others, faces undone, eyes sometimes reddened, followed him with their heads down. Beïka didn't lower his head. When Belma had noticed her partner's absence, the truth had rained on them all.

"That little motherfucker, that fucking monster! He killed him, he killed Mora! Your son has no father because of him. My mother should have let him die in her womb instead of giving birth to him." Beïka had spat out his hatred, mad with rage, crying. No one had had time to stop him. The damage was done. Everyone knew what crime Domino had committed. Ero himself had come out of the infirmary to clarify the facts, both to clear Domino's name and to announce the news, the one that would overshadow Mora's death.

The death was there, however, implacable and crushing, like a massive blow to the ribs. Gus couldn't afford to think about it for even a minute. He didn't want to think that by following them on this hunt, he might have been able to heal Mora. He didn't want to think about the void his absence would leave.

What could he do about it? Nothing at all. Right now, Domino was his priority.

"I have to go back there," Gus said as if the conversation they'd just had never occurred, brushing aside Matta's objections with a wave of his hand.

"Wait until tomorrow morning," Matta advised. "You should eat —"

"I'm not hungry."

"I can imagine. Sleep, maybe. No? I realize that must seem out of reach at the moment," she added when he glanced at her with a dark expression. "You won't get anything from them tonight. It's up to them to deal with it. Make yourself as small as you can, for a few hours at least."

So he was still there, having to remind people of his usefulness or pretend not to exist at all. Tonight, more than ever, he felt helpless. An outsider.

To tell the truth, he wanted to protect Domino, reassure him, offer him a shoulder to cry on, but he needed his friend just as much. Now that Mora was no longer here, apart from Domino, who would stop Ero from kicking him out? Gus's gift was a significant safety feature. However, the boy kept telling himself that one day, this gift would no longer be enough. Ero would remember that nichans had survived without his help for thousands of years, and that they would do just fine if Gus disappeared.

For a moment, Gus blamed himself for being so dependent on Domino. He blamed himself just as much for reducing their friendship to a necessity. Domino was so much more than that . . . and Gus needed to see him.

You must stay out of it, Matta had said. And she was right.

Gus thought it might be a good idea to take this advice and wait until daybreak. Not a minute longer, though.

Back in the hut he shared with his friend, he stood in the middle of the room for a long time, staring at the empty bed he'd been reluctant to make that morning. Normally he and Domino would have been in the sanctuary finishing their supper, or in the baths, exhausted from their day of swimming, running, and climbing trees. Gus was indeed exhausted, but he hadn't eaten, hadn't bathed, and Domino was painfully inaccessible.

After long minutes of staring at the undone sheets, he lay down on the right side of the bed, his friend's side. Domino's smell lingered on the pillow. If he closed his eyes, Gus could imagine his friend was here too, beside him. He didn't close his eyes. He refused to miss daybreak, even though it wouldn't be there before long.

Gus hadn't seen Domino's true form. His true nature. A beast.

A real nichan.

A miracle.

That didn't surprise Gus as much as he thought it would. Domino had always been special to him, but not only that. The other kids in the clan had always run away and rejected Domino. Without knowing what it was all about, could these kids feel a difference in him?

Domino talked about it sometimes, less and less as the years went by, as the matter seemed to lose importance to him. But Domino still cared—the sorrow in his black eyes spoke volume.

"They can't hate you, they don't know you," Gus had told his friend, who had just explained that even when he and his brothers lived in Kaermat with their mother, children had always refused his company.

"It feels like hate, though. As soon as I approach, they run away, they look at me as if I just pissed at their feet. You know it, you've seen them." The sadness on Domino's face sickened Gus. Inside, he was boiling. He dreamed of throwing himself at those kids and tearing them down, one by one, even if this was but a fantasy.

Now Domino had grown up. He was no longer a child, but some things hadn't changed. Kids still avoided him without the command seeming to come from their parents, as if their instincts were taking over.

"Do you think there's something wrong with me?" Domino had asked a few months earlier.

There's nothing wrong with you. You're perfect just the way you are, Gus had thought to answer. Instead, he had turned to his friend, who was distractedly pulling out weeds, his gaze lost in the valley below leading to the bamboo forest.

"I'm here," Gus had said. "I'm not running away."

"You were before," Domino recalled.

"I was running away from everyone. I'm not running away from you anymore. Is this worth anything?"

Domino had returned his gaze, the shadow of a smile on his lips. As always, actions were more important than words, Gus knew that. It had taken effect and Domino had seemed reassured, or at least diverted from his dark thoughts. "Are you implying that you're more important than the rest of the clan? More important than the kids who run away when I show up?"

"That's exactly what I'm saying," Gus had said in all seriousness.

Domino had smiled for good.

The phenomenon persisted, but now the shadow of an explanation was emerging. Animals felt nichans' proximity at a remarkable distance. They could discern the presence of these powerful predators and move away from them without further ado. Did nichan children share that sixth sense, that survival instinct not yet regulated by reason that told them to stay away from Domino?

Would this first transformation change anything to that phenomenon?

The vision of Domino's skin turning black flashed before Gus's still-open eyes. And the muscles and bones of his back waving, changing, remodeling themselves . . .

On taking Domino back to the village, Ero had summoned Muran and Gus to the infirmary. Once back in his human form, Ero had been forced to stun his nephew. A precaution, considering Ero had no desire to bury another of his protégés today, he had said.

But the inconspicuous bump left on the back of Domino's

skull was only part of the problem. Still stunned by the news and Beïka's hateful cries, Gus hadn't immediately noticed the piece of fabric attached to his friend's leg.

Not attached.

Gus recognized the blue linen of Domino's pants. As if out of a heavy sleep, he'd reached out to close his hand on the fabric.

Ero was quick to push it away. "I tried to take it off. It's stuck in the calf."

Gus and Muran had then started to work. No matter how confusing the sight of those thick fibers trapped in the flesh and skin was. No matter that no one knew how the cloth got trapped inside Domino's unharmed leg. Muran had cut open the calf, revealing inch by inch the bottom of the pants creased between the muscle cords. The foreign body had been removed, and Gus had closed the wound. Once his work was done, he couldn't find the strength to get away from Domino, to take his hands off his friend's leg and skin. This contact alone wasn't enough to provide meaning to what they'd all just experienced.

Once again, Matta was right. Gus knew nothing about his friend's true nature, or even the nature of other nichans. He could speculate to exhaustion; he would get no answers.

GUS SLEPT LESS than two hours that night. The rooster crow brought him back to reality before the sky turned from black to dusty gray. He waited a few more minutes, got up, and set off.

The village was waking up. A few nichans entered the sanctuary to have their first meal of the day. A small group headed for the baths in the village heights, clean clothes shoved under their arms. Farther on, he heard the sound of claws sharpening wood. The coolness of the night still lingered. It grazed Gus's bare arms and face, still puffy from sleep. Facing him, across the central square, the infirmary was dark.

He knocked gently on the door, a weight pulling at the back of his tongue. Ero appeared on the other side, scowling. He looked down at Gus and seemed to hesitate between closing the door in his face and finishing what he'd started the day before. Gus swallowed hard and remained calm. Ero took up all the space in front of him; it was impossible to see if Domino was still asleep. The human had to come in to be sure.

"I don't remember asking you to come." Ero's voice was hoarse and tired. He'd probably stayed up all night, keeping an eye on his nephew, tightening the ropes, Gus thought.

There was a pause during which Gus took a deep breath to give himself courage. "I won't cause any trouble."

"You're wasting my time. That's what you're causing."

"Please."

If those words grazed his tongue, they grazed his pride even more. If anyone in this clan didn't deserve to be begged, it was Ero. But did Gus still have a choice?

Ero waited.

Gus resumed, his teeth clenched, "I won't touch his bonds. I'll follow orders. You won't even notice I'm here."

For a moment he thought of begging Ero again, for the man would probably enjoy the sound of his despair. He threw the idea away and waited patiently. The clan chief's gaze was heavy on him.

The door opened, and Ero stepped aside to let him in. With a cautious step, Gus crossed the threshold, went around the bed, and grabbed the little bench on which the herbalist was always the only one to sit. He pulled it to the bedside and sat down next to his friend.

Domino was asleep. A trickle of dried saliva stretched from the corner of his mouth to his jaw.

On the other side of the bed Ero untied the bonds holding Domino's wrists. Despite his surprise, Gus held back his reaction. Ero went to the ankles, then finally to the rope wrapped under the teenager's ribs.

"If things go wrong," Ero said, rolling the ropes on themselves, "you'll be the first to suffer the consequences. He didn't wake up yet, but when he does, it might be a bloodshed. It better be all right with you because I won't stand in the way if he rips your throat."

A threat. Typical. However, even though Ero scared Gus, his words didn't.

"Let him," he said.

Ero nodded his head and returned to sit in a corner of the room.

Gus placed two fingers on the side of his friend's throat. Domino's pulse was normal, steady and strong. He breathed easily, clenched his fists occasionally, wiggled his toes. The only apparent abnormality was the amount of sleep. Normally, three to four hours of sleep were enough for him. Today, even the rough hemp tightly knotted to the point of leaving marks on his skin wasn't enough to disturb his rest.

As day broke, Orsa visited the infirmary, holding a bowl of cassava for her partner. She noted Gus's presence, kept her comments behind her teeth, briefly massaged the nape of Ero's neck as he ate, and walked away after receiving a kiss on the back of her hand.

The door slammed, and Domino's breathing changed. Gus, who was choking back a yawn, stood.

Domino's eyelids fluttered and then opened. "Mora."

Gus found his friend's hand and squeezed it tight. Domino's black eyes were dead when he turned them toward him.

"Hey," Gus whispered.

He applied gentle pressure on the nichan's fingers. It was not enough. After that night of anguish he wanted to hug Domino tight against him, to let himself go in his arms. As if the same need was awakening in him, Domino rolled to the side to face his friend, turning his back on Ero, who merely watched them in silence.

Domino's eyes were already blushing behind a veil of tears. "Tell me it's a nightmare. I . . . I'll wake up. It'll be over. Just say it. I'm begging you, Gus."

Gus gritted his teeth to keep his own tears at bay. He bent down and placed one kiss and then another on Domino's fingers. There was nothing to say because nothing would change what had happened. But Domino had to know that Gus would stay with him. Whatever he'd done, whatever he was, whatever the others', Ero's, or Matta's opinions, Gus would take care of him.

Sobs carried Domino away, irresistible, filling every space in the room. Unable to hold on, Gus drew Domino to himself, providing all the comfort he had to offer. Domino buried his face in his neck, Gus stroked his hair. Closing his eyes, relegating his suffering to the back of his mind, Gus hugged his friend in his arms and closed his valid wing around them as much as he could.

Soon after, Ero stood and left them alone.

A few minutes passed, then Domino's body stiffened. He backed away suddenly, sitting halfway down on his bed with terrified round eyes. "No. You have to get out."

Still leaning over the edge of the bed, Gus froze. "What is it?"

But Domino spoke over his words. "I'm dangerous. You have to get out of here."

"No."

"You have to stay away from me."

"Domino, stop—"

But the nichan was getting up. His long legs were confused, as if trapped in an invisible net, and he lost his balance. Gus stood up to help him, but it scared Domino away, and he leaned against the opposite wall. He reached a hand out in front of him to keep Gus away.

"Domino," Gus repeated, cramps in his stomach.

His friend had never pushed him away. Whatever the reasons, it was a situation Gus had never thought he would ever have to face.

He took a step, opening his arms slightly to welcome Domino into his embrace. It was all right; they could get through this. Together. But Domino, releasing a new flood of tears, panicked as if the human was threatening him with a blade.

"Gus, please, no!" Domino begged. Gus stopped, a cold sweat running down his back. "Don't come near me. Get out of here."

"Where do you want me to go?" Gus didn't know what he was saying anymore. He meant *don't leave me, let me take care of you.* But his thoughts tripped on one another.

"Anywhere I can't hurt you," Domino said in a trembling voice, tension tightening the muscles of his neck. "I'm sorry. I'm sorry. I'm—"

"Don't apologize," Gus whispered.

He had to pull himself together or he would fall apart too. Gus was in pain, but Domino couldn't know that. The burden the nichan carried on his shoulders was heavy enough to crush him and prevent him from ever getting up again.

So Gus obeyed. One step at a time, he forced himself away from the one person he wanted by his side. Then he went outside.

He sat for a long time behind the infirmary, where no one could see him, where Domino's incessant weeping reached him for hours on end.

XIV

Domino stayed in the infirmary for two more days. As the mournful silence gradually gave way to conversations that didn't require murmurs, and as the nichans patrolled more than ever around the village, in the valley, and the hills to the north, Domino ended his convalescence with the agreement of the herbalist and his uncle.

Physically, he felt fine. After lying in bed for days, his legs lacked exercise. He hadn't eaten since the accident and the bottom of his stomach felt as if it were covered with mud, but he wasn't hungry. His muscles were slightly sore, as if they'd been stretched too hard. Apart from that, he wouldn't have been able to detect the slightest change in his system—perhaps because there was none and what was inside him had always been there. He didn't wish for an answer. If he could walk and run, so much the better. That beast in him would stay where it was: hidden.

Gus had tried to visit him. He'd come by that morning, food in hand, only to be denied access to the infirmary. Ero, who'd stayed with his nephew most of the time, had ordered him to leave. Gus had said something that Domino hadn't heard.

"You're really looking for shit," Ero had replied.

Then Gus was gone.

His smell, recognizable among a thousand—a subtle mixture of soap, warmed leather, and human sweat—had evaporated with him. Turning his back on the infirmary door, Domino had sighed with relief as well as misery. He'd begged Gus to stay away from him, but half his thoughts were focused on his best friend. He wanted to see him. He needed to see him.

He was about to leave this room of thousands of heady, sometimes disgusting scents, and was putting on the clothes brought for him, when Ero stood in his way.

"Just a moment," Ero said, leaving enough distance between them so his intervention wouldn't be interpreted as a threat. Domino didn't bother to look up at his uncle. "How's your leg?"

"It's fine." Nothing but the truth. He didn't want to bring this subject back. The concept of his own clothes trapped beneath his skin was as sickening as being a murderer. Part of him wished Ero had never told him about it.

"Good," his uncle said. "I know things haven't always been easy between us."

That was an understatement that under other circumstances would have made Domino chuckle. The blade skillfully slicing his cheekbone, missing his eye by a hair . . . Ero had made the decision to mutilate him on a whim. The gesture had only served to punish Mora, to teach him a lesson the hard way. If Ero and Domino had ever had a chance to get along, to understand each other, Ero had trampled on it before spitting on it.

Domino let his uncle continue.

"But I know what it feels like to lose someone you love."

Do you know what it feels like to have killed them yourself? Domino thought. He didn't want to have this conversation, not now, not ever. But he lacked the strength to fight his uncle, or even tell him to fuck off. So he'd endure what the man had to say to him, and then he'd leave to mourn his brother somewhere else.

"You probably have no reason to do this, but you can come to me if you need to," Ero said. "We are family." Domino bit the tip of his tongue. "All that happened . . . it's a terrible burden on your young shoulders. Your true nature has been revealed, and you haven't learned to live with it. We may be nichans, but we've forgotten what it feels like to be pure blood. To be . . . complete. But there could be good, in the end. Someday. This is an amazing opportunity for you —"

"I'll stop you right there," Domino said, finally looking his uncle in the face. "There's nothing amazing about this."

"Domino —"

"This shape . . . I'll never transform again. Never."

He gritted his teeth and pulled away when his uncle's hand rested on his shoulder. It was Mora who used to reassure him with a hand on his shoulder and words of utter tenderness. Ero could keep his compassion drawn out of nowhere and put it wherever he wanted.

"It's all right. No need to talk about it now," Ero said, raising his hands in a sign of peace, a reaction he would never have had before today. "For now, try to eat. Get your strength back. Get some rest."

"Can I go now?" Domino pressed him, eyes on the door behind his uncle.

"Of course." Ero stepped aside, and Domino left the infirmary, sneaking through the barely opened door.

First he turned and headed for his hut by pure reflex, then he stopped in the middle of the square, patch of black smoke drifting low in the sky. Gus would probably be there. Domino was dying to see his friend. Gus cared about Mora. They should mourn together. But that wasn't all. Domino was afraid. Afraid of himself, afraid of what it would change in his life, in Gus's life.

Without being able to determine how his entire existence had crumbled under the weight of his actions, he knew that nothing would ever be the same again.

He wasn't ready to face it.

He resisted the need to seek comfort, to return to where he would feel safest, and turned away from that path.

Soon, discomfort wagged in him, all around him, like a shift in the atmosphere. Something had changed beyond his brother's overwhelming absence.

With a single circular glance, he noticed the clues. The few nichans in the square or in front of their huts looked at him. A woman sitting on the step of her porch sharpened a short blade without taking her eyes off him. A couple scratched the crust of earth on their vegetables before washing them, interrupting their conversation to observe him from a distance, slipping quiet words to each other. Arms laden with animal skins, Memek stopped not far from Domino, studying her cousin with her mismatched eyes.

Where once was indifference grew mistrust. Curiosity too. Perhaps everything was different. Now he was the clan's real nichan. The clan's miracle.

A baby started crying in a nearby hut. It captured Domino's attention. The cries came from Mora's house.

The clan's monster. That's what he was.

Domino could no longer stand those looks on him, fearing he'd vomit under all those stares of nichans who would find no answer to their questions in this contemplation.

He decided hastily, without thinking. He turned north. One step ahead of the other, again and again. His legs seemed to weigh a ton, as if sucked into the earth. He ordered them to press forward. He wasn't to stop, or he'd collapse and might never get up again.

When he reached a large house of stone and wood, the suffocating heat of burning water enveloped him and obscured his view. With the door still open behind him, daylight playing with the clouds of steam, Domino froze. There were people inside: a hunchbacked, dark-skinned, hail-stained nichan dean, and a middle-aged man, his son, who helped him dry his feet. The younger one turned around to greet the newcomer, looking indolent. Like the others, his expression tensed as he recognized Domino. After a short moment of hesitation, the nichan picked up his clothes and his father's, and guided the old man to the exit. The entire time, the man kept his distance. The door slammed shut behind them.

Water dripped lazily on the stone. A draught came through the back window, making the shutter creak. Domino loosened his fists and finally realized where he was. The baths. The fountains on the opposite walls, the cold-water basin almost empty, the other, larger, filled with steaming water despite the ambient heat. It was the most outlying building in the village. Like the two men who'd just left, whoever would come up here for their ablutions would find Domino standing motionless in the middle of the fog.

He stayed like this for a while, long enough for sensations to abandon the soles of his feet, then he settled down by a fountain. And he waited. He couldn't stay here forever. Other nichans would come in for a bath at some point. It was rude to force them all to accept his presence or run away.

The clan's monster. The one who'd killed his own brother.

He would have liked to cry, but for the first time, he was unable to summon any tears. He felt empty, both locked out of his body while trapped inside his own thoughts. A ball in the bottom of his throat, he raised his hands before his eyes. His palms were pale, rough. The other side, darker, was a little dry but without a scratch.

Panic gripped his throat when he noticed the blood under his fingernails.

Blood.

His own?

Mora's?

An image materialized before his eyes, like a memory. It wasn't a memory, but rather a projection of his imagination, an insidious thought. Domino saw himself in the bestial form of an ordinary nichan—not the form Ero had spoken of. Not that of a beast. So it couldn't be true. Yet the image filled every gap in his mind. His clawed hand slitting the air before it meeting his brother's throat. A movement so violent Domino could experience the shock reverberating through his muscles. Mora's head going backwards, the wound spreading like a fan, coral blood splashing around...

Domino flinched, breathless. The image then repeated itself, all the more violent.

Sudden nausea overcame him.

He pushed back this flash, this thought that, because he was desperate to suppress it, gained in power, in verisimilitude.

"Stop it," he begged in a tearless sob.

His pulse raced. He scratched at the dried blood, trying to reach and dislodge the orange-red filth. He couldn't do it, as if it'd become one with his fingernails.

No, it's got to go!

Bumping his back against the faucet of one of the fountains, the metal scraping his skin to the point of drawing blood, he straightened up and searched frantically around him. Under a pile of dishcloths he put his hand on a scrubbing brush. Domino abruptly activated the pump. Water flew. He wet his hands hastily and rubbed harder and harder. The harsh boar bristles helped. Not enough. It would never be enough. He could taste the blood in his month. A metallic yet sweet taste, like an overripe fruit.

He rubbed until his own blood appeared and mingled with the one he wished to erase. And he rubbed. A groan came out of his throat. What was he doing? It wasn't working. It would never work. That blood would stay there forever.

"*Fuck!*" he shouted. His fist hit the wooden wall reinforced with stones and lime.

He struck again and again as his perverse imagination spilled his brother's blood in his mind. His skin peeled from the meat and bone of his hand. His own blood ran down the wall.

It had to stop. He hit the wall again, this time with the corner of his head. He didn't count how many times his forehead collided with the wood. He just slammed his head hard, begging for unconsciousness. A little dazed, he slumped into the drainage ditch, dark spots replacing his thoughts before his eyes. Breathless, blood-pulsing nails drilling into his skull, the joints of his hand raw, he stared at the wall in front of him.

Time lost its substance, impossible to quantify, but Domino remained conscious.

If anyone visited the baths in that lapse of time, Domino didn't hear them. He curled up on the slabs for long hours, his hand closed against his chest, the other dripping on the floor, blood crystalizing ever so slowly on his knuckles. He would have wanted it to break, for every bone to pierce the skin. This hand that would remain forever stained with his brother's blood. He opened it, closed it. In his condition, he couldn't even tell one pain from the other.

When he woke up much later, it was dark. He summarily rinsed out the crystallized blood between his swollen fingers, tried to ignore the blood under his nails, and looked for a place to spend the night. He wouldn't go back to his hut. He wouldn't go to the sanctuary. No one was to see him or come near him.

A COOL, fine rain bounced off his face and stuck his hair to his forehead. Someone was coming.

"Domino, can you hear me?"

Always the same question.

Each drop seemed heavier than the last. The boy half-opened his eyes, and Ero's features appeared behind a sleepy haze. Domino put a hand to his forehead. He grimaced as his fingers met the open, swollen flesh on the edge of his scalp.

His uncle's hand then grabbed his wrist and he inspected the boy's fingers. "Can I leave you alone for two minutes without things going out of control?"

Domino tried to yank his hand back. Around him, the leaves of the trees under which he was lying swayed as the wind and the rain increased in intensity. Domino stood up, struggling to remember how he'd landed here. He'd wandered for a while in the village woods. At that time it wasn't raining yet. He'd probably considered this tree and the black ferns surrounding its base to be an appropriate bed.

"You spend the night here?" Ero asked.

Domino pulled on his hand again for his uncle still refused to release him. "Let go of me." He tried to get up.

But the blows he'd inflicted on his own skull tripped his balance—like when his mother had given him a sip of almond liquor when he was little to soothe him to sleep.

"Did you eat yesterday?" Ero said, studying his face more closely.

"Leave me the fuck alone."

Before this day, Domino would never have dared to utter such words. Ero was the chief of the clan, his Unaan. Domino's tone was close to blasphemy. He felt it in his core, in that part of his being attached to the man, bound by the blood oath. It squeezed, contracting his muscles, pressing against his rib cage, wrenching a groan out of him. For an instant he shivered, pressed himself against the trunk of the tree under which he was slumped, and stopped pulling on his arm.

Facing him, Ero shook his head. "It's unpleasant, indeed," he said, guessing what discomfort was tormenting Domino. "I'll let this insubordination pass. Just this once. Now, you'll get up and follow me."

"Don't order me."

Domino heard these words spoken by his mouth, expelled from the depths of his soul. He hadn't anticipated them. Yet the fear was there, oppressive. The fear of being forced to eat, to return to his hut, to a normal life, in plain sight. Fear that his clan leader would order him to transform. Domino would do it. The oath he'd sworn was that powerful. He would try to resist, of course, with all his might, but only to break under his uncle's will.

This too Ero seemed to have guessed. His hand released Domino, and he sighed long and hard before wiping the beads of rain from the surface of his black beard. "I won't do that," he said. "I'm not here to torment you, so stop playing the martyr. I just want you to get better."

What if I can't get better? What if what you see here is all that's left of me?

"Are you going to stay here long?" Ero continued, as Domino remained quiet.

"There are worse things."

"For a wild beast, yes. But nichans don't hide. We don't run away."

"In that case I'll go back to the village. We'll see if I'm a nichan . . . or a wild beast. Let's see who I'm—who I'm gonna kill next. How's that sound?"

Ero clicked his tongue and stared into Domino's eyes. "Are you done?"

"It's too dangerous," Domino said.

"So you're going to stay here, like the village idiot everyone hears about but never sees? Will you steal food at night when everyone's sleeping, like a rat?"

Fuck off, Domino wanted to answer, but the words didn't cross the barrier of his lips.

Ero sighed and shook his head. "You must eat. Your brother wouldn't want you to starve to death. You think he came between you and this dohor for you to throw your life away?"

Domino's chest swelled.

"There's a meal waiting for you. As long as you are part of this clan, there'll always be one." Ero stood up. "You don't have to talk, you don't have to do your chores for now. But out of respect for all your brother has done for you, don't let yourself fall apart. I won't let you. And before you start shitting yourself, no, that's not an order, just a reminder."

"Respect," Domino repeated, forcing a bitter laugh. "Is that what it's called when you stick a blade in a child's face?"

There was silence. Domino stared at his uncle with a look so bitter the challenge it raised twisted his guts.

They'd never had this conversation. Domino had always avoided the subject. To forget, to forgive, to move on. He'd achieved none of this.

Ero stared back at him. "You want to talk about this? Now?"

Domino said nothing, didn't look down.

"It was a mistake," Ero said.

"True. Now you're gonna tell me you were blinded by sorrow."

"I won't."

"You don't regret anything, do you?"

"We're done with this conversation."

"Unlike you," Domino continued, ignoring his uncle's answers, "I'm not hurting anyone by falling apart."

"Your Vestige is looking for you everywhere."

Ero's remark struck him like a slap in the face. Domino instinctively stood and looked around.

"I sent him back to his chores," Ero said. "I was tired of him snooping and begging just because you're avoiding him."

Domino relaxed a little and looked down at his injured hand, whose swollen knuckles restricted his mobility. Had he been here, Gus would have grabbed that hand between his own and applied some of his gift. That one touch, at once cool, tender but numbing, would have been enough to persuade Domino to return to him. Knowing that Gus was looking for him and asking after him crushed his heart. Gus never asked for anything from anyone. Ever.

Domino took his head in his hands.

Ero sighed again. "It's raining, Domino. Why don't you get up and eat? I'm sure you can decide how you want to waste your life on a full stomach."

So Domino followed him and ate. Then he was gone again.

XV

NEVER BEFORE HAD A BOY AS YOUNG AS DOMINO BEEN INVITED to attend the village council.

He'd spent two more nights outside. The first had seen him rolled on his side in a sheltered corner of the kitchen, deserting it before breakfast was prepared; the second he spent between two henhouses. He'd never imagined that after so many years he'd come back and get stuck between these pens. He'd crawled in there with difficulty, enjoying the comfort of the warm boards, the smell of straw, and the constant clucking of the chickens. When the rain returned in the early morning, he had no choice but to seek another shelter, a dry place away from the other nichans, away from anyone prone to talk to him.

But he couldn't escape his uncle so easily. Ero had grabbed his arm, preventing him from going back to the baths, and brought him to the auditorium.

The room was located in the sanctuary, above the great hall, and was intended for various uses, always approved by the Orator or the Unaan. The village councils were held there, private ceremonies whose nature remained vague in Domino's mind. He'd understood that it was also here that the village Orator inked the tattoos honoring the dead. It was accessed by a staircase at the back of the sanctuary, out of sight.

Domino had never set foot here. The room was more private and exclusive than any other place in their territory. Nichans had to go to the Prayer Stones to pray and honor the faces of the missing Gods during the Callings; the banquet hall was a place of gathering, announcement and sharing. But the auditorium only opened its doors to a few privileged or mournful people.

Domino entered with apprehension, holding his breath. Seeing the columns surrounding them, the imposing wrought-iron brazier in the center of the room, the deep, richly colored carpets all around the flames, he first thought he was going to receive the marks. A touch of excitement mixed with humility warmed his heart. He wanted so much to honor his brother, to bear the marks that would help support Mora's soul to the Gods, to keep his memory intact through eyes that from now on would glance at his tattooed skin.

Many of the clan's nichans were tattooed. After the premature death of a family member, a nichan would always receive the marks. Beïka would do it if he hadn't already. So would Belma. She'd probably wait a few years to bring Natso up here, so that he'd be old enough to endure the brutal pain of the needles and understand the value of this ritual.

Domino was ready. At that moment, it was all he could do for his brother. He'd never get forgiveness, could never go back. The marks were his last gesture to the one who'd raised him longer than their mother had had a chance.

The Orator stood in the center of the room, throwing handfuls of spices into the blaze to perfume the air. Although he'd never spoken to him, Domino had seen the man many times over the years. His name was Issba. He looked barely older than Ero and wore his hair long, very long, in a thin twist reaching his calves.

The sides of his skull were closely shaved. The pocked skin around his ears and on his cheeks was evidence of a skin disease cured years ago.

He briefly raised his brown eyes to Domino and Ero as they entered the auditorium and then returned to his spices, sorting them in the palm of his hand before letting the flames consume them.

Issba was a man of the Gods, entirely devoted to the divine word, to remember and share with his fellow nichans the memory of a time when the Faces of the Gods still brightened the sky. The Orators' role had changed after the Corruption's arrival. Before that, they'd been nothing but men and women praying all day long to thank the Gods for the blessing of life. Since the other nichans were busy hunting, roaming the world, and breeding, their people needed someone to pray continuously on their behalf. In days of old, Orators were the only ones who remained exclusively in their human forms. A necessary renunciation to love the Gods. Then the Gods had disappeared, and the Orators had gained influence. After all, they were the sole bearers of their Creators' memories. They always prayed for their kind, usually alone, but it was said that only the Orator of a clan wasn't accountable to the clan chief.

It was only today that Domino faced from up close this thin man, dressed in a faded, black linen shawl.

Ero pushed his nephew to the carpet and motioned for him to stay there. Domino obeyed and knelt. Issba still ignored them, even when Ero passed by and threw into the fire some spices collected in a round golden bowl.

Then Orsa arrived, repeated the same process, and sat down on a carpet farther away. Within minutes, three more nichans joined them. They all took their places, Ero included. As the flames crackled, the Orator kept them waiting. He then settled on a cushion on the floor on the other side of the brazier, across from Domino.

"My young apprentice is ill," said Issba in a voice that carried effortlessly to the other end of the large room. "This is very unfortunate. He shouldn't miss an event like this."

"You explicitly asked not to wait any longer," Ero reminded him, annoyance folding the skin of his forehead.

"I know what I said."

"Have you changed your mind then?"

"We don't change our minds. One of you will have to visit Tulik during the day to report back to him the content of our conversation. I do not have time for that."

There was silence around the fire. One of the nichans sighed. It was Omak. "I'll take care of it," she said.

"They will be eternally grateful. What we are witnessing in these dark days may never happen again. The Gods' will is mighty and beautiful, but it weakens if we forget to—"

"The days are short, Issba," said Ero, and everyone turned their eyes to the Unaan, even Domino, who until then hadn't been able to veer his attention away from the Orator's hollow face. "If we're to climb to the Stones, we better hurry."

Issba then set eyes on Domino, whose heart beat stronger and stronger. The man got up, walked around the blaze—more stifling than anything else at such a time of year—and positioned himself in front of the teenager. There was sweat on the man's chest, forehead, and short nose. He rubbed his hands, bent down, and lifted Domino's chin with his fine, delicate fingertips. He pushed back the dark, wavy streaks falling on the boy's forehead. "This is a beautiful face," said the man for himself. "How old are you, boy?"

"Thirteen. Soon fourteen."

"Thirteen. You already look like a man. You're growing up well. Your eyes are frank, though full of doubts. But the signs can't escape me. You already have a proud stature. Let me look at you. Get up. Take off your clothes."

After a long hesitation, Domino complied. He got rid of his tunic and trousers and laid them at his feet. Nudity rarely made him uncomfortable, but in the middle of this room, with all eyes resting on him, facing the Orator and his piercing scrutiny, Domino knew what humans felt, what their modesty dictated to them. He resisted the urge to hide his sex behind his hands.

Issba studied him from head to toe, settled a finger on his waist, then his hip, going up in a firm pressure to feel the fine muscles of his arms. "You have a good build, good shoulders. You will become a beautiful man, I can attest to that. Are you a virgin?"

Domino swallowed heavily. "Yes," he said, heat washing through his face.

"That will have to be taken into account," Issba said louder, as if addressing someone other than Domino.

"Indeed, he'll need a good girl for his seasons," said a nichan named Anon two places farther down the circle, his forearms decorated with thick honorary tattoos.

Domino knew that the man had lost his partner even before Domino and his brothers arrived in the clan. The two men had been part of the council since before Ero became Unaan of the Ueto clan.

"I was worrying more about cultivating that virginity," Issba replied, turning Domino's face to the left, to the right, bending slightly to touch the curve of his throat and the bone pointing under the skin. "Losing it could alter his abilities."

"Maybe review your judgment on that," Ero said.

"Do you know what is good for him, Ero? Do you know our ancestors' nature?"

"He's a pure blood. I saw his true nature with my own two eyes, thank you. It will be torture if you forbid him to take a woman during his seasons. Since he has to go through this, I see no reason to impose any abstinence on him. It's part of us. At least leave that to the boy or you'll kill him."

"He's probably above that."

"No one's above it."

Orsa smiled, and Omak glanced obliquely in Domino's direction. A gaze that didn't fail to emphatically detail the teenager's anatomy. Omak had always looked at Domino with insistence and curiosity. Or want—he couldn't have said. For his part, Domino tried to remain dignified in the face of this conversation, which had become too personal for his taste. He rather lost track of it.

He now knew that there would be no marking. The Prayer Stones were their next destination. Domino already sensed that he wouldn't like what would happen there.

"I can't forbid him from doing anything," Issba resumed after a pause. "I am only here to offer my advice and knowledge." He lifted Domino's chin again between his fingers, forcing their gaze to meet. "Our Almighty Gods have set their eyes on you and they have made a choice. They do no such thing without purpose. You will have to prove yourself worthy of it."

Domino's eyes wandered. Ero looked at him, as did the other nichans in the auditorium. The boy looked down. Were the Gods really responsible for this? By accidentally taking Mora's life, had Domino disgraced their offering? None of this felt like a gift. Whatever it was, he was sure he was no longer worthy of anything. He'd failed the Gods. He'd failed Mora.

"Come on, boy," the Orator said, shaking Domino's face. "You don't have the choice. Don't you want to make our Gods proud?"

The man seemed to be waiting for an answer. For once, Domino was at a loss of word. Issba added, "And your people, your clan. Everyone is counting on you." He let go of Domino and stepped back several paces, opening his arms wide as if to take flight, a slight smile arching his lips. "Honor them, boy. Reveal your smile."

So that was what this was all about. They expected him to transform? Here? Had they lost their mind to request such—

For fuck's sake! He was responsible for his brother's death. Were they all craving the same end?

They don't care. They think Mora was weak, that they can survive this beast . . .

Domino forgot the man who stood before him, his charisma, his title, and pushed away in a powerful strike everything that made up his being. No more nichan smile, Domino even dulled his senses.

His answer was sharp and final. "I won't do it."

Ero folded his arms across his broad chest. He'd already been offered this line.

Issba raised his eyebrows, somewhat surprised. "Come on, I know it's intimidating but there's no reason to be shy. You are safe now. Don't be scared. Let's see it."

"No."

The Orator lost his smile and his arms fell along his body. He stared at Domino accusingly and less forgivingly than Ero had a few days earlier.

"That is not an acceptable answer, boy. Whatever grief you are going through, you have no excuses. You are almost of age to be raising children. Act like an adult." The lack of a positive reaction from the boy forced the man to show more authority. "Besides, that is no way to stand. Come here. Here, I said! Do not resist. Stand there. Stand up. You think this is a way to honor the Gods? No, look at me."

Instinctively, Domino had turned his eyes to Ero, begging for his help. How ironic to have only his uncle to rescue him at this moment. His uncle who had insisted that Domino accompany them on their cursed dohors hunt.

Ero's expression darkened, but he didn't move an inch, his jaw muscles rolling under his beard.

Once again, Issba moved back to give Domino enough room for a transformation that didn't come. "Reveal your true form, be proud," said the Orator.

"No." Domino stood on his feet, jaw clenched, his anger rising. "No, that's a simple enough word. I think anyone in the rest of the world would have understood it by now."

His hands trembled as he struggled against the urge to run away, to scream at the man to let go. He had to keep his calm, and insolence was all he had left to restore his strength.

A resounding slap smacked his cheek. Domino opened his eyes wide as Issba pointed a finger at him, the burning tongues of the flames shining in his eyes.

"I won't accept this answer," he said. "You dishonor the memory and the infinite goodness of our Creators. I will not tolerate it any longer. Transform yourself immediately!"

"I will not."

Another slap.

"Transform at once!"

"No."

Then another one.

"Don't waste my time."

"*No!*"

The Orator's hand went up, quick as lightning. The blow didn't burn Domino's cheek. With a firm grip, Ero had stopped Issba's hand.

Issba exhaled in surprised. "What's the matter with you?"

"Stop hitting him," Ero ordered wearily.

"You dare defy the way of the Gods?"

"I don't intend to watch my nephew slaughter you, so reconsider your attitude before it gets ugly."

"I am not afraid of him."

"Your courage does you honor, but it wouldn't save you."

"Indeed."

Issba got his arm back and, despite being a few inches shorter, looked at Ero with the luminous gaze of a man who fears no harm, who bends to no law. Domino had taken the opportunity to step back. In the auditorium, the nichans watched the exchange in silence. Orsa had stood, ready to defend her partner.

"This boy has to wake up," said Issba.

"He will, but not under your will. Last I heard," Ero recalled, "I'm still his Unaan. And in his mother's and brother's absence, he's my responsibility."

"You think you can solve this problem without me?"

"I've achieved a lot without your . . . guidance."

"In that case, get out."

"You said you wanted to go to the Stones—"

"That's not the case anymore."

"I thought you Orators didn't change your minds."

"The boy refuses to obey. Unless you force him to, it would offend our Gods to go up to the Prayer Stones under these conditions. I will not do them such an insult. Are you going to force him?"

Ero took a brief glance at Domino over Issba's shoulder, brief but long enough for the hesitation lingering at the edge of his mind to show.

Domino would leave his clothes here. He would flee before the order fell.

"It's interesting that you fear the effects the loss of his virginity could have," Ero told the Orator, "but that you don't care what shock his being might suffer if I ordered him to go against his greatest fears. The blood oath isn't without danger to body and mind. You already know that. You Orators refuse the oath for that reason. Given what he is, it's impossible to say what—"

"So you refuse the Gods' gift?"

"I will not risk wasting it. The Gods have blessed us. I won't spoil the hope they've given to our clan. It'd be more sensible to cast you out and lose your teachings than to follow your advice. Domino's life is more valuable than yours. The Gods would agree with me."

Issba raised his chin and looked away. He turned on his heels, grabbed another handful of spices from the bowl, and threw it into the fire. "Out. I'm tired of repeating myself."

Domino grabbed his clothes. He was putting on one leg of his pants when Issba's voice rose once more.

"You know what you have to do, Ero. You know the best way to restore the true color of a nichan's blood."

"He's too young," Ero answered.

"He's almost a man."

"Barely. He hasn't yet reached the age of his seasons. Once it's past, everything will be easier for him."

His seasons, the rut, a mandatory step for all male nichans. A trivial subject, and yet it made Domino's heart cower in the depths of his chest. Mora had gone through it. So had Beïka.

His turn would come.

Domino stopped dressing before taking it up again, passing an arm through one of the holes in his tunic. He was hot with nervousness, but the fabric was a protective shell he felt had been split when he undressed in front of the Orator.

"Do you think so?" asked Issba. "There is a beast in him. He should learn to embrace what he is before he reaches that turning point. His future is uncertain—you told me so yourself."

"Enough."

Ero's order once again slipped over the Orator's will like water on a swan's curves. "You've been afraid of him since he was sworn in. You've always felt there was something different about him. That power, that savage force we all yearn for. The truth is, you are afraid he might dominate you. Fear no more, Ero, for he will. You cannot fight against the will of our Creators. Do not attempt to sabotage their work."

Silence fell yet again. Ero was calm, his eyes locked on the Orator's arrogant face. In an instinctive move to protect their leader, all the nichans of the council had risen when Issba braved the Unaan's order.

In the suffocating atmosphere, the Orator never looked away. Both men stared at each other. A puff of smoke rose from the everlasting brazier.

Behind Ero, Domino came out of his torpor. It was too much. He had to get out; he had to leave this room and its rage-filled air. Without closing his tunic, he walked out with great strides.

Issba's words still echoed in his head as he ran down the stairs. *The truth is, you are afraid he might dominate you. Fear no more, Ero, for he will.*

Was this what Ero really feared? That Domino would take his place? Had Ero really told the Orator that he had been afraid of Domino since the day of the blood oath? Afraid. Such a deep word. Afraid of a six-year-old who had fainted at his feet? Afraid of a teenager unable to control his true nature?

Domino shook his head and rubbed his eyes. He hated people talking about him behind his back, as if he weren't there, as if he didn't have a say in the matter. If his opinion mattered so little, why should he worry about other people's opinions? No one cared about his fears, his grief, to know how he felt. He was responsible for his brother's death, for Gods' sake! All Ero, the council, and Issba cared about was what to do with a pure blood now that they had one on hand.

And Domino, in all this, would one of them ask him what he needed? Probably not.

Without further hesitation, he went through the village woods, and found the breach. No one had closed it yet. He pushed the bamboo logs out of the fence and slipped out of the village. He'd come all the way here without thinking, driven by an overwhelming desire for truth. He wouldn't get far. If others saw him and punished him, he would accept it. It was worth it.

The rain was still falling, masking the smells, transforming them, awakening many others. Domino navigated between the trees, trusting his fragmented memory. He advanced with a determined step. But the closer he got to the place, the more his confidence weakened. It had been raining for several days; perhaps the tracks had been washed away.

He hesitated and stopped dead in his tracks. In front of him, a tree had been cut down. Not with claws. Not with a saw as humans did. It was broken in two. The wood fibers were still clinging to the rest of the trunk lying in the grass. Much of the top bark had been brutally torn off, as if something as hard as rock had smashed the poor tree. Probably the cause of the fall. It was a beautiful specimen, thick, at least fifty years old. Domino released the breath he'd held against his will and approached. He had the feeling that he knew what had caused this tree to fall.

On his right he recognized the place where Ero had fought and finished the first dohor. On his left, the place where he and his brother had stood, listening to the cries of the other creature who'd probably already spotted them. No blood on the ground, as Domino had expected.

No blood, but something else.

Impressive lacerations in the earth. Deep, irregular, awkwardly drawn.

You saw the dohor. You transformed and attacked it. But . . . your movements were messy. You could barely stand on your feet, as if you'd never learned to walk, like a child. Ero had not lied. These grooves could attest to that.

Domino bent and grazed the wet earth with his fingertips. He closed his eyes and concentrated. If only some pieces of this moment could come back to him. Anything would do to give momentum to the rest of his memory.

The missing spots of his mind remained out of reach.

Nothing.

He breathed as Mora had taught him, soothing his nerves, delving into his mind.

Still nothing.

He opened his eyes again. How could he have forgotten?

The upside-down tree.

No, even a blow to the head wouldn't have been enough to make him forget. And even if it had, then his memories were not really lost, only buried deep in his head. Yet Domino felt as if he had none, as if the accident and his transformation were a lie, or as if his mind had refused to hold onto even a single second of these events.

He peered at the scene one last time, moved closer to the tree, and rubbed his palm against its skinned trunk.

Nothingness. Not an image, not a feeling outside the suffocating emptiness that dashed all his hopes.

It was a lost cause. How could he ever accept what he'd done and what he was if none of it seemed real? But Mora's absence was real, as was Belma's grief, Beïka's grief, and his own.

He'd come here for nothing.

XVI

DOMINO TURNED TAIL AND RETURNED TO SURHOK, SOAKING wet all over. He opened the wall and crept inside the village. A familiar scent shook him with surprise.

First appeared his asymmetrical dark wings, then his light hair, like no one else had here. It was soaked and dripping on his bare shoulders. He turned his back to Domino, motionless, his arms at his sides.

Domino watched him silently, enjoying if only for a moment the peaceful presence of his friend. He was seeing Gus for the first time in days. An impulse was urging him to get away from him. Another implored him to never leave him again.

Gus turned around and sighed imperceptibly. Shadows rimmed his eyes. As Domino noted this detail, Gus's expression hardened. "I thought I'd stay here, in case anyone else followed you."

Domino wanted to thank him but remained silent. He'd avoided Gus for days and yet Gus was here, watching over him, covering him as Domino was defying the clan's rules once again. A mere "thank you" felt uncalled for.

"Did you find what you were looking for?" Gus asked.

The truth wouldn't hurt, so Domino answered. "Not quite."

Risks taken for nothing.

"Everyone's been looking for you lately," Gus said. "They keep asking me where you are. I never have the answer. What a shame."

"It's better for everyone."

"Who said that?"

"I did. I don't want to hurt you." The words came out of his mouth, desperate. "I've already taken Mora away from us. I don't want to do the same to you. I won't survive it."

That confession stole a sob from the bottom of his guts. He missed Gus so much, he missed Mora even more. In an instant, the thought of losing them both was unbearable, more palpable than the rain pouring down on his skin.

"I'm not afraid of you," said Gus, his jaw tightened.

"I am."

Gus turned completely to Domino and reached out his hand. Something was trapped inside his fist. He opened it, revealing a piece of dried sap carefully tied to a long, soft leather cord. Domino had forgotten that piece of amber sap, the one that reminded him of Gus's eyes, as he'd told him.

Domino had dared share this confession. After showing it to Gus, he'd told himself that he could do it. To cross the few inches between them would have been enough, as well as a hint of courage. He would have moved slowly enough to reveal his intention, to give Gus a choice. If Gus had given him permission, Domino would have kissed his lips. But everything had gone upside down and a beautiful day had turned into an endless nightmare. Now, would he ever dare get that close to Gus again?

"Come home with me," Gus said.

Domino looked at the palm of his friend's hand. He was weak and couldn't bear the thought of being alone.

So he grabbed the necklace, slipped it around his head and hung it to his neck. In the end, he'd quickly decided which part of him he wanted to listen to.

When Gus marched back to the village, Domino followed suit.

HE FOUND his hut identical to what it'd been before the accident. As always, the bed was undone, the blankets—useless in this season—pushed back to the foot of the mattress. A plank of wood had been laid on the braided floor, not far from the small extinguished brazier. A few sharp tools lay around. Inside, silence reigned, barely disturbed by the drops hammering on the roof.

Domino gently sniffed the air. He recognized smells of vaguely familiar plants—not the kind he associated with his home. Apart from that, everything was normal. As normal as their lives could be after the recent events.

He walked into the room and stood there, uncertain what to do with himself. Gus sat on the edge of the bed. He must have realized he was soaking wet, for he got up suddenly and started to change, finding dry clothes in a wicker basket by the window. After a moment of dull wavering (what was safe or not?), Domino did the same and hung his wet clothes from the rope running across the corner of the room. Water dripped on the floor.

Gus stood beside him. Maybe too close. "Your hand," he said, taking an extra step.

Domino's right hand was slowly healing. The still swollen knuckles tore at each movement. "It's nothing," he said, disposed to step back if necessary.

"If it's nothing then it will only take me a second." Domino clenched his fist and partially hid it behind his back. "Domino . . . "

"You don't have to heal me every time. I can take responsibility for my mistakes."

Gus looked up at his friend's cut and bruised forehead. He clenched his jaw and a trembling exhalation left his chest. "It's been five days. I want to do this."

Five days since Domino had begged him to keep his distance. Five days since Mora . . .

Burying his fears deep inside himself, Domino relaxed his hand and let Gus close his on his flayed skin. As expected, the process lasted only a handful of seconds. Domino's muscles tightened and a coolness as gentle as water flowing between his knuckles carried the pain away. Gus raised his eyelids and held his friend close to him, palm to palm. Even though he'd noticed the harm Domino had inflicted to his head, Gus only focused on his friend's hand.

Domino should have taken his hand away. He left it there for a moment, appreciating the softness of Gus's skin and the comfort that infused peace into his body.

Then he tore himself away from the soft grip. "Thank you."

"You're exhausted," Gus guessed. "You should get some sleep."

He didn't ask where Domino had been the last few nights. If he wanted to know, at least he gave the nichan a chance to keep his secrets.

"I don't know if I can . . . if you stay close to me. If I have a nightmare . . . " Domino remembered then that it was still early and Gus wouldn't come to bed with him.

Gus didn't react. "We can talk about it if you want."

"I can't. I don't remember anything," Domino confessed, knowing what Gus was referring to.

"Nothing at all?"

"It's all gone. Everything."

"Even what happened before?"

A pause. Domino stepped away from his friend and leaned against the wall. Tears were already returning, burning his tired eyes.

"I panicked," he said. "There were two dohors, not just one. The first one that jumped us wasn't the one from the cave. Ero got it so easily. At least it looked easy. I still panicked, I . . . I've never been on a real hunt. I almost shit myself like a fucking child." His eyes went to the infinite stitch of the floor. He paused again and focused on Gus's heartbeat. Steady and balanced. "There was another one left, the one who'd marked me as its prey. The one I —" Domino took the time to wipe his wet face and nose and sniffed. "The other one attacked and . . . I don't know. I felt weird. I felt like I was breaking into pieces. It's blurry, like a dream. I can't remember. I'm . . . I'm afraid I can't tell the difference between reality and my imagination."

"You need sleep."

"Is it even safe? What drives me crazy is that I don't know if this house will hold up if I transformed in my sleep. Can I transform in my sleep? How could I know? I don't want to do it. I don't . . . I don't want to hurt you. I don't want to be a pure blood, I—"

Suddenly his breath ran out and he turned away from Gus, resting his forehead against the wall. He pressed his fingers against his eyelids and, in a desperate effort, tried to swallow his tears. He was tired of crying, of feeling so febrile and helpless. He couldn't take it anymore.

"I took plants from the infirmary," said Gus, his voice softer than before. "They can help you, soothe you. You'll get a dreamless sleep." He took a longer breath. "No one's expecting you to go back to your chores today. And if they do, I'll take care of them."

"It's not your responsibility," Domino whispered, still facing the wall.

"It is. I was one of the dohor's prey. I should have been there to . . . You did nothing wrong."

"I killed Mora," Domino cried, pressing his fits hard against his eyes, as if shoving his eyeballs to the back of his skull would end the pain for good.

"It wasn't your fault. You panicked. Your emotions were out of control. That's when you transformed. That's right? Domino." And that name, uttered in a breath, was like a gentle caress to the nichan. "The more you wear yourself out, the more likely you are to lose control."

Long seconds passed during which Domino absorbed Gus's words. When he turned around, his friend was already holding a cup between his slender fingers. Domino nodded, and Gus gave it to him.

The water inside had a bitter taste. It made his tongue raspy. Domino swallowed it in one warm gulp, returned the cup and let himself go against the wall again. "I don't want to talk or think about it."

"Then don't."

Gus walked over to him. The room lacked light; Gus had only turned on one lamp, which was now on the floor. Domino could barely see his friend's eyes.

"Don't let me think about it," he implored.

"Come on."

Gus walked across the room and settled on the floor in front of the wooden plank. Domino joined him, sitting on the other side. He could feel every inch separating them, wondering if his beastly shape could fit all the way into the hut, if Gus would have enough time to rush out before that happened.

Domino shook his head and grabbed one of the wood chisels lying around. He knew this wooden plank placed in front of him. A closer look revealed drawings and lines carved into its uneven surface. Gus spent a lot of time leaning over this board. When Domino would go away for days at a time for hunting training, it was by carving that Gus would fill the silence. The shapes he traced ignored the grain of the wood. They veered, rushed, and circled, some straight and precise, some curved and interlocking. None of them matched the other, proud of their independence. The end result was a chaos born of long hours of work. Neither beautiful nor ugly. As Domino knew, this was just a way for Gus to kill time.

Domino had never carved anything on this board. Gus had offered to let him do it, but the nichan had turned it down. Even though Gus didn't seem to care much for the work, it belonged to him. It was up to him to finish it. This time, however, Domino held the chisel in his right hand and placed its point against the wood in the lower right corner.

"What can I carve?" he asked, already regaining control of his voice and emotions.

"Whatever you want," said Gus, who was already scratching the surface with his own blade.

"Show me."

Gus looked up. His dark eyes met his friend's and he probably understood the message. *Don't let me think about it*, Domino had asked.

"A circle," Gus said. "Not too big. It's a good way to practice, to take the chisel in hand."

"Okay. There?"

"Yes."

"Am I holding it right?"

"Yeah. Just carve the circle into the wood, just on the surface, gently. It doesn't have to be deep. There you go. You can rectify it here."

"Right here?"

"Yes. Now you know where to dig. Take a hammer. You hit

here. Make sure you point it in the direction you want to go. Not too hard."

"I'm gonna mess up."

"Don't worry."

"Wait. Here. Show me."

"The chisel in the direction you want it to go. Like that. Ah!"

The hammer met his flesh, which opened immediately. Blood beaded on Gus's hand as he laid down his tools in front of him. But the damage was done.

Going beyond his thoughts and resolutions, Domino reached out. He captured Gus's hand and, giving the lead to his body, his instinct taking over, he brought the wound to his mouth and licked it. The gesture was natural, benevolent, one of a nichan protecting one of its own, caring for its wounds as an animal would do with its offspring. The sole accomplishment of this gesture slowed Domino's racing heartbeat. He tasted the blood's metallic, salty flavor, and felt a desire to protect rise within him, more intense than ever.

Before he realized the significance of his action, Gus withdrew his hand, looking shocked. "Don't do that."

Domino opened his eyes wide, more stunned than his friend was. Gus told him he wasn't afraid of him. Apparently, that wasn't entirely true.

"I'm — I'm sorry," Domino stammered, about to back away.

"Don't apologize. Just don't do that. There's no telling what my blood might do to you. How do you feel?"

Confusion overcame Domino. "What?"

"I'm a Vestige, even though we spend our time pretending we don't know it. My blood . . . "

"What about it?"

"Don't touch it."

"I don't get it."

Gus's hand still bled, but he ignored the red drop blossoming then running down his white skin, even as it dripped onto his board.

"You're afraid I can't transform anymore," Domino said, for it was all that mattered to anyone else lately. "It's because of what I am that you—"

"I don't care if you're a pure blood, Domino." Gus cut him off, firmer but also colder, as if his friend's remark had just offended him. "Do you think it makes any difference to me?"

"It should."

"I'm right here. I'm not running away. I would have said the same thing to you a week or a year ago. You're not the problem. I am."

"You? Why? Gus, you've proven more than once that you're not dangerous."

"No one knows what Vestiges are made of. The Blessers say we stole the Light from the Gods, that we defiled it. Others say we are the dogs of the Corruption."

Others. Did he mean nichans? "This is bullshit," Domino said.

"The truth doesn't matter. My blood could hurt you. Maybe it's poison to nichans." He paused, finally looking down at the superficial wound marking his pale hand. Like Domino, he watched the blood finally stop flowing to clot. Lowering his voice, Gus said, "Do you remember the men who hanged me?" The question made Domino's chest uneasy. Of course he remembered. Gus didn't give him time to answer. "They'd eaten something, a plant they found on the road. They thought it was beautiful, they'd never seen one like it before. Its leaves weren't black like other plants. They were dark red, like raw meat. It was beautiful and . . . I think I recognized it. It was different. It was like me. Another Vestige. It was just too different to be normal. It should have scared them that it was that different. They thought its fruit must be a delight. They loved the taste. They ate every last berry.

"That night, one of them started shitting blood. Then they

231

both spat blood, as if something was rotting inside or . . . melting their gut. They devoured the fruits of a Vestige, and if your brothers hadn't killed them, those men would have died anyway. Maybe it was unique to this Vestige, or maybe it's part of all of us. Maybe all Vestiges are really tainted from the inside."

"You can't believe that."

"I don't know. Do you? If I was chopped into pieces, would they find the same organs as in another human?"

"Don't say that." Pain grew in Domino as the renewed idea of his friend's death barreled through him.

But Gus kept going, forcing this reality to take form in Domino's mind. "Look at my eyes. Do they look normal to you?"

Yes, Domino wanted to answer, but he was afraid of angering his friend. The truth was inescapable.

"And my wings," Gus added before taking a moment to think. "The Blessers have a sacred book. The Artean. It speaks of many things: good, evil, the Gods. Nichans and . . . Vestiges. It talks about us in very colorful terms."

Domino had never heard of this book until now. He wanted to ask how Gus knew of it. Another dangerous question that he chose to keep for himself, for the answer scared him.

"What does it say?" he asked instead.

Gus looked up at his friend. A certain distress shone behind the hardness of his delicate features. "After meeting you, I realized that what the book said about nichans was just a bunch of crap. You're nothing like what the book describes."

"What makes you say that? What does the book say?"

"Doesn't matter."

Gus sighed then wiped the dried blood off the back of his hand, rubbing it with the thumb that he'd just moistened on the tip of his tongue.

"The book says you're tainted," Domino guessed, bitterness growing inside him. "Is that it?" Gus said nothing, continuing to wash away the blood. His skin reddened under the brutal friction. "Why believe what's in the book when it comes to Vestiges, but when it comes to nichans, it's just bullshit?"

"Because I saw it with my own eyes." Gus sighed softly and let his hand drop. "I've seen what a Vestige can do. I take a risk every time I touch you."

"What if this plant was no Vestige at all?"

"Well, there's no way to know."

"You would never hurt me."

"Some people would disagree. That's why they kill us."

"They kill us because they believe it will bring back the Gods. And because they're fucking insane. Especially because they're insane. That's all it is, Gus. This has nothing to do with you or what you might do to them."

"I don't know what's inside me so I can't really argue with them. Maybe they're right."

Gus stopped there, having made himself abundantly clear. Anger and grief grew into Domino at the same time.

Domino had often wondered where exactly Gus had come from, who had raised him until they'd met. Questions he had never dared ask for fear of crossing a line that would shut his friend's heart. If Gus didn't talk about it, it was because he didn't want to. So Domino had speculated in silence, had invented a past that defied logic. He'd imagined parents for Gus, a man and a woman with golden hair and the same eyes as their son. It was idiotic. Human Vestiges were born of ordinary humans; only Gus had such eyes and wings. Then Domino had stopped imagining, accepting that this truth didn't belong to him.

But he would have never imagined that Gus had such thoughts, that he saw himself as a permanent threat. Everything he'd just said was true, no one could deny it. Gus was a potential risk even though Domino refused to admit it.

Domino blamed himself for never having been able to guess his friend's internal turmoil.

Strangely, and for the first time, he felt like he understood Gus. They were more alike than Domino could have imagined. Whatever the risk—whether or not there was one—he was willing to take it as Gus took it by staying by his side.

"I'm not afraid of you," Domino said, repeating the words Gus had used earlier.

Gus returned his look.

The herbs took effect soon after. Domino grew dizzy and holding his chisel became laborious. He put it down and Gus helped him up—a seemingly risky but necessary physical contact —and into bed. As he sank, and Gus closed the window shutter and blew out the lamp, Domino thought one last time about that kiss he'd wanted to give him a few days earlier by the pond. This desire had survived the tragedy he'd just caused.

As promised, Domino didn't dream and slept peacefully. When he woke up in the middle of the night, Gus was sleeping right next to him.

XVII

THE LITTLE BOY WAITED AT THE EDGE OF THE WOODS. HE WAS less than half Domino's height, had black hair awkwardly cut around his protruding ears, and round cheeks reddened with small pimples. Something was trapped in his hands, against his heart, like a treasure.

Arms full of logs, Domino stood still. When he spotted the child, his heart leaped into his chest. He looked around and then returned his attention to the boy.

Then, joy took off. Domino smiled.

Facing him, three-year-old Natso was smiling as well.

"Hi there," Domino said.

He hadn't spoken to his nephew in months. Belma was doing a great job at keeping her son away from Domino. A fulfilled promise. If the woman caught Domino so much as breathing in Natso's direction, she would end it without delay. Apparently not enough efforts were put to the task. The little boy sometimes slipped through the net, making such meetings possible.

Domino ignored if his nephew knew what they meant to each other, if his mother or even Beïka had agreed to reveal to the child the bond they shared. But at that moment, as he was about to take some wood to the sanctuary's kitchen, Domino had only one thought in mind: Natso looked more and more like Mora.

"What are you doing here?" Domino asked, not daring to approach for fear of alarming the child.

Under the dark sky, legs buried up to his knees in the grass, Natso stretched out his hands in front of him. Something was sticking out between his round little fingers. Half a dozen steps away, Domino made his decision. He walked at a measured pace toward the child. Domino came within three feet of his nephew, put his wood on the ground while crouching down, and studied the child's face. Domino hadn't stood so close to him since Natso's baptism on the day Mora had—

Domino pushed the thought away and forced his smile to linger. He didn't want his nephew to leave, that like all the kids Domino had met throughout his life, Natso felt that his uncle was different. Dangerous.

Not him. Faces, please. Don't let him fear me.

But Natso didn't bat an eyelash, always showing his pearly teeth in a touching smile.

"What do we have here?" said Domino. The young man wasn't expecting a verbal answer. He knew, both from his brief experience and from the rumors circulating in the village, that at three years old, Natso had never uttered a word. But the boy understood what was said to him, so he opened his hands, revealing a tiny lizard with smooth, bluish skin. What was left of its falsely severed tail was pinched between Natso's thumb and forefinger.

"Look at that. Here's a great catch!" Domino congratulated him and the child's joy lit up his face.

Though no doubt treated with the little delicacy that children showed at such a young age, the reptile was still alive. Through his and Natso's heartbeats and breaths, Domino could make out the tiny pulses animating the lizard's body. They wouldn't last long.

"It's beautiful," Domino said when Natso brought the animal close to his uncle's face, proudly displaying the fruit of his hunt. "Where did you find it?"

Closing his fingers on the lizard, the little boy turned around and pointed to a pile of lichen-covered stones.

"And you caught it by yourself?"

Natso nodded.

"Well done! A real hunter. You'll have to give it to your mom. She needs to see this."

But at these words, the little boy shook his head and handed the dying lizard to his uncle.

"What? For me?"

Natso nodded again.

"You want . . . to give it to me?"

Another nod.

Emotion burned deep in Domino's eyes. It was but a half-dead animal. Yet coming from his nephew, whom he dreamed of knowing and whose company he sorely missed, the young man felt as if he were receiving a token of both love and forgiveness. He wanted to hold the child in his arms to thank him, maybe in hope of hiding the tears threatening to run down. Having not received the permission to do so, Domino raised his hand to tousle the child's hair, as Mora had done with him countless times.

"Natso!"

Domino's hand froze in midair and then withdrew. Her cheeks covered with honorary tattoos, Belma ran the last few yards between them, grabbed the child's arm, and shoved him behind her.

Ice coursing through his veins, Domino stood and took a step back, forgetting his abandoned fuel in the grass.

Belma glanced blackly at Domino and then leaned over to her

son. "Go back home at once. Dadou is waiting for you to eat. Now, Natso-sanoa."

Sanoa, meaning "my son," or in this case a clear way for any Torb to remind a child who was in charge. Joy had deserted Natso's features, but he wasn't told twice. With his hands still full, he turned around and, throwing a last glance over his shoulder, walked away from the woods, scampering toward the heart of the village on his little legs.

"We were just talking," Domino said.

"Talking?" Belma said, pointing to the nil probability of such action when it came to her son.

"No, I . . . He just wanted to show me a—"

"Do I look like I care?" A breeze passed between them. "I told you to stay away from my son. I meant it. I may not be a hunter, but I'll make you regret it if you keep going."

If he kept going? A ball of frustration swelled inside him. He'd never gotten too close to Natso before. Belma had made herself clear, but it was guilt that had held Domino back. But for some reason outside of his control, the child kept coming back to see him.

"He came to me," Domino said. "What was I supposed to do? Send him away? Ignore him?"

"Don't put the blame on him."

"That's not what I'm doing."

"You're just making excuses, as always. Last time he lost a sandal."

And Domino hadn't lied. The shoe had been lying there, a few leaps from the front porch of Belma's hut where Natso sat and played by himself. Domino hadn't taken two steps in his direction before Beïka, the asshole, had appeared to stick his oar in.

"So now what? Killing our brother wasn't enough? You want to settle the score with his son too?" Beïka had told Domino, proudly displaying on the whole surface of his neck, jaw and torso the marks honoring Mora's memory, marks that Ero still denied Domino for fear of damaging his transformation abilities.

It was useless to defend his case. Belma wouldn't give in. But in the face of the anger growing inside him at the mention of this incident, Domino couldn't keep quiet. "I would never hurt him." A poor defense. He'd killed Mora, even though it was the last thing he wanted. Domino added, for it was all he had left, "I . . . I'm his family."

Belma shook her head. "He already has a family. He has the clan, he has Dadou, he has me, and—"

"And who? Beïka? With him around, no wonder the kid can't talk yet."

No . . .

Belma's eyes sprang open as if Domino's fist had just lunged at her gut. Domino froze in fright. He'd replied without thinking, without considering the harm his words could inflict. The point had been to insult Beïka, to support his brother's terrible influence on all the children left to his care. Instead, he'd just insulted Belma and her ability to raise her own son—the son she was raising by herself because of Domino.

"I'm sorry," Domino said, red with shame. He still couldn't believe that he'd had the audacity to speak such words.

"Go fuck yourself, Domino," Belma answered.

She stared at Domino's imploring face for a moment. Nothing he would say could save his case. He'd just ruined his chance to be a part of his nephew's life.

I'm just a fucking jerk.

Belma turned around and left him there.

Darkness crept in between the trees, and Domino picked up his wood.

Tomorrow he would go on a hunt because Ero had allowed it. Ero still hoped Domino would change, that Domino would stop being afraid of the nichan inside him—that real nichan that had taken Mora from him, that today kept him away from his family.

Three years earlier, Domino had made the decision not to transform anymore. He could live without that part of himself. He had to live without it. But to live without his family was unbearable.

When he left Surhok at dawn the next day, he took one last look at Belma's hut, where Natso was probably still sleeping.

———

SO MUCH BLOOD. Gus couldn't have missed it.

The nichans swarmed into the village, a small group of five individuals. In the middle stood Ero. In his arms, his face pale and agonizing, was Domino. His leg was bloody from the thigh down. A crude bandage covered the wound.

Again? Gus thought.

In the three years since the discovery of Domino's true nature, the nichan had been wounded at least four times during the hunt. Given his condition, this misadventure wouldn't be without consequences. If this continued, Domino would lose his right to hunt with his own people.

Gus ran to them, lungs squeezed tight between his ribcage and his pounding heart. Ero had ordered him to join them in the infirmary. Gus was already on his way. It was becoming a habit.

The mattress on which Domino had been laid quickly became soaked in blood. Domino gritted his teeth and twisted the sheet into his fists as its fibers were drowned in the oily, coral liquid. He was livider than ever.

Keeping calm, Gus laid his hand flat next to the soiled bandage. He didn't need to watch the wound, for he'd see it properly in a few seconds.

"I'm fucking done with you, Domino," said Ero.

He paced the small room, fists on his hips, sweating. He kept his eyes downcast, as if one look at his nephew would have been enough to set off his temper. Gus imagined him tearing off the bandage and letting Domino bleed out before their eyes.

Domino didn't respond, breathing laboriously, his pain and strength leaving him.

It had to be done quickly.

Gus closed his eyes and concentrated. The process was now a part of him. But the silence he needed to allow his gift to unfold remained out of reach.

"You're incredibly lucky that we're so close to the village. A little more and you'd be dead, you little prick!"

"I'm sorry," Domino hissed between his teeth.

"A grave, is that what you want? You want to join your mother and brother?"

"Stop! I already apologized. What else am I supposed to say?"

"If what you want is to get killed, you should've said so earlier. We can dig a hole in the middle of the village, nothing easier. I'll throw you in there myself. We'll put a stake in it and engrave, 'Here lies the village idiot. We gave him everything, and he refused everything.' Sounds just like you —"

"Shut up!"

The injunction didn't come from Domino, but from Gus. He opened his dark eyes and looked up at Domino and then at his uncle. He didn't care about the repercussions. If they didn't let him do his job, Domino would die. To his left, Ero rose to his full height, as massive and intimidating as ever.

Gus wasn't impressed, as if facing a wall instead of a beast. "I need silence."

Without further ado, he closed his eyes and took care of the wound that appeared to him in all its splendor. It was deep, perhaps deeper than any wound he'd ever healed before. He immediately spotted the affected artery that the bandage was severely compressing. Not enough to stop the bleeding, but enough to buy Domino time.

Halfway through his treatment, Gus emerged partly from his trance. "The bandage is in the way. Take it off."

He was obeyed, and he resumed after swallowing a large gulp of air. Once the wound was firmly closed, he batted his eyelids and Domino reappeared before him, his breath steadier, his hand clutching his necklace and the piece of sap hanging to it, the other relaxing on the bed.

Ero grasped his nephew's jaw, forcing him to look into his eyes. Despite the fatigue, reacting without giving it a second thought, Gus reached out his hand to intervene. With a sharp slap, Ero pushed the young man's arm away. Gus clenched his teeth, holding back a scream. Ero rarely restrained his blows.

"Look at me, you worthless shit," said the man, his eyes paralyzing Domino. "No more hunting for you. You hear that? It's over. I'd rather kill you myself than put up with your fucking act."

Teeth clenched, Domino breathed heavily, the flesh of his cheeks constricted. "If it's so hard for you, why didn't you let me die?"

"You just wasted your last chance," Ero continued, speaking over his nephew's voice. "Don't come crying to me when I'm forced to take more drastic measures."

Domino's breathing stopped. He stared at his uncle with the same tired but inflexible look, yet a cloud had just cast its shadow over his face.

"Drastic measures" was but another way to remind Domino that a few words from his Unaan were enough to bring him to heel.

To transform.

Without adding anything more, Ero released Domino's face

and left the room, taking with him his rage as suffocating as a brush fire.

Eyes on his friend, Gus took a step back and let himself fall onto the nearest bench. His hands shook, damp and tired, like the rest of him. As always when he used his gift on Domino, he'd drawn only from his own strength, refusing to use the strength of the body he treated. It would have been easier, however, for Domino's energy felt endless. But Gus wouldn't allow himself to rely on it.

A decision Ero would have wholeheartedly approved.

After it was discovered that the Ueto Clan had a pure blood in its ranks, Ero came to find the human. "Your gift, how does it work?"

The gift was an intimate part of Gus, as much a curse as it was a precious possession. He was unwilling to share the details with the clan leader. But even though he'd mastered his gift, it remained a mystery to him.

For all these reasons, Gus had only spoken a few vague words in response to Ero. "I use my energy, sometimes that of the patient, to speed up the healing process."

Half a lie.

Gus had been in the sanctuary kitchen cleaning a huge cast-iron pot in which vegetables were cooked every day. The boy could have fit in there in his entirety. This was Domino's task, but at the time he'd still been recovering from his brother's death, and Gus would have done anything to lighten his friend's burden.

"The patient's?" Ero had asked.

"My own strength is limited," Gus had explained to Ero.

A bit of a shameful confession. Amidst all those huge, powerful nichans, he sometimes felt as fragile as a twig. Ero seemed to have had the same idea. He had sneered before shaking his head. "I see. Well, no more of that with Domino."

"Which means?"

"Meaning you're going to have to toughen up. Domino is special. I don't want to take any chances. From now on, if you find yourself doing your Vestige tricks on him, you'll have to settle with your own energy. And it will have to be enough. Do we understand each other?"

Ero may not have pulled a blue stone out of his pocket, but Gus didn't need it to be convinced. The memory of the Op crystal still shone in a corner of his memory, like the sparkle of a blade.

To tell the truth, Gus had long since stopped using Domino's energy, and not because Ero had threatened him once again.

Domino stirred on the bloodied bed.

"Lie still. You've lost a lot of blood," Gus told him.

His friend fell back on the mattress and sponged his face with a clean corner of the sheet. "I'm sorry."

"Don't apologize," Gus said to him between two deep breaths.

"How's your hand?"

"Probably better than your face." Domino breathed a short laugh then massaged the curve of his reddened jaw. Heat pulsed in Gus's fingers. It was nothing, whereas Domino's face . . . Gus knew from experience how merciless Ero's grasp could be. "Do you want me to look at it?"

Domino shook his head and winced, running a shaky hand through his black curls.

"So what happened?" Gus asked, wishing he had enough stamina to stand at his friend's side.

"That's today's biggest question. I have no fucking clue what happened, beside messing around. I just . . . I can't concentrate lately. The boar stuck his tusks in my thigh before I had a chance to see its ugly face. I didn't even hear it coming. I was all numb and out of it." Domino hesitated. "It would please Belma."

"What about her?"

And Domino told him about meeting his brother's former partner two days ago. He stared at Gus, as if waiting for an answer. Not just an answer, or even a comment. He was hoping for Gus to call him on his mistake, to remind him that as usual Domino had spoken and acted without thinking. He wanted to be punished for his harsh words to Belma.

Gus would do no such thing.

"I ruined my chances," Domino said. "I'm just an idiot. I should know by now. I've been told thousands of times."

"Why don't you get some rest? You almost died."

"Hardly."

But his eyelids were already drooping.

Domino was exhausted. Aside from this accident, he was already pushing himself too hard. Now that he'd chosen not to transform, he knew he was losing a considerable advantage. He was lagging behind his nichan brothers and sisters. Their semi-transformation exacerbated their already highly developed senses. It improved their reflexes and speed. Not to mention a strength that no human could match. Stuck deliberately in his human form —his camouflage—Domino was giving up all these benefits.

So he'd set out to strengthen his body as much as possible. He ran from one end of the village to the other before daybreak, again and again, pushing the limits of his system. He carried heavier and heavier loads, in his arms, on his shoulders, sometimes risking injury. Within a few months, his body had become accustomed to these exercises, inspiring him to increase his efforts. He'd now been doing them for over three years.

Now, at only sixteen, Domino looked more like a man than a teenager. His features had hardened. His slender silhouette had thickened, with dry muscles despite the large amount of food he ate at every meal.

"If I become strong enough, if I prove that I can hunt and fight like them, maybe Ero will get off my back," Domino had said one night in the baths, struggling to soap his exhausted arms and legs.

"Maybe," Gus had replied, even if the evidence was obvious in the tone of his voice.

"Yeah, a man can dream."

None of them were duped. That didn't stop Domino from aiming to his goal. Some days, Gus would run by his side. He wasn't sure how to reassure his friend, but he would be here for him, even if it meant fainting or vomiting his guts and lungs out in the attempt.

Moreover, the constant effort had another advantage: it cleared Domino's head. *Don't let me think about it*, Domino had begged back then. They were both working on it. After all this time, thinking about Mora was still too painful.

They remained silent for a while until they regained their strength. Domino dozed off, then fell asleep. Gus stayed by his side and took the opportunity to clean the blood before it dried on Domino's skin. His own human blood was easy to clean (even though Gus rarely spilled it). Nichans' blood was lighter, volatile in its own way. Like dry oil. It settled everywhere and crystallized like honey as it dried. It would take a lot of work to wash the blanket on which Domino slept right now. Gus was used to the task.

After a cursory cleaning, Gus examined his friend's thigh. The scar was pale and pinkish in the middle of this brown patch of flesh. Not his finest work, but time had been running out. One more scar, he thought. Without thinking, he massaged the skin and the muscle, felt the newly stitched rigid tissue roll under his fingers. It would regain its elasticity in no time.

"Admit it, you can't help touching me," laughed a lazy voice.

Gus smiled without looking at Domino. If he did, he would blush. He wasn't taking advantage of his friend, only checking, as he often did, that he'd done a decent job. What he saw during his trances seemed so insane that when he opened his eyes again he was amazed that it was real. Yet he withdrew his hand, unhurriedly, but a tinge of guilt tickled the side of his mind. Gus wouldn't deny it; he greatly appreciated the feel of Domino's skin. It was always warm, soft, and supple despite its thickness, typical of nichans' physiology.

"You don't have to stop," Domino whispered without losing his smile. He'd regained color even though his lips were still bloodless.

Gus felt the warmth show on his cheeks and thanked the dusk for its auspicious arrival, hiding his confusion. "I'm beginning to think you're getting stabbed by wild animals on purpose. I thought my hands were too cold. Now you're asking for more."

Gus should have kept his mouth shut.

What was now going on between the two young men had started about a year earlier. They were looking for each other. Flirting. Mostly it was just a matter of words and glances shared around their meal, teasing each other on the edge of the river to lighten the atmosphere, to discover each other's limits.

Nothing more than a game

"I'm so hot," Domino said. "Your hands feel good."

"You're hot?" Gus placed his hand on Domino's forehead. "You must have a bit of fever."

"Really? What a pity! Will it ever end? Will I even survive this unfair trial of misery?" Domino opened frightened eyes colored with a glimpse of malice.

"That's a dramatic way to describe it."

"Oh, but that's exactly how it feels."

"Yes?"

"Yes. Nothing but misery."

A smile curled Gus's mouth. "You'll be fine."

"Maybe my leg is infected. I can feel it. Right here. Here! Come on, touch it again. Quick, before the agonizing pain crawling through my veins reduces my flesh to a mound of rotten meat. Oh, no! No!"

Biting against the laugh shaking his chest, Gus sighed. "What now?"

"It's too late. My poor leg. We'll have to cut it off!"

"Shut up."

"Gus, will you take care of me when I get my leg cut off?"

"It's your tongue we should cut."

Domino bit his lip. "I could still have use of it."

The shared allusion in this whisper warmed Gus to his core. "No need to cut."

"My leg or my tongue?"

Silence.

"Your tongue," Gus said, accepting his friend's meaningful words, the echo of a shiver tickling the back of his neck. "The leg's probably fucked up already." Domino's smile widened and Gus exhaled a laugh. "Your leg will be numb for days. You'll have to massage it. Would you like me to show you how to do it?"

He finally dared to turn his black and amber eyes toward Domino. The young man was panting lightly, ready to respond to the advance. Gus really should have kept his mouth shut.

Domino sat up in spite of his weak condition, bringing his face closer to Gus's while giving him a chance to slip away.

They'd come to this point more than once. Each time, Gus had put an end to it. Domino had never seemed to take offense, as if the little Gus offered him was enough for him. In the ten years they'd known each other, some things hadn't changed. Domino was still content with what people were willing to give him.

Gus matched Domino's breathing, not backing down. It was getting darker, and he hadn't bothered to light a lamp. But he could still sight his friend's eyes resting on him, his lips half open, his broad chest and shoulders tensed by his sitting position, his belly rising and falling close to his hand.

Handsome.

"I promised myself I wouldn't let you heal me anymore," Domino said softly.

The confession took Gus by surprise. "When?"

"You think I remember everything? Gus, you're too good to me."

"All right, keep your secrets."

Domino smiled, the tip of his tongue running along the edge of his lower lip. "We were just kids. I think I was eight. I cut open my palm. Just here," he said turning his hand upward, displaying a straight scar at the base of his thumb.

Aware that the pounding of his heart was probably deafening for his friend's sharp hearing, Gus allowed himself a hint of audacity. He reached out. His fingertips grazed Domino's palm. "I forgot this one." He swallowed hard as he imagined himself bending over to press his lips to the hollow of the nichan's warm hand. "You have too many scars."

"Not my fault. Like I said, my life is a trial of misery."

Gus smiled and drew circles on Domino's skin with the tip of his thumb.

"You told me it exhausted you to use the gift," the nichan went on. "Strangely, I mistook it for pain."

"It's not painful."

Their voices were nothing but murmurs now. And Domino's fingers gently closed on Gus's. "Are you sure?"

Kiss me...

No, it was too risky. Leaving his hand in Domino's was as well. Yet Gus failed to find the strength to retreat.

Not yet.

"It's just tiring," Gus said, "like I told you. But I like it."

"You do?"

"It's exciting."

Slowly, Domino wet his lips. His eyes searched Gus's face,

studying his every reaction. They also stopped regularly on Gus's mouth. Stirring on the bed, Domino came half an inch closer.

Gus stood still. He wanted this moment to last, to know how far Domino would go before they reached the point of no return, if only to taste Domino's breath against his lips. Nothing more. Gus trusted his body to react and end their game at the right moment.

Domino smiled and tilted his head, revealing in the twilight light the vein pulsing wildly in the corner of his throat. "Exciting. Really?"

"You'd like that," Gus said.

"Too bad you can't show me. I'll have to settle for the massage then."

Unintentionally, Gus moved to the side. The back of his hand met Domino's bare thigh. The nichan gasped in surprise. A muffled sound, almost an uncontrolled moan.

It was time.

Gus calmly retreated and pulled with one hand on the sheet stuck under his friend's body. "I'm going to change that," he said nonchalantly, brushing aside the moment. "Then we'll go eat. If you can walk."

His heart was beating faster than he thought possible. His hands were sweaty, his belly a little knotted. Even so, he could pretend it was nothing, that he wasn't taking any risks.

Domino smiled at him—as always—shook his head to set his mind straight, and did his best to get up. But his efforts weren't enough.

He spent the night in the infirmary. Gus stayed by his side.

XVIII

GUS'S WINGS EXTENDED FROM EACH SIDE OF HIS SPINE, TWO arched branches protruding under his skin. Because of them, he rarely slept on his back. The discomfort always led him to roll onto his side, consciously or not. But not that morning. For once, his wings fit the curves of his body, sinking deeper into the old mattress than into his shoulder blades.

He stretched his arms above his head with a sigh of comfort and opened his eyes. It was already daylight. However, a significant difference lay right next to him. Domino was present, propped up on one elbow, watching him.

Domino gazed at a precise point. His mouth was half open, his breath steady but panting. In the warmth of the hut, sweat beaded down his face. Domino always woke up and left before dawn. Yet he was still here, as still as a statue, as if he were in a trance. He didn't so much as blink.

Without a sound, Gus followed the trajectory of his friend's gaze. Down . . . Gus's heart skipped a beat. He immediately discovered what captivated Domino. As the human turned on the bed, the blanket had slipped, revealing the intimate shapes of his body. And beneath the thin linen of his night pants, Gus's morning erection was unmistakable, rising to the rhythm of his breathing.

He looked up at the other young man. Then looked down. And up again. This was indubitably what captivated Domino.

Swallowing despite his dry mouth, Gus searched for his words. His head was emptier than ever. A hot flush rose to his face. His heart hammered.

He waited.

A voice in his head told him to move, to get Domino out of his contemplation. Another was begging him to ask for more. For an indulgent moment he imagined his friend untying the front of his pants, working his fingertips on the belt with reassuring confidence. Then the pressure and warmth of Domino's palm against his lower abdomen, slowly diving down, caressing the line of blond hairs . . .

Gus's body responded to the thought. A shiver shook him, his sex quivering beneath the fabric, beyond his control. Next to him, Domino clenched his fist on the bed and released a hot breath that caressed the lines of Gus's pale chest.

"Domino," said Gus.

The nichan blinked and seemed to come back to him, sniffing hard. He looked at Gus and went from dizziness to horror in a snap of the fingers. What he was doing had obviously not escaped him. He straightened on his arm, squirming awkwardly, probably to get out of bed. He was already pushing away the woolen blanket covering him. In his agitation, it fell off, sliding against his strong legs. Gus noticed the long bump on his friend's crotch.

"Domino," Gus repeated as his friend discovered at last his own state of arousal.

"I— By the Faces, I'm sorry, I . . . I didn't—"

Someone knocked on the door, pounding angrily. The hut vibrated around them. The two boys stared at the door.

Heart at the edge of his lips, Gus rolled to his side, turning his back to the front door, hiding his condition. It took Domino a moment to regain his wits and leave the bed, still a little awkward.

He opened the door. "What?"

"What the fuck are you doing? We've been waiting for you for an hour."

As always, Beïka was talking to his little brother like he was shit stuck underneath his shoe.

"I overslept," lied Domino, being as rough as his brother.

Those two had never learned to appreciate or speak to each other. Since Mora's death, the situation hadn't improved, to say the least. Domino had long since stopped trying to fix it. There was no way out of this. Beïka treated him like a dog and blamed him for the bad crops, or his own bad mood. Without Mora to mediate, their relationship was doomed for failure.

"I don't give a shit," said Beïka. "The others have already left. Now move."

"It's fine. I'm coming."

"You'd better. We shouldn't have to endure your whims and wait for you to —"

Beïka studied his brother up and down then took an unwelcome look inside the hut. His gaze crossed Gus's. Domino immediately blocked the view with his own body.

"You overslept, my ass!" Beïka said.

"I said I was coming. You can go now."

"Sure. Just remember to clean your mouth and cock before joining us. You reek of human."

Blood rushed to Gus's face.

"Fuck off!" With that, Domino slammed the door in his brother's face.

As he walked away, Beïka smashed his fist against the front of the hut, probably to get the last word.

Gus waited silently. Domino breathed heavily, his back

muscles tensing under his skin, one hand on his forehead. He'd gone from one emotion to another far too quickly.

"Hey," Gus whispered.

Domino glanced over his shoulder. His expression was calm, though his face glowed with sweat. "I'm sorry." His face was full of guilt and stupor. It was as if Beïka hadn't interrupted them even though his vulgarity lingered in the air. "I don't know what came over me. I wasn't going to—I wouldn't touch you."

You could. I'd let you.

"It's all right. It's nothing," Gus said instead.

"I'm sorry, Gus."

"Domino, it's okay. Don't worry about it."

Domino nodded, unconvinced. "I don't know what Beïka's going to say to— Do . . . do you want me to tell him something? That he's wrong?"

"Don't bother." Domino's silence remained too long. Gus tensed on the mattress. "Would it be so shameful? To bed a human?"

Bed me.

Domino sucked on a breath and swallowed hard. "No." Then he turned in haste, his hand brushing the front of his pants. "I've got to go."

He grabbed a pair of dusty pants he kept for his dirty work and took off the ones he was already wearing to trade. Gus looked away. Normally, neither of them cared about their nakedness, but after what had just happened this morning . . .

A year earlier, they had agreed, implicitly, not to ever sleep completely naked again. They'd done this throughout their childhood; they knew each other's bodies as well as their own. But they were no longer children, and all the means were good to avoid having to sleep in separate rooms.

There were looks, a hand staying longer than necessary on a shoulder, a waist. They were attracted to each other. Gus had always kept things from going any further. He was still afraid to find out what his own body could inflict on Domino. Maybe nothing. Maybe the worst. But as time passed, his determination wavered. He wanted Domino to touch him. He was dying for it to happen while having always strongly opposed it. Sometimes he thought he could let him, that he wasn't allowed to touch, but Gus and Domino's respective boundaries didn't need to align. It was risky, of course, but some days Gus just wanted to play with fire and see how much it'd burn. And more than anything else, he wanted to feel on his body and in his whole being that this desire was mutual.

Once he was ready, Domino took one last look at Gus. He stopped as if to say something, to no doubt apologize again, but swallowed his words. When the door closed on him, Gus sighed long and hard and pushed his thoughts away once more.

DOMINO DIDN'T KNOW what was going through his head. Or his body. He'd woken up before dawn, spent a little more time in bed, forgetting his obligations, his training, enjoying the peace and quiet of his hut. Turning around, he'd noticed Gus's condition, the length of his sex resting along the base of his thigh. From that moment his entire world had revolved around this point. There'd been no looking away or thinking of anything other than what he wished to do with Gus, if Gus would allow it. The urge to take off his clothes and Gus's had paralyzed him entirely, saving him from waking up his friend to share his sudden want with him.

And he thought about it all the rest of the day.

And the next day . . .

Things didn't get any better after that. As the summer's end went by, as burning hot, sweaty, dusty days passed, Domino's concentration decreased. He felt more awake than ever. Every muscle prepared for the effort, but again and again his mind wandered, diverting his body from its purpose. It became difficult for him to perform simple tasks. He often found himself standing on his own, separated from his own thoughts, as if a fever had melted them.

The Uetos went hunting again, without him. Domino began to lose sleep.

This time, he couldn't blame his discomfort on any encounter that had gone wrong. Something had changed in him, something that not even reason or rest could alleviate.

He lay down at night, struggling to fall asleep, each limb inflamed, his heart pounding in his chest with the energy of despair. When he finally managed to fall asleep, he'd become agitated, troubled by dreams he could hardly remember, and woke up drenched and excited. He resisted the instinctive urge to touch himself. Next to him, Gus was motionless, but Domino wouldn't be able to tell if he was sleeping or pretending. He turned his eyes away, his mind and body burning with a painful desire to hold Gus close to him, skin to skin.

Domino opened his eyes one night, his pants stuck to his flesh, breathless, groans stuck in the back of his throat. He'd ejaculated in his sleep. As quietly as he could, he left the room and after a welcome bath, he spent the rest of the night outside. The newly returned cold water of the baths soothed him for a while. No more. In the early morning, his ache still persisted.

When Domino noticed that women's proximity aggravated his condition, giving him untimely sweats, triggering his arousal, he had to face the facts with agonizing frustration. He'd just reached the age of his seasons, as all male nichans did at the close of puberty. He tried to relieve himself alone, finding a secluded corner in the back of the village. It was no more than a fleeting comfort. Helpless, he repeated to himself that this situation wouldn't last, that it would lessen on its own.

It was unlikely to happen.

He felt so stupid.

He returned to his hut one night, hoping to get some clean clothes as he had nothing left to wear. He could have stayed naked; no one would have been offended since he was hiding most of the time in the depths of the Surhok's woods. Impossible. Once naked, he spent all his time seeking his pleasure, trying to silence the appetite that choked all others. An exhausting yet unsatisfying effort.

As he entered the hut, he was relieved to find it empty. Gus hadn't returned from his chores in the infirmary yet. However, the first thing he noticed was his friend's scent. In fact, it almost jumped down his throat. Domino ignored it as best he could and went through his belongings looking for clean clothes. He'd wash the ones he was wearing later tonight—if he could keep his thoughts in order.

Then he realized that he was holding Gus's clothes in his hands. His friend's heady scent must have attracted him. Putting all his will into it, he set the fine tunic down. He wanted to bury his face in it, as much to scream as to fill himself with Gus's smell.

The door opened on the other side of the room. Like a trapped animal, Domino turned and shoved himself against the wall. Gus gently closed the door and stood on the threshold. Could he sense Domino's distress? Feel the burst of pheromones? The nichan probably looked awful. He hadn't slept for several days, couldn't remember the last time he had eaten.

"I've been looking for you for a while," Gus said quietly. "Can you explain? Did something happen?"

His voice was tinged with worry and maybe a little bit of blame. It was always hard to tell.

"No, I . . . I'm sick. I don't feel well."

If there was someone Domino couldn't convincingly lie to, it was Gus. "Sick? You want me to take you to the infirmary? Do you need anything?"

"No. It's not—damn it!"

Domino ran one hand over his face, then took advantage of the darkness to place it on his crotch. He felt himself getting harder and wanted to hide it. His hand wouldn't be enough. He had to get out of here.

"Domino," Gus said, trying to be reassuring.

The nichan could trust Gus. There was no judgment between them. Domino wasn't responsible for his condition, his nature only reminded itself to him.

He took the plunge. "I . . . My seasons have just begun. The rut. It's hard to control it."

He didn't have to reveal anything more. Gus knew as much as he did about the subject—which was little but enough to know what it all came down to.

Gus remained silent for what seemed like an eternity. When he opened his mouth, Domino was startled, on edge. "I see. Is it painful?"

Yes. "It's . . . uncomfortable."

"Are you going to end it?"

Domino hesitated. "I'm not sure if . . . " Another silence only disturbed by Domino's jerky breathing.

"You must go to Ero."

This announcement from Gus was so unexpected that Domino burst out laughing. The sound was close to a cry, but in his condition he overlooked it. "Your sense of humor is a delight today." He laughed, pressing against his erection, which was still growing in his pants.

This attempt at cheerfulness was met with silence. Gus walked across the hut and raised the shutter to allow the lanterns shining outside to provide light. In his state, Domino was too slow to react. A golden glow lit up Gus's face. The human's jaw contracted and Domino knew he could see the symptoms. Other than that, Gus didn't show any signs of confusion. As always, his thoughts were impenetrable behind his impassive appearance.

"I'm going to stay out all night until it calms down," Domino said.

"It looks painful."

"There are worse things, as you can imagine."

"I'm serious, Domino. Go find Ero."

"It's complicated enough as it is. I doubt he'll help me."

He still couldn't believe Gus had made that suggestion to him, but he had to face reality. Ero was the leader of the clan, it was his duty to help his protégés. Even though he'd sometimes strayed from this task, he did it every day. Domino didn't trust him—he never could—but Ero was the only nichan he could turn to right now.

He had to. Unsatisfied seasons could lead to impotence, among other sequela.

"You look terrible," Gus said, brutally honest. "And I suspect you feel a lot worse than that."

"Can't get anything by you."

"It's late. Stay out all night if you feel more comfortable. But don't leave things lying around. It's awful to see you in pain."

Gus would never admit to that kind of feeling. If something hurt him, he kept it to himself.

That was enough to convince Domino.

DOMINO WAITED until late the next morning to follow Gus's advice. He avoided the sanctuary, the baths, any confined space where anyone other than his uncle could see him. He watched the small garden behind the clan leader's house and approached when

Ero appeared, the frame of his brazier in hand, preparing to clean it.

Fortunately, Domino was still decent when he got close to his uncle. "Can I . . . can I talk to you?"

Ero lifted his nose from his task, surprised to see him arrive in his garden straight from the woods.

The next moment, the scent of a woman captured Domino's attention. Before the young man realized who was approaching, Ero grabbed him by the elbow, pinned him against the wall of his house, and held him firmly with one arm under his chin. Memek entered Domino's field of vision from the other side of the hut, scrubbing brushes in her tattooed hands. She then discovered her father, who was violently pushing Domino against the bamboo facade.

"I'm disturbing you, I see," she said after a moment of surprise.

With his nose full of his cousin's perfume, Domino couldn't resist, to his great despair. His body responded.

Ero growled, "Leave us, Memek."

"So you don't need my help?"

"We'll do that later. Leave us alone."

She sighed, baffled, and lowered her eyes as she turned tail. She finally noticed Domino's poor condition and frowned, barely holding back a grimace of disgust. "What the fuck is —"

"Get out of here!" her father shouted, and she threw her brushes to the ground before obeying him.

The wind washed away her scent and Ero directed all his attention to his nephew. His uncle's face didn't express the same disgust as Memek's. Just anger and something else harder to pin down.

"All right, will you be able to talk, or do I turn you on too?"

What a bad idea to come talk to him. Domino was already regretting his choice. As a reflex, he'd put his hand on his genitals to hold them down. This simple touch combined with Ero's comment turned his stomach. Being excited by his cousin was the last of Domino's wish. His body betrayed him in a nauseating way.

"How long has this been going on?" Ero questioned, still holding him in place, as if Domino might go after Memek. He had no intention to do so.

"One, maybe two weeks."

Ero chuckled without losing his seriousness. "By the Faces! You really like to complicate your life. Two weeks, huh? No nichan with any sense would let himself suffer for that long. You know it can end badly, right? What's wrong with you?"

Domino remained calm even though his blood was boiling in his veins. "I just need a solution. Something to make it stop."

"Don't pretend to be dumber than you are. You know exactly what you need."

Yes. A woman.

The very thought almost got him swearing, for it made his blood boil hotter.

"You may not have noticed, but I'm not very popular," Domino said. "No woman would want me."

"First, yes, I'd noticed. And let me tell you, if you took on what you are, you'd be spoiled for choice and, trust me, you wouldn't know in which bed to sleep at night."

"Are you done?"

"No. Your body's sending you a message. It's pretty clear, but for your own sake, let me translate: it's telling you that you're ready to breed, and it's going to keep doing it, and it will get worse than you can imagine. Do you want me to tell you what it can do to your balls?"

"I'd rather die, thanks."

"So let me be clear: until you stick your cock up a cunt, you're gonna stay that way."

"Oh, it was clear already, don't worry."

"So what's your problem? You're not attracted to women?"

"I am."

"Then stop moping and hurting yourself. I'll find you some women."

"Some?"

One more snigger from Ero. "Yes, *some* women, you idiot, because it's been two weeks. And as I know you, it might be even more. Just one will never be enough for you. At this point, you'll find it hard to stop. One woman would exhaust herself before you are half satisfied, and you'd spend the rest of the day crying like an infant."

He paused, lost in thought. Domino said nothing, his own thoughts trapped among naked bodies and intertwined limbs. He took a deep breath. If only Ero could let him go. He didn't want to associate this kind of idea with his uncle.

"We'll finish it tonight," Ero said.

"Tonight?" Domino repeated, confused.

"When there's shit to eat, you better swallow it as fast as you can. In the meantime, you lie under a tree, you cry, you jerk off. I don't give a shit. You distract yourself as best you can. I'll find anyone who's willing to help you. I'll come and get you when I'm done. You got that? I don't want to see your face in the village."

Domino didn't have to hear it twice. "I get it."

Ero finally freed him and Domino raced away to the trees and the relative privacy they offered.

NIGHT WAS FALLING when Ero found his nephew sitting in the grass, head trapped in his hands as if the pressure could free his mind. Domino listened to the verdict. He expected his seasons to kill him, but his uncle was bringing good news.

"Two women will join you later in the auditorium."

Two women. Domino didn't dare ask which ones. "The auditorium?"

"It's clean, neutral, and big enough for men to keep watch without being too conspicuous."

Domino was stunned. Nichans were going to watch him have sex? He was going to lose his virginity before their very eyes?

Ero continued before his nephew had time to react to the information. "Your season partners say they're not afraid of you, but you never know what might happen. These men will still be there, for safety. For the women's and yours. They've been through this. They'll know when to end it."

A bitter taste crawled up the length of Domino's tongue. He returned to the essential question. He feared the answer, but since he had to go through it, he might as well find out in advance.

"Who agreed to it? I mean, the women."

"Ensun and Omak."

The first was a beautiful, discreet young woman in her late twenties, the kind of woman Domino would have looked at more if his mind hadn't already been elsewhere. The other belonged to the village council and had shown unwelcome interest in Domino more than once in the past. In the midst of the excitement that suddenly overtook him, Domino remembered that Omak was about twenty years older than he was. However, in view of the urgency of the situation, the thought lost its relevance.

"Come on, get up," Ero said. "I had the baths cleared. You're going to wash yourself from top to bottom, then I'll accompany you to the auditorium. No, I won't stay in the room," he said when Domino froze, close to vomiting. "I don't want to see that."

XIX

DOMINO RUBBED AND RUBBED WITH HIS SPONGE, GETTING close to burning his skin. His penis, which he avoided touching — apart from purely hygienic gestures — or even looking at, was swollen with anticipation, painfully hard. Cold water had long since ceased to relieve him.

He was so impatient to get it over with.

He dried himself, tied a long skirt around his waist, and leaned against the wall. His heart was beating so fast he was sick to his stomach. He felt like he wouldn't survive the night. *Breath in. Exhale.* Over and over again. He was both exhausted and more awake than ever, nerves frayed, muscles close to breaking down. He slapped himself to put his brain back in place. And he went for it.

Ero, who was camping in front of the bathhouse door, accompanied him to the auditorium. Fortunately, they went through the woods to reach the door of the building at the back of the sanctuary. No one in sight. They climbed the steps, his uncle opened the door for him, and Domino entered.

"At least try to enjoy it," Ero said before closing the door behind him.

They'd prepared a bed of thick blankets near the brazier. The blaze was extinguished, but several lamps hanging from the columns or sitting on the ground framed the area dedicated to the fucking. Domino, searching for his courage, spotted the four men discreetly kneeling in the shadow of the pillars. They were far enough away so that their smell wouldn't disturb him, but their presence didn't fail to intimidate the young man. Apart from that, a heady scent of fruity alcohol floated in the air.

Domino walked towards the blankets. He knelt on them, facing the front door, skin ablaze and itchy wherever the fabric of his skirt made contact, and waited. In the silence, he could only hear the thundering beat of his heart. Then the creaking of the door.

He looked up. The two women entered, one after the other.

Omak led the way, an amused smile on her wide mouth. Ensun stood at a distance, pushing back the long black hair falling over her bust. Both wore thin tunics that left little room for imagination. Domino guessed the tips of their breasts under the linen. And the smell . . . Their scent pervaded him, and he swayed on his knees, sighing with both delight and impatience.

Ensun stood back for a while, half in the shade, visibly curious but cautious. Omak wasted no time. With a straightforward gait, she opened her tunic, let it slide to the ground, and knelt naked before Domino, close enough for the smell of her to erase his name from his memory.

Omak was beautiful, small for a nichan, with coppery skin, muscular thighs and small round breasts. Domino was already holding them in his hands, had moved without even realizing it, driven by a desire he could no longer contain.

Omak grinned, biting her lip. "You like them?" Then she shook her shoulders, as if to chase a shiver.

Eyes focused on the woman's body, Domino remained quiet. Talking made no sense anymore. Only flesh did. His fingers kneaded her tender breasts, whose nipples were hardening in his palms.

"I think so." Omak laughed and moved forward to appreciate the contact of his hands on her skin. "I've wanted you for a while, you know. How old are you again? Sixteen? Yes, so young. With such beautiful skin. Look at those hands. And this body. You're a gorgeous man, has anyone ever told you that? Come on, let me see the rest of you."

Undoing the cord holding Domino's skirt, she leaned forward, opened the sides of the garment and revealed Domino's cock, leaving the fresh air and the pheromones she was releasing caressing its surface. The young man groaned and his body reacted accordingly.

"Yes, it's coming," said Omak, shivering again, a light moan on her lips, coming ever closer to Domino. She grabbed his hand and guided it to the dark triangle of her own crotch. "Have you ever touched a woman like that before? How badly do you want to feel my sex? You can touch it, I want it."

Domino's long fingers found their way into the flesh. He gasped and leaned toward Omak, his hand getting lost between the slippery lips that seemed to want to suck him in whole. The woman was already wet and kept smiling and panting. For a moment, she guided Domino's fingers deeper, then out, and inside again. She moaned at the touch.

Out of pure reflex, responding to a desperate and vital need, Domino withdrew his hand and reached for his erect sex.

Immediately, Omak stopped his gesture, grabbing his wrist forcefully, and frowned. "Don't even think about it."

Just like talking, thinking was impossible. He was acting solely on the impulse to meet his needs, to put an end to his suffering. And driven by that same need for relief, he sobbed at the refusal to do so.

Letting go of his arm, Omak closed her fist around the young man's erection and caressed him without restraint. "Let me see the beast," she whispered.

Normally, such words would have repulsed Domino. But nothing was normal about him anymore. So he grabbed Omak by the waist and pushed her to the ground, on her back. He leaned over her in a hurry, spread her legs and penetrated her with a long movement. She gasped, eyes wide open. Then a resounding laugh came out of her throat. She clung to the blankets above her head as Domino moved inside her. The pleasure overwhelmed him like a tidal wave, and he came almost immediately, grunting like the beast she wished to see. But he continued to move in great thrusts, trying to go ever deeper. His erection remained, his pleasure grew. After less than a minute, he ejaculated inside her again.

He quickly lost all sense of time and space. All he could see was Omak's body, the warm, moist slit he came and went through, her breasts bouncing with his own hip movements. He didn't know how long he'd been inside her, how many times he'd already come, when Ensun approached, panting, eyes locked on Domino. Without slowing down the pace, gorging himself with Omak's unbridled screams and moans, he looked up at the second woman and climaxed again as Ensun undressed in front of him, revealing one by one her generous curves, her heavy, pointed breasts, then the arch of her wide hips, and finally a patch of black hairs that Domino was eager to explore.

He continued to move.

Ensun sat down next to him. Ever so slowly, her hand wandered onto his arm, going up to his muscular shoulder, then down his back, following the line of his spine. She then grabbed his ass with her fingertips and brought her lips closer to

Domino's. By the Faces! She smelled so good. She kissed him in spite of his movements, and he groaned as the young woman's tongue slipped into his mouth.

He'd never kissed anyone before. He'd never been kissed either. It was terribly good. She was so beautiful. He wanted her so badly.

Omak trembled, finally reaching orgasm.

"My turn," Ensun whispered before licking Domino's lips, caressing his chest and abdomen. "Fuck me."

And he did. After another rushed kiss, she turned around, leaning forward, kneeling on her elbows and knees. He grabbed her waist with one hand, her neck with the other, and entered her with blissful ease. The sound of flesh knocking flesh filled all his thoughts. His heart followed this steady pace. Ensun contracted her muscles, tightening around him, intensifying their pleasure. Domino saw stars and spread himself inside her.

And he did it again. Over and over and over again. He kept coming, lost track of it. He clung to his relief as much as to the hips of the two women. One then the other. He didn't even give them time to get up after catching their breath. He moved from one body to the next without a break, feeling a raging frustration during the brief interval when his body was separated from theirs. Bathed in sweat, tears in his eyes, he took everything they gave him, always wanting more. He didn't immediately hear the voice telling him to stop. He pushed it away, clinging to the body he was rocking back and forth and that gave him so much pleasure he could have died from it.

"Let him do it," said one of the two women.

"Ensun's done," said a man's voice. "It's over."

"Are you deaf or something? Ah! Faces above! Let him finish!"

Domino swallowed and tried to understand where these

voices were coming from. His comings and goings continued, unstoppable.

A hand was placed against his wet chest and with a suddenness that took his breath away, he was pushed back. He lost his grip and fell backwards, his shoulder hitting the wood. And he considered the scene without understanding: Omak knelt on all fours, her reddened crotch facing him. She looked annoyed, blushing hard. Next to her, Ensun gathered their clothes, hair tangled in the back of her skull, fingerprints marking the skin around her thighs and hips. With one hand, she tried to hide the transparent liquid dripping between her legs.

"I'm so . . . I'm sorry," Domino stammered, lying on the ground, not daring to make the slightest gesture. "I'm sorry."

He didn't know why he was asking for forgiveness. Everything was foggy, and apologizing seemed to be the only reaction to this turn of events.

The men all approached, one helping Omak get up, another placing her tunic on Ensun's shoulders. Those who remained stood between Domino and the two women, as if he were a ferocious animal and they his prey.

The bile rose up his throat.

"Why do you care so much? I told you to let him finish," Omak said before freeing her arm from the nichan who helped her to her feet.

She knelt back, sweating, and progressed toward Domino, who would have backed off if he'd had a clue of what was happening. Before his consciousness reached his mind, Omak straddled him, attempting to awaken his instincts with both hands. He then realized that this hand on his chest and this other hand on his genitals were bothering him. He didn't want that anymore, didn't see the point. He'd already received what he needed.

When Omak leaned in to kiss him, Domino retreated, turning his face away.

"Come on, we're not stopping there," the woman whispered against his ear, clutching his penis with far too much force. She approached, eagerly seeking to capture Domino's mouth, which he again evaded. "What if I tell you that Beïka lasted longer than you did? Will you mount me again?"

Beïka? What the fuck is . . .

"No!" Domino pushed Omak away as the reality punched him in the face.

The woman struggled for a moment, refusing to accept his rejection. She pushed Domino's hands away, going for his crotch, landing a slap on his jaw when her effort remained ineffective. She was strong but no match for Domino.

"Omak, leave him be," said one of the guardians, taking a step in their direction.

The woman yielded. She sat up, released her grip, and sighed. Then she gave Domino a disappointed look. "Come back to me when you've become a nichan," she said, standing.

But she couldn't hide the weakness in her legs, which wobbled under her weight, and forced herself to walk slowly as she dressed and left the auditorium with Ensun and their guardians.

A moment passed, silence froze the place.

Domino sat painfully and buried his face in his hands. He was still hard, but his blood cooled eventually, matching the radical drop of his mood. The urge to vomit hadn't left the pit of his stomach. He breathed softly, contracted his legs to stop their shaking. To tell the truth, his whole body was shaking.

Sexually, he was recovering. Part of him wanted more. He could feel that his desires hadn't been fully satisfied, but the worst was behind him.

However, the discomfort in his core was only growing. He felt dirty, as if coming out of a sick dream, at the same time cloudy and yet as clear as reality. He could still hear the sounds he'd made—an embarrassing echo in the back of his head.

It felt as if Beïka was in the room, standing behind him, laughing.

Domino shouted repeatedly, fighting to expel his rage and the disgusting images trying to invade his brain. It took a few minutes for him to calm down.

In the flickering light of the lamps, he looked at the pile of crumpled, damp blankets. He could still feel the soft, warm skin of the two women against his own.

He'd just offered them his first kiss. His first time. It wasn't fair. Those he'd saved for someone else.

His throat tightened.

Still tense, he stood, blankets rolled into a ball in his arms. After throwing them by the door, he tucked his skirt up and left. Once back to the baths, he soaped himself more than once.

THE LINES CARVED into the wood were more erratic than ever. Gus gave a sharp blow to the back of his chisel. The point skidded to the side and went out of bounds of the board. He sighed through his nose and scratched his forehead. He should have been in bed hours ago. But Domino hadn't reappeared since the day before, and Gus needed answers.

With a controlled movement, he pushed his hair back behind his ear, blew the wood chips away, and placed the blade back on the board.

At his back, the door opened. Domino entered after a short hesitation, as if the hut wasn't his. His pitch-black hair was wet, curling.

"Hey." He stopped on the doorstep. His gaze was troubled,

seemed to avoid contact. But he'd come home at last and looked in better shape.

"Hey," said Gus.

Domino rubbed his chin and walked into the room. Once seated next to Gus, he looked down. He smelled of soap.

Gus combined the information he'd just received, and his belly contracted.

Domino was doing better.

He'd done what was necessary.

"Have you eaten?" Gus asked to avoid the subject.

"No."

Gus got up and brought him the plate sitting on the table by the bed. He'd piled fruit, nuts, and pork strips on it. He put it by Domino and sat on the floor. With a trembling hand, Domino grabbed a lychee. The fruit never touched his lips, rolling clumsily between his fingers for several minutes.

Unable to hold on, Gus asked, "Have you talked to Ero?"

"I don't really want to talk about him, right now." Domino inflated his lungs and breathed out slowly, as if to calm his nerves. Then he said, "I spent the night with two women."

Gus didn't blink as the truth took form.

Women. Domino had just spent the evening with them. He had touched them. They had touched him too. Had he liked it? He had. Of course, he had.

Gus swallowed in silence, forcing his thoughts to shut up now, for many were rising. Domino didn't need to know how much the confession affected him.

He's better now. He's done what he needed to do.

"Feeling better?" Gus asked.

Domino pursed his lips and squeezed the lychee between his thumb and forefinger. He stopped when the gray shell of the fruit gave way, revealing the white flesh underneath, like a deep wound.

"I think so," he said, his eyes still lowered. "I'm not too sure. It wasn't— That's not how I . . . "

"Tell me."

Another pause during which they both held their breath.

"I felt like I wasn't myself, like something was controlling my body, my thoughts. Like I was . . . an animal. I know it's the rut. I know it's normal. I've waited too long. But . . . I feel empty."

He threw the fruit in the bowl, sending it rolling with the others, and passed a feverish hand through his hair. Not once had he looked at Gus.

Look at me, Gus wanted to tell him. *I'm here, you don't have to feel empty. Just let me . . .*

Gus clenched his fists.

Let me show you that you don't need them.

Instead of echoing these thoughts, Gus chose silence, his eyes resting on his friend's face. In the dim glow of the lamps, Gus followed the line of his nose, the little bump that curved the bridge. A little farther on, he spotted the scar under Domino's eye, the one from when he was seven years old, the one that dug into his cheekbone when he smiled. He descended to his frank and square jaw, then moved up towards his round lips. Gus imagined himself reaching out to his friend, if only to put his hand on his shoulder.

Don't leave me.

A weight still rested on his chest. After a long silence, Gus knew what he had to say.

"You're not an animal, Domino. That's why you feel bad, why it's not enough for you. Someone like you needs somebody to take care of him, to reassure him." A pause. "If you want, we can go to bed and lie down. Together. I'll hold you, and you can do the same with me. If you feel comfortable, if you feel the need, you can pleasure yourself. I don't mind. We'll keep our pants on. You can hold me. I'll be right here. I won't run away."

Slowly, Domino finally turned his eyes toward him. He seemed taken aback by Gus's offer. His chest rose faster and faster.

"My seasons are over," Domino said.

"I know." *Don't leave me.*

"You would do that for me?"

I would do anything for you.

Gus remained quiet and moved his hand closer to Domino's. Their fingers met and intertwined. Domino squeezed his hand, his gaze never leaving Gus's face.

It was risky. It was the kind of situation (though not quite) Gus wanted to avoid. Once in Domino's arms, he would be weak. And Domino, who without saying so, had just confessed to having had sex with several women. Would the ghost of their lovemaking intrude on their bed? This whole idea was probably bad, but —

Gus silenced his thoughts and smiled, a nervous but genuine smile.

Domino was still watching him. He could have refused. He hadn't yet.

Gus stood up, inviting him to follow. "Are you coming?"

A few seconds passed. Domino's fingers closed tighter on his own. The nichan stood up to follow him, and a relief beyond suspicion restored courage to Gus's muscles.

Domino still held Gus's hand between his long fingers when they stopped by the bed. He looked at the sheets, then at Gus. The blond boy retrieved his own hand and passed it over his back. Without breaking eye contact, he pulled on the laces closing his sleeveless tunic and took it off. The fabric slipped off at the base of his wings. He repressed a shiver. His tunic fell to the ground without a sound.

Domino looked down at Gus, at his slender torso, his contracted abdomen. Gus knew exactly what he looked like. He was a skinny, pale human surrounded by tall, power-filled nichans. He still looked like a boy where Domino, about the same age as him, had the build of a fine man. If Domino wanted a man, Gus wasn't the best choice available around.

Flirting and wanting were two different things. One was a game. The other carried a much heavier weight.

He questioned himself, felt ridiculous for thinking that his friend could desire him as much as he craved his touch. Though still wearing his pants, Gus felt barer than ever, as if his raw heart was on display. Yet he held his head high, his gaze steady, and didn't retreat as Domino contemplated him.

"What . . . What am I allowed to do? Hum . . . I mean, to touch?" Domino asked, licking his lips.

"Anything . . . I'll tell you."

"All right," the nichan whispered in a trembling voice.

Less than an arm's length separated them. Soon there would be nothing left.

On this thought, Gus lay down on the bed, soon joined by Domino. They settled down as they did every night: Gus on the left, Domino on the right. Lying on his side, Domino hesitated. Gus then moved closer to him, quickly assailed by the heat emanating from his friend's powerful body. Domino did the same and wrapped one arm around Gus and then the other.

He kept his distance, didn't dare.

"Do you want to stop?" Gus asked.

Domino shook his head and pulled the other boy to him. Their torsos touched, and he sighed. Immediately after, he hugged Gus tighter. Gus tentatively returned the embrace. He had to remember that he was doing this for Domino and not for himself. For a moment, Domino's breath swept across the top of Gus's skull, his hands wisely placed under his wings.

Domino's first hip movement surprised them both, subtle but obvious. Gus spoke before his friend backed away. "You want to lie on top of me?"

Yes, Domino wanted to.

They rolled awkwardly on the bed, separating for a moment. When Domino lay down on him, Gus felt his breath leave him. He rested his hands on Domino's shoulders and realized that the position of their body wasn't quite right. The problem didn't come from his wings, even though they were pressing unpleasantly against his back. It was something else.

The bed creaked at the movement of their tangled limbs. Gus spread his thighs. Domino's legs moved into this offered space and the position suddenly became more comfortable, more natural. They exchanged glances, said nothing. The innuendo was eloquent enough.

Domino buried his face in Gus's neck and his hips resumed their motions. They were light, timid. Then Gus felt Domino's lips on his skin. They laid one on top of the other and it was impossible for Gus to hide the jolt that coursed in his veins and shook his whole being. It echoed into his hands, which closed over Domino's shoulders.

Feeling the change, Domino raised his head, his cheeks rosy. He'd stopped all movement. "I'm sorry."

Gus thought he'd die of shame, for if Domino put an end to this now, he'd be forever sorry to have suggested it. Their friendship becoming uncomfortable had always been one of the reasons to limit themselves to harmless flirtations. This wouldn't be harmless.

"It must feel strange to you," Domino said, his breath warming the space between their faces. "You don't have to . . . Do you want me to stop?"

"No. Just tell me how I can help you. Tell me what I have to do to make you feel good."

He meant, *to make you stay.*

"Hold me," Domino said.

Gus did. His hands moved up Domino's neck, one of them

getting lost in the curls of his thick hair. He then pulled Domino down against him and ran his fingertips along his scalp. A soft moan escaped Domino's lips, and he let himself go against Gus, pressing their foreheads together.

"Like this?" Gus asked, running out of oxygen.

"Yes. Just like that. That feels good."

Gus continued his massage, slow and delicate. As his body warmed, he felt Domino harden against him. *Good.* That was what Gus wanted. If Domino felt good, then it suited him.

Don't leave me.

As if suspended on the edge of a precipice, Gus let himself fall, no matter how painful the impact. "You can kiss me if you want."

Domino's eyes opened. He could probably hear the frantic beating of Gus's heart.

He'd dared to offer it.

Looking disheveled and blushing, Domino seemed to be contemplating for the first time this concept that had been floating between them for years. "You want to?"

The nichan was watching Gus. But then and always, his gaze rested on the human's thin lips.

Gus couldn't hold on any longer. "Kiss me."

A handful of seconds passed. When Domino leaned over, Gus held his breath. The contact of Domino's lips lasted only a brief moment. It was a gentle kiss, careful of the reactions it would trigger. Gus trembled with pleasure, adrenaline erupting in his chest. Domino retreated a few inches, panting. Then, as their breaths mingled, he did it again. This time his lips lingered until Gus returned the kiss. It was a caress, as light as moth's wings, and hesitant at the same time, but it set Gus's mind ablaze.

With their eyes still open, the two young men exchanged another kiss. And then another. And another one, ever more urgent, longer, hotter. For a moment that seemed to stretch, they did just that, blushing, sweat beading on the surface of their skin. One kiss after the other, always more yet never enough.

Then Gus opened his mouth, full of an intention that couldn't be mistaken. The next moment, Domino's tongue found its way in and caressed Gus's own.

One of them moaned; Gus couldn't tell who. His arms tightened around Domino's neck, driven by a primitive, possessive instinct. In response, the only one appropriate, Domino let himself go completely, no longer holding his weight on his elbows, and captured Gus's mouth without restraint or shyness.

Gus couldn't believe that Domino was kissing him. That they were kissing. He'd wanted to for a long time. This feeling . . . Like walking on air, pulse dripping on itself everywhere. In his palms, his lips, his crotch. Gus hadn't anticipated the effect it would have on him. He couldn't control his hands. They cuddled the nape of Domino's neck, grabbed his hair, kept their faces as close together as possible. And he opened his legs even more, giving Domino enough room to press himself harder against him.

Domino's hands touched his sides, whispering along his ribs, holding his thin waist and hips as he rubbed himself against Gus. These same hands eventually found the hem of Gus's pants and began to push it away to undress him.

"Domino," Gus blew against his mouth.

It was another invitation, like the one to see their kiss deepen. He wanted more. But Domino seemed to take that as a warning, for he interrupted their kiss, his lips swollen, and lifted the garment he'd tried to remove.

"S-sorry," he stammered, his gaze veiled, his eyes still on Gus's mouth. "I wasn't thinking."

"Okay," said Gus, his heart struggling to escape his ribcage.

Didn't Domino want it too? Maybe Gus was moving too fast. Maybe he understood his friend's ardor the wrong way. Was that possible? Gus felt that he was losing his footing, but also that he was failing in his resolutions. He wasn't certain of anything anymore, didn't know if he should care. All he wanted was Domino.

"Can I kiss you again?" Domino asked.

"Yes."

The kiss resumed and the brief embarrassment was pushed away. Domino's mouth was so warm, so tender, his tongue so soft. It made Gus forget all his doubts. His own pleasure was rising, hard against Domino's. They moved together now, only separated by the fabric of their respective pants. Then Domino moaned harder, took his lips off Gus's and put them on his throat. The movements of his hips slowed down, pressing hard, but didn't stop.

"I . . . I'm going to come if I keep going," Domino warned him, his voice muffled by the flesh.

Gus took only a second to find an answer. "Keep going."

Domino didn't seem to want anything else.

With his face buried against Gus's wet throat, Domino kissed him, licked the feverishly pulsating skin, sucked it off. There would be a mark. Gus didn't care. He wanted there to be one, so they'd know what they'd done once it was over.

Domino's moaning was only getting louder. It rose and rose and rose, and then Domino growled, arching his spine, pressing the most sensitive spot on his body right between Gus's legs, where the two boys could have fit together if they'd had the audacity to try.

Out of breath, Domino went still. He had come.

Like dead weight, he collapsed on Gus, catching his breath; a minute passed, maybe more. Gus, whose desire hadn't been satisfied, finally closed his eyes and concentrated on anything but the beautiful body pressing on him. He wasn't to move. He had to control himself.

As if his body weighed a ton, Domino pushed on his arms with a grimace and moved out of the way to make room for Gus. Fresh air rushed through Gus's sweat-soaked chest and belly. But he lay still, except to turn his head. By his side, Domino was slumped on the mattress, his face soaked, his lips red.

I did this. My mouth was there.

As he marveled at the sight and idea, Domino opened his eyes, exhausted, as if all the fatigue of the last few days—and especially of this night—was finally collapsing on his shoulders.

"You . . . you didn't finish," Domino mumbled.

"It's fine," Gus said, still motionless. "Sleep."

Domino's eyelids closed. A few seconds later, he was asleep.

Next to him, Gus took much longer to recover. His body cooled, his skin and clothes dried, but his mind was trapped in the moment. The way Domino had touched him, kissed him . . . The feel of his tongue in his mouth, the pressure of his sex so close and yet beyond reach.

Things could have gone further. Gus would have accepted it. If Domino had wanted to, Gus would have offered himself to him. But Domino hadn't needed it. He'd had women. By the time he'd come into the hut, the madness of his seasons had already found rest. What they'd just done, however, was because Domino wanted it, and not to silence instincts inherent in his species. *Right?*

Gus could no longer concentrate on one thought at a time. He took a moment to calm down. When he failed, he sat up. He didn't dare leave the bed for fear of waking up his friend.

Tomorrow, what would Domino tell him? Gus himself didn't know what he'd say. He didn't regret it, he'd wanted it; he still wanted it. That didn't guarantee that his feelings were shared.

What if he gets sick because of me?

But Domino seemed fine, and he was strong. They'd just kissed. Nothing more.

But such kisses meant something to him, and he knew his friend well enough to . . .

Gus had to put his fears out of his mind at all costs. The worst that could happen was to have hope and have it taken away in the morning.

With a heart heavier than it had been before their embrace, Gus looked up at the ceiling and let the lamps burn.

His living wing was all numb, as were his lips.

———

GUS WOKE the next morning to a knock on the door. With his hair spilled all over his face, he opened his eyes and found the place next to him empty. Normally, it wouldn't have bothered him. Today it did.

There was another knock.

Mouth pasty, stomach painfully hollow, Gus left the bed and opened the door. The daylight, though shy, assaulted the back of his eyes, and he winced. Matta was on the other side, a basket loaded with laundry under her arm. She looked at him from head to toe.

"Here you are," she said in a tone that didn't match her words.

"What is it?"

"Come and help me with the chores. Don't stay by yourself."

That was a first. By himself? Gus always did his chores alone or with Domino. Since when did Matta get involved?

"What?" he said, his voice hoarse.

Matta remained silent and studied his face. Her expression then changed, becoming deeper. "Domino is gone."

Gus must have misunderstood. He repeated himself. "What?"

"Early this morning, he left the village with Ero, his brother, and Memek."

"What?"

He couldn't think of anything else to say. He opened the door wider, as if it countered the proper course of his thoughts.

"They went on a pilgrimage," Matta said. "For Domino. Nichans do that sometimes, to reconnect with their roots. They live in the wild, far from their clan."

The words finally made sense. Gus stood up. His heart raced. "How long will he be gone?"

"Weeks, months. I couldn't say. It all depends on Domino." The news hit Gus right in the face. He hung on to the door. "Maybe you should stop by the baths before breakfast. You've been . . . marked."

Marked. Like a stain impregnated with the urine of a feral cat. Marked, by Domino. Imbued with his scent.

In the midst of this senseless situation, Gus responded thoughtlessly. "We haven't —"

Made love. He kept it to himself, both the confession that something had happened and the fact that Domino had refused to take him.

He was gone.

"It doesn't matter," Matta said, lowering her voice. "Even I can feel it. I'll follow you to the baths. My scent will probably cover yours. If someone smells it . . . you'll get funny looks. You don't want that."

Domino was gone. Gus didn't care about anything else. Let the rest of them watch. He'd hold his head up high, wouldn't let himself be stepped on, as always.

"Get your stuff. I'll be waiting outside."

Matta's voice seemed to come from afar. Gus moved by reflex, pushing the door, grabbing his clothes, his shoes. His gaze then caught sight of an orange glint on the other side of the bed.

Domino had left without even saying goodbye. The Domino he knew, his best friend, would never have done that. And yet the sense of abandonment he felt then drained Gus of all his strength.

Gus walked around the bed and grabbed the necklace with the piece of sap hanging from the end of it, the one Domino had worn every single day for the past three years. This morning, as he'd left the bed, as he'd left the village, Domino had left the necklace behind as well.

He left me.

Fingers stiff, Gus put the necklace back down and left the hut.

PART THREE

LONELY SOULS

X X

Domino had stopped looking back two days after their departure.

That morning, Beïka woke him up with a kick in the calf. Domino, just like the day before, remembered where he was. Almost a hundred miles west from Surhok. He also remembered how his uncle and brother had ambushed him as he came out of the baths. He hadn't understood at the time, had taken their arrival as a setback.

Then Ero had made it clear. "We are leaving the village and the clan for your pilgrimage. Naturally, you're coming with us."

Domino had resisted at first. Beïka held him by the skin of his neck as he made his way through the dawn darkness and the fleeting mist rising from the ground. He was strong, brutal, but nothing insurmountable. Domino could defend himself, and since a nichan never transformed against one of his own, Beïka could do nothing to increase his superiority over his younger brother.

Then Ero's order had rang, tipping the scales. "Stop resisting and come with us. It's time to turn you into a nichan. That's an order."

Nothing in Domino could fight his words. Coursing through his veins, flexing his body to his uncle's will, the command was absolute. Domino had walked in his brother's footsteps, his screaming mind struggling to regain control. (After two days, this part of him was still fighting.) Every step had seemed so heavy to him, his body acting against his deepest wishes. He wanted to stay in Surhok; the blood oath made it impossible.

Disoriented, his nose had begun to bleed, as it had so many years earlier in the great hall of the sanctuary, as his uncle wiped on his tongue the blood collected from his nephew's arm. As he arrived in the heart of the village, Beïka's heavy hand still clinging to his neck like a tick on the back of a wild dog, Domino had turned his eyes to his peaceful hut. His body was trapped, but the order wasn't meant to silence him. Domino had screamed. To ask Ero to release him, to remind him of the unfairness of the situation. And to wake everyone around, Gus included.

It hadn't been enough. One more order, and Domino had found himself unable to produce a single sound, as though his tongue had been nailed to the palate of his mouth.

Near the village gate, Memek and Orsa waited for them. Memek had followed them outside, offering to her father one of the saddlebags she carried; Orsa had stayed inside after kissing her partner and her daughter goodbye.

Domino hadn't been so lucky.

After his frolics with Gus, he'd fallen asleep in his own semen. Exhaustion had won him over, reducing all his concerns to barely visible points on the horizon. When he awoke, Gus slept right next to him, so close that one of his hands rested on Domino's waist. The nichan had smiled, unable to take his eyes off his friend's serene face. What had happened between them was still so clear in his mind and warmed him with an unprecedented happiness. That feverish embrace; the right to kiss, to lick and taste every inch of Gus's mouth; their clumsy bodies, only separated by a bit of cloth at the crucial spot, leaving them free to appreciate each other's skin and curves, the pleasure they gave to each other. The rest had been clear in his mind. He'd come with the imaginary feel of his body diving deep . . .

It hadn't been the right moment. His body was still tense from his previous fucking. Gus deserved better than to share this moment with two other women.

Domino had wanted to stay in bed, to wait for Gus to wake up. But he was dirty and needed a quick bath. After that, he would have gone back to bed without a sound, to contemplate Gus's awakening at the crack of dawn. If his friend had accepted, Domino would have kissed him again. No excuses, no rut. The meaning of that kiss would have been crystal clear; Domino would have appreciated its full value.

He'd gotten up to wash with a confidence and happiness freshly gained, his heart beating with enthusiasm. Yet the moment he'd been waiting for so long never came.

All the day after, he'd emptied his stomach contents on the roads chosen by Ero. The Unaan's order was still in effect. And Domino was still failing to get around it.

As the opening day of the journey came to an end, Ero had sent Memek and Beïka on a hunt for food. He'd taken Domino to the nearest water point and forced him to drink and rinse his mouth. The acidity of the bile he'd regurgitated every hour since dawn had scoured his throat. Domino had drunk greedily and threw the whole thing up almost immediately.

"You really need to stop being so contrary," Ero had said, the perfect portrait of boredom.

"No doubt warning me in advance of your plans would make me less contrary," Domino had grumbled.

He wasn't done vomiting, but he still drank again before sprinkling mud-flavored water on his face.

Ero had immersed his hands in the water to cool himself down too. "You think I enjoy this? You're leaving me no choice, Domino. I've been preparing to take you on a pilgrimage for three years and it still pisses me off that it had to come to this. I'm getting to know you. You don't want to transform, you don't want to sleep with a woman, you don't want advice from your elders. It would make your life so much easier if you knew what's good for you. But no, of course not. Why would you? You're so stubborn you can't even see you're hurting yourself. You remind me of your mother."

Domino had clenched his fists. He had felt the nausea return, this time for other reasons. For a long time he'd wanted someone, anyone, to tell him more about his mom, to fill the blanks of her life, to erase the blurry patches concealing her face every time he tried to summon the memory of her. But not today, and not from Ero.

Luckily, the man hadn't continued on this path.

"You're not the center of the world, you know. This pilgrimage is as much for you as it is for Memek." Domino had looked up at Ero, surprised. "We all know what your problem is, and I hope to do something about it, because we won't set foot in Surhok again until you've grown up. But you and Memek have another problem, one that all nichans share." He'd splashed his face and rubbed with vigorous hands the scarred surface of his head. "You know why the elders established the pilgrimage when the Corruption came?"

"To travel around," Domino had replied, tense and reluctant to cooperate.

"Clever boy. The rest of us had forgotten who we were, what we'd lost. Can you imagine for a minute what it felt like for our ancestors when it suddenly became impossible for them to return to their original form? The Orators' sermons say that they felt as if they'd been stripped of their identity. At first they believed that they were being punished by the Gods out of hatred and human jealousy. Nichans had lost their names and faces overnight. Others said their souls. They were even doubting their pasts and the Gods . . . I think that's bullshit, but I know the feeling.

"The pilgrimage was an ordeal, a way to reconnect with nature, to rediscover the true color of our blood. We're not human, but we've modeled much of our way of life on theirs. It makes me sick that it's come to this."

"You hate them, but humans are as much creatures of the Gods as we are."

"That doesn't mean we have to pretend to be them."

"We're not. We just needed to . . . adapt."

"Oh, I heard that before, you know? Your grandmother, when she still ruled the Ueto Clan, thought we had to adapt too. She had plumbing put up all over the village, made foolish deals for furniture and all kinds of crap we could do without. She wanted her protégés to learn the art of blacksmithing and weaving. 'These are the Gods' plans,' she used to say. She wanted to turn us into humans; it's as simple as that. She refused to acknowledge the Corruption's doing, even when its shit was raining on us. I stopped this nonsense before it went too far. Some nichans would be content with that, you know? Those who aren't built for hunting or fighting. They no longer see the point of going back to our roots, of understanding what makes us different from humans. The pilgrimage forces us to turn away from the easy way out, from human habits.

"Now, many things have changed. There's a threat hanging over us. This pilgrimage is here to prepare you to face it. I lost a son because we underestimated the Blessers and the hatred they spread everywhere. I won't lose my daughter or my clan, as well. Even you, as annoying as you are — I'll kill to protect you."

Memek and Beïka had returned. Ero had nothing more to add. Domino had stopped vomiting. Resignation it was, then. But until sleep took over, his gaze had turned east, to Surhok, to Gus.

After being violently pulled out of his dreams, Domino stood and rubbed his eyes. In front of him, her braided hair ruffled by sleep, Memek nibbled a stick of sugar cane, a frugal breakfast before the hunt. Beïka wasn't far away, turning his back on them to urinate against a tree. Ero was nowhere to be seen. When Domino asked after him, Memek threw a stick at her cousin and wiped her hands on her legs.

"He went scouting," she said.

"That's no excuse for dawdling. Get up and get ready to leave any minute," Beïka added.

Domino kept his eyes away from his brother, still filled with disgust. The sound of Omak's words still echoed in his thoughts. *What if I tell you that Beïka lasted longer than you did? Will you mount me again?*

Domino ate, using water from a skin sack to wash his face and rinse his mouth. He rubbed his teeth with his fingertips and chewed black, round *bathia* leaves whose acidic taste wiped away any other flavor on his palate and tongue. Only then did he get up.

But Ero delayed until the sky was at its lightest shade of dirty gray. The other nichans heard him approaching before they could even see his head sticking out through the foliage. The bottom of his pants and shawl were wet with dew.

He watched his daughter and nephews. "There's a farm to the southeast. Humans."

"Friendly?" Memek asked.

"I only saw a woman outside tending goats and some geese. The yurt is small. There are several humans inside."

"A family?"

"I doubt it."

"How many humans?"

"Too many hearts beating for me to count. At least four. The woman was acting strange. She was tense. Maybe her age puts her in this state; she's not a young girl anymore. I kept my distance to not scare the animals. Something's going on over there. I want to check it out."

"What do you expect to find?" Memek said.

"I don't expect anything. I'm just taking the lead."

In front of him, Beïka took a step. "Whatever it is, we don't have to be afraid of a bunch of humans."

Ero glanced at him but didn't react. He deflected his gaze to Domino. "You're coming with me. We're going to talk to this woman."

"Aren't you afraid to scare her?" Domino asked.

Two nichans and an old human isolated in the middle of the woods. Domino had never been this far southeast—or anywhere else—but knew that nichans only entered a human village if they were invited. A verbal invitation, most of the time, was enough but necessary to avoid trouble. Many nichans resented the company of humans. The opposite was also true.

"A red cloth is nailed to the door of her house," Ero said. "Some humans show their sympathy for nichans this way. But let's be careful."

"You're going without us?" Beïka asked with indignation.

"You and Memek will wait under the cover of the trees. No one must see you. You'll stay within earshot."

"You're sure you're not overreacting?" asked his daughter. "It could be the family of that old human."

"I don't think so. The smell of them . . . I don't like it."

"Have you ever liked the smell of humans?" the girl grumbled.

Ero's plan then found its purpose in Domino's mind. Nichans rarely traveled alone. The case of two nichans showing up at the home of a human ally would be quite ordinary. If danger presented itself, Memek and Beïka would come as reinforcements with the effect of surprise on their side. Domino, however, hoped his uncle was being overly cautious.

A few minutes later, the yurt appeared through the dark vegetation. It was a little larger than Domino and Gus's hut, with a black moss-covered roof. Strangely enough, the house had been built around a tree whose dense foliage protected the animals and farmers from the corrupt sky and the weather. The woman Ero had mentioned was still there, caressing with a caring hand the head of a suddenly agitated goat. The other four goats began to snarl, nervous. They felt the presence of the nichans close by. In a separate pen, the geese reacted to the goats' panic.

Yurts were mostly owned by nomads. They were simple dwellings easy to assemble and transport. However, this one seemed not to have moved for years. Plants climbed on its facade. A nest was perched on the edge of the roof, threatening to fall. The people who lived here were now too old to carry on traveling, Domino thought.

With a gesture from Ero, the group split up. Domino and the Unaan moved slowly toward the farm, trying not to cause more anxiety in the animals. The woman noticed the change of mood of her protégés and looked around. Her skin was dark, like that of the Uetos, her hair silvery, and her eyes were bright green. She was tiny, her back was bent like a hook, and she wore simple gold bracelets on her ankles. For a human, she seemed to be between seventy and eighty years old. Domino wouldn't have been able to estimate her age correctly; the life expectancy of humans was much shorter than that of nichans. At the age of one hundred and thirty, Dadou was in better shape than this human.

Her face crumpled with wrinkles as she noticed the two nichans standing a few steps from the pen. But soon she seemed to change her mind, and her features, although worried, softened on her forehead.

"Ohay," she greeted them, clutching the hemp collar of the anxious goat she had been caressing seconds earlier.

"Ohay," Ero said, and Domino nodded, readjusting on his

shoulder the skin satchel Memek had given him before they parted, making him look more like a traveler. "I see the sign," Ero said, pointing to the ruby cloth hanging from the yurt's door.

"Yes."

"We haven't found water in two days. Do you have any for travelers? Or some milk, maybe?"

"Yes," repeated the woman without taking her eyes off them. "Yes, I have milk. Come closer. Not too close. My animals."

"Of course."

It was useless to tell her that nichans, without water, could last for months by drinking the blood of the animals they hunted. If the woman was aware of that fact, she said nothing of it.

Ero and Domino took a few more steps. At the other end of the enclosure, the goats crowded together, sticking their heads between the fences, looking for a way out. Their owner pulled out a stool, a bucket, and started milking. The animal she chose tried at first to escape the grip of her owner, but she let herself be milked.

"That's very kind of you," Ero continued in the tone of the discussion. "With this drought, all the streams are dry."

"I understand," said the woman.

She was devoted to her milking, and yet Domino could feel the distress emanating from her, from her mechanical yet irregular movements, from her voice on the verge of breaking. Nonchalantly, he looked around and listened. At first nothing, then he perceived against his eardrums the beating of hearts — fast, human — and breaths. He didn't know how many. He sniffed the air but didn't detect anything coming from the house. The wind was blowing in the wrong direction, working against him.

The woman got up from her stool and pulled the half-full bucket. Ero took out his recently emptied goatskin and uncorked it. He bent down low enough to get on the same level as the woman. With a trembling motion, she tipped her bucket over and the milk flowed into the bottle neck.

"Is everything all right?" Domino asked her in a low voice.

Hearing him for the first time, or perhaps because of his question itself, the old woman was startled and milk dripped to the ground, in the dust. She looked up at him, but immediately lowered her eyes.

"You look nervous," Domino said, even lower now.

A little farther away, his brother and his cousin could no doubt distinguish his words. The humans in the house couldn't.

"Visitors are rare," the woman whispered.

"What about human visitors?" Ero asked.

The milk stopped filling the bottle, for the woman was now shaking too much to keep her bucket on the right axis.

Domino wanted to offer to relieve her, realizing how thin her wrinkled arms were, but Ero spoke before he had time to do so. He bent over a little more and spoke firmly. "You live here alone?"

"With my husband," the woman said, trying in vain to tip the bucket.

"Is he inside?"

"Yes." Her voice was now but a breath lost in the breeze.

"Who are the people with him?"

She spoke faster than Domino had expected—like a cry for help. Or a trap. "They arrived two days ago. They said they found nichans heading east. They think . . . from here."

"Did they come from here?" Ero asked.

"It's possible."

"They've retraced their trail."

"They said the Blessers punish those who help your kind. When they realized your people sometimes pass through our house, they decided to stay. I wanted to give them some animals.

They don't want them. They said they'd leave once they'd killed more nichans. They said they would forgive us."

"How many of them are inside?"

"Four."

"Do they have pistols? Strange weapons hanging from their belts, some kind of small mechanical tool," Ero explained as the woman didn't seem to recognize the word.

"I think one of them has that, yes."

Domino clenched his jaw and refrained from looking up at the small opaque window of the yurt facing the sheepfold.

"Thank you very much for the milk," Ero said in a normal voice. He closed his water-skin, put it back in his satchel, and smiled at the woman. "I have some meat on me that might spoil, killed this morning. Do you have any salt? Or maybe you have something to smoke it with? I know it's a lot to ask. I could offer you some of it, as a thank you for your good services."

As her breath became panting, the human raised her eyes towards them, paling slightly. In the bucket, the surface of the warm milk undulated under her shivers. Ero had just revealed his intention to enter her house. The signal had been given, as much to those hiding inside the yurt as to Memek and Beïka.

After a long time, the woman put down her bucket. "I have salt, yes."

She opened the gate and led them to the entrance of the house. Domino prepared for everything. He could feel the warmth and tension sweating from his uncle's muscled figure. The man was preparing for battle. Hidden in the thickets, Memek and Beïka followed their movements. They wouldn't appear until the last moment. The Blessers' partisans hiding inside needed to believe until the end that they would have only two nichans to face.

They had at least one gun, enough to do some serious damage.

But this damn weapon had a weakness. Although Domino had

never seen any with his own eyes, he'd been told that the Sirlha's pistols got dirty after each detonation. The partisans, much like the Blessers, stuffed the cannon with small fragments of Kispen crystal, a mineral with fairly flammable properties and whose shards were as sharp as razor blades. The heat from the gunshot produced fragments as thin as ashes that stuck to the walls of the barrel, clogging it. The gun was then too hot to be touched, so it was necessary to wait a few minutes before scraping the inside and then reloading it. A devastating but limited weapon. If the humans waiting for them inside thought they would only have to deal with two nichans, perhaps they'd save their ammunition. Domino hoped so from the bottom of his heart.

The woman reached out to open the door, but Ero stopped her and pulled her out of the way. *Good*, Domino thought. If she stayed close to them, she risked being hurt. Ero opened the door, bent down to enter.

One step was enough. A sword flew across their field of vision, missing Ero by an inch.

Domino entered, shoved inside by Beïka and Memek, who appeared to take care of their opponents. Bent in half under the low ceiling, Domino avoided the next blade that passed close to his arm. Without thinking, he struck down. His fist crashed into the nose of a long-faced man, splashing blood everywhere with the amplified sound of a cracking egg. The man fell to the floor as another, larger and bathed in sweat, hastened to replace him. Domino hesitated, frozen on his feet. But unlike his companions, his nichan smile didn't appear. No transformation on the horizon.

As if he'd just noticed it, the human took his chance. He turned and grabbed an old human lying on the ground next to his fellow bloodied partisan, using the old man's body as a shield. The elder was missing half of his left leg, his teeth, and his hair. Probably the farmer's husband. The partisan brought his blade close to the old man's throat.

Fury grew in Domino. As quickly as his human form allowed, he grabbed the partisan's arm, his grip as strong as a steel bracelet, and mowed the legs of the two humans facing him. The old man collapsed on the dirt floor, escaping the partisan's hold. The partisan remained standing, without balance, hanging from Domino's fist. Domino clenched the human's wrist tighter. The man lost his sword, which bounced off the ground in a metallic clink. He growled as a yelp rose and died in the yurt. Then another, right behind Domino. The nichan veered his eyes. Dark human blood drenched the bottom of his pants. More blood on the ground. A clicking noise snapped close to his ear. Domino turned to the man he was still holding. The next moment, a silvery glow reflected the light coming through the open door. Domino's eyes widened. A circle as black as nothingness presented itself to him.

The mouth of a pistol.

The end of the barrel aimed at him between the eyes.

A clawed hand whistled in the air, and a dark stream of blood dashed around. A long trail partially blinded Domino and ran down his eye. Then the cannon disappeared as the man, his throat slit to the bone, exhaled before his eyes. The human's head fell to the side, opening the wound like an oyster.

Still in shock, Domino didn't realize until several heartbeats later that he hadn't let go of the dead man's wrist. He forced himself to unfold his fingers. At his feet, the old man held his shoulder, crawling away from the tree around which his yurt was built. Its trunk vaguely resembled the shape of human legs...

A tree ... with human legs. There's blood on its knees.

What was he thinking?

Domino wiped the blood leaking inside his right eyelid and looked around. Memek stood beside him. She panted through the rows of fangs, her ebony hair and skin blending in with the darkness of the yurt. She shook her hands and blood slid down her black claws. In this form, it was impossible to make out her tattoos.

Behind them, Ero and Beïka wiped their faces. The humans at their feet no longer breathed. The fight had lasted less than a minute.

A gasp broke the silence. The old woman entered her battle-ravaged yurt, her knees bumping in fright and exhaustion. She sailed among the shredded human corpses, the overturned furniture sprinkled with blood, and joined her companion, who found the strength to stand upright.

"Are you all right?" he asked, to which she replied with a kiss on his bald, sweaty forehead.

"Pick that up," Ero said, bringing Domino back to reality.

His uncle pointed to the bodies. They had to be buried. Domino avoided Memek's heavy gaze, and they both obeyed. If he'd been quicker, he would have stopped that human from drawing his weapon and sticking it under his nose. And a glance in Beïka and Ero's direction as they carried the corpses outside told him that the two men had witnessed his blunder.

They gathered all the limbs and guts, put them in the ground, and recited a brief prayer before returning to tell the farmer that the job was done. Even though she didn't chase them away, she closed her door on them without a goodbye. As the nichans turned on their heels, picking up their saddlebags, Domino noted that the piece of red cloth had been snatched from the door.

They were no longer welcome.

XXI

Contrary to what they'd suggested, the entire region wasn't dry. They found a small brook a mile to the south and washed themselves in it. The red blood of the humans stained the swirl as the morning heat continued to rise.

Domino moved away from the group. He used no pretext, just walked along the shore, and sank into the shadows of the trees. He couldn't leave the area. Ero's order was still acting on him, like an anchor stuck deep in the sand, limiting the range of his movements. He could feel it getting heavier as he went along. Each step became more difficult and hazardous. So he stopped and looked up at the sky, trying to distinguish the shape of the clouds among the thick foliage.

Domino could have died today. The cannon would have exploded in his face, spewing millions of sharp, incandescent shards. His unrecognizable-faced body would have been buried in that forest he didn't know the name of, far from Surhok. From Gus. Ero would have returned to the clan without Domino.

He took his face in his hands and groaned in frustration. What would have happened if he'd transformed? Would he have controlled his actions, his emotions? Would he have killed a family member again? It was of little comfort to know that Mora's death was an accident. Mora was still dead.

He looked down at his hands. This morning he'd fought humans for the first time in his life. He'd reacted instinctively, taking only a second to study his opponents and find the quickest way to neutralize them. Up to a point, he'd succeeded. But there was a simpler way to beat a Blessers supporter. Memek had shown him.

Had she ever killed someone before today? She hadn't hesitated, her movements of dazzling speed, as precise as Ero would have been. Memek was only two years older than Domino, but the gap between them was tremendous. Well, she was the clan leader's daughter, after all. And as for her father, a human had taken Javik, her older brother. It was hardly surprising that she showed so little mercy.

"Are you going to do this often?" asked a voice behind him, and Domino tensed from head to toe.

He turned his head vaguely without facing his brother. "What do you want?"

"Right now? I'd gladly break both your legs. Then you'd finally have an excuse for your bullshit."

Beïka had just taken what he thought was a commanding tone. He wasn't emulating Mora's behavior—a calm and compassionate mother figure—but Ero's. Even his choice of words was vaguely reminiscent of something their uncle might have said. But in Beïka's case, these words, as always, sounded hollow.

"Why don't you find somewhere else to be?" Domino replied.

He didn't fear his brother, hadn't in many years. Nothing that united them was like the bond he'd shared with Mora. Beïka had always repudiated Domino.

Like the other nichan children . . .

When Domino came into the world, had he turned Beïka's life upside down? Had Beïka grown up with fear in his stomach, turning it into hatred because, unlike other kids, he couldn't run away from his own kin?

It was possible, though Domino wouldn't ask his brother to confirm. Beïka was way too proud to admit that Domino's existence had had such an impact on his life. True or not, nothing was enough to justify the odious way Beïka had always treated him. But at least he understood. Domino's true nature was nothing but trouble.

"I'm fine just here. Look at me when I'm talking to you!" Beïka cried out.

Domino didn't make a move. "Fuck off."

"You think you're above everyone, right? Domino, the pure blood, his people's hope. I don't see any nichans in front of me. And to think the Gods chose you, that they gave this gift to you. That's twisted! Look at you, they made you human. Incapable, a coward, weak. If I were you, I'd feel like shit. Tell me, does your weakness suffocate you some days? Does it make you want to end your fucking life?"

This time Domino turned around. He was already tired of this day, and it was just beginning.

Why had Ero asked Beïka to accompany them? As backup? As an older brother? In that moment he was only stirring up the grudge Domino had buried deep within himself since childhood. The sight of the honorary marks covering Beïka's throat and chest intensified this resentment. Domino should have been marked. He and Mora had formed a family, a powerful and genuine bond to which Beïka was a stranger.

"Look at you," Beïka continued in disgust, scrutinizing his little brother. "A waste of time and space, that's what you are. You and your puppy eyes. If I'd not seen it with my own eyes, I'd refuse to believe that a brat like you ripped off our brother's head."

No . . . Did I do that? His . . . head. I . . .

Just like Ero, Beïka knew Domino had no memory of the events of that day. Was he lying right now? He was Beïka. The words leaving his mouth were only venom and hatred.

The same hatred grew in Domino. He caught it in flight, filled it with his warmth, and let it give him strength. "Is it jealousy I see? And you think you're strong and brave. Oh no. It's not brave to be jealous, Beïka. It's me the Gods have chosen, you say? So what? You think you would have made a better candidate? The rest of the clan probably would have taken you down by now if you were in my place. Do you know why?"

Beïka walked toward him, his teeth clenched. "Shut the fuck up, you little shit!" He stopped within a hair's breadth of his brother's face.

Not the least bit intimidated, smelling Beïka's hot, raging breath on his chin, Domino continued in a calm, unhurried voice. "Ours would have taken you down because it would drive you crazy to be what I am. Because you don't have what it takes. You can parade as much as you want in front of Ero, pretend to be him, imitate his every move, kiss his ass. You're wearing yourself out. There's a crowd of nichans more capable than you to succeed him."

"I'll make you shut your fucking mouth. Is that what you want?"

Domino looked right into his brother's eyes. They were the same height and knowing that Beïka had finished growing where Domino hadn't made him gloat. Domino didn't care much about his own height, but such a detail mattered to his brother.

"Whatever happens, I know at least one thing about you. They would never have chosen you," Domino said, pointing to the skies. "And I'll tell you something else I know, because we share the same blood: one of these days, when you realize that you're less than a bug, you'll fall on your knees before me and beg me to forgive you for being a dick. You—"

Beïka's fist crashed into Domino's temple. His head went to the side but he regained his balance, throwing himself on his older brother, no longer containing his rage. He struck Beïka's stomach with his fist, once, twice. The man retreated a step, groaning all the air from his chest. But he resisted. His knee flew up, right for Domino's crotch. Faster than him, Domino blocked the kick with his left palm. He pushed his brother's leg to the side, and his fist struck harder under Beïka's ribs.

Suddenly he felt the change as much as he saw it through the dark stars surging from every corner of his sight. Beïka's skin was turning black.

The asshole is transforming!

"Enough!"

Ero.

Domino let go of his brother. As he returned to his human form, Beïka took a step back. Domino did the same.

Ero approached, frowning. His gaze shifted from one man to the other but stopped on Beïka. "Go back to Memek right now and wait for me."

Beïka obeyed immediately and disappeared between the trees. He was replaced by Ero's silhouette, more massive, indestructible. Still vibrating with anger, a pain pulsing in the soft corner of his face, Domino lowered his eyes. If he raised them to Ero, the blood oath would make him nauseous again for daring to look at his leader with the fierce hatred now tensing his body.

"You still want to leave?" Ero asked. "Go back to Surhok?"

Domino was surprised by the question. "You know I do."

Ero nodded. "Let's say you go back. Let's say you give up on the idea of one day accepting what you are. What do you think will happen?" Domino remained silent, for his uncle was about to lecture him once again. "You've seen these humans just as clearly as I have. They're worse than the one who killed my son. They travel around, looking for nichans to slaughter, humans to punish for looking at us without spitting in our faces."

"I've never fought a human before," Domino said, knowing where this speech was leading them, feeling the need to defend himself. "I just need more experience."

"No, Domino. Any nichan would have known what to do without any training. You know that, so don't even bother making up excuses. Mora was no hunter, yet he didn't hesitate to kill to protect you. He was your age when he did it for the first time. He knew what to do. It is part of who we are. We don't hesitate. And you lost that. You're so afraid that you've destroyed day after day what makes you one of us."

"I'm still nichan," Domino said shaking his head.

Stuck in his human camouflage, refusing above all to accept his original form—that of his ancestors, the true form of all of them—could he still claim to be nichan?

I am nichan, no matter what shape I am. I will always be nichan.

"The Blessers are going to invade our lands one of these days," Ero said. "Not pathetic followers, but those who inspire them and make them believe that by getting rid of us, the Gods will return. It is their hatred that ruins the lives of nichans and Vestiges." Domino swallowed hard at the sound of this word. "How long do you think you'll survive against their weapons? Take two seconds and imagine that. You're barely faster than them. Barely stronger. They'll kill you effortlessly because you didn't do what needed to be done. They'll kill you, your family, and your Vestige."

Domino suddenly looked up. He ignored the cramp that forced in his spine to bend him and struck Ero with his eyes. "Don't talk about him," he raged through his teeth.

An order. The cramp twisted his stomach, and he breathed faster, a vein hammering against his swollen temple.

Ero had an amused grin. "You want to hit me, don't you? Answer me."

"Yes."

"Of course, you do. No one touches your Vestige. It belongs to you."

"He belongs to no one!"

Domino was feeling worse and worse. The anger he directed at his uncle was unhealthy, going against the oath that bound a nichan to his Unaan. But he couldn't calm down. Imagining Gus at the end of a rope still made him sick. Anyone who touched Gus —human, Blesser, or nichan—would pay for it.

His uncle knew exactly where to hit to hurt.

"If you attack me, you'll regret it, and I don't have time to wait days for you to recover. So I'm gonna do you a favor, and we'll move on. How's that sound?" Ero spread his arms. "Hit me."

Domino didn't react, shocked by this request that he never thought he'd hear from Ero's mouth.

Ero left him no choice. "Hit me!"

Domino shouted as his hand collided with his uncle's face. One blow, just one, in the nose, exactly where he'd imagined it to land. Ero's head went backwards as a crackling sound echoed through the woods.

It wasn't enough, hardly a fragment of what his uncle deserved, and yet it did Domino a lot of good. He shook his hand, waiting for the aftermath of his attack. But the cramps were gone. His guts unraveled. By responding to Ero's order, an order he dreamed of carrying out, Domino had silenced his torment. Or at least part of it.

His uncle straightened his head, wiped the blood from his broken nose. At the base of the bridge, the shattered bone threatened to pierce the skin and break free. But Ero didn't blink at the pain. He stared into Domino's eyes. He took a step, placed a protective hand on his nephew's shoulder, and struck.

Domino wasn't as tough as his uncle. He bent in half, Ero's fist still buried under his ribcage. Its power drove the air out of his lungs. His belly contracted. Domino collapsed at his uncle's feet, close to vomiting and crying. He managed not to cry.

Here it was—the aftermath.

"Join us when you can walk. Don't come back crawling. A nichan doesn't crawl in front of anyone," said Ero, his voice distorted by his blood-clogged nostrils.

HOW LONG DO you think you'll survive against their weapons? You're barely faster than them. Barely stronger. They'll kill you effortlessly because you didn't do what needed to be done. They will kill you, your family, and your Vestige.

Slumped to the ground in the fetal position, Domino tried to push his thoughts away. Amidst his nausea and the headache resulting from Beïka's blow to his temple, Ero's words pulsed through his mind like blood in his ears, like acid in the pit of his gut.

They will kill you, your family, and your Vestige.

It would happen, no matter how it was done. Domino had seen the barrel of a pistol up close today. He'd been close to meeting his end. The beast inside him, the nichan he truly was, wouldn't have feared the bite and the burning of crystal shards. Domino would have killed this partisan before the idea of using his weapon even occurred to him. He could only assume, only believe, that the beast that Ero and a handful of nichans had seen three years earlier was capable of this. That beast had killed a dohor. When Domino had awakened that night, he hadn't a scratch on him—only a bump offered by his uncle. The dohor hadn't had time to touch him.

A nichan as powerful as their ancestors were before the Great

Evil. In this form, only the Gods knew what Domino was capable of.

Natso, Belma, Gus . . .

Things were clear.

It was time to stop resisting.

By the time Domino found the strength to stand up, almost an hour had passed. He went back to the stream to rinse his mouth and to clean his face, chest and arms. One more moment of solitude and calm wouldn't have hurt him. He reluctantly returned to the others.

When he arrived, Ero was no longer bleeding and had put his nose back in the right place. As much as he could. "All right, let's go." He picked up his satchel, Memek threw the other one on her shoulder, barely paying attention to Domino, and father and daughter went on their way.

Something was missing.

"Where's Beïka?" Domino asked, following in their footsteps.

Ero looked over his shoulder without stopping. "On the road. I sent him back to Surhok. We don't need him."

XXII

Eight days had passed since Domino's departure when the village sentries opened the doors. The one who arrived, alone and unescorted, wasn't supposed to be here.

Word spread faster than the wind. It reached Gus all the way down to the river.

Beïka had returned.

The bar of soap slipped from Gus's hand, missing to slide to the bottom of the creek. The young man bent down, retrieved it, and stood up quietly. The only nichan on the riverbank, back arched above the water, busy scrubbing greasy kitchen towels against a washboard, glanced at him from the corner of the eye. The nichan kept his mouth shut, but the curve of a smile appeared on his face. Gus knew what was being said in Surhok, what this man thought of him, like the rest of his peers. Gus knew what people called him: Domino's human. Domino's Vestige. And he'd received more than one conspicuous look since his friend had gone on his pilgrimage.

On the way up to the baths that day, following in Matta's footsteps, whose presence was supposed to cover the scent of the two young men's intense kissing, Gus had averted his eyes from more than one indiscreet glance. Walking behind Matta had obviously not been enough. Even though his skin was dry, it was still covered in Domino's sweat, his saliva, and probably the vague trace of nichan pheromones. The last was probably the cause of everyone's sudden attention.

"Domino made quite a racket when he left the village this morning," the woman had said when they arrived at the large, deserted bathhouse. "Everyone knew what was going on even before Orsa explained that she's now in charge of the clan. I'm surprised it didn't wake you up. Your friend clearly didn't feel like leaving."

Gus hadn't answered anything back, stepping resolutely into the shack, immediately assaulted by the clammy atmosphere.

After wetting himself from head to toe with a bucket, he'd frozen in the middle of the steam and the receding, dripping water.

Did this really happen?

The question, popping up out of nowhere, had momentarily slowed his movements. It swelled inside him, pouring a flood of doubts into his veins and mind. Had he imagined the events of the past night?

Without thinking, Gus had slipped his hand between his legs. The village forbade sexual practices of any kind inside the bathhouse. With this thought, Gus had initiated his own pleasure. One hand leaning against the wall, the other focused on the right pace, a sudden rage had taken hold of him.

Rage against this place that imposed more prohibitions on him; against those nichans who probably thought that sharing their bed with him—a Vestige—was as disgusting as fucking an animal; against Domino, who had taken these women and then sought comfort in Gus's arms . . .

It's my turn. Fuck them all.

And he'd stroked himself harder, summoning the memory of his friend's frank hip strokes against him, begging for an answer.

After coming, part of him dripping on the soaked stones, Gus had felt stupid and childish. The events of last night were his doing. He was the only one to blame for what had happened. He'd always known that it would be a mistake to engage into this kind of intimacy, that somehow he would end up overwhelmed with regret.

He'd stayed in the baths longer than he had planned to clean up the evidence of his misstep. The next nichans who entered wouldn't fail to notice the foreign smell of his sperm. They would know what he'd done. He'd soaped his spot more than once.

Domino was gone, whether he'd wanted it or not. He would be away for several months. Since they'd met a decade earlier, the two boys had never been apart for this long. It was obvious to Gus that Ero had only one idea in mind: Domino had to transform himself. But Domino had been struggling against his true nature for more than three years. He'd muzzled himself with as much resolve as he'd fought the guilt strangling him every time he dared think of Mora. Gus feared that this pilgrimage might not be enough to change his friend's mind on the matter.

It was all he could think about. Day and night. He couldn't focus on anything but the silence and loneliness that surrounded him. As soon as he entered the sanctuary to take his meal, eyes would turn in his direction. Gus would sometimes surprise a few words: "I remember when it was just a wild beast."

"I guess Domino managed to tame it." Laughter.

"Is it going to get wild again?"

"Humans get rabies, don't they, like animals?" More laughter.

Some of them didn't even bother to whisper.

Several times, Matta had invited the young man to join her during meals. Gus had refused. He didn't need company. He just wanted Domino back.

But Beïka was home. Only Beïka. Why only him?

Gus had to know what was going on.

He wrung the sheets fresh from the water as hard as he could and tossed them over his shoulder. The water ran down his dead wing, down his back. He barely noticed the coolness that would otherwise have soothed the effects of the late summer heat. But Gus's heart beat too fast; questions assaulted his mind. Nothing else mattered. He left the riverbank and returned to the heart of the village.

Beïka was there, near the now-closed Surhok gates. He was talking to Orsa, his face closed, his arms folded over his tattooed chest. As rumor had it, he was alone; not a sign of Domino's presence.

His laundry dripping in the dust, Gus stayed out of sight and continued to observe them. He told himself that any moment now, the doors of the village would open again, revealing the silhouette of his best friend. His fears would then be allayed.

But that didn't happen. Beïka finished his conversation with the temporary clan leader and left her to return to his own hut, eyes dark and his jaw clenched.

Night fell a few hours later. No one showed up at the gates.

When Gus got up the next morning, nothing had changed.

HE NEEDED TO KNOW. Where was Domino now? Was he okay? When would he be back? Gus wouldn't ask Beïka to go into details. The important thing was Domino's safety. He wasn't so distraught as to nag the man with a hundred useless questions. People didn't need to believe that Gus couldn't take care of himself without Domino around to wipe his ass.

Domino's Vestige . . .

Gus didn't need anyone. He could survive on his own, unlike the rest of them who absolutely needed an Unaan to feel whole and protected. But it had all happened so suddenly. One moment they'd been kissing—somehow things had gotten even further than that. A few hours later, Domino had left without warning, as if nothing had happened.

The only person who could answer him right now was Beïka. And Gus wanted to talk to him as much as he wanted to see that blue crystal again. Orsa might know some details, but Gus had never spoken to her. She was Ero's partner, after all. She probably shared the same displeased opinion as the Unaan about humans walking freely on their territory. But he kept in mind that she was still a valid option.

Gus sat where he and Domino normally ate all their meals: at the end of a table away from the others. His food, illuminated by the flickering light of the grease lamps, had cooled. The vegetables had shriveled, the meat juices had congealed. He hadn't touched it. His eyes were on Beïka at the other end of the dining room. The man was eating with two nichans a little younger than him, scraping the bottom of his plate with his spoon, laughing at the words of one of his friends. He stood up, nodding to his companions, took his dishes with him, and retired to the kitchen.

Gus had already made up his mind.

He left his table and followed Beïka.

When he arrived in the kitchen, lit only by the oven and a lamp hanging above the sink, he found the nichan activating the fountain above his dirty dish. He looked up as he felt Gus approaching. His unkind glance was filled with a deaf anger that Gus detected despite the poor visibility.

One question, nothing more. It would only take a minute. And whatever if Beïka didn't answer it.

Gus advanced and stopped a few steps away from his best friend's brother.

Beïka and Domino had a slight family resemblance, something

in the curvature of the bridges of their noses, in the shapes of their long faces. The resemblance went no further. Beïka had hair cut flush with his skull, fleshy lips, thin eyebrows, and a round, hollow scar in the middle of his forehead (result of a bad fall during his first hunt with the Uetos). And then there were the honorary marks that covered a large portion of the man's neck, chin, and chest. They undoubtedly changed his features, making his neck and his jaw look narrower than they were. In the end, Domino and his brother didn't look so much alike. Especially not when Beïka's eyes betrayed a deep disgust as they landed on Gus. Domino would never have looked at him that way. Was he even capable of looking at anyone like that?

"Is Domino okay?" Gus asked.

He could have greeted his friend's brother, asked him if he'd encountered any danger on the road. He preferred to avoid false pretenses. Might as well get to the point.

In the kitchen, you could have heard a pin drop.

What he expected happened. Beïka threw his half-rinsed plate into the sink, sending water splashing against the wall and his light pants, then he turned around. He walked toward the door leading to the courtyard.

Gus had thought he would accept the lack of response, for he'd prepared for it. He'd lied to himself. The silence only strengthened his resolve. He wouldn't have the patience to come back and question Beïka later. He insisted. There was already anger in his own voice.

"I just want to know if your brother is all right."

In an instant, the air in the room froze. Beïka turned around. It took him but a second to walk through the kitchen and grab the hem of Gus's shirt. Gus gasped, too slow to retreat. He always forgot how fast nichans were.

"Don't even talk to me," Beïka said through his bared teeth, drawing Gus to himself, dominating him from all his height, chin up. "Get it? And don't look at me. Look down!"

His collar trapped in Beïka's grip, Gus looked up at him. The man wanted Gus to submit himself, like a nichan facing his Unaan. *What's next?* Beïka was no Unaan, and Gus wasn't nichan. Beïka would have to make him. Gus had long ago broken free from that compulsion. *Don't look*, used to say the woman who'd raised him in that basement. *Don't look down*, Matta had advised him to help him regain his dignity. Of the two paths, he knew which one he wanted to walk.

Beïka's grip became more urgent. "I said, look down."

Gus didn't. He'd stood up to Ero more than once. He would stand up to anyone.

Beïka's hand engulfed Gus's face. Brutal, it closed like a vise, half on his throat, half encompassing his cheeks. In his surprise, determined not to give in, Gus didn't immediately understand what was happening. When his back and wings hit the wall behind him, he finally tried to break free. Beïka was all the more violent. His strength wasn't as overwhelming as his uncle's, but Gus was certain it could crush his bones, tear his jaw off.

"Don't look at me," Beïka whispered.

He turned Gus's face to the side, forcing him to look away. Gus resisted. His head still turned to the right, revealing the side of his face and his old burn scars to the man. A burning pain spread to Gus's cheeks, his head, his spine. He didn't scream, he didn't say anything, although his heart was pounding at a desperate pace, hard enough for everyone in the sanctuary to notice. Apart from his constant resistance, Gus was helpless.

Beïka's breath swept across his ear. "You're just like him. You think you're better than me. But what are you without my fucking brother to protect you? I'm gonna tell you: without him, you're an insect among gods. You're nothing. Eventually, someone's going to step on you. So a word of advice: you better hide and pray. Next time you get in my way, you'll feel it coming."

He pressed both sides of Gus's face one last time. He was trying to wrest a complaint from him. Gus kept his teeth firmly clasped together. When Beïka finally let him go, Gus looked up at him, provoking. He trembled. Tears blurred his sight.

A simple effect of pain, he told himself.

Either the nichan didn't see his defiant gaze in the dark kitchen, or he was done with him. He gauged Gus for a second, then turned.

Gus stood there a little while longer. As if dazed, his mind slipped away. He didn't know what to do now. He should have left the room. Nothing happened. He stood on his feet, his wings against the wall, his body refusing to awake. He was still trembling.

He took a deep breath.

Everything was all right. Ero had done much worse to him. Those two humans had done worse with their rope. Beïka was a small fry, a loudmouth. If Domino had caught him laying hands on Gus, he would have taken down his older brother . . .

Gus straightened up. What a silly thought. Domino wasn't his protector. Gus could take care of himself. He wasn't going to stand there shaking like a kid until his friend protected him. Protect him from what? From whispers and rumors, from nichans, from Beïka?

He'd get through this without the help of anyone.

XXIII

A DETONATION CRACKED IN THE DISTANCE. IT ECHOED OVER the surface of the blackened grassy plains here, yellowed there, blended with the wind, crept between the rocks that lined the stream. When the echo reached the sleepy little camp, no one flinched.

Domino opened his eyes. The same blast had surprised them a few days earlier, and the sound had become the new anthem of the area.

The family had entered the Osska Lakes region, moving closer and closer to the capital, Papema. They'd been resting at the exit of a sanctuary when the blast had resounded and alerted all the travelers who weren't yet aware of the last local news. They had been quickly filled in on the situation.

It was rumored that a crystal deposit of considerable but undefined size—for it was still largely buried underground—had just been discovered nearby, by the Ukatehontasan Lake.

"Another Matron," had said the keeper of the sanctuary, nose close to the tanned skins Memek offered to his expertise in hope of compensation. "Can you imagine that, one of those things in

Torbatt? It'll bring all the Blessers and their supporters 'round here if it gets out."

Ero had turned his eyes toward a cloud of black smoke that rose like a tower toward the equally dark, puffy clouds. "This din, it sounds like the gunshot from a pistol."

"For sure, sounds like it. It's nothing but the picks of the idiots who gathered around that giant rock. Every time they hit it, it makes this noise. I guess they'll stop when they all go deaf. The smoke comes from the camp they established there."

"What are they trying to do?"

"Apart from this never-ending mess, you mean?" had said the other nichan, concentrating on the merchandise. (He'd occasionally glanced furtively at a group of travelers pitching a tent near the sanctuary.) "Some say they're trying to tear this thing to pieces. Only way to kill it before it manifests itself. They say this is how the Blessers took over the east, by tearing the Matrons to pieces. People around here probably want to kill the rumor before it spreads. Can't blame them."

"Do you have an Unaan? What do they think of this initiative?"

"An Unaan? No need for a big word. Our protector came by to check it out. She said there's no danger. They're just frightened humans. I get how they feel. We nichans don't need a Matron, either."

The man had spat on the ground, a bored pout on his brown face, and traded food for half the skins brought by the Uetos.

Domino had remembered Matta's lessons. She was a Santig'Nell, one of the Matrons' daughters, a chosen one. She came from the east, from Laranga, the Sirlhain capital, the exact place where the Blessers had first struck nearly twenty-five years earlier. According to Matta, there remained one Matron in D'Jersqoh, south of the Coroman Continent, across the sea, and two Matrons in Ponsang, the capital of Meishua. And according to the sayings, destroying the usurpers, as they called them, was their divine mission.

Many people considered these powerful crystals to be new Gods, worthy successors. A blasphemy to many others. If a Matron emerged in Torbatt . . . Domino had understood the initiative of the local people without approving it. He pictured them with shovels in one hand to excavate, picks in the other to break up the deposit of inestimable potential. The Matrons were sentient. Matta had described their intelligence as superior to that of the most evolved beings in the world. Instead of destroying such an entity, a creature of the Gods, it would have been better to go east and close the border to block the way to the Blessers. But not everyone possessed the soul of a hunter, and Domino doubted that these Torbs, frightened by the sight of a giant crystal, would be able to repel an impending invasion.

The small group had stayed several days at the sanctuary, using the time to sell the furs they'd hunted, to trade some food. Not enough to their liking, despite Memek's efforts—no one negotiated with as much verve as she did. Domino had come to her aid with little result. The other travelers clung to their possessions as they did to their own offspring. They probably thought they could get a better deal in Papema.

After that, it'd become clear that their journey would turn all the more difficult.

"The Road of the Gods is two days away from here. People are heading up to the Arao. I like this one," the sanctuary's guardian had told them, pointing at a bearskin. "If you want to sell more, you have to go through the city."

"No, thanks," had said Ero.

"As you wish. Otherwise there's Kepam. It's in one of the chasms of the Great Evil. It's connected to Papema by the Road of the Gods, but it's quieter, and cheap, as you can imagine."

"We're going south."

The news had surprised Domino. The guardian had seemed to find the idea preposterous. "Then you'll need all the luck in the world. You better line the road or the west coast. Things are getting messy down there. There are a few nichans clans, if you need help. Some of them aren't exactly kind, though. Not sure they'll open their doors for you."

"A nichan never lets his brothers and sisters starve," Memek had said.

"You can still try," had said the guardian. "But there are almost as many Blessers' partisans out there. They're clearing the way to Ponsang. Lay low, friendly advice."

The lake region was fragmented into many rivers, ponds, and large lakes of unpronounceable names. Here and there, a few woods offered better shelter for the night. It was in one of them that Domino, Ero, and Memek had decided to rest. They'd left the last sanctuary that morning, yet the echo of detonations still chased them.

Lying under a lamp hanging from a branch, one arm as a pillow, Domino observed the bottomless sky. He felt that this night, although disturbed by the distant detonations, would be one of the last peaceful nights he'd know. The Blessers hadn't yet reached Torbatt, but those who adhered to their whimsical ideology were preparing the ground for them. Here, a semblance of war was already in progress, apparently. It seemed so strange. They'd only left Surhok three weeks ago.

Domino sighed, agitated, and passed a hand over his stomach. For a moment he imagined it was Gus touching him, taking care of him, safe in their hut, warm, with a belly full of a good meal.

He was still full of Gus's almost imperceptible moaning, like the chant of water. His small and delicate body. The exquisite arching of his back under Domino's fingers . . .

Domino forced himself to interrupt the thread of his thoughts. After all those weeks away from his friend, he couldn't divert his mind from this particular moment. He thought about it every night. But this wasn't the time or place for such daydreams. Better wait to be on his own for that.

He reopened his eyes a second before another blast rang in the distance.

Faces, make them stop.

Impossible to sleep.

Domino straightened up and rubbed his face. Behind him, Memek was sleeping, lying on a pile of unsold furs, snoring slightly. Next to her, spread under the glow of the lanterns that would burn all night, Ero kept his eyes open. One look in Domino's direction, then he returned to his thoughts.

As promised, they were heading south, toward trouble. Ero probably hoped that this initiative would awaken Domino's lost instincts, that in the face of real danger, the young man would react and set the beast free. A curious strategy, for coming close to dying at a partisan's hand hadn't helped. But at least Domino had announced his desire to try.

"What if I don't have enough willpower? Who says I can control this thing?" had dared to ask Domino after making his decision, a couple of weeks ago. "I don't remember anything. It's like a hole in my memory. This beastly form may be some kind of . . . second state beyond my control. What happens in this case?"

"In that case you'll die," Ero had said, calmly, his piercing gaze on Domino. "You keep telling me you're nichan. For sure you are, the purest blood I know. You're also a hunter. Whatever happens, you will fight. That's your thing, even when you can't hold a candle to your enemy. You know what it's like, the longing for action. We hunters are born for that. But that isn't the form in which you'll win. Nichans aren't made to fight in human form. So if you do, you'll die."

Domino had laughed softly. A speech without detours or illusion.

"Well," he'd said as he stood, ignoring the pain that still tugged at his belly after his uncle's debilitating punch, "at least neither one of us is in denial."

"It's not my kind. We'll end up finding bigger trouble than we've ever encountered before, Domino. These assholes won't spare you just because of your shortcomings. If you don't transform, you'll be the first one they kill."

"Then I'll have to transform. And if I can't, I'll try to take at least one of them with me to the grave."

They hadn't really spoken that much ever since. They'd repeated themselves enough already.

Domino waited silently for another moment, looking up at the lantern and the flame whistling on the surface of the melted nohl fat. When Ero's snoring groaned next to him, the young man stood without a sound.

DOMINO CLOSED his eyes to block the golden glow of his lantern. A breeze ruffled his hair, constant whistling, waving the thick leaved branches. It carried a pungent smell in its wake. An animal had marked its territory nearby. Nothing Domino couldn't ignore. He clenched his fists and then relaxed them, laying his palms flat on his lap. He concentrated on his heartbeat, as he'd done so many times since his youngest years. The cool air caressed his neck. Cooler than a few weeks earlier. The season was advancing, leaving the heat behind for good.

Domino released a long breath and raised his hand to his chest, clutching the empty space where his necklace would have been if he hadn't left it at Surhok. How unpleasant, as though he'd left several of his bones back home. The missing weight against his heart was unsettling.

I should never have taken it off.

Domino lowered his hand. He was not to let it distract him. He would get his necklace back. He would see Gus again. Everything was fine. He was safe. So were the others.

He passed his tongue over his lips and swallowed. In the distance, an owl accompanied the silence of the night, encouraging.

Domino had made up his mind. It was time.

He remembered Mora's lessons. At the time Domino had only been ten years old and something was wrong. He'd never transformed. He was the right age, everyone said so. So Mora had given him a push.

"It's like stopping yourself from running down a slope. There's . . . it's like a stream flowing through us, keeping us in our human camouflage. You must feel it inside you."

"Where?" Domino had asked back then.

"All over you. No, don't look, you won't see anything. Close your eyes. Come on. Breathe in, relax. It's like the beat of your heart. It's there, constant, both in your chest, in the pulp of your fingers, in your toes. You never think about it, but it's there; it lives inside you. Tell me what you feel."

"I feel . . . it's tingling."

"Okay. That's good. Focus on that. Just tell me what it is."

"I don't know."

"What does it look like?"

"I can't see anything."

"Even things you can't see have an image, a texture, a taste. Think about it. Take your time."

Domino had done so. Through his endlessly repeating pulse and breath, he'd perceived a shadow with golden reflections. It had no name, no shape, except that of Domino himself. And something else.

"It's buzzing," he'd said.

"A buzzing tingling," Mora had concluded, a smile in his voice. "I like it. Come on, let's keep going. Listen to the buzzing, follow it. Hold on to it and stop it."

"Stop it?"

"Yes, to stop the flow, keep it from trapping you in human form."

In the middle of the woods, motionless in his amber bubble lost in complete darkness, remembering word for word his brother's advice, Domino opened his eyes. His breath quickened, an icy sweat ran down his back.

The buzzing, he couldn't feel it anymore.

It was impossible. It had to be there somewhere. Domino had to concentrate harder. His eyelids drooped, he blocked out the trembling threatening his concentration and the steadiness of his posture.

A buzzing tingling.

The dark stream of the Corruption in his being, as everyone said. To transform, one had to push back that flow, to block and filter it.

Nothing. It had to be there. Domino was nichan, and though he'd forgotten it, he'd already transformed before. Completely. After that fateful day, he no longer had tried to block the flow, to reach his natural shape. Quite the contrary. He'd let it run free inside him, seeing it as a bulwark against the beast that had killed his brother. A protection.

He'd shut down all the rest. He'd . . . muzzled the beast.

Why did he feel nothing now?

"Come on," he said in a shaky breath.

He had made his decision. He was ready. Taking his puck with him, an oval plank with handles to protect modest travelers from the potential black rain, he'd moved away from where his uncle and cousin slept so as not to run any risk, finding a quiet and open place to give his bestial form the space it required. He still had time to practice.

For long minutes he searched inside, but soon the sham of his heart pounding in his chest overshadowed everything else. Then another shock in the distance.

Breathe. Don't panic...

If he had to transform again—and he had every intention of doing so—Domino would do it on his own terms. Calmly, entering into communion with himself, not under the yoke of fear.

Several hours passed. Silence. Emptiness.

Footsteps approached. Light, a little clumsy. Domino opened his eyes for the first time in quite some time. Dawn was approaching, no doubt, but darkness still reigned.

Behind him, Memek sighed. "What are you doing here?"

"I couldn't sleep," he lied. Lies it would be, until he'd made progress.

A lump formed in his throat. He swallowed it.

I'll get there. I can do it. I just need time.

"You didn't sleep at all?" Memek asked.

He turned to her. She'd hung her own lantern from a branch and was unravelling her braids ruffled by the friction of her head against the animal skins. Her hair was long and slick, like Mora's . . .

His legs were numb from kneeling half the night. Domino slowly got up. "Is Ero awake?"

"He went back for water. He told me to find you."

"You did."

"Yes, and you look like a man who hasn't slept in weeks."

Domino rubbed his face and ignored the comment. Weeks was a little too strong. Days, however, was closer to the truth. Days that felt like weeks.

"My father is right, you know," said Memek. "You're hurting yourself for nothing." She sighed, threw her long black hair behind her shoulders, and stretched out with a grimace. "Faces above! I want a fucking bed."

And she turned. Domino followed her. He hoped very much that soon he would be able to reassure everyone by regaining control of his body. The remarks would finally stop. Then they would go home.

***

IT WAS REPORTED in the small town of Kepam that partisans farther south in the country were raising funds for a monster hunt. The monsters in question were nichans, of course.

Standing on a bench, a human brandished a poster she'd brought back from her last errand south of the Osska Lakes. For those who couldn't see it as well as those who couldn't read at all, the woman read aloud.

" 'The Great Evil spares no region. Don't let it slip under your bed. Join us or make your contribution. The beast must die.' "

Everyone in the inn was silent.

Set at the bottom of a ravine overlooked by the rest of the village, welcoming guests on three floors for food and lodging, the inn was full of humans and nichans at all hours of the day and night. And no matter their degree of inebriation, none of them wished to hear about the partisans or the Blessers.

"That's on everyone's minds and lips lately. You can't drink or take a shit in peace anymore," said one customer before emptying his pitcher with a single, heavy sip.

"You're taking a shit right now?" asked his table neighbor.

Still perched on her improvised dais under the tired gaze of the owner brewing tea and warming up wine in a pot, the human, bearer of bad news, continued. " 'The beast must die. May we give Light back to the Gods . . . ' They translated the rest into Meishuana. Looks like Meishuana. Whatever. Just warning everyone, in case you're going south or east of the lakes. And for anyone who needs to wipe their ass, I'll leave this here."

She came down from her perch and put the crumpled poster on the counter. It quickly disappeared without anyone caring who'd taken it.

Sitting at a small table not far away, Domino scratched his head before repressing his gesture. He dreamed of a bath as much as his cousin dreamed of a bed. They would have neither. Unlike the rest of the region, the town had no hot springs. There were indeed baths heated by wood fire near the entrance of the town, on the Road of the Gods, mainly reserved for travelers, but following an epidemic of lactic fever, the kivhan—or major—of Kepam had forbidden access to nichans. A simple precaution, it was said. The place would be reopened to everyone soon, the kivhan promised.

Ero and his family had been directed to the inn, unlike the establishments controlled by the kivhan and his council, open to anyone whose purse wasn't empty yet. Domino had rejoiced.

To reach the inn, one had to go all the way down to the bottom of the ravine that adjoined the town. It was reached by a wobbly staircase anchored in the rock.

A most unusual place. The Kepam chasm had appeared on the day of the Great Evil. An unimaginable tremor had wiped out half of the town, leaving the rest miraculously intact, as if the gigantic foot of a God had trampled the landscape, stamping a deep imprint forever.

As Memek had approached this perfectly circular crater of smooth rocky walls, she'd opened her eyes in amazement. "Faces and tits! Look at that. Looks like this was cut with a knife by the Gods themselves."

His heart pounding, Domino had approached the railing,

smiling, feeling insignificant before this incomparable view. "What do you think did that? Not a knife, right?"

"Who knows? Maybe the Gods fell from the sky, right here. Or maybe that's the world's butthole. What if the Corruption came from here?"

"There are other chasms of the Great Evil. In the rest of the world, I mean," he had said, catching a questioning glance from his cousin. "A big part of Netnin is full of them. That's a lot of buttholes."

Memek had seemed both curious and doubtful. "Well, that's a fucking big world. So that's not the only one?"

"No."

"Faces above! Sounds like you know a thing or two."

"You think I'm playing you?"

"No, I wouldn't dare." She had bitten her lip and glanced down into the depths of the pit. "Does Netnin look like this? Like a huge hole full of rubble?"

"Don't forget to mention the inn."

She had smiled at him before she pursed her lips, as if to stop herself from doing so. So Domino had decided to tell her more, to share the few insights he'd gained years earlier from Matta's lessons.

"Netnin doesn't quite look like that, actually. There are many chasms, an incalculable number of them, even though I'm sure those who live there have counted them. But they're connected to one another by channels. The ocean and the Tuleen sea flow into them. They're no longer chasms, they're lakes in the middle of cold plains. And from what I've been told, there is another difference, and a big one at that." Memek stared at him, her eyebrows slightly frowning, hanging onto his every word. "Over there, wherever you find craters like this one, above these plains and these round lakes, are hills floating in the air."

Memek's impression had then changed from interest to boredom. "Because you've been there, of course?"

"No. I've—"

"Then stop talking like you have. Bragging doesn't look good on you."

"I'm not bragging."

"Why don't you focus on your transformation instead? Transformation. Sounds familiar? And don't try to educate me about things you don't know shit about. It makes you sound like Beïka."

Domino was silent, a knot in his stomach. Memek had then turned away from him to join Ero, who hadn't bothered to stop to admire the landscape.

When they'd arrived at the inn, their excitement was shattered. The establishment was full. Apart from a meal and a drink to forget their setbacks, they wouldn't be entitled to anything. Only guests staying overnight could enjoy the private baths. So was life along the Road of the Gods. Cluttered.

Domino took a sip of his mulled wine. Facing him, Ero rummaged through his satchel. Since they'd left, its sides had swelled like expecting women's bellies, as had Memek's bag, which now lay at Domino's feet. Under the tired gaze of his daughter and nephew, Ero pulled something out of the bag, something Domino was seeing for the first time. Ero looked at the long object, weighting it in his large hand, and placed it on the table in front of Domino. The young man shivered.

It was a hunting knife. A thick weapon protected by a sheath of boiled white leather.

"What's that?" Domino asked after swallowing his wine.

"It's a knife, you idiot," Memek said in a whisper, peering at the weapon with unmissable annoyance.

"No shit?"

"You said you wanted to make yourself useful in the hunt." Ero cut them off. "Here's your chance."

Domino froze. Close to him, Memek straightened up as if to put some distance between her and the blade.

"Are you kidding me?" Domino said. "I don't want that thing."

He surely didn't. As heat rose in his face, he scanned the room with a circular gaze to make sure no nichan saw him when he touched the knife to push it toward his uncle. The man grabbed the weapon and slammed it down in front of Domino, making the handle vibrate against the wood on the table.

"This thing will come in handy once you get your hands on it," Ero said as several pairs of curious eyes turned to them, attracted by the shock. "Stop fighting me on this. You're not a child anymore, and I don't like to check over my shoulder every five minutes to make sure you're still alive. You still haven't transformed, so you don't have any weapons on you to protect yourself."

"Protect me?" Domino laughed, suddenly suffocating in his own skin. "Oh, yeah, of course. Protect— Be honest, Ero. You're just trying to humiliate me. Don't act like—"

"Like what? Like I care? Like I took an oath to protect you?"

"You care? I'm touched, Ero. Really, you have no idea. My heart is leaping with joy."

"Good," Ero answered, ignoring his nephew's sarcasm.

"I don't want that stuff." And Domino was ready to repeat it over and over again.

Nichan hunters didn't carry weapons, ever. On them, they would have been a sign of weakness. Nichans were weapons, even with their incomplete transformations. Blades were made for humans, or for nichans who had resigned themselves to a human life.

As if he'd caught the thread of his nephew's thoughts, Ero

said, "I thought you liked humans. Since you spit on this gift the Gods have given you, you should feel no shame."

"I told you that I will transform—"

"And yet here I am, wondering if I should believe you. What are you waiting for to try?"

"I'm—it's dishonorable for a hunter to carry this."

A hunter. Domino saw himself as such, as a nichan made to fight for his people, to protect them. Until today, for obvious reasons, he'd been a poor hunter. Yet he knew he was meant to be one, not to be left behind to tend the crops or raise children. He was a nichan hunter, even though Ero now provoked him by insinuating otherwise. This weapon was dishonorable and repugnant to him.

Ero laughed and grabbed his pitcher to empty it. "You'll speak of honor when you have honored your clan. Until then, take this knife and keep it with you. That is an order."

"Of course," Domino said, bile in his throat. He grabbed the weapon, leather groaning against the palm of his hand, and hid it under his tunic, pretending not to care what the nichans in the inn would think.

But in the core of his mind, his pride yelled at the blow it had just received.

XXIV

"WHAT DOES A REAL NICHAN LOOK LIKE?" GUS ASKED.

Facing him, Domino smiled dubiously and rubbed his nose, spreading on its rounded tip the red makeup running across his face. "We're real nichans."

"But the ones before?"

"Before the Great Evil?"

Gus nodded.

On the other side of the village, across the rows of huts, a loud cheer partly covered Domino's answer. Someone had probably just won the last fight.

The Koro—the summer solstice celebrating the rising point of the year—would last until the next morning. For the moment it was still daylight and the two children didn't feel like joining the rest of the clan for the festivities. Like everyone else, they were made up in carmine—shoulders, cheekbones, forehead and the top of the head—and had put on their most colorful clothes to catch the eyes of the Gods. If, as nichans hoped, their creators had noticed their effort to attract their holy attention, they surely wouldn't blame the two children for preferring quiet to collective excitement.

Domino repeated himself as the screams faded in the distance, replaced by laughter. "You mean when they were in their true form?"

Sitting on the edge of a stump, Gus bent his knees against him and nodded again. "What were they like?"

Domino bit his lip, hesitating. He rubbed his earlobe and quickly moved his hand away. His ears had been pierced the day before, and he'd been scratching them ever since. Once the holes healed — Gus had to let this process happen naturally — Mora would help Domino enlarge them by gradually increasing the size of the wooden rod piercing his flesh. For the moment, half a golden ring hung from each side of the boy's face. The loops were a good match for his complexion. Gus liked them.

Domino rubbed his nose again. "To be frank, I don't know."

"No one knows?"

"Yes, some people do. The Orator knows. He knows everything about the Gods and the time before the Corruption. He must know that too. Ero, he must know."

An icy finger ran down Gus's spine, and he tightened up to suppress it. Domino must have felt it, for he moved to his friend's side, sat closer to his stump, then passed a hand over his own right cheekbone. The outline of his scar appeared beneath the red pigments.

"I think I know," Domino announced.

A *distraction*, Gus thought. His nichan friend often did this when a disturbance came between them, menacing to raise a shadow over their good mood. He would tell a story, something, anything, as long as they forgot what was haunting them. Above them, a bird squeaked as if interested to know more as well.

"Mora said that we used to be big beasts," the little boy said, opening his arms in a circular gesture. "Where we nichans pray, there are very, very big rocks and they are shaped like beasts."

The Prayer Stones. Gus wasn't allowed access to them. The sacred place belonged to nichans and nichans alone.

"How big are the beasts?" Gus asked.

"Almost like the sanctuary."

"You all? You were that big?"

"No! No, not us," Domino laughed. "The beast-shaped rocks. They're huge, as if they're trying to touch the sky. Sometimes they do. The clouds are so low that the Stones disappear in them and we have to go back home. Because the clouds hurt."

"Like the black rain," Gus whispered.

Domino nodded. "Yes, the clouds, they either choke people or… or they burn them."

"Like in the Arao."

Matta had told them about this place a few days earlier, about these lands perched high up in the middle of the country where once humans, nichans, and dohors used to go to touch the skies with their fingertips, to caress the Gods' faces, to praise their creators. With the Corruption, the clouds had become poisoned, taking on the morose hue of death, forcing people to migrate to the outskirts of the Arao, to abandon their homes, their sanctuaries and their temples.

In order to get closer to the Gods, nichans had once located their sacred place at the top of a hill. The Prayer Stones. It wasn't far from these that the Uetos came to establish their clan two generations before Domino was born.

Gus tried to imagine them. Rocks shaped like beasts. But what kind of beasts? The little boy knew so few of them apart from the village chickens and the rooster. The others would end up on his plate without him having had time to see what they looked like before they were stripped of their skin and bones.

He could see in his mind, however, the dense, puffy, dark

clouds that occasionally let only thin streams of ochre light pass through, never reaching the land.

What if Domino went there when those clouds were too low? What if he was hurt?

Gus was very good at imagining that. His heart raced. "It's dangerous to go."

"It's okay."

"Don't go there."

"We don't go when it's like that. No one wants to go in the clouds."

In the village, the cheers exploded again, startling Domino. "I wonder who's winning," the boy blew as he glanced toward Surhok's heart.

But Gus didn't care about the shouting and laughter. All that mattered to him in this moment was getting that promise. He didn't want Domino to go there, to put his life in danger to pray to the Gods who'd abandoned them all. The Gods' love didn't matter. Only Domino's friendship mattered.

Mother would have been furious if she'd heard all of his blasphemous thoughts.

"Don't leave me," Gus begged, reaching out to Domino.

"Get him out of here."

This voice. It wasn't Domino's. Gus turned and darkness rose all around him, leaving but a flickering flame by his side. Wrenching pain twisted his insides. Cold and yet as burning as hot iron shoved into his flesh.

"Let me see him," he said and two arms reached out from him, thin and bathed in sweat.

The scars lining his forearms . . . He couldn't think of them now. He couldn't let his shame distract him from his goal. He had to hold him. To see him. The end was close, he could feel it, had heard them announce the price of his mistake. Soon it would be too late.

"Please," he begged again in a wet breath, blood coating the surface of his tongue. "He's . . . he's mine. Please . . . "

But he was alone already. A baby cried in the distance, first calling of his life.

"No," Gus sobbed. His arms curled around his aching belly. More blood flowed between his legs and his weeping intensified. "Don't take him…"

The baby screamed again and the door was slammed shut.

Domino. Don't leave me . . .

A FIGURE APPROACHED and Gus came out of his torpor. With a pasty mouth and heavy eyelids, he straightened his back and opened his eyes. One more second lost in his memories and he would have fallen asleep in front of his full plate, in the sanctuary.

The place was almost empty, quieter than the village had been on that particular Koro, years ago.

Domino had promised that day, as Gus had asked him to. But Domino, barely eight years old at the time, had quickly realized that such a promise was impossible to keep. Under Mora and Ero's authority, he'd returned to the Prayer Stones again and again. The path followed by nichans had no regard for the fears and promises of two children.

The rest . . . The baby's scream, the pain turning his guts inward . . . In the end, Gus had fallen asleep while eating, long enough to dream of pure nonsense.

With a foggy mind, as if after too short a night, Gus grabbed his cutlery, mechanically mixed the vegetables and fish cooling on his plate, and tried to ignore the silhouette walking in his direction.

He recognized her without even looking up. A little smaller than him, with skin much darker than anyone else in the village, Matta slid onto the bench across from Gus yet without sitting right in front of him. But the Santig'Nell was within earshot and briefly glanced in his direction—obviously in hope of initiating a conversation. He ignored her. He'd woken up drenched in sweat after a nightmare, hadn't found anything clean to wear, having neglected his laundry chores for too long. After that bad meal and the resurgence of his old memories, both of which left a bitter taste in his mouth, Gus was in an unfriendly mood.

He grabbed his plate and got up from the table. Matta had taught him years earlier that a well-bred person who was given food and shelter without any compensation should leave nothing on his plate. Another lesson he chose to ignore.

"You shouldn't—" began the woman, leaning slightly to him.

But the sound of the village bell covered the rest of her words. In one motion, all faces turned to the sanctuary's front door, through which a flock of nichans rushed in. They patted their bare arms and shook their wet hair.

The bell. It hadn't rung for over a year.

The Corruption Rain!

His dishes in his hands, Gus walked at full speed and reached the kitchen door in a couple of heartbeats. It may have been too late to return to his hut, but there was more than one shelter in the village. Anything would do. Anything except staying in the sanctuary for hours with the Uetos waiting for the Corruption Rain to stop.

With a flick of his shoulder, he pushed open the kitchen door and stormed out. Several nichans camped here. Two lit a few lamps to ward off the sudden darkness. The rest watched the black rain from the only door leading outside. They were chatting heartily. Two of them noticed Gus's presence. However, the uninviting glance they cast toward the young man was enough to thwart his plans. Walking tall, he went to the sink to empty his still full plate and rinse his cutlery. As he pumped to draw water from the deep source underground to the faucet, the others noticed his presence as well as all the food the boy was wasting.

Heat rose to Gus's face and ears. But he kept acting as if nobody was watching, as if the shame festering in his stomach wasn't as strong as his need to escape everyone's attention.

No chance of getting out that way. Outside, the downpour was getting heavier, forcing the nichans to back up to avoid the splash. Gus took advantage of the distraction and turned back.

The sanctuary had meanwhile welcomed a few more individuals. When the front doors closed, Gus flinched. He was trapped here with the others.

Damn it!

He'd spent all of the Corruption Rains he'd known in Domino's company. Not this time.

No one came in anymore, yet the number of nichans seemed to grow endlessly, filling all the available space. A figment of his imagination. It was so dark in here.

Dark enough to hide him from sight.

Without wasting a moment, Gus walked to a corner of the large room. No one on this side, and no lantern to reveal his position. He sat on the stone, tasting its coldness through the worn linen of his pants. At the table he'd left two minutes earlier, Matta still ate, her back to him.

And he waited.

Voices rose from the four corners of the room in a permanent humming punctuated by cutlery pounding, laughter, throat clearing, and interjections. A group of young men laughed near the front door. Farther away, two children ate alone, sitting next to each other. At the end of a table, a large group of nichans of all ages had gathered around one person and one child. This person was talking, sitting on the edge of the bench as if it were a much more comfortable seat. His back straight, wearing a black tunic, this man seemed to want to dominate the others who drank his every word, nodding gravely. The twist of hair falling down his back was so long it brushed the ground with every flicker of his head.

Even with his poor eyesight, Gus recognized the man. Issba, the Orator of the clan. Gus had never spoken to him, but he knew the man. By reputation only. Domino wasn't fond of him.

Someone at that table jerked his chin in Gus's direction. The others turned their eyes to him. Issba too, soon imitated by the child sitting next to him—his apprentice Tulik, also dressed in black. There was no gentleness in their eyes. Maybe a spark of curiosity here, a lack of interest there.

The Orator's brown gaze settled on Gus, piercing, as if coming to a realization. Nearly a minute passed without either of them breaking eye contact. A silent encounter.

Around the Orator, the nichans had gone back to their nonchalant chatting now that they'd lost the man's attention.

Issba suddenly raised his hand to impose silence to his disciples. He obtained it the next second. "A perfect example, indeed, for the defilement has already crossed our threshold," said the man.

His voice rang effortlessly and covered those of the other conversations in the sanctuary. The last voice died with a questioning murmur. Heads turned, first to Issba, then to Gus, whom he was still observing, hardly blinking at all.

"A defilement marked out by the Gods," said the Orator. "They wished for us to know, to see the Corruption at work. Look at him." All eyes were now on Gus.

The boy trembled and gritted his teeth. He stared at Issba as the man stood from his bench, his long twist of hair similar to a rope dangling from the back of his skull.

"His appearance alone highlights the flaw in our enemy's strategy. The stain is no match for the Gods' might. Those eyes. Those wings. Impossible for this thing to mingle with the rest of the population. The Gods have marked it, and mark my words, none of us failed to heed that warning."

A few nods of agreement, whispers of approval. As a reflex, Gus raised his chin. He was still trembling.

Issba approached, sliding like smoke under the light of the lamps that reinforced the prominent angles of his features and the hollow scars on his cheeks and temples. "Your defilement will not reach us. It has no power, for we see you for what you truly are. A deception. Where the rain fails, where the dohors fail, you will fail too."

"This boy has no use for your sermons."

Alone at her table, smaller than everyone else, Matta had turned on her bench and looked at Issba with a placid but unsettling gaze. The crystal replacing her left eye shone in the darkness of the sanctuary. An immediate reminder of her blasphemous identity.

Issba raised a hand in her direction, as if to stop a projectile. "Don't address me, vile creature! The Unaan may tolerate you, but I am not fooled. I will always recognize an evil minion, no matter its appearance."

"An evil minion," the woman repeated. "Young people use and overuse fancy words these days."

She seemed so relaxed, more relaxed than she'd ever been in Gus and Domino's company. Whether her attitude was honest or woven of pretense, she gave the impression to not take Issba seriously, as if he were but a noisy child on a whim.

"Silence!" Issba scolded, suddenly calming the ardor of the nichans around him. "The Gods do not —"

"An evil minion?" she cut him, directing her attention to Gus. "This boy is full of the Gods' beauty. This beauty — this Light — has been saving lives in this village for more than ten years. You should be ashamed not to recognize the work of our creators."

"The Corruption's maneuvers take the most subtle forms. You and your eye are undoubtedly the proof of it."

Matta chuckled and went back to her meal. Motionless, Gus remembered to breathe when Issba's attention was drawn back to him.

The man detailed him up and down. "I will not waste any more of my time with a creature like you, but I will add this: the taint calls for death. It will find you."

The answer left Gus's mouth without his being able to hold it back, strong of a truth he'd accepted a long time ago. "I know."

A smile stretched the Orator's mouth, widening it so much that, for an agonizing second, Gus thought the man would transform. But he just smiled and turned to his own.

"The only words worthy of an abomination, are they not?" Issba found only the attentive silence of his disciples. He turned to Gus. "Your time will come, and may the Gods forgive you."

The man returned to his table and after a few frantic heartbeats, the buzz of conversation resumed. Outside, the rain was still pouring down on the building.

Gus had clenched his fists so tightly his joints were now sore. He rested his palms against his thighs when he saw him. At the other end of the room, Beïka stared at him with his depthless eyes. Gus hadn't noticed him until then. Unlike Issba, Domino's brother stayed in his place. No one was interested in the object of his attention. Gus decided to do the same.

He veered his gaze to the opposite wall, stopped it for a moment on Matta sitting a little farther away, and waited for the rain to pass.

NIGHT HAD FALLEN QUICKLY after the storm passed. Gus was exhausted from scraping the black, slimy shit of the Corruption with the others, yet he couldn't sleep. He'd been going over the same heady thoughts for hours. Domino, Issba, Domino, Matta. It promised to be a long night.

As he sat up in bed to get a sip of water, the door of the hut opened then closed almost immediately. It was dark—rays of light slipped through the shutters. Someone had come in. Gus could make out the outline of their tall, strong figure. He could clearly hear the raspy breath surging from their lungs. And though he couldn't discern their features, Gus knew exactly who had just burst into his house uninvited.

He stood motionless, not even bending his arm still reaching for his bedside.

The crash broke the silence without any warning. It spun around Gus in a downpour of disheartening sounds and furious heartbeats. The world exploded around him. Fragments of wood, terracotta, glass. They splattered everywhere.

Then the bed shook.

In an instant as brief as the jump of a flea and at the same time interminable, his home was wrecked by Beïka's silent anger. Not having moved an inch, Gus forced himself to calm his breath. His heart threatened to climb up into his mouth. He was close to vomiting.

Don't show him anything. Don't give him that pleasure. If Domino was here he—

Cowering in spite of himself, he suddenly choked his thoughts. He didn't need Domino to save him. Gus forced himself to talk, to take back control. "You're good? Feeling any better?"

Beïka punched him in the face. It shoved Gus against the bed. Nothing could have prepared him for that. He couldn't have prevented it, either. Blood slid from the inside of his cheek ripped open against his teeth. The metallic, salty taste invaded his mouth.

Lost in the darkness of the night and the pain palpitating throughout his skull, Gus realized that Beïka had crossed the distance that separated them when a thick wad of spit landed near his eye.

"Next time you insult our Orator or any of us, I'll kill you," Beïka said. "Then I'll tear this country apart to find my brother and show him your fucking head."

He bit his lip, perhaps holding back from carrying out his threat in the moment. He could have done it. Folded in on himself, fighting in vain against the terror knotting his throat, Gus would have had no choice but to accept his own death. Amidst the sparks that flew before his eyes, he was able to contemplate it. He'd always been able to contemplate it.

The taint calls for death. It will find you, Issba had promised.

To his surprise, it didn't come. Beïka only turned around, stepping on the broken furniture, and walked out.

Gus sat on his bed immediately. How could he have cowered like that, like a frightened beast, like a helpless child? With a wave of his hand, he wiped off the spit glued to his skin and grimaced as pain pulsed down the side of his face. His eyes suddenly burned. Pain wasn't the only matter. No, it was something more insidious, more intimate. Humiliation. He felt it in his whole being, in the bloody wound following the curve of his molars, in the smell of dried saliva on his cheek.

His muscles tightened, his jaw contracted. He pushed back the tears with all his might.

I said no! he scolded against his own weakness.

He slapped himself, the contact brutalizing his already bruised nerves, and pushed back the tangled hair stuck in his eyelashes. He sniffed hard and stood up.

Of course the lamp had been knocked over with the rest.

Never mind, I know this room like the back of my hand.

Gus held back a scream as the sharp pottery shards made contact with the soles of his bare feet. He fumbled on the ground, found his woven savates and put them on after shaking them of their possible contents. He had always been messy, but this was something else entirely. This wasn't his home.

Nothing insurmountable. Gus was no longer a child. He was a man. He'd let go once dead and gone.

In the next few minutes, repressing the suffering that made him sway from one foot to the other, he fully opened the shutter, bringing some light into the room. He picked up his laundry, tied up the rope to hang it back up, gathered up the pieces of his bedside table, refilled his clothing chest, swept the pieces of terracotta scattered all over the place, pushed it all close to the front door to take out at daybreak. Finally, he drew water from the fountain behind his hut and washed his face twice. He rinsed out his mouth, spattered red water on the cobblestones, and then did it again, ignoring the soft open flesh, the raw nerves, and the molar he could tilt with the flick of his tongue.

When he went back inside, he checked that no one had taken advantage of his absence to invite himself in again.

The hut seemed soiled, as if Beïka had taken a shit in the middle of the room.

Back in bed, Gus was now certain he wouldn't sleep that night.

XXV

"WILL YOU STOP MAKING THAT FACE?"

Memek's voice caught Domino off guard. He looked up, making sure his cousin had spoken to him. Memek, half transformed, skin as black as a midnight sky, stuck her claws under the thick scales of the saurian she and her father had just killed. She spread her arm away with a sharp movement, and the skin peeled off from the rest of the beast's powerful muscles. On the other side of the campfire, Ero piled up enough wood to warm them all night. He didn't react to Memek's words.

"What face?" Domino asked.

"The face of a sulking child," the young woman said, returning to her human form. "You should have cut the legs off by now."

Indeed. It was essential to retrieve the skin and claws of the huge reptile before its flesh turned cold. Both were sold at a significant price, and if Domino didn't hurry, the fragile scales would soon become inseparable from the rest of the animal. They needed the money if they were to sleep in a real bed by the time they reached the next village. If only someone allowed them to do so.

None of the villages they'd passed through since Kepam had offered them the shelter they longed for. And south of the capital, nichan sanctuaries were becoming increasingly rare.

"Papema is a quagmire," Ero had said as they advanced through the fields on the outskirts of the massive city. "If we walk in there, we'll never get out. So forget it." Just like that, Memek's everlasting request to join the capital had been rejected.

Papema had been built along the border of the Arao, forming one whole with the villages and other towns that had developed at the foot of the holy land. The Torb capital stretched for hundreds of miles, crossing part of the country. It was now, according to the natives, a muddle of merchants, beasts, whores, and refugees trying to reach the Meishua without being able to leave the city afterwards. Anyone who entered the capital got lost, robbed, and found a way to incur several debts in the process. It wasn't Ero's habit to give credence to peasant gossip, but he obviously wanted to avoid setting foot in Papema. Memek had kept her eyes on the big city of warm, golden tones. She seemed to care nothing for the wind-waving steppes that stretched as far as the eye could see, or the lines of mountains of frozen peaks that could be seen beyond the sharp buildings and through the low clouds. She wanted a bed, and in the weeks that went by, her mood only darkened.

Domino readjusted his grip on the handle of the damn knife he'd received from Ero. He'd eaten all his life with cutlery, knew how to handle tools for gardening and building a house. But something was preventing him from holding that very tool properly. Even though most of his anger targeted his uncle, he couldn't deny that his lack of goodwill was probably at fault.

He picked up where he'd left off. Once again, the perfectly sharp blade slid and slashed the surface of the precious greenish scales.

"Damn it," he swore between his teeth.

Memek reached out and pushed the hunting knife away,

preventing her cousin from doing any more damage. "That's at least thirty heads you just wasted," she raged.

"The fucking blade slipped out of my fingers."

"Poor thing."

"You think I did that on purpose?"

"I think you're only doing what you want to do, and it's costing us a fucking lot. Silver doesn't just fall out of the sky, you know."

"Since when do you care so much about money?" Ero asked, leaning before the golden flames gradually taking over.

"We need it," his daughter reminded him, arms and back stiff, her clenched fists pressing on her lap. "To sleep with a roof over our heads. To—"

"We're on a pilgrimage, Memek. We're not visiting the country."

The girl paused, her bloody hands soiling her pants, her eyes fixed on her father. They'd gone from anger to a cold impassiveness. "To sleep with a roof over our heads," she repeated, drawing her father and Domino's attention for good. As far back as he could remember, Memek had never been so restive with Ero. "To eat, because soon all the meat will be gone for winter. To wash. I'm pretty sure Domino and I have lice. Is it so ridiculous to try to make this trip a little more comfortable?"

"We're on a pilgrimage," Ero said, repeating himself, mirroring his daughter's way of speech.

He stared at her, calm. Memek sent a quick glance at Domino and pointed to him with a wave of her bloodied hand before turning back to her father.

"And what a pilgrimage! You might say we've made great progress."

Domino stuck his knife into the cool earth beside him and sat up. "If you have a problem with me, talk to me. I'm right here."

"I have a problem with you and with you," she said, flashing her eyes at Domino and then at her father.

There was a silence that only the crackling of the fire disturbed. Ero hadn't looked away from his daughter for a second. "I'm listening," he said.

"It's been almost two months since we left," the young woman said, raising her eyebrows. "You bought him a knife. A fucking knife. I mean, we don't take him hunting anymore. He just stays here guarding the camp, Papa. If that's not called resignation, I don't know what it is."

"Tell me what you want from me, Memek."

"This pilgrimage had two goals: to knock some sense into him, and to prepare us to fight the Blessers."

"That's not changed."

"We're going in circles! We go from village to village. We hear about these partisans who learn to fight, who raise money to murder us. And we don't move a finger. That's why you wanted to avoid Papema. You're running away from rumors, from the news from the east. It would only remind us of the mess at the border. You don't want to hear about the partisans. Well, fuck that! Those rumors are everywhere. Every time we are turned back to a village, it's their influence that gets in our way. And we just walk around doing nothing when we should be cutting them to the bone. For fuck's sake, have you forgotten that it's one of their kind that killed Javik?"

She suddenly fell silent, tears of anger in her eyes.

Facing her, Domino stopped breathing for a moment.

At first he'd expected Memek to complain about him, expected her to ask to go back to Surhok. She must miss her mother and her family. No doubt she did, but her frustration went far beyond that. For the first time, his cousin's violent desire for revenge was like frost in his veins. She wanted to get rid of partisans; Domino was a burden preventing her from doing so.

Domino was no match for those fuckers. Not with a knife he could barely handle to defend himself against their sabers and pistols.

"You have a lot of nerve asking me this question," Ero said to his daughter without losing his calm. "Your brother died before my eyes."

"Why are we heading south?" Memek asked, changing the subject abruptly.

"It's part of the pilgrimage."

"Stop saying that!" she shouted and stood, wiping her sticky hands on her pants. "We don't fight. And he refuses to transform. If you don't order him to do it, what's the point of all this? Might as well go home and wait for these assholes to come and get us."

She was right. Domino looked down and searched for the flow within him. The spark of his essence, the taint of the Corruption . . . Anything would do. Again, no buzzing. Just an overwhelming void.

Ero stood up and stepped over the campfire. "Domino," he said, his authority restored. "Finish butchering this beast. Keep the fire burning. You"—he pointed at Memek—"you're coming with me. We'll go for a walk, hunt some more meat."

"I—" started the young woman.

"Do as I say, Memek. Nobody likes saurian meat anyway. Don't argue. I have to talk to you."

She hesitated, arms folded, still full of resentment. Eventually she accepted, and father and daughter turned their backs on Domino before disappearing between the half-naked trees.

Once again, Domino found himself alone.

You got yourself into this shit, a voice said in his head. *It's up to you to make it right.*

Responding to the order coursing through his body, he uprooted the knife half-buried next to him and took care of retrieving the scales from the saurian without turning the task into a massacre. The day was waning when he grabbed the skin of the beast, removed the remains of flesh, and hung it on a branch to dry. After extracting the animal's fangs, Domino emptied its mouth of the tongue and a gland as big as his fist, capable of producing venom even after death. He collected enough meat, rekindled the fire, and began to dig with his bare hands to bury the remnants of the reptile underground. A waste of meat, but Ero was right: nobody liked saurians, and its meat was only kept in case other animals went missing.

His body moved like a tool dealt by his uncle's hand. Efficient, fast, and lifeless. His promised future if nothing changed.

A growl interrupted Domino in his task. He tracked the source of the noise, but the curtain of scaly skin blocked his view. He sniffed the air. Animal, young, male. Big. Another growl, closer. This time he heard the paws treading the ground, the claws scraping the rocky earth with each slow, heavy step. A shadow passed under the animal skin. Domino stood up and stepped back, his senses alert.

It can't be.

An animal, so close to him, less than five paces away. It grumbled as it appeared on the other side of the dark scales swaying in the wind. Domino froze. It was a bear. Its brown fur was wet with all kinds of filth. The smell of the animal intensified.

It shouldn't have been here. Animals, all but birds, feared nichans. Larger predators could smell them from hundreds of yards away. As a result they fled as far as they could. They always did. That was why nichans hunted for miles and miles. It was the effort it took to flush out, catch, and kill the prey.

But not this one. This bear was definitely right here, just a few steps away from Domino.

The young man looked for his knife. The thing was by the fire where he'd left it with the meat. Slowly, without taking his eyes off the animal, Domino moved toward the flames casting vivid shadows in all directions. Not a single threatening move. The bear reacted as if it was. It growled, straightened up on its hind legs, and growled again, louder, just in case its intention wasn't clear already. Domino stood still. Another nichan would attack. So attack the bear it would be, as his instincts urged him to do.

Using all his speed, he ran to the fire and slid on the rocks and dirt. When he jumped to his feet, the knife was in his hand. The bear charged at him, and its clawed paw swept the air. Domino struck with a circular motion. None of their blows were effective. They both charged back in a second attack.

Blood splashed all around. Coral blood. An icy wind forced Domino to the ground. His ass and back crashed on the rocky earth, and his breath got stuck in his throat. But nothing could have outmatched the ache piercing his stomach. On reflex, he raised his hand to his side. Warm blood flowed between his fingers.

No! No!

Facing him, the shadow of a scratch circling its drooling mouth, the bear came for retaliation.

Get up! Get the fuck out of here!

Domino gathered his senses and obeyed his survival instinct. He couldn't fight. Nearly four years earlier, he'd transformed himself in the face of danger. Now he had no time to even try.

He got up and ran as fast as he could, but the pain slowed him down. He dared look back. The animal chased him, its gait heavy, enraged by the stab that had sliced the corner of its snout. Domino forced his legs on, his heart missing a beat with each step, blood spilling out from under his ribs.

Suddenly, the ground slipped from under his feet. He fell, and the world swirled around him, made of branches, sharp rocks, and thorns. He couldn't find anything to catch himself as he rolled down. A muffled crack ripped a gasp out of him. He continued to fall down the steep hill. On and on and on.

Then his back hit an obstacle. His descent was abruptly interrupted.

Breathless, his first reflex was to find his wound again and cover it with the flat of his hand. A scream escaped from his throat. His shoulder hurt terribly. He clenched his teeth, not wanting to know why he was in such pain. He had to move, check that the bear was gone, stop the bleeding. With his left hand, he pressed against the open cuts. With the strength of his legs, he sat back up and searched for the animal around him. Domino could vaguely distinguish the slope he'd just descended. Quite a height. He sniffed the cold dusk breeze, no longer found the musky smell of the bear. The damn thing obviously didn't want to follow him down here. Good, because a glance was enough to notice the crooked angle of his right shoulder—dislocated, no doubt—and the waves of blood gushing from his belly.

He swore through the pain.

How could something like that happen? If he considered the knife Ero had put in his hands a disgrace, being attacked by a bear and losing to it was deserving of death. No nichan had a skin thick enough to endure such shame.

Ero and Memek would soon return. They had to.

Domino tried to get up. He dismissed the possibility. He was already weak, completely dizzy. He pressed harder against his wound. If he called his uncle, if he shouted to bring him back, would that be enough? Would he risk attracting all the hungry animals in the area?

I'm going to bleed to death and die like an idiot.

Gus.

Domino couldn't die here. Not like this—disgraced, helpless, empty of what made him nichan. And alone.

Gus.

He wanted to see him so badly.

"No," he whimpered, still pushing on his legs, which refused to carry him, and in a last spark of hope, he screamed his uncle's name. It was all that separated him from his end.

He shouted it again and again, pressing ever harder on his hatched belly, calling until his vocal cords snapped.

"Domino!"

Memek. Her silhouette stood high up in the darkness. Domino called again. Another dark figure appeared. Ero. With the same impulse, both nichans threw themselves down the slope. As they reached him, Domino pushed away the urge to let go and fall asleep. He wasn't saved yet; he had to keep fighting.

"By the Faces!" Memek cried out, adding her hand over Domino's. "What did that? A dohor?"

Ero knelt on the other side and briefly examined his nephew's shoulder. "Who cares," he said. "We have to get him a healer. We have to go back to the last village."

"You think they'll have a healer?" said his daughter.

"A—a bear," Domino stammered, struggling to look up at his uncle.

"What?"

"It was . . . a bear."

"That's impossible," Memek said.

"Don't let me die," Domino growled as she moved her hand away to take off her shawl and roll it into a ball.

Domino recognized her intentions but couldn't take his hand off his abdomen. More than ever, he wanted his blood to stay inside. But Memek's iron fist forced him to uncover the wound. She immediately covered it with her shawl.

"Don't let me die," Domino repeated.

"Why didn't you transform?" Ero's anger was almost a caress compared to the pain. He put Domino's good arm around his neck. "Why are you so stubborn?"

"I can't do it. I've tried. I can't do it."

The pain in his arm soon climbed to his head. Well, as long as he was in pain, he would know he was alive.

His uncle spoke. Memek did too. Nothing made sense, yet he clung to the shapeless words floating around him. He just concentrated on the pain as well—no way to ignore that bitch.

He was lifted from the ground, and the rest of time and the world presented themselves to him intermittently, in the form of fragmented lights, smells, and cries.

The lapping of the water. The scent of rain. The freshness of the rain. The voices of men. Knocks against the wood. Muffled responses. The creaking of a door. More voices. A plea. Memek? The stench of alcohol. Moaning and moaning and moaning, more and more timid. His own voice.

Then he ran out of strength and fainted.

XXVI

Domino dreamed of Gus. He dreamed of that day when they were eight or nine years old, when they'd decided that their world wasn't quite right.

It was a challenge, a way, once again, to cut themselves off from everyone. From Mora, who didn't want to play with them anymore because Belma offered him things that only grown-ups understood. From Ero, who pretended not to see them but who Domino and Gus still feared. From Beïka, who jumped at the slightest opportunity to mess with them. From Matta, who filled their heads with lessons that would never teach them to be strong and to fight the Blessers.

So they'd decided to live in the woods. They were still within the village walls. No houses on the horizon. Domino could only smell his own scent and his friend's. They gathered wood for a fire, found berries and fruits, and stocked them in a lotus leaf they'd picked by the river. They counted them. Enough for two. They marked the border of their territory with stones. No one would enter, not relatives, not wild animals, not even those dohors everyone was talking about although the two children wondered if the thing wasn't just a lie meant to keep kids in line.

They spent their day preparing for a life where there would be only them. Gus smiled, moving the stones to reduce their territory. Domino agreed and smiled just as much. They didn't need that much space. Sitting face to face, they ate the berries, throwing them into each other's mouths. Then they engaged in a mock hunt, Gus spreading his wing open to act like birds of prey while Domino made himself as small as possible, running naked through the wilderness, using his skirt as a shelter whenever Gus approached, laughing. Gus laughed so hard. Domino was happy.

The day waned; the temperature dropped. They lay on the ground, close together. Above them, the sky soon disappeared, swallowing the world, only sparing the warm bubble surrounding their bodies.

"You should be my partner," Domino said. "Would you like that? Being with me always?" He'd never asked, neither that day, nor the ones that came after.

Next to him, silence stretched for seconds, hours, years, myriads of lives. Then, "You left me," said Gus.

Domino turned his head, but he was alone.

He opened his eyes, and flames blurred with tears burned his eyes. He lay on his back, his head tilted to the side. For a moment he stood still, bathing in the heat of the fire. Then the memories resurfaced like a mudslide, pouring over his exhausted mind. A cold tremor washed over him.

The bear, the fall.

He looked around and wiggled. He was inside a tent. The canvas hung over him in brown curves. A brazier in the center, different from those used by his clan. This one was narrower and screened. On the flames was a kettle. Domino rolled on his bed to widen his field of vision. The pain racked him. He shuddered and clung to the sheets on which he lay.

"Hey, be still," someone said to him.

Domino followed the voice, his head pivoting. A scarf held his right arm firmly against his body. He remembered the alarming protruding joint of his dislocated shoulder.

Memek was next to him.

Her eyes tired, her hair loose, his cousin pursed her lips in a thin line. The delicate loops of her tattoos appeared more clearly to Domino. Triangles outlined with delicate petals. Honorary marks were supposed to mean something about the dead and the living who wore them. What was the meaning of the black shapes covering her skin?

"You're so stupid, Domino," she whispered in a tense breath, bringing him to the harsh reality.

"Fuck you too," he replied without thinking, tired of receiving the same insults over and over again for so many years.

To his surprise, Memek smiled and laughed lightly, lowering her head. When she lifted it up, her mismatched eyes shone with tears. She reached out her hand and gently tousled Domino's curls. Such tenderness from her took the young man's breath away. He and Memek had never been close, yet at that moment she seemed as worried and relieved as if they'd come out of the same womb.

"What are we going to do with you?" she said in a low voice, sitting on the edge of the bed.

He took a breath. "I tried to transform myself. I've been trying for weeks. I just can't do it. I don't know why I can't. I just—"

"I know. You told us."

"I did?"

"You cried it, actually, while we were bringing you here. You kept repeating it, as if it could save your ass."

So Ero knew. Domino tried to rise to a sitting position, but the dizziness swaying in his head sent him back to his pillow. He swallowed with a grimace. His saliva was as irritating as sand. "Where's your father?"

"He's gone back to the camp to get our things. He should be back soon."

"What's this place?"

"Somewhere safe, with one of our own. The human healer in the village wouldn't help us. 'I don't know how to treat nichans,' he said. My father almost broke his door down. Some travelers gathered to send us away. And then Feanim opened his tent and offered to stitch you up."

"Feanim?"

"Well, someone had to get your shit together since you were too busy leaking from every hole," a nichan said.

He stopped in front of the fire to stir the contents of his kettle with a wooden spoon. He looked Ero's age. He had short hair tucked back, a slender figure and neck. He turned his head toward Domino, revealing gray eyes half hidden under thick glasses that narrowed his gaze. Like his body, his face was thin and hollow. His brown skin was tanned by the sun.

"Don't worry," the man continued as he approached. "I've done this all my fucking life. Your guts aren't the first I've had to shove back in place. Don't give me that stupid look. You're still breathing, aren't you?"

He then lifted the soiled cloth covering Domino's left flank. Domino held his breath as the fibers stuck to the crystallized blood pulled at his swollen skin. He released a heavy sigh of pain then was able to see the damage the bear had caused. Four long, parallel cuts now sewn with clean, even sutures. This Feanim knew what he was doing, indeed.

Finally looking at the rest of the circular tent, Domino discovered the clean, folded cloths on a hanging shelf, the bottles filled with various substances, the metal tools, most of which were unknown to him.

"Your first stitches," said Feanim. "You'll live to celebrate them."

Domino looked at him, baffled by this remark. Feanim bent over to take a closer look at his wound over his round spectacles. "You're covered in a lot of scars, kid. They're nice, clean. Not a damn stitch in them. Whoever healed you would have a few things to teach me. Just when I thought I was good."

He finally looked up at Domino. His expression showed nothing but justified weariness at this time of night.

"Yeah," Domino said. He didn't have to tell him about Gus, so he refrained. Next to him, Memek hadn't flinched.

With that thought intertwined in the mess of his memory, Domino rested his head and closed his eyes. The image of the bear jumping in his face immediately came to mind. The beast had approached him. It had...

Natso.

Domino opened his eyes. Everything was suddenly so much clearer. The truth struck him harder than a punch: in the last few months, Domino had managed to get close to his nephew. The little one hadn't run away from his uncle, where all children had always had the reflex to do so over the years. Domino hadn't thought about it, or maybe he'd purposely ignored the reality, too happy to be a part of Natso's life. Now he understood.

The nichan in him was gone. Gone.

Did I do that? Did I kill the nichan in me by blocking it out all these years?

Such a thing couldn't be possible. Someone couldn't just decide not to be anymore what the Gods had made them, right?

I'm still nichan, Domino thought as Ero's voice echoed, low and deep. "I brought this back for you."

"I hunt my own meat, you know," Feanim said. "No need to be a hunter to get a snack."

"Think of it as a thank-you gift."

"You shouldn't have bothered. Big change isn't so bad either, you know."

Feanim looked around him with a long sigh and abandoned the dead hare hanging limp in his hand next to the fire.

Close to him, Ero was dripping with water. The rain still drummed against the tent canvas. The man got rid of his wet belongings, wrung out his beard—which had thickened over the past few weeks—and quickly laid his eyes on the camp bed where Domino was resting.

"It's late. Go back to sleep," he said.

"I'm sorry."

Ero sighed and looked away, taking off his rain-darkened clothes. "I'm tired, Domino. We'll talk tomorrow."

WHEN DOMINO WOKE, Ero and Memek were nowhere to be seen. Neither was Feanim. Sharp gusts of wind shook the sides of the tent. The timid daylight intermittently pierced the darkness. Domino, himself heckled by a shiver, stood. He pressed his hand against his bandage, as if to make sure his guts wouldn't spill out through the sutures. He hadn't slept this much in years. Even his seasons hadn't worn him down as much. Yet he didn't feel as awake as he would have liked. His vision was blurry as he looked around, his mouth pasty as he swallowed through his parched throat.

As slowly as possible, he pivoted on the camp bed. A grimace and a furtive thought. After what had happened the day before, could Ero and his daughter have left without him?

They wouldn't dare . . .

Voices seeped through the thick tent, and Domino listened. One was unknown, tense.

"Everyone agreed to this. The other nichan told me so when he left. One day should be enough to pack everything up, right?"

And another that the young man had memorized in no time. Feanim's. "And you think I can carry all this crap on my back? Do I look like a damn turtle?"

"Please, be reasonable. We're only trying to prevent trouble," said the other. His heart was human. It beat hard and fast, all wrapped up in the characteristic breath of low stamina.

Like Gus, every time he tried to keep up with Domino's long strides.

"You be reasonable," said Feanim as Domino stood.

Wearing only pants, a sling supporting his arm, and the many strips protecting his wounds, he walked through the tent with a not-so-steady pace that kept shaking him from left to right. He opened the entrance. The midday light fell on his eyelids, forcing them to crease. Close by were a pair of men. Beyond them lay a small village covering the side of a hill. Domino and his family had left that place two days earlier. This emergency had delayed them.

Feanim, turning his back on Domino, continued, "We have a wounded boy in there. You would send him to the wilds? With his guts out? You want him dead or what? Give this kid time to recover. He can't even stand up. So walk . . . "

The human facing him—a man with round cheeks reddened by the cool breeze—looked up at Domino, who stood at the tent's opening, and sighed.

Feanim glanced over his shoulder and his bored look turned darker than the sky above their heads. "Fuck me! Your timing is a real problem, kid."

"He seems fine to me. You nichans are rough-skinned," said the human. "Tomorrow morning, then. Do not force the kivhan to visit you himself."

"Or what? What's he gonna do about it?"

The human kept his mouth shut and walked away from them, his brown hair tossed back at the top of his head by the wind. Feanim sighed and took off his glasses to polish them off on the corner of his sleeve.

"Tomorrow morning," Domino said in a hoarse voice. "What's going on?" He already had a vague idea.

"We made too much noise last night. And that mess tends to attract partisans like shit attracts flies. They're kicking us out."

It was Domino's turn to sigh. "You too?"

"Aren't we nichans popular these days? I didn't plan to stay here. Don't particularly like the view. But leaving tomorrow . . . Fuck, why did I sell my wheelbarrow?"

"I'm sorry."

"I'll get another one. I'm used to it. We all make mistakes. The Gods have a nice sense of humor. They probably thought it'd be more interesting if we were all a bunch of idiots." Feanim looked down and walked back to the tent. "And you're not responsible for everyone's problems, so quit apologizing all the time. Keep that for when you truly mess up."

"I was attacked by a bear, because I never learned to transform," said Domino. He wasn't sure why he felt the need to tell the healer.

Feanim looked him up and down, frowning. "What's wrong with you, kid?"

Domino laughed and grimaced as his belly contracted. "At this point, what isn't?"

Feanim returned the laugh. "Well, for sure you're a strong beast. With all the blood you left behind you, I don't know how you're even standing right now."

"You heard the man. Us nichans are rough-skinned."

"Yes, and my ass is made of goose meat." Feanim sighed again and threw a glance over his shoulder, toward the village. "The Gods really tried. They made us look human to fit with the others, but in the end . . . Might not be possible for the lot of us to live together."

Domino trembled as another gust of wind swept his bare skin and penetrated in the tent. Would Gus have agreed with Feanim? He who had grown among nichans, who had let Domino cross the threshold of his intimacy.

"Maybe everyone just needs to try harder," Domino said.

Feanim shook his head, eyelids heavy above his steel-gray eyes. "Quit being naive too, kid. There's a reason why people don't try." He folded back the entrance of the tent and stood at Domino's side, close enough for every single wrinkle of his face to show. "They don't try because they don't want to."

―――――――――

BEFORE LEAVING, Ero asked the healer how long it would take Domino to recover. Sitting on the bed, letting Feanim free his arm from his sling, Domino looked up at his uncle. Ero continued to ignore him. Unable to decipher his uncle's expression, Domino looked away, giving up on receiving sympathy from his chief.

Feanim had gathered his belongings for departure. Domino didn't know how long the man had lived in the village. Feanim said nothing when the question was raised.

"Whatever," he grumbled as he checked the young man's stitches. "Half of my herbs are good to throw in the fire. Might as well restock before shit happens. Or more shit."

"So? Where will you go? You have family somewhere?"

Feanim shrugged before writing a smirk on his thin lips. "Who gives a shit? I'm not going to run out of nichans to treat, considering this mess."

In the corner of the tent, a new wheelbarrow waited to be loaded. It'd follow Feanim wherever he'd choose to go.

"Give him two short weeks," the healer told Ero, palpating

Domino's shoulder. "He's young and healthy. Next month he'll have forgotten about the damn hunting accident."

A hunting accident. Not what Domino would have called it. His failure felt more accurate.

In the meantime, there was no going back on the road. Domino couldn't do it and knew his uncle wouldn't risk traveling with partisans roaming the countryside, not if the situation was as critical as they'd been told.

"Two weeks . . . We'll avoid the roads," Ero concluded.

"Are you heading west?" Feanim asked, lifting Domino's elbow. A spasm stirred the boy's arm. He grimaced.

"Not west, no," said Ero.

"No?" Feanim continued to manipulate Domino, making him bend and unfold his arm, pushing his shoulder with his palm.

"We're continuing southeast," Ero said.

Sitting on the floor, packing up their supplies, Memek didn't react. The conversation she'd had with Ero the night of the bear attack seemed to have persuaded her not to doubt her father's decisions today.

So the pilgrimage hadn't reached its end yet. The Unaan hadn't changed his mind or given up. After being attacked by a bear, Domino had feared a turnaround and had almost seen Surhok appear on the horizon.

Deep relief filled his chest.

Domino jumped again. His arm kept going numb and contracting in an untimely manner.

"Push against my hand, kid," Feanim told him in a lazy tone.

Still troubled by Ero's news and the discomfort running up and down in his arm bones and muscles, Domino had to focus to perform. He pressed his hand against the doctor's long fingers. A pain pierced his right shoulder and his hand slipped from his grasp. His fingers bent, both soft and out of control.

"Damn it," Domino swore.

"Easy, calm down," Feanim said in a relaxed voice. "The nerves are probably damaged. It happens. It's fucked up, but it happens."

After long seconds, Domino was able to bend his fingers again. As his thumb closed around his fist, another spasm ripped a grunt out of him, and the healer placed the scarf back on.

"Stop it, kid. If you seek trouble, that's all you'll get. Give yourself time to heal."

Time to heal. Domino was running out of time. Ero didn't intend to interrupt the pilgrimage, but he would eventually change his mind if Domino's situation remained hopeless.

Whatever was happening in the south, with all those partisans on the warpath, Domino had to be ready to face it. He had to find a way to free himself from his own shackles before it was too late.

XXVII

BEÏKA SEEMED TO HAVE HAD AN EPIPHANY. HE HAD ALWAYS been a violent person, even as a child. Gus remembered very well the kick that had sent him into the river; the violent slaps that used to smack Domino's cheeks. There had been some pinches strong enough to leave bruises. These gestures from adults had always appeared harmless—the punishments of a not-so-delicate older brother, nothing more. Mora had sometimes surprised such gestures, had interfered. Never mind, Beïka had learned a very simple lesson: to make it a secret.

An epiphany.

Sitting against a tree, palms pressing against his eyes, fingers buried in his bright hair, Gus struggled with nausea. He'd already emptied his stomach next to him, still the twitching of his belly was unbearable. A slight spasm twisted his insides; he gnashed his teeth. He could barely swallow for fear of throwing up. So he brushed his tongue over his teeth, collecting the acidic remains staining the inside of his mouth, and spat at his feet, drooling partly on his chin.

His shaking was out of control. He was soaked with sweat. It still ran down his back, between his wings.

Come on, move. Don't stay like this.

The young man sniffed and uncovered his eyes. Not far from him, a beige spot in the middle of the dark vegetation caught his eye. The sheets from the infirmary.

Beïka had dragged him by the wrist from the riverbank to the depths of the village woods. Gus hadn't had time to get on his feet. One hand holding the human, the other carrying the sheets the boy had been cleaning seconds ago, Beïka had applied the lesson he'd learned from years of persistent cruelty: he'd found a discreet spot to keep this a secret.

No reason was given to justify what happened, but did he need one anyway? Gus could see the nichan's face, the pleasure he took in dragging him behind him, pulling his hair, throwing him to the ground. Gus had tried to run away. A breathtaking blow to the gut had interrupted the foolish attempt. A punch, a kick, he'd never know. And as he'd run out of breath and as his heart threatened to stop in the midst of his jolts, Beïka had slammed his pale face into the wet earth for long seconds. No more air or light. The nichan hadn't even said a single word. Once released, Gus had immediately started to vomit.

Then Beïka had released his dick from his pants, turning away from a still gasping Gus. The freshly washed sheets were now covered with cold urine.

Beasts! They're beasts. Words of which Gus thought more and more, remnant of a past that, in the moment, could have belonged to another man. Right now, he wasn't sure anymore of who he was, of when he'd last breathed normally, and why the earth beneath his feet still felt so close to his scratched face.

A silence sob bounced in his chest.

No one would look for him, there was no rush. He could sit

here a little while longer. So Gus did, until his stomach recovered enough to allow him to walk again.

THAT SAME EVENING, in the brazier of his hut whose door he kept an eye on every night, Gus burned the sheets he refused to clean.

To clean Beïka's piss . . .

Over my dead body.

MURAN COMPLAINED. Her sheets were missing. She asked Gus what he had done with them. Nothing, he said. He'd washed them and put them back where they belonged. The sheets were missing, though. Gus suggested she might have moved them and forgot. The nichan turned sour. She drank enough to forget half her actions of the day.

"Washing the sheets is your responsibility," the woman recalled.

"If you say so."

The woman's hand rose. Gus retreated with a flutter of his eyelids, his chest compressed by a start. She was going to hit him, his mind told him. A mistake. No blow reached his face or hurled his guts up his throat. She was instead pointing to the door to kick him out. She barely noticed his confusion and the fear that had bleached his face.

As he walked away from the infirmary, Gus found himself on the threshold of a home other than his own. Built on stilts, the hut was a little larger and better maintained than any other in the village. The steps leading up to the front door had been swept away. The door itself appeared to have been brushed, and several birds had nested under the woven bamboo stems.

Watching the surroundings through the heavy darkness of the evening, Gus raised his fist and knocked.

The front door opened, revealing a tidy, incense-smelling interior. Matta's countenance darkened as she discovered Gus's face. The young man's cheek was still covered with small gashes after being pressed so violently against the ground. The bruises, several weeks older, still colored his cheekbone like gushes of purple and yellow ink. His thin, white skin marked way too easily.

So what? His cheek would heal. For the moment, he had only one thing on his mind, and his determination couldn't wait another minute.

"Good evening," Matta said, obviously trying not to examine the young man's wounds too insistently. "What can I do for you?"

"I have a favor to ask of you," said Gus.

"Why, I'm all ears."

"Teach me how to fight."

The woman paused, licking her lips, staring at the boy. Gus stood still, waiting without showing any sign of impatience. But he hoped she'd bring him in quickly. He didn't want anyone to see him, even though no one would know—or care about—the purpose of his late visit.

When Matta stepped aside to invite him in, she seized the opportunity to take a good look at him from head to toe. Gus pretended not to see anything and crossed the threshold.

Before agreeing to Gus's request, Matta offered him a seat at her table, which took up almost half the space of the small hut. She brought to the table the grease lamp, placed a second one not far away, and then lit it. The golden flame stretched in flickering waves and warmed an earthenware vase filled with a bunch of twisted branches. A heady scent reminiscent of an overripe melon tickled Gus's nostrils.

Sitting on the edge of a small bench, waiting for his answer,

Gus watched the woman bustle around the room, remaining silent, suddenly wondering if his idea wasn't downright absurd.

He didn't want to involve anyone, for his problems with Beïka were nobody's business. But he lacked a solution. Beïka would come back. He was enjoying himself way too much to stop. Gus could feel it in his abdomen, still tense with pain and anticipation.

When the Santig'Nell finally sat down next to him, in her hand was a round tin can. She opened it, and a scent of arnica rose to the boy's nose, blending with the other smells filling the hut.

"A boost to the healing process. May I?" Matta asked, pointing with her chin at Gus's face and then at the jar of ointment.

Gus had more than once taken small amounts of herbs and balm for his own or Domino's use, but never a whole jar. With his gift, he didn't often need a remedy. He was surprised to find that Matta had also stolen something from the herbalist. Arnica only grew in the heights, outside the village, and, as far as he knew, Matta had no access to it.

"No need," Gus answered.

He figured it would have been better if he hadn't come. He'd missed the chance to weigh the pros and cons, had only felt a strong need to learn how to defend himself. The way Matta had tried to get him out of Issba's clutches some time earlier had influenced his judgment. But the more he considered it now, the stupider it felt.

Him, defending himself against a nichan? What a fool.

It was the request of a desperate man, and he hated more than anything to have come to this point.

"Tell me about it," Matta said. "You seemed to be in a hurry to talk, but I can wait. In any case, I'll only speak once I've applied the ointment on the wound that poses as your face."

The reproach in Matta's words was as thick as mud, though

she was careful not to raise her voice. But anxiety mixed with anger passed into her eyes, both the brown one and the blue one. Worry or pity. He wanted neither.

"Keep your ointment for a better use. I'm all right."

"It's up to you, but the best thing would be to let me help you," she added.

The ointment was no longer the issue, and Gus had figured that out. He could heal by himself; he had plenty of time for that. A sermon was the last of his needs. Most of all, he didn't want to be touched. Not while he could still feel Beïka's hands on him.

Unsure what bothered him most, Gus got up and walked away. Might as well do it before Matta asked any more questions he certainly wouldn't answer.

"Is it so hard to let me help you?" Matta asked him, and Gus stopped in his tracks. "Does it cost you so much to admit it?"

"I didn't come here for treatment—" He couldn't even look at her. The bruises of his skin spoke a truth different than the one he needed her to accept.

"You come in here covered in marks and scratches. Your face, your wrists." Gus resisted looking down. He hadn't even noticed his wrists, but the mention of their bruised appearance immediately drew his attention to the tightness in his forearms. "This isn't right. Do you know how worried I am about you, Gus?"

"Then stop worrying."

"If I could, I would. But it's not in my nature to look away from a child in need."

"A child?"

"At my age, that's what you are. Please, come back and sit down. And talk to me."

Gus breathed harder, and the ferrous taste on his tongue intensified.

He couldn't take it anymore.

"Forget that I came," he said as he left the hut, ignoring a last call from Matta.

He slammed the door behind his back. Silence came back.

What a fool! What would she have to teach me? She wouldn't be able to resist a nichan, no matter how powerful her bloody Eye is.

He should never have involved her in this. Now she would come back at him with her silly questions and worries.

Gus immediately returned to his hut. He made no detours to the sanctuary. Since that blow forced through his gut, no food had passed his lips. The evening had just begun, but he was tired. He might as well go to bed now and try not to think about the Santig'Nell. He'd send her away if he had to. Nothing easier than that. Matta was a good woman, but . . . She didn't belong here. She would leave too.

They all did.

He reached his hut, grabbed one of the matches left under the nearest lantern, and set it alight. Protecting his flame against his heart, he entered his house, pushed the door shut with the tip of his foot as he went by, and quickly found the lamp lying by his bed.

He noticed the gaze following him in the dark only once it was too late. The glow of the flame was reflected in two black eyes. Gus started (did he cry out?) and took a step back. One step too far.

Probably thinking he was about to run away, Beïka leaped up from the bed on which he was sitting.

"Where do you think you're going? Well, well. Aren't you feisty tonight?"

"Let go of me."

"I'm the one giving orders. Shouldn't be so hard to understand?"

Gus's arms were already stuck in the nichan's grip. To restrain him was child's play.

"Let me go," Gus repeated, retreating to be pulled back in place the next moment, trying to keep control of his voice and nerves.

He was already sweating profusely and the pain of the previous assaults woke up everywhere in him, feeding his terror. He didn't give up, however, and pulled harder to regain his imprisoned wrists. Without even thinking about it, Gus sent a forward kick that hit the nichan's tibia; it wasn't what he was aiming for.

"You want to play this game?" Beïka laughed as he leaned over Gus, insensitive to the attack. "Then let's play. Yes? All right. Let's give you exactly what you're asking for."

With a gesture so quick it blended into the darkness, Beïka released one of Gus's arms, clasped the nape of his neck and held tight. The next second, the man twisted the human's arm, turning it inexorably. With a loud bang, Beïka slammed him against the wall and tore a handful of his hair in the process.

Breathless, the wood flaying his face still swollen and stained from the previous strikes, Gus groaned. He complained all the more when Beïka's hand closed on his dead wing. The nichan touched it, but Gus didn't know exactly what he was doing with it. This little atrophied wing was devoid of sensation from its base. Gus could only wince as the weight of the limb fluctuated against his scapula. If Beïka had cut the skin, Gus wouldn't have felt a thing. But then Beïka moved on to the next wing. And the twisting and pulling started.

Unable to turn around, Gus hit the wall with his free fist.

"What? Does it hurt?" Beïka asked in a lazy voice.

A searing pain arched down Gus's back. He didn't know what Beïka was doing to his wing, but he wanted it to stop. It had to stop. With anger vibrating through his entire body, Gus forced himself to keep his teeth clenched, even as Beïka tested the strength of the thin, sensitive membrane by squishing it into his grip.

"We should cut it, what do you say?" said the nichan as he opened and pulled at the trembling wing Gus was trying to fold against his back. "That shit would make a nice fan."

You motherfucker! I'll make you pay for this!

Gus's lips remained sealed. One more word, one more complaint, and Beïka would get exactly what he wanted. But as he tugged and tugged on the wing, as if to lengthen it, Gus couldn't help but struggle, contracting the limb made of fine bones and fragile cartilage.

"You're right, monster, we shouldn't rush. What about taking some time to think instead? We'll cut it off another day," Beïka promised.

Then his hand went down the middle of Gus's back, down his spine, and forced Gus's pants down. A sharp, violent movement that ripped the seams holding the fabric. The cool night air bit the young man's exposed flesh, urging him to move, to free himself. He wanted to scream.

Until now, Beïka had never undressed him. Hitting Gus, insulting him, spitting on him, had always seemed to be enough. Tonight he'd just crossed a line.

Without warning, Beïka rested his hand on Gus's ass. His fingers were hot and dry, cracked from work. "I really don't get why he likes you so much. You look like shit. Look at that ass. What came over the Gods' head when they created humans?" Beïka's palm came and went on Gus's skin, pinching the flesh, snapping it with the flat of his hand with enough force to leave a rash. "Hey, tell me. Did he fuck you? Come on, you can talk, it's just the two of us. Did my stupid little brother have the balls to lay you on your stomach and fuck you?"

The touch as much as the words revolted Gus. He growled. A

thick sob of hate and disgust clutched his throat. And Beïka's hand slipped between his cheeks.

"Let me go," Gus hissed through his teeth. Immediately, the hand slipped farther in. "No!" He twitched his muscles, wiggled. Unable to get free, he squeezed his legs. Behind him, Beïka laughed, happy to finally get that lively reaction he'd been waiting for so long.

Then he inserted a finger inside Gus.

I'm gonna kill him! I'm gonna kill him! I'm gonna kill him . . .

"Domino wouldn't like it if someone else fucked you," Beïka whispered in his ear, his breath reinforcing Gus's nausea. Pressure grew as another finger was added. "But maybe I should help myself, too. Stop moving, or I'll find something other than my fingers. There's plenty of branches outside."

His fingers sank even farther, more threatening, pulling a strangled moan out of Gus. Then Beïka insisted beyond what anatomy should accept and pressed his full weight against Gus. The pain grew as Gus contracted, refusing the penetration. Caught between the wall and the nichan, he stopped breathing altogether. One breath, and he would call for help. It would be the end of him. No one would come to help him. Beïka's satisfaction would reach new heights.

"You disgust me. It's not my thing. Men, I mean. But I could do it," Beïka mused, giving a brutal jerk that hammered against his hand like a mallet on the back of an ice pick. "I could mount you like an animal, make you scream and bleed, just to spite him. Then he'd understand that I'm not to be toyed with. My brother wants me on my knees. I'll get him on his knees. I'll make him beg me." Another push of the hand. "Or maybe you can beg for him. To give me an idea. Are you gonna beg? Are you? Come on, to please me. Just do it. Beg me!"

His fingers folded on themselves, and pain radiated all over Gus's body. His mouth opened against his will. "Stop it!"

"Again!"

The pain intensified in furious shocks, again and again and again . . . Choking under his own skin, Gus whimpered, "S-stop, please! Please!"

They stayed in this aching pressure for a few more endless seconds.

Beïka giggled. "I wish he'd heard you. Faces! You were born for that, monster. We'll practice again, don't worry. I'd hate to disappoint my little brother." He freed his hand, wiped it on Gus's shoulder, leaving a trail of blood, and let go the next moment.

Gus stood still. Yet his instincts told him to react, to flee, to get away from the predator, to hide. He couldn't do it. Facing the wall, half-naked, he waited with his heart suspended on the edge of his lips.

He didn't see Beïka leave, only heard the door creak and close. He then pulled up his trousers with hasty gestures, his sweaty hands both clumsy and tense.

Gus remained in the middle of the room for a long time. The tension in him threatened to break him in half. Standing on wobbly legs, he was expecting the door to open any second. When nothing happened for the next few minutes, he thought about going out. He couldn't stay here. He had to leave.

He walked toward the door and stopped. A voice in his head told him that Beïka might be on the other side, that he might have anticipated Gus's next move. So the young man hesitated for an eternity.

Brace yourself. Don't let yourself be caged.

But he was in a cage, and Surhok was his prison.

Domino's passage, the hole in the wall . . .

Gus hadn't been there in years, hadn't thought about it for just as long. After the accident that had lured the dohor to the village and hastened Mora's death, he and Domino had avoided leaving the territory again. But Gus had closed the passageway after they returned from their trip outside. Maybe that breach still existed. Gus could do it; he could run away. Or at least plan his departure.

He had to make sure of that.

Still tense with fear, he grabbed the lamp and forced himself to open the hut door. In the narrow gap, he couldn't detect the slightest movement. In the distance, through the song of the night breeze, voices echoed from inside another house, and even farther away, laughter. But the place was deserted. Without further ado, the young man went out and cautiously walked away from his home. He didn't run into anyone, but stopped several times, hiding, becoming one with the shadows, to make sure he was alone. When the woods finally opened up in front of him, he quickened his pace after peering over his shoulder one last time.

His lamp offered him little light, but he soon found his way and the section of wall Domino had opened for them three years ago—at least, Gus was sure it was here. Beneath the branches hovering above him and swaying in the wind, he approached the bamboo ramparts and pushed. He pushed harder, testing one after another, the trunks thicker than his own thighs. The wall resisted and never shifted an inch.

Harder.

He found a safe spot to place his hot lamp and pressed against the bottom of the wall with both hands. That wasn't enough. Domino had struck. So Gus struck. He used his shoulder on different portions of the wall, over and over again. After a handful of minutes, he'd moved so far away from his lamp that he couldn't even see the wall standing a few inches under his nose. He returned to the trembling flame and cleared the plants growing at the base of the trunks, in order to spot the breach and stop wasting his time. His efforts were disappointing yet again. The bamboo seemed deeply embedded in the ground. Even when Gus scratched with his fingernails, pushing away the earth teeming with insects, nothing revealed itself to him. Not a single gap betrayed the location of Domino's opening.

With his heart pounding harder and harder, Gus pressed both hands on the wall and pushed anyway. He couldn't stop. He just couldn't.

But reality came over him. The wall had been repaired. The nichans would never have left such a flaw in their ramparts.

The young man's throat tightened. He was trapped. He could go all the way around the village to find a weakness in the wall, but the result would probably be the same.

In a cage. With a pair of wings unable to carry him to the other side.

Still leaning against the wall, Gus felt his strength running out. His breathing became faster and faster, stronger and stronger. So why was he suffocating? Why was air not enough anymore?

Just breathe, you fool. Breathe!

He'd said the almost same words to Domino dozens of times, maybe more. Domino, who panicked, who lost control, who let his emotions get the better of him. Domino, who cried.

No, that can't be it . . . that can't be . . .

His chest tightened, making his breath hiss.

No, I'm stronger than that!

His throat was painfully sealed.

I don't want to. I don't want to.

His eyes burned.

Unable to resist any longer, his eyes filled with tears. A violent sob shook Gus. With a trembling hand, he forced his mouth shut to compel himself to silence. The next sob bent his spine, and Gus groaned through his fingers pressed hard against his lips.

He had held on all these years. It was now beyond his capacity.

Tears streamed down his face, getting lost in the weeds.

Shaken to his core, Gus hit the wall with his fist. The hollow wood absorbed the shocks, so he hit harder, yielding to anger.

How could it have come to this? He'd always told himself he wouldn't let anyone break him. He'd been hanged, he'd been given a taste of the power of the Op Crystal. But all it took was for Domino to go away to leave him defenseless. He'd survived the rope because of Domino. He'd survived the crystal because of Domino. But this time, there was no guarantee of escape. With Beïka lurking in the shadows, Gus might not survive until Domino's return.

If he ever comes back.

He hated to think like that, but he had to consider it, prepare for it. Gus had always thought he would be alone, that the ones who mattered to him would forever abandon him. Then Domino had managed to convince him otherwise.

Now he was alone. Again.

His tears subsided after endless minutes. He uncovered his mouth, wiped the saliva from his palm against his pants, and got himself up on his legs, ignoring the pain between them. The young man wavered forward, suddenly weak. He hadn't slept or eaten since . . . He couldn't tell. A fleeting thought crossed his mind. He could lay here, sleep on the ground, away from the village. A ridiculous idea. Any nichan could smell him. And what little dignity he had left had to be preserved. Since there was no hiding or running away, he might as well not humiliate himself trying.

He grabbed his lamp and slowly retreated to the village heart.

XXVIII

"Don't make excuses for me to follow you. I still have all my common sense, and I'm telling you this: going south is as clever right now as diving headfirst into a pile of fresh shit." Feanim got up and put the bandage he'd just removed into one of his boxes.

At his feet, sitting in the dewy grass, Domino closed his tunic and sighed. After more than a week camping in the woods, doing nothing but resting, he was more than eager to get back on the road. But his body didn't agree. His belly was still sensitive, and Domino was afraid to stand up straight and reopen the wounds that healed with a slowness Gus's care hadn't prepared him for. Next to him, Memek stared thoughtfully at the scratches that extended over ten inches on his skin, then she sighed. Was she thinking the same? They would have left this camp much sooner if Gus had gone with them.

A place like this is too dangerous for him. He's safe in Surhok. That's all that matters.

The group gathered its belongings and set off at a moderate pace. Feanim joined them for a while in silence. After the last few days in his company, it had become clear the man had no intention of opening up about himself. Then he diverged at a crossroads to take the westward path.

"Don't get killed," he said, turning around, pulling his wheelbarrow behind him in no hurry, its wheels cutting furrows in the wet earth. "And you—be careful with your shoulder."

Domino nodded, realizing he was massaging his shoulder, which still caused him to lose control of his arm from time to time. He would get better, he wanted to believe it, but Feanim had remained vague on the subject. And now that he was heading for the most dangerous part of the region, Domino had no choice but to deal with it on his own.

He turned away from Feanim and forced his legs on to keep up with his uncle and cousin.

They skirted the last southernmost lake in the Osska region for several days under a dense drizzle and a sky speckled with black spots, heralds of a Corruption Rain. The rain came from the north, forcing them to halt and find shelter. When they resumed their journey hours later, Domino's right arm spasmed incessantly after carrying over his head his wooden puck, which had gotten heavy with black, sticky residue.

But now that they were on their way again, nothing could have stopped Ero, not even the sky falling on their heads.

At the end of that first week, they met a couple of exhausted humans heading north. The news was the same as the ones the group had gathered in Kepam or even faced themselves: unpleasant. Although Ero kept a suspicious look on these humans, he listened carefully to what the two travelers announced.

A small nichan clan had been attacked farther south. Partisans had set fire to the village and killed many people before being hunted down by their victims. The two travelers preferred to turn back, fearing to be caught in the crossfire.

They added, however, that a fishing village called Noktchen, several leagues to the south, treated nichans well—from what they'd witnessed—and had hot springs. A glimmer of hope filled Memek's eyes.

Senses on the lookout, the Uetos walked along the waves for several hours—a cold wind swept across their faces—and found the village. Noktchen was more a hamlet than a village, however. Its few black wooden houses on stilts faced the waters, and only a wet net recently pulled out of the lake was evidence of the presence of inhabitants.

They slipped between the houses. Not a soul in sight but many hearts beat through the wooden walls. At least Domino hadn't lost his senses. And he couldn't deny the performance of his nose as a particular smell floating through the ruffling sea spray drew a wince to his face.

Rotting fish. By the Faces, Domino hated the taste of fish as much as the smell, and the early years of his life spent by the sea hadn't improved his distaste.

The scent burned his nostrils, and Memek smiled. "That's all they'll have to eat here. You'd better get used to it," she said, pushing him toward the biggest house in the village.

Ero was already knocking on the door. A moment passed. The panel slid out, and an elderly human with long, graying hair tied in a catogan examined them one by one. He wiped his hands on his apron. Blood. Fish blood. Domino resisted the urge to cover his nose.

"Ohay," said Ero.

The man's nod was his only answer as he found a way, despite his small size compared to the three nichans, to look down on them.

"We're looking for shelter for the night," Ero continued. "We have furs to sell, or to trade."

"I don't buy, I don't trade," said the man in an equal tone.

"All right. Does anyone in the village offer food and lodging? We might have enough to pay."

"I have room. Six heads for three people."

The breath of the sea wind whistled in their ears as the man announced his price. A little expensive for a small fishermen's village. But the clouds in the sky kept getting darker, and it was likely to rain again, which was clearly a common occurrence in the area. Night approached. Ero must have been thinking the same, for he pulled his purse from the inside of his tunic and presented the six silver coins requested of him.

The human accepted them and stepped aside to let them in.

Five men and three women sat at a low table, playing cards. One of them seemed to have fallen asleep, eyes closed and chin resting on his chest. They all wore shawls made of bear or sheep fur, and the cotton of their ponchos was of a more or less faded red ochre, depending on the individual. Another thing they had in common: they all looked suspiciously at Domino and his family when they entered.

The room was small, dark, already crowded, and fogged with a long pipe the humans shared between themselves, taking turns spouting curls of smoke.

The owner showed the newcomers a corner where they could sit. All that remained was a small bench facing a low table. A bench on a human scale, far too small for more than one nichan. As Unaan, Ero claimed it, letting Domino and Memek sit on the woven hemp floor. As the owner returned to them with a steaming tureen and three spoons, Domino sniffed the air. The scent of fish was everywhere. In the customers' clothes, in the carpets on the floor, on the nets hanging on the walls, in the soup Ero eyed behind his thick eyebrows.

But there was something else. A different smell that even rotting fish or tobacco couldn't hide. A smell of death. Not the fish's.

Domino decided at that moment, regardless of his dislike for fisherman's cooking, that he wouldn't touch the soup. Facing him, Ero and Memek ignored the food with the same suspicious expression. Something wasn't right.

Out of the corner of his eye, Domino checked the men and women sitting at the next table. They looked like travelers, with their swollen pouches and rolled-up tents. Yet none of them carried a weapon. All human travelers the Uetos had met since they left Surhok had a stick in hand, or a knife, for the wiser ones. Not them. It was as if these people had relieved themselves of their weapons on the way here. It was as if . . .

More hearts pounded, like a diffuse rumbling. Impossible to count them. Domino felt them approaching. Outside.

He barely had time to question Ero when the humans at the next table rose in one motion. Worn metal whistled in a dissonant harmony as they all pulled long machetes from under their table. Near the stove, the host pulled a pistol from behind his workbench. The metal glowed through the smoke.

The nichans leapt to their feet.

"Don't let them attack!" shouted one of the humans.

They all charged at the same time. Domino drew his knife from the inside of his clothes; Ero and Memek transformed. The door slammed open and a group of armed men entered, joining the ambush. At the same time, Memek and her father stood in front of Domino.

His heart stopped. They were surrounded.

They needed a way out.

Now!

A way out!

His brain considered the options. The wide opened door. A narrow window on the other side of the house. At least twenty humans blocking the way to both issues. There was only one solution left. To create another exit.

Domino turned and banged his healthy shoulder against the wall. The wood was reinforced but worm-eaten. He could break it, even in his human form. As the hiss of blades clashing nichan claws rang behind him, he hammered again with all his might. On the periphery of his vision, a first man collapsed, the glistening tubes of his guts exposed, the white fur of his shawl turning crimson. A woman dropped dead the next second, the side of her head pierced with five holes. This didn't discourage the other humans, who split the air with their machetes, avoiding Memek's and Ero's attacks.

No time to waste. Domino struck again. The wood gave way, revealing the dim light of day on the other side. Soon after, a gunshot rang out, and Memek screamed.

Time stopped.

Terror compressing his heart, Domino turned. Metal danced in the air, reflecting the colors of the shed blood filling the room. A blade spun before his eyes and hit Domino on his left shoulder. No pain, or so little that it could be ignored—a scratch compared to what the bear had done to him. But it was enough to awaken Domino's rage. His body reacted faster than his mind, suppressing everything but his survival instinct and strength. He thrusted his leg forward, heel first, aiming for his opponent's knee. The bones broke and the leg bent in an unnatural angle, like a twig. The man fell to the ground, screaming his lungs out, and Domino froze. A step from him was Ero, a machete stuck in his foot, two more blades threatening his throat and nape. Farther away, Memek lay on the ground, howling in pain. Her rust-colored blood mingled on the carpet with that of two slaughtered humans.

Then hands grabbed Domino. A blade slipped under his chin, meeting the throbbing skin of his throat.

"On your knees!"

Domino complied, hands up in surrender, letting his own

knife slip from his grasp. He glanced at Ero, who never took his eyes off his daughter, his face drenched with human blood. Several watchful men were already tying Memek's wrists. Her leg bled profusely. The bottom of her trousers was shredded, her calf riddled with fragments of Kispen crystal.

Then they tied up her father. Hands behind his back, another rope around his torso to immobilize his arms. The machete hammered in his foot kept him nailed to the now-soaked floor. The ropes were then wrapped around Domino's wrists and chest, and Memek was forced to stand despite the severity of her injury. When she failed to get on her feet, crying and grunting at her aggressor's face, one of the fuckers decided that dragging her on the floor if necessary was a valid solution.

Then a linen bag reeking of sweat and dirt fell on Domino's face.

Trusting his ears, his nose, the length of his every step, Domino kept track of the following events in his mind. They were pushed out of the house, then through the village. The partisans both led and closed the procession. Apart from Memek's panting and moaning, the dragging of her injured body on the ground, and the lapping of the swell, only silence. No one spoke, not Ero, nor the many humans who obviously didn't come from this village.

The smell that Domino had detected—the stench of death— came back to his memory. It was a similar smell that emanated from the dead wild pigs the Uetos brought back from the hunt. Domino was certain that if he'd searched Noktchen, he would have found the roughly buried bodies of the real inhabitants of this village.

These were numerous, well-trained Blessers' partisans. The human couple who'd encouraged them to stop by Noktchen to rest was probably in league with them.

Those assholes. *We have to run*, Domino thought. *There's too many of these motherfuckers for us.*

"Don't touch me!" Memek wailed between grumbles.

A few steps away, Domino was hurled flat to the ground as the clash between Ero, Memek, and the humans resumed. Heavy breathing, grunting, muffled sounds of fists and blades biting flesh. Domino thought about getting up. Even blinded by the damn bag, he could use the distraction to strike back. But two feet crashed heavily into his back. A human had just climbed on top of him with both feet, pinning him to the ground, limiting his mobility. Domino gritted his teeth when pain awakened in his violently crushed belly.

The next second, Ero growled. Then Domino jumped at the shock of a huge mass crashing right next to him with an abrupt gasp.

"Papa!" Memek shouted as Domino recognized Ero's scent close to him.

Memek would bleed to death in no time without a tourniquet. Ero could carry her, even with an injured foot . . . if running away was still an option. They were tied up, surrounded. And Ero seemed to have lost his position of power for good. His status as Unaan no longer meant anything in the face of the death reserved for them.

After a brief minute, Domino was put back on his feet, pulled by the ties that held his arms behind his back. Memek's moaning resumed. Ero's breath, barely noticeable among the heavy steps, the waves and rushing wind, was now fickle, modified by pain.

Or fear.

A blade still pointed in their back, or slitting their throat, they marched forward. Then they were thrown to the ground in one blow behind the knees. The bag remained on Domino's head. The next moment, something closed around the nichan's neck. He recognized the rough texture of the rope, its weight, its smell—a mixture of hemp, dust and sweat.

A fucking rope...

Those men were going to hang them, just like those assholes who had hanged Gus.

Don't you dare!

Domino immediately struggled.

Omitting the sharp pain beneath his ribs, he leaped to his feet and charged the nearest man with all his weight, with all his strength, still relying on his senses. His hip and bloodied shoulder smashed into the chest of the partisan he was aiming at. Domino heard his target fall and bellow in shock. He let the asshole's screams empower him and moved into position.

He was blind, but he had to fight. He wouldn't die without giving his all.

He sniffed the air, trying to spot his uncle and cousin through the cloth. They were close.

The next moment, someone pulled the rope wrapped around his throat. Air failed to reach his lungs, but Domino resisted, straining all his muscles, starting with those of his neck. He stepped back sharply to unbalance anyone clinging to the other end of the rope. They pulled harder. The rope tightened and this time Domino collapsed. His head hit the ground. Pain and blood ragged inside his skull. They kept pulling on the rope. The young man was dragged through the tall grass by the neck. Someone shouted to get it over with. His bonds were impossible to break. In his true form, Domino could cut them. He knew it.

Impossible to concentrate, to even try.

Then his body rose. Pulled up by his neck, Domino flapped his legs.

No! Not that!

A blast from his past came into him amidst the emptiness and terror overwhelming him. Gus, small and frail, soaked in alcohol, hung from a tree, his legs jerking in spasms as oxygen abandoned him. This time Domino couldn't get out of the bushes to save him.

Gus.

His heart pounded in his ears. His head seemed to be gorged with too much blood. It would just explode, separating from the rest of his body. He couldn't breathe or tolerate it.

Before long, he would be dead.

He felt the heat and the hissing of flames.

Death by fire and pain, Mora had explained to him. The Blessers' purification.

Air, air. Faces above!

A distant, diffused roar rose, as if the world itself was rebelling. The next second Domino fell and crashed heavily to the ground.

Air.

Air filtered down his throat, spread through his chest. Beneath his panting body, the world shook harder.

Something was coming.

"It's here! *Run! Run!*"

Domino felt the humans running around him, then racing away. They were all heading in the same direction. North.

A scream erupted. Slumped to the side, Domino instantly forgot his injured shoulder, the rope still wrapped around his neck, Memek, and Ero, whose fates remained unclear to him.

This howling entwined his innards like a snake twisting itself around its prey, paralyzing him. He'd never heard such a call before. And yet . . .

It was both his earliest and deepest memory, stronger than the first cry of a newborn, sharper than a blade detaching the flesh from the bone.

Human and nichan screams added to the tumult. Fighting everywhere, human blood streaming, saturating the earth. It didn't last long. Within seconds, the humans all stopped running and yelling. The echoes of their heartbeats died with them.

"Are they conscious?" asked a deep voice.

"Take the masks off," said another one.

Domino waited, motionless, full of the call that had just filled him with fear but also hope. Then the bag that covered his head vanished. The raw light of the sky and the steppes irritated his eyes. He didn't care. A nichan leaned over him, untying the rope that bound his torso, and reduced his breath to a trickle of air. He didn't care either. He looked around him, on the lookout. Nichans everywhere, most of them transformed, a few in their human forms.

Then he saw the creature. Time halted its course.

It looked at him with its black, shining eyes, in the depths of which burned a bluish spark. The creature was as massive as a dohor but thicker, as if shaped in the purest essence of strength. It was black as nothingness, so deep no light could cling to its skin. Its powerful legs were longer at the front, like muscular arms. The claws disappeared into the ground and blended with the earth, smearing it with dark traces the way water flows between rocks.

A golden ring surrounded the beast's mouth, like a necklace.

No, not a necklace.

This ring floated without making the slightest contact with anything other than air.

Faces above . . .

And that smile . . .

Domino stood up without thinking. Someone called him. He walked toward the creature who only had eyes for him, who was waiting for him, motionless. He sniffed the breeze by instinct. The creature was female.

Domino stopped one step away from her. He looked at her entire body, filling his mind with all the details he could capture, plunging his eyes into hers. He didn't need to ask. He knew, he felt it in his whole being. The humming had returned, not in his own body, but in that of the creature. Domino could hear it.

The tingling buzzing.

Not the taint of the Corruption, but pure nichan essence.

A pure blood, no different than their ancestors from before the Great Evil. This was what stood before him.

Hands still tied behind his back, the rope hanging from his neck dragging behind him, he took a deep breath. "Can you feel it?" Domino asked in a hoarse voice. He coughed briefly.

The beast came a little closer. Her nostrils were invisible in the black expanse of her face. Nothing could be deciphered except her eyes and the threatening dark spikes of her smile. But she sniffed him nonetheless and tilted her head to the side.

Domino continued, enthralled. "I felt you approaching. Do you feel it too? I am . . . I'm like you. They say I'm like you. I . . . I can't transform, but I'm like you. You know that, right? Do you feel it, too?"

A hand grabbed Domino by the arm and forced him to step back and fall to his knees. He was too out of his own body to protest. But the beast reacted on his behalf to the distance placed between them. She growled at the person who had just separated them, and the hand holding Domino moved away. Still unaware of his pain and the rest of the world, Domino got back on his feet, once again, and waited. The beast peered into his eyes. Domino was sure that this nichan understood him, that they both felt the force binding them to each other, like the surge of a forgotten past suddenly restored. If that was the case, then it meant one thing: his essence, what made Domino a pure blood, hadn't disappeared. He was still the same. Whole.

A smile spread across Domino's lips. For the first time, he understood what the others meant when they spoke of miracles.

"Lienn," said a woman near Domino. "Is he telling the truth?"

The beast made a hollow sound that echoed around them like

the rumble of thunder, then nodded slowly. Whispers rose up everywhere. Domino finally dared to look away from her and scanned the area. Among the small crowd of nichans, he spotted the gibbet from which he had just been hanged, and then Ero who, ignoring his own injured foot, carried Memek in his arms. The Unaan had taken off his shawl and tied it around his daughter's thigh in a tight garrote.

Domino's and Ero's eyes met. The man's expression was indecipherable but tense.

The beast remained motionless for a while, staring at Domino. His wrists were still tied and he struggled against its restraints.

"Leave it to me," intervened the nichan next to him, a tall woman who, under her armor of skin and metal bands, seemed as muscular as Domino.

She untied the ropes, and Domino pulled the one hanging to his throat and threw it away. By the time he looked up, the pure blood had turned tail, unhurriedly moving away in a graceful gait, as her hunters followed. The rest of them were already busy burying the dead as the air around them filled in a black mist.

Domino watched the beast. He wanted to follow her. He resisted the impulse.

"Our camp is a few leagues farther south," the woman next to him announced, her eyes troubled, studying Domino's still flushed face through the dark particles. "Can you walk?" The young man nodded. "Good. If it's all right with you, come along."

That most certainly is.

"Domino!" Ero called out to him. "Go get our things."

The order brought Domino out of his bewilderment. The cold crept in and blew a gust of wind through his sweat-soaked hair, biting the cut still drooling blood down his arm. Returning for good to reality, he rubbed his neck to chase the sensation of the rope from his flesh.

Is that what Gus feels? Every time he has a nightmare, he feels this bloody rope around his neck?

Well, now Domino knew the feeling. The anger inside him boiled over again.

The scent of human blood rose from the bodies lying in the golden grass. Before the eyes of several curious nichans, Domino set off, passing his uncle and his cousin, returning to the fishermen's village where they'd been attacked.

As he arrived there, alone and out of sight, his heart fluttering, he smiled. Then a hysterical laugh carried him away and Domino let himself forget everything that had gone wrong for months. In fact, for years. Before he knew it, he leaned against a house and cried through his laughter.

Today, he'd once again felt the kiss of death. But today he might have been saved for good.

PART FOUR

PRECIOUS BLOOD

XXIX

THE CAMP PRESENTED ITSELF TO THEM A FEW HOURS LATER AS the night gradually deprived the world of its light. Beautifully crafted leather tents lined up in several straight rows. They edged a modest, twisted pine wood on the other side of where steep, rocky hills gushed out of the ground.

Armored nichans guarded the camp. They welcomed the hunters who returned unharmed, greeting them warmly with a hug or a relieved handshake. The beast, who had guided the group for hours, walked quietly between the tents and then moved out of sight. Walking in his uncle's steps, Domino looked for her, scanning the darkening area, ignoring the glances cast at him and his family.

The woman who had untied him after the ambush came to meet them. She had short black hair and icy gray eyes. A scar ran across her lower lip, slightly deflecting the slope of her mouth. When she spoke to the Uetos, Domino noticed a missing incisor on the lower part of her dentition.

"Let's take care of your wounds. Follow me, please."

In a tent heated by braziers, Memek was attended to

immediately. Her wound was nasty, the crystal splinters deeply embedded in her partially shredded muscles. Ero squeezed his daughter's hand, and a nichan who introduced himself as the camp physician proceeded to retrieve all the shards. None were to be left. The damage was already serious enough to make the young physician pale.

After pulling several screams from Memek, the man concluded that the situation required more careful attention. "I have to make an incision to—"

"I don't care about that," roared Ero. "Just do what needs to be done and do it now!"

"Papa, stop," Memek breathed, sweating profusely, out of breath. Despite the tourniquet, the young woman had lost a lot of blood in the last hour. Her face was terribly pale, her voice agonizing. "I don't want that shit under my skin. Just don't . . . "

Ero squeezed his daughter's hand harder as her voice died and bent to kiss her fingers, as if to stop himself from talking. Standing behind him, Domino remembered an Ero overflowing with hatred after his son's death. An Ero so devastated he'd lost his sanity. Domino had no desire to see that man again. They were far from home, outnumbered by a small army of hunters in armor and a pure blood. If Ero went after this healer, no one would forgive him on the pretext that he was worried about his daughter.

She's going to live. It's only her leg. She's going to be okay.

But Domino was concerned too. Once again, his uncle and his cousin had shielded his body to protect him. The young man refused to let his cousin lose her leg—or her life—for him.

The physician put Memek to sleep with a handkerchief soaked in a smelly liquid that twisted Domino's stomach. Then he took out new instruments from a brown leather-covered wooden box and proceeded.

A few steps behind his uncle, Domino looked up, the back of

his neck and skull relaxing. Something had changed in the air, something familiar. A shiver mixed with the warmth of blood pumped by a powerful heart. That presence . . . The pure blood, she was close.

Domino looked toward the entrance. The wind shook the sides of the infirmary tent. The aura was getting closer. Domino swallowed hard when a woman with ashy blonde hair pushed the skins open and entered. The outside breeze came in with her, stirring the flames into the braziers. Domino was seeing her in this form for the first time, but he recognized her essence, like an imprint in fresh earth. It was the same beast who had saved them from the partisans and brought them here.

She stopped at the entrance and looked at Domino with dark brown eyes. She was as tall as he was. Her olive skin was lighter than that of the Uetos. She had a long face with a broad forehead. Her thick lips opened up for a moment, then closed again, lips on which a tattoo began, extending down to her chin, her throat, getting lost under the fabric of her tunic.

The young woman wore honorary marks. This detail troubled Domino without his knowing why.

"You'd better come with me," said the woman without taking her eyes off him. He himself couldn't look away. "This isn't the most appropriate place to talk."

Domino opened his mouth but Ero got up and stood in front of his nephew. Such a reaction announced his position of Unaan with a single movement. Annoyance rolled under Domino's skin.

"I don't think I know your name," said Ero. "Or your intentions. So my nephew won't follow you anywhere."

The woman remained completely insensitive to Ero's refusal. She still forced herself to look at him before continuing. "I'm Riskan Lienn, daughter of the chief of the Riskan Clan."

"Ueto Ero. My daughter." He pointed to the bed where the

sleeping young woman was being treated. "Ueto Memek, and my nephew."

Surprisingly, he didn't introduce Domino, as if to hinder what was happening between Lienn and the young man.

Domino took care of it himself. "I am Ueto Domino."

Lienn turned her attention back to him and nodded. "My intentions will be inconsequential. I only want to discuss without disturbing your child's rest, Ueto Ero."

"This can wait," the man said.

What was his game? Why so much mistrust? Lienn and her clan had just saved them from a terrible fate.

"I've been waiting ten years to meet and talk to another . . . to someone like me," said the young woman, determined despite the exhaustion burdening her eyes.

"Waiting a few more hours shouldn't be a problem, then. I want to be there when you talk to him."

"You're ridiculous," said Domino, his face warm, a discomfort falling into the pit of his stomach as he pronounced those words.

"Say that again."

"You're ridiculous." This time the discomfort disappeared and Domino shook his head, a bitter laugh shaking him. He was tired of his uncle's games. "What do you think they're gonna do to me?" he asked in a low voice, even though everyone in the tent could hear him without having to pay attention. "Let me talk to her, just for a few minutes. Please, Ero. They saved us. They are taking care of your daughter."

Ero's angry expression didn't change. It also betrayed the pain rising up his leg and making him shake. His foot had been pierced through, and no one had yet examined him.

"Get treated," Domino said. "In the meantime, I'm going to have a chat with our host. You can indulge yourself when I come back and order me to tell you every single detail. I won't even complain."

Ero's hand then rested on Domino's shoulder, heavy, close to the wound left by the machete, like a warning. "You don't know her, you don't know what she wants, and yet you're ready to trust her and follow her?"

A bitter taste ran down Domino's tongue. The taste of betrayal and scorn. It was almost amusing to hear Ero speak of trust. What did he know about trust when he himself had broken his oath by sticking a blade in Domino's face? Since then, he'd insulted, beaten and humiliated him.

"I'm still with you," Domino said.

Indeed, despite all that Ero had done to him, he'd remained in Surhok even though the idea of running away with Gus after Mora's death had crossed his mind more than once. He'd thought that despite his behavior, Ero would protect him. He had, but at what cost? Ero was pulling the strings and manipulating in every way possible the blood oath tying them to each other. There was no trust between them; only a bond of necessity.

Domino continued. "There are nearly a hundred hunters in this camp. You probably know that; you're not the kind of man to overlook that kind of information. If she wanted to hurt me, or capture me, she would have done it by now. She wouldn't lower herself to politely asking your permission first."

The young man's words hit the nail on the head. Ero let go of him. All anger appeared to have left him. On the surface, Domino knew.

"Go. Then come back here."

Without showing his relief or impatience, for Ero's every decision had consequences, Domino took a step back and turned to Lienn. She stared at them, slightly frowning. She took a deep breath and left the infirmary, Domino on her heels. As he passed the exit, the young man refused to look back.

He followed Lienn between the tents, conscious of the glances being cast at him through the warm light of the torches, of the muffled murmurs carried in the wind, and the hunters on the alert waiting for them at the exit of the infirmary. They followed in Lienn and Domino's footsteps, as intimidating as a whip about to strike.

They entered a small tent, leaving their escort outside. However, the nichans scattered to surround the tent. Their heartbeats were as loud in Domino's ears as those that echoed in his own chest.

A brazier awaited them inside, along with a huge armchair covered in fur and multicolored fabrics richly decorated with circular patterns. *This chair*, Domino said to himself, *isn't for just any ass.*

When Lienn turned to him and observed him again, he gathered his thoughts and took a deeper breath. It was strange to look this woman in the eyes, to see her soft, tired face, and at the same time to feel the power lurking inside her.

"Thank you," he said. "Thank you for rescuing us."

"Your thanks will come after you forgive me."

"Forgive you for . . . "

"For almost acting too late." She filled her lungs, joining her hands in front of her. "My clan has been after these partisans for weeks. They're organized, with what we believe to be spies scattered throughout the region. We spotted them and were about to attack, hidden away, when you and your family arrived."

Domino tried not to lose track as the new information got tangled with his growing excitement. "You mean . . . you were already there?"

"I felt you, but I didn't recognize you. What you are. I'd never felt it in anyone else."

"I only felt you when you got closer to stop those humans."

"The transformation heightens all my senses. I found myself as if paralyzed . . . and frightened. The others waited for me to attack. They waited for my orders. And I almost didn't give this one."

Resisting the urge to touch his throat, Domino nodded slowly. "It's a chance the Gods gave me a strong neck." He managed to smile even though the fate he might have met a few hours earlier hardly amused him.

"I'm sorry," Lienn said. "I really am."

"Well, you gave the order. That's . . . what matters."

"Yes."

"If you hadn't arrived . . . " He paused, aware that he was talking to fill the silence and hide his bitterness. He didn't want to blame the woman. "I think we both know what would have happened. There is nothing to forgive. Let's leave it at that."

"Let's leave it at that?" she repeated. "What, already? Is that all you have to say to me?" She smiled, a glimmer shining in her eyes, no doubt amused at his confusion.

Domino sighed, laughing in spite of himself. "To tell you the truth, I'm having . . . some difficulty thinking tonight. The rest of the time, I'm less of a fool than I look."

"You don't need to justify yourself. Domino." She said his name as if to get used to it. She moistened her lips. *Pretty lips.* "How old are you?"

Domino took a moment to think about it. The last two months had passed by at breakneck speed, yet he felt like he'd been traveling for ages.

"Seventeen."

"You're younger than you look."

"So I've been told."

She seemed pensive. "Have you been through your seasons?"

Domino raised his eyebrows. "Is that all you have to say to me?" he repeated, and Lienn lowered her eyes and smiled.

"Forgive me, once again. That was . . . inappropriate." He couldn't deny it but kept the comment to himself. The blush on her face was enough to confirm the sincerity of her words. "Where are you from? A much more decent question, right?"

"Right," Domino smiled. Once again, thinking too much about the creature in front of him, his thoughts became confused. Yet the questions were simple. "I'm from Surhok, a village north of the Osska region. It . . . it seems like the end of the world to me today."

"Are you hungry?" she asked then.

This was a question he could answer without difficulty. He nodded. "Yes."

"Calico!" called Lienn out loud, and seconds later, the broad-shouldered woman who had guided them to the infirmary entered the tent. "Somebody bring food to my guest."

"Yes, ma'am," nodded Calico, and she came out as quickly as she'd entered.

"We will do the same for your uncle and his daughter once they've been treated," Lienn added to Domino's address.

"Thank you."

"You don't need to thank me."

"One can never be too polite these days."

"In that case, thank you. You have . . . brightened up my day."

She seemed serious, always half-caught in her thoughts, maybe even a little intimidated, but Domino laughed anyway. "Brightening up the day" was an expression used sparingly among nichans. It was comparing a person to no less than the sun itself, the sun whose light everyone dreamed of seeing again one day—a light so intimately related to the lost Gods.

Such a compliment was strong.

"I could say the same to you," Domino replied.

"Would you like to sit down?"

"No," he said, still smiling.

He was exhausted, but his legs, like the rest of his body, were full of energy he wouldn't have been able to soothe even if he'd tried.

"What makes you smile like that?" she asked.

"I . . . I'm not sure. Exhaustion, maybe, but . . . we met, and I told you I couldn't transform. Yet here I am. You took me in without proof of what I am."

"I felt your aura. I still do."

"I can't transform."

His smile was gone. He had to make sure she understood that this situation, though miraculous, wasn't ideal. It wasn't just for her that he was repeating those words, but also for himself. He was too enthusiastic. He was in unknown lands, surrounded by strangers. He couldn't foresee what the future would bring after such a meeting.

But she had felt his aura, his presence.

Lienn quickly looked at him from head to toe. "What's the reason for that?"

Domino hesitated and opted for a half-truth. The real one was none of her business. "I've stopped myself from doing it for many years. For safety's sake."

The tent opened, Calico entered. She held in her hands a tray of salted meat and dark bread sprinkled with pumpkin seeds. She placed it by the fire and disappeared again. Domino was hungry, but he ignored the food for a while, sorting out his priorities.

"I want to transform again," he said. "I practice every day. I know I can do it. With your help—"

"Not with your uncle's, for sure."

"Probably not," Domino conceded after a pause.

"He's your Unaan," she said. "But you're a *Liyion*, a pure blood. You shouldn't have a leader. We're not suited for that."

The look they exchanged sent a wave of questions through Domino's head. Then an idea bloomed, watered by the lasting silence. He looked over Lienn's shoulder. The chair. Or rather, the throne. Had the young woman brought him here for a reason? he asked himself. In an instant he understood what she was keeping quiet while making herself clear.

Lienn said she was the daughter of the chief of the Riskan Clan. The power he felt in her, however, went beyond that of a pure blood meeting another.

She might as well have been the clan leader.

Maybe because they were identical, Domino could sense it. How could it be otherwise? All those hunters were following her, protecting her. The lie she'd told in the infirmary was meant for Ero.

What did she have in mind?

She added, "But my mother is a good leader. She has my absolute trust. We do understand each other."

The young woman's gaze intensified, supporting her words as much as what they concealed.

She'd just spoken of trust—as had Ero a few minutes earlier— reminding that her mother was the clan chief.

A lie.

Trust.

The blood oath.

What if Ero, once this conversation over, asked Domino to repeat everything to him. Every word pronounced by Lienn. Domino would say it all, he would have no choice. But none of Lienn's words betrayed the truth. Her dark eyes staring into his did so, as did the tent in which she had chosen to speak with him in private.

Am I reading too much into this?

"That's yours?" Domino asked, jerking his chin at the massive chair behind her.

The woman didn't turn yet answered, "Always. Do you see what I mean?" she asked then and the pieces of the picture fell into place. Lienn was the Unaan of the Riskan Clan.

The message grew inside him. For a reason he didn't know, Lienn wanted to hide from Ero that she was the leader. The other nichans of the Riskan Clan were probably ordered to keep it a secret.

Ero was right about one thing: Domino couldn't trust Lienn yet. But she'd just confided in him, either to prove her trust or to test him. Nevertheless, he trusted the young woman more than he trusted Ero, perhaps wrongly so.

He wouldn't tell his uncle the truth.

"I see," Domino said.

Lienn nodded. "We'll arrive in Visha in two days. We'll get to know each other better then. I guess your Unaan is looking forward to hearing your report. Eat, go back to him. Then get some rest. The journey is still long. In the meantime, I hope your uncle can cool his blood," Lienn added.

Domino raised an eyebrow with a sigh. "He would tell you that the warmth of his blood is none of your concern."

"Not on these lands."

Then she bent, grabbed and offered him the plate of food. He accepted it without taking his eyes off the young woman.

Liyion. That was what she called them both. Pure blood.

Then he realized how little he knew.

XXX

A LONE CLIFF, A DROP IN THE COASTLINE THAT ROSE ABOVE THE dark waves. It could be seen on the horizon from miles away. In the fading light of the day and a drizzle too fresh for the season, Domino stared at it, swallowing back the surge of excitement inviting him to speed up and take a closer look.

The hunting party, their guide, and protégés had been traveling for two days, but their goal was finally in sight.

Visha, the stronghold of the Riskan clan.

A fortress and its stone ramparts were built on the end of the cliff the group was heading to. At the top of the fort was a tower, a lighthouse which, as night approached, didn't shine. The fort turned its back to the sea, its main gate facing the flat, golden land to the south, but also a town. The city, three to four times larger than Surhok's heart—as far as Domino could judge from afar—had been built from the valley to the fortress, covering the whole surface of this cliff in length and width, clinging to the steep slope like lichen on the trunk of a tree. Approaching it, one could see houses made of black wood and square stones. Their tiled roofs colored the city a rust hue. In spite of the magnitude of the task in the face of the Corruption Rain, the people of this city worked to keep their roofs clean.

The Uetos had long since stopped bothering about what Ero called "a triviality." Houses didn't need to be pretty, only to offer a strong shelter, he used to say.

Well, the Riskan had decided to do both, and why not?

Still led by Lienn, the troop of nichans took a winding path of earth and sand up to the main entrance. From the ramparts, sentries, also dressed in leather and metal armor, opened the gates. On the nearly fifteen-foot-long wooden doors appeared the signs "Sky" and "Sea." The gusts of wind that swept over the cliff blew ever harder, rushing between the streets of the city, welcoming the newcomers with an iodized kiss.

Lanterns burned all over the city and on every street corner. Around every house, no matter how big or small, a flame guided the inhabitants. The main street glittered, enveloping the newcomers in a welcoming warmth. Pine trees with black thorns, bare roots, and twisted branches grew here and there between the houses.

His family's saddlebags hanging to his shoulder, Domino shivered. This place left him speechless. The city climbed in front of him, as if to reach the Gods' realm, adapting to the natural growth of the pines; the thick railings, erected like the bars of a cage, through which the horizon of the raging sea could be admired; the seagulls circling above their heads in a chaotic dance; the gigantic fort of unbreakable walls...

Domino stopped in his tracks again and closed his eyes once the beauty of the place was carved in his mind. He breathed in deeply, nostalgic of the delicious scent of the endless waters. His throat tensed. Tears filled his burning eyes as emotion gripped his heart. He hadn't seen the sea in eleven years. Just like his mom.

Not now.

He would think of this another day, at a more appropriate time. There was too much to focus on. The Riskans, Lienn, Ero . . .

At his feet, bigger than a pheasant, was a blue-plumed peacock with a trail of green and flowery feathers. Domino had heard of it but had never seen one with his own eyes. The majestic animal walked past him as if the fort belonged to it, its beak high, not caring the least about the arriving nichans.

Indeed, too much to focus on, enough to lose track of what was at stake, and to fall into traps.

Domino turned from the colorful bird and embraced the sheer size of the fort looming on the other side of the town. The nichans of yesteryear didn't build fortresses. By the sight of the stones polished by rains and salty winds, this one was ancient. It probably dated from long before the arrival of the Corruption.

Who owned it before the Riskans moved in? Had they used violence to claim it as their own?

Lost among the crowd of nichans returning from hunting, Domino looked for a familiar face, someone to guide him and answer his questions—Lienn, or even Calico. Now that they'd arrived, he and Ero would soon meet with the Riskan clan council.

"My mother will want details," Lienn had said that morning, before taking down and leaving their camp for the last time. "She'll summon the council, and we'll make decisions quickly."

"Domino is a Ueto," Ero had recalled, calm now that Memek was no longer bleeding, even though he'd had to carry her on his back for the rest of the journey.

"I already know that. What are you getting at?"

"He belongs to my clan. We raised him and protected him. Whatever your leader proposes to us, my consent, or my refusal, will count as Domino's."

Domino had laughed quietly, disgusted but not surprised by his uncle's attitude.

Lienn had merely nodded before turning to Domino. "Is that fine with you?"

Domino had smiled so as not to let anger ruin the day's journey. "You should ask him. He probably knows better than I do."

Memek had pressed them to leave, wiping away the tension growing between Domino and his Unaan.

The people of Visha didn't seem to have noticed these strangers coming from the Gods only knew where. They went about their business, welcoming their nichan brothers and sisters back alive with open arms. Despite the commotion, Calico found the Ueto family waiting on the edge of the main street. She led them to a house larger than the Surhok's auditorium. It had two floors with several rooms, and the humbly furnished ground floor could have contained five huts like the one Domino had built.

Ero laid Memek on a sofa near the extinguished brazier. The young woman grimaced, her face tired and closed. Covered with multicolored blankets, the furniture didn't seem as comfortable as she would have liked. Domino noticed that the bandage around her leg was stained with blood. Once again, he couldn't help but think of Gus.

Domino came out of his thoughts and lit a fire in the brazier. At the other end of the room, Ero was watching the place with a circumspect glance. About two months of traveling separated them from their home, yet there was little here to remind them of the life the Uetos had built for themselves in Surhok.

Because these nichans aren't led by the same chief. They don't hide in the woods, isolated from the rest of the world.

Nothing but guesswork—Domino had to admit it. But something about the Riskans and this town seemed particularly . . . human. The armors, the fortress, the elaborate tents. Ero and his disciples had always made it a point of honor not to behave like humans, to stay close to their ancestors. However, Lienn was closer to their nichan ancestors than anyone else they knew.

The three had barely had time to adjust to the size or even the smell of the house when Lienn returned to them, alone, more clothed than she'd been until now.

Because she changed from one physical form to another throughout the day, the young woman, until today, had appeared in human form only dressed in a thick tunic, decorated with fur at the collar, which she tied at the waist. A glance at her had suggested to Domino that she was wearing nothing underneath. A garment easy to put on and take off between each metamorphosis.

Now she wore sandals with wooden soles, hiding her toes. Ribbons held them on her feet, wrapping around her ankles in a simple knot. She wore dark woolen trousers, topped with a long shawl similar to the one the Uetos wore in winter. Hers was a warmer variant, pleated at the bottom and hemmed with ermine fur and elegant embroidery depicting clouds of birds. She also wore a white shirt—Domino had never seen such a white cloth—crossed over her chest and neck, hiding most of her honorary tattoo.

Domino stood up and greeted her with a nod and a smile.

She returned the nod, gaze going from his face to the embers reddening in the hearth. "This is one of the best houses in the village." She stopped on the carpet that marked the entrance to the room. (A village. Domino pursed his lips. He'd never seen such a place and would have felt ridiculous calling Visha and its fort a village.) "I hope you'll be comfortable here."

At last the blaze finally caught fire. Near the door he'd just closed, Ero observed Lienn, his eyes unreadable but unkind.

"It's perfect. Thank you," said Domino. She finally returned his smile. "You live in the . . . village?"

"I live in the fort," the young woman said.

"You do? Isn't it intimidating to live under all those stones?"

"It's a dark and unfriendly place." Words spoken in such a severe tone. She paused, lips parted, as if at a loss of word. Unsure why, Domino smiled at her. For a second she looked him in the eye, the shadow of a grin curling her mouth. Then her eyes turned to the rising flames—but still too shy to warm the room. "Few of us live there. The fort once belonged to the Kaibalars, according to the notes we found on our arrival. When my clan settled here a century ago, it was in the hands of a pack of very territorial dohors, provided these horrors remembered the place and what it once meant to their kind."

Domino nodded, still a little distracted by Lienn's unease.

Matta had mentioned the Kaibalars. From the little he'd listened to, being eager to go out and play with Gus in the village, Domino had remembered that they were once dohor riders, sometimes humans, who traveled on incredible mounts. They ranged from the majestic winged bull, to the mighty pony of D'Jersqoh, to the Verns of the even more distant deserts, so far beyond any horizon that these beasts lost between the saurian and the owl seemed to be nothing but a creation of the woman's imagination. Matta had also mentioned dragons, huge legendary beasts able to fly without wings. It was said that there was one left in the Meishua now—even though everyone called it Calamity and not dragon. Then Gus had doubted the woman's words, breaking his usual silence to let Matta know of his skepticism, and Domino had seen it as the perfect excuse to leave the Santig'Nell and go have fun.

"The majority of the fort is made up of stables for the animals," added Lienn. "I'll take you on a visit. Those stones can be intimidating, indeed." She turned to Ero who hadn't moved from his spot on the threshold. "You stay close to the door, Ueto Ero. Are you in a hurry to leave?"

Lienn didn't express herself with any gentleness. By repeating Ero's full name over and over again, she placed a distance between them that even the respect due to a clan leader didn't require.

"A visit to this fort is a must," Ero said. "To meet the council and its chief, perhaps."

"That's why I'm here," said Lienn. She veered back to Domino. Again, she devoted most of her attention to him. Liyion to Liyion. Ero wouldn't appreciate this habit lasting.

Putting an end to it, Domino nodded and wiped his charcoal-stained hands on his trousers. "Then let's go visit this fort."

LIENN HADN'T EXAGGERATED the description of her home. The inside of the fort turned out to be as austere and cold as an ancient grave. Windows were scarce and probably required the use of a ladder to be open considering how high they'd been placed. Dohor's-eye-level high. Numerous goatskin lanterns illuminated the dark corridors and the vestibule but failed to pierce the darkness clouding the ceilings. Even the colorful carpets woven with white patterns didn't provide any sort of comfort.

Armored nichans stood guard at each tall door, sliding them open to let Lienn, Ero and Domino through, closing them behind them right after to stop the course of the cold air. Their ancestors came from the northern icy lands of Torbatt and Netnin. But as he stood between these gray stones, a whistling breath snaking into his collar, Domino wondered if his kind hadn't forgotten what it was to be truly cold.

He suppressed a shiver, clinging to the idea that past nichans had once lived on frozen hills, and moved along.

Lienn led the two men into a room that reminded Domino of the interior of his village's auditorium. Although the room was smaller, it was surrounded by several carved pillars, along which hung red banners embroidered with a nichan smile and a spiky circle of branches, or what he interpreted to be a sun. In the center of the room was a hollow circular table. Its core was reinforced with metal and a bright fire crackled in a bronze vat, sending gleams of amber and gold onto the face of a woman already present in the room.

"Welcome to you," she said.

She got up as they arrived and circled the table. No mistake about it, she was Lienn's mother. Their two faces were almost identical. Only years of experience marked a difference. The woman had the same dark brown slanting eyes, the same fleshy lips, the same broad forehead. Her short hair was dark blond and curled around her prominent cheekbones. Like Lienn, the woman exuded a charisma that irresistibly attracted Domino's eye. She wasn't a pure blood—Domino could feel it—but she would easily pass for the Unaan of the clan in Ero's eyes.

Domino bowed respectfully to her, quickly imitated by Ero, and she gave them back their salute as her daughter stood by her side, taller than her mother.

The woman studied them one after the other, her fingers playing with a long necklace of pearly beads hanging from her neck.

"I am Riskan Vevdel," the woman introduced herself. "I presume you're the leader of the Ueto clan?"

"I am, indeed. Ueto Ero."

"And this is the boy."

Vevdel looked up at Domino. He smiled and bowed again to give himself a little composure.

"This is Domino," Ero said as his nephew opened his mouth. Mother and daughter glanced at Ero and a chill passed through the shaky shadows undulating in the room. "I thought I was to meet the council of your clan," said the man. "Is it only the two of you?"

"The council knows of Lienn's intentions. They support them and didn't wish to corner you like a court of law. Discussion, chief to chief, should be enough."

Lienn's intentions.

Ero frowned. "And what are your intentions, Unaan Vevdel?"

Vevdel smiled and turned her eyes to her daughter for a brief moment. "Forgive the confusion. It is a precaution we would take with anybody."

Ero indeed seemed confused. "What precaution?"

"I'm not the Unaan of the Riskan Clan," Vevdel confessed. "This responsibility is my daughter's."

Domino pursed his lips, forcing himself to keep quiet about what he'd already guessed. To his left, Ero lifted his chin and flashed his eyes at the two women.

"You have a strange way of welcoming your people and gaining their trust," he said slowly. "What's more, their respect."

"We both know that the best way to weaken a clan is to kill its leader," said Lienn.

"Did I threaten you?"

"No."

"Right. I didn't."

"I don't know you, Ueto Ero. I can't swear to your intentions as you can't swear to mine. I wanted first to find the safety of these walls and my protégés before opening myself to you. A mere protocol. Nothing personal."

"A wise lie, even though I doubt I'd be a match or a danger to you." Despite being the tallest of the four nichans gathered in the room, Ero wasn't the most dangerous beast in Visha.

Lienn laid eyes on Domino, sizing him up, and then returned to Ero. "Right. Not you."

Ero clenched his jaw tight. He had control of Domino. One command would be enough for the man to send his nephew at Lienn's throat.

But the reason of Ero's current expression was probably different. "I'm not the kind of man to bite the hand that feeds him."

"Good. It would be unfortunate to try."

The temperature dropped all the more. Neither Lienn nor Ero flinched as they stared at each other. Domino swallowed and cleared his throat. For once he wished he had enough authority to put an end to this encounter.

His uncle turned to Vevdel. "What about you? Are your daughter's abilities hereditary? Should I prepare for more surprises?"

"I'm only here to support and advise Lienn," the woman assured, her calm and friendliness intact. "Unlike her, I haven't been blessed by the hands of the Gods. This doesn't prevent me from being her mother and fulfilling my role."

Vevdel invited the two men to sit at the table and offered refreshments, which Ero declined with a wave of his hand. He still seemed to have difficulty processing the truth, or rather the lie he'd believed for days.

"No need to linger," Ero said. "My daughter is waiting in town and I don't want to leave her alone for too long."

"I can send someone to her. Calico, maybe," said Vevdel, turning to Lienn.

"Just like you, I know how to take care of my child."

It was hard to know whether these were the words of a worried father, or an excuse to cut this meeting short. Or even a way to question the Riskans' reliability.

"All right," said Vevdel. "We're very busy, and the days are short."

Her words made Domino smile. He'd only heard them from Ero's mouth until today. "The days are short" was a saying of the elders, of those who'd known the world before the Corruption. Indeed, since the Great Evil, days were getting darker too quickly and seemed quite short.

"In this case," Vevdel said as she sat, "let's get to the point. An alliance." She announced it outright as she let herself go in her armchair.

Near her, Lienn studied Domino's face. The young woman added, "Two Liyion united to lead our men and protect them."

"Slow down," Ero cut, looking relaxed despite his right fist, which he kept firmly closed.

"Yes?"

"You don't know me. I don't know you."

"Indeed."

"See, that problem is mutual. So let's take the time to know each other first, or at least to think for one minute. An agreement between two clans doesn't come about on a whim."

"I understand and agree with your statement," Vevdel said, not moved that her daughter had been interrupted by her guest in her own home. She put a hand on Lienn's shoulder. Vevdel's gaze was filled with a pride and a tenderness that clenched Domino's heart. "My dear Lienn revealed herself to us at the age of twelve. A late but providential first transformation. We'd lost hope and yet, here she was, the first Liyion in almost two centuries. We didn't hesitate to pledge our oath to her. After ten years of work, she became the future of this clan and, as you can imagine, our most precious hunter. Many of us would have died without her. When my daughter goes hunting with her protégés, I can look after the rest of our clan without worrying about their lives . . . until recently."

The woman was speaking on behalf of her daughter—the true authority in this place—yet Lienn didn't mind. Quite the contrary. Sitting next to her mother, the young woman seemed more peaceful than ever, as if relieved of a burden and reassured to let someone she trusted carry it for her. At least that was the impression Domino had when he laid eyes on the two women.

"You're from the north of the capital, right?" Vevdel asked.

"Not quite. The forests north of the Osska region," Ero rectified.

"A brief respite. I heard the situation beyond the capital is still manageable—correct me if I'm mistaken." Silence met her words. "Here as elsewhere, over the last five years, the number of sympathizers for the cause of these blighted Blessers has been in constant rise. They are everywhere, like weeds. Impossible to differentiate them from other humans. We can't flush them out, only wait for them to show up at our door, or to kill our children."

Domino bit his tongue and glanced at Ero sideways. The loss of a child by the partisans was a subject his uncle knew all too well.

However, the man remained unmoved and turned to Lienn. "Don't you have anything to say, or must I still doubt your title?"

"Pardon?"

"I understand that you're young, but you're Unaan, not a child. Right? Can't you speak for yourself?"

Lienn returned his gaze, unshakeable. "My mother is my right hand. She knows the situation perfectly well. She's also more eloquent than I could ever be. Whatever our title or influence, we should never underestimate our flaws."

Ero clenched his jaw and Domino resisted the urge to move away from him.

In the distance, the sound of the crashing waves challenged the crackling of the fire in the middle of the table to lure the tense silence away.

Vevdel resumed. "This immediate reaction to your nephew's presence isn't rushed or thoughtless. When your men are killed by weapons faster than they are, you start making plans. For years we've been taking in isolated nichans to expand our troops. The very idea that another pure blood would come along seemed delusional to us. That didn't stop Lienn from foreseeing what to do should it happen. The way forward is what we present to you: an alliance between our two clans, sealed by the marriage of my daughter and your nephew."

Domino blinked, and his heart skipped a beat. A reaction no one here would fail to notice. Swallowing the news, he turned his attention to Lienn, who stared at him peacefully. This announcement, this alliance, were they all her ideas? Was it for this reason that she'd asked him his age and whether his seasons had passed? She was older than he was—around twenty-two—but Domino had indeed gone through his seasons. In the eyes of nichans, he was an adult.

Old enough to marry, but not enough to be told before anyone else, apparently . . .

Torbs had united major human families in such fashion for many centuries. A marriage celebrated under the eyes of the Gods. Some nichans had even adopted the tradition after the Gods had given them access to their human form a long time ago. The Gods had disappeared, but the tradition had survived.

A marriage. The concept went round and round in Domino's mind, revealing itself to him from every angle. In principle, this union meant three things: a shared life in the same place for the Ueto Clan and the Riskan Clan; the creation of an heir born of both names; a vow of fidelity pronounced by the spouses to the skies to receive the Gods' blessing.

Domino's heart was overwhelmed. Still too excited about Lienn's very existence, he hadn't considered what the young woman intended to do with him.

What about Gus? Gus, whom Domino had kissed, whom he still desired as much on this day despite the distance and the months of separation.

"Liyion, no less. Their nature could be passed on to all their children," Vevdel added as if to drive the point home.

Domino couldn't hold back a disillusioned laugh. "I have a feeling that in a moment you will tell me the names of my future children."

Nobody said anything, as if to give him time to digest the news.

Domino's heart beat harder. He had to calm down before saying something stupid. This alliance was exactly what his clan would need in the near future. And Domino needed Lienn. It was a good thing. It was . . .

"Did Lienn explain to you—" he began in a voice that he managed to control.

"About your affliction?" Vevdel ended, incredibly perceptive. "Of course. My daughter insisted very strongly that she feels your aura, so I'm not giving up hope. Your training should start as soon as possible. It's a long process, and it could prove to be quite arduous, given your current condition. But after a few years, you'll finally be ready. Then the wedding will be celebrated, and your clan will join ours."

"Hang on. A few years?" Ero looked between the two women. "You can't be serious."

"It took me a long time to learn my true form," Lienn said. "In the beginning, the transformation alone was painful, traumatic. Then I had to relearn how to walk, run, fight, all in a body five times stronger, faster, and bigger than the one I grew up in. You cannot imagine the danger Domino would pose to your nichans if he were to launch an assault on the Blessers without having tamed his original form. And from what I gathered, it is fear for his people's safety that now imprisons him in his camouflage."

"Domino is no longer a child. A few years, as you anticipate, won't be necessary."

"Make no mistake, Ueto Ero."

"You're asking us to stay here indefinitely. My clan awaits my return. This pilgrimage wasn't supposed to last forever. We don't have years."

"A messenger will be sent to explain the situation," said Vevdel.

"A messenger is not what my people needs. They need me."

"If you don't wish to stay away from yours, nothing stops you from going home yourself to inform them while Domino starts his training."

"And leave him to you? Do you take me for a fool?"

Domino clenched his fists. Once again, like that day in the auditorium when Issba and Ero had been debating his future, they all talked about him as if he weren't here.

He'd had enough. "Ero, come on. I—"

"Shut up!"

The order had the effect of a rock forced down his throat. In front of Lienn and her mother, Domino fell silent. He lowered his eyes to the table, unable to face the two women.

Treated like a child, no matter what.

"Ueto Ero," Vevdel said, still calm, sitting up in her chair. "The peoples of Torbatt have governed themselves alone since the Gods disappeared. No Matrons, no kings. You already know that. It's an everyday struggle, but we survive this scourge. I look at these two young people at this table, and I feel hopeful. I look at you, and all I feel is suspicion." Ero raised his chin, chuckling ever so slightly. "I don't know anything about you, about your past, about your clan, about your plans for your protégés. Yet my daughter is ready to welcome you and yours as if we all belonged to the same family. We don't consider you an enemy, or a stray sheep in need of protection. Above all, we see nichan brothers who almost lost their lives a few days ago, and who found salvation in the help my people gave them without the slightest hesitation."

She paused, leaning towards Ero. Her previous kindness was now but a memory.

"For the moment, our agents report that the Blessers still face strong resistance from the Sirlhain population. Attacks regularly break out, killing so many that the survivors have barely enough time to bury the dead."

"Some towns have been destroyed by the Blessers, then abandoned to the Corruption and spirits," Lienn added. She noticed Domino's alarmed gaze and turned to him. "The Blessers mock spirits and the danger they pose when their numbers are too great. They believe that once the Gods return, everything will revert to the way it was."

"And they believe wholeheartedly that their return will grow from our ashes," said Vevdel. "They won't give up. And their followers don't care about borders; they're born on our lands. The Blessers will soon try to cross them. They will."

Ero frowned. "You think I don't know that? This condescension is almost insulting. Careful. One might actually think you take me for a fool."

"Rest assured, I don't, Ueto Ero. Quite the opposite. You know what we're up against. You also know that once the east attacks, our country and our people will go to war, and the southern Torbatt, of which your village is a part, will be the first to fall unless you join forces with us. Our people's survival is all that matters."

And the silence returned. The echo of Vevdel's voice, soft and deep, was broken by the scraping of a chair on the stones. Ero stood. The others sat motionless, dumbfounded.

"A beautiful speech," he said. "I'll think about it, and you'll have my answer as soon as possible. Domino, come with me. We're leaving."

THEY LEFT THE FORT, found rain and night, and crossed the main square, the only paved area outside the wide alley splitting the city in two. After returning home, Domino closed the door behind him and tapped into everything that constituted his will and freedom to speak. Ero's order was dispelled, but a cautious part of Domino advised him to keep quiet. He had no intention of doing so, not after having been trapped in silence throughout most of the meeting.

"Are you going to refuse? It's a chance we won't get again, Ero."

Standing in front of the brazier, taking off his shawl as the house had significantly warmed, his uncle glanced at him. "What do you know about it? The two of you may not be the only ones."

Domino ran an exhausted hand through his hair. "Are we playing this opportunity on speculation now? Are we? You'd risk waiting forever just to find out if there's another clan as powerful as this one with a Liyion in its ranks? It's a fucking miracle Lienn exists, you know it as well as I do. Look at the sky, Ero. Miracles are as rare as sunlight. I get the feeling you want to antagonize the Riskans."

"We're here because of me, don't you forget that."

"Because of you? Because you dragged Memek and me all the way south, hoping those partisan-infested lands would trigger a reaction in me? You know, Memek was right. We were going around in circles."

His uncle sighed and turned away from him. Just as Domino thought the conversation was coming to an end, Ero searched one of the saddlebags and fished something out of it. Then he reached out to Domino, roughly took his hand and stuck a piece of paper in it. "Do you think chance has anything to do with that? That I am playing with your life and my daughter's life?"

Domino unfolded the crumpled piece of paper. He didn't immediately recognize it, although it was familiar. It was a propaganda poster inciting whoever reading it to join the fight against nichans. Ero couldn't read it, but Domino could.

"The Great Evil spares no region. Do not let it slip under your bed. Join us or make your contribution. The beast must die," said the slogan beneath a monstrous caricature of a nichan face.

"I'm lost," Domino said.

"Everybody thought it's a portrait of a nichan. I thought so, too, at first. And then I paid attention to this. This circle." Ero followed the edge of the sketch with his fingertip. "Does it ring a bell? Because I haven't forgotten the day you transformed to kill that dohor. The memory of that beast will remain forever engraved in my mind. A beast that looks like your bride, black as death, with a smile on its face and a golden ring floating around its mouth."

Domino lowered his eyes to the poster. Anyone would have considered this circle as the frame of the portrait. But not Ero. When the man looked at the drawing, he saw Domino—Domino's true face.

"He sees everything and knows everything," Domino whispered to himself. "You could have been wrong."

"It was a risk worth taking. I'd been following this rumor for a while. It's a sometimes-useful characteristic of humans: they love gossip and share it with everyone. When I saw that woman holding up that poster, I knew, and I figured if I'm going to take a chance, I might as well go for it."

Ero had been hiding this from him for weeks. Perhaps warning Domino would have been enough to give him hope, to find what was hidden deep inside him. Instead, he'd almost been killed by a bear and then by partisans. He'd been hanged. Indeed, the gamble had paid off, but at what price? Domino had almost given up . . . Given up on himself.

He gave himself a few seconds to get his thoughts in order. Between this revelation and the news of their alliance with the Riskans—and his marriage—he felt as if his skull was about to burst.

What was done was done. There was no point in dwelling on the past.

"Finding the beast on that poster was your goal, right?" he said, shaking the sheet under his uncle's nose. "Yes? Well it's done, we found it."

"You can thank me."

"If that's what you wanted, why are you making such a fuss? Because Lienn is the leader of her clan?"

"No."

"Then what is it? You were hoping to find a lone creature to recruit, someone willing to swear an oath to you?"

"You really don't understand anything."

"What I understand right now is that you're just screwing with them for the sake of it."

"Watch your mouth. I'm tired, and my patience is running thin today."

"Then I'll make it short. Accept this alliance so I can start training. I'm ready to get married and have children for—" He paused, this reality momentarily cutting off his voice. Becoming a father was the last thing he'd intended to do. He pulled himself together. "You want a pure blood to fight for the Uetos. Guess what? I'll fight. I know exactly what the partisans are capable of," he said, pointing to his throat still reddened by the rope. "Lienn is my only chance. Our only chance, unless you'd rather get ours back and flee to the other side of the world."

"You have no idea what you're talking about. Joining another clan is a long-term agreement. It completely redefines the life of the entire community. They want us to come and live here, to leave our village, these lands we have cultivated, these houses we have built. Our way of life will be completely overwritten by theirs."

"Well, look at that," Domino whispered, both amused and bitter. "Houses and cultivated lands. Here you are caring about such . . . human ways of life."

His voice was still echoing in his mouth when Ero grabbed Domino's collar. The young man found himself two fingers away from his uncle's face.

Once again, Domino should have thought twice before speaking. Yet each reply that was sent back to his leader's face filled him with ecstasy, like a takeover, despite the risks. He clenched his teeth to hold back the satisfied smile that attempted to betray him.

"Stop playing games," Ero advised him, each deep scar on his face reminding everyone of what he'd survived.

"We won't be the first to leave our home because of this conflict."

"In case you haven't noticed, I'm doing everything I can to avoid it."

"With the Blessers coming, it's gonna happen anyway."

"I need to think about it."

"What are you afraid of?"

A memory. Words. They popped into Domino's mind: *The truth is you're afraid he'll dominate you. Fear no more, Ero, for he will.*

Issba's words spoken more than three years ago. Fear that Domino would dominate him. By being at the heart of the alliance between two clans? By fighting alongside Lienn? By regaining control of his life and body?

Yes, Domino thought. Deep down inside, he knew that Ero

was afraid of all this. His nephew growing stronger. Stronger than him.

"This isn't the first alliance I've tried to forge," his uncle replied, releasing him. "And the last time, nichans died, and your mother turned her back on me."

Ero grabbed the poster and threw it into the fire. The paper burned down in the blink of an eye. Domino barely noticed it.

"Why? What happened?" he asked.

What did you do to her? he meant.

"It doesn't matter."

"By the Faces, just tell me. For what it's worth, it matters to me."

Apart from a few complaints about his older brother, Ako had never explained in detail what had motivated her departure. By leaving her clan and turning her back on her chief, she'd become an orphan. Her essence, once tied to a whole community, had been forced to live in solitude. His mother had Mora at the time, so she wasn't entirely alone, but the oath was a powerful vow. It took great mental strength to break it. Domino suspected that it was for this reason that Ako had lost sleep, for this reason that his memories of a happy mom were scarce.

He took a step toward his uncle, desperate to learn more. "Please. At least tell me your side of the story. It's not like my mother would contradict you where she is."

"It's late, Domino. Go to bed and let me handle this myself."

BUT THE NEXT MORNING, as Domino joined Memek for breakfast —a tray of black bread, boiled eggs, and smoked fish that Domino ignored—the young woman told him in a few mumbles that Ero had left before dawn to talk with the Riskan Clan chief.

Domino was pacing around the room, making his cousin dizzy, when Ero reappeared and announced the news.

He'd just accepted the alliance and set the terms with Lienn. One of them gave the three Uetos the right to go wherever they wanted in the city, to act as if they were Riskans. Ero kept the rest of the negotiation to himself.

I see, Domino thought. He badly needed to find Lienn and talk to her.

Alone.

XXXI

THE WINDOW OF GUS'S HUT DIDN'T REQUIRE HIM TO TIPTOE UP to look outside. In building the small house, Domino had measured what he considered to be the optimal height for the two friends to enjoy the outside view. The calculations hadn't taken into account how much Domino would grow along the years. Before he left, when he wanted to take a look out the window, he had to bend in half. He would still grow in the years to come. A youthful mistake, he'd laughed.

Standing in front of the window, Gus thought of the day he'd taken his few belongings to his hut. Asking where to put them, Domino had approached, grabbed the clothes, and thrown them into the reed box at the foot of the bed, along with his own.

"I'll try not to confuse your things with mine."

"You'd never fit into my clothes," Gus had said.

Domino's face had brightened with a mischievous smile. "Are you challenging me?"

The seams on the sides of Gus's pants had cracked when Domino put the garment on forcibly. Both boys had laughed their heads off. Gus had put on the nichan outfit. He was swimming in it. Anything Domino wore could fit two men like Gus without either of them feeling cramped.

Gus looked down at the tunic he held in his hands. It belonged to Domino. He'd just washed it with his own clothes. The tunic hadn't been used since Domino's departure, yet Gus continued to incorporate it into his laundry.

He put it in the wicker basket, took off his own tunic and dressed himself in Domino's. Still wet and cold, the linen clung to his skin. The cloth had no slits to fit the Vestige's wings. It didn't matter. Gus tightened the tunic around his flanks, his hand disappearing inside the long sleeves, filling his chest with the soothing scent of soap. On Domino, it reached halfway up his thighs. Today, it hid Gus's knees.

A seductive glimmer shined in the corner of the room. An amber glow. Domino's necklace. Gus stood still for a long time, his gaze piercing the transparent resin riddled with bubbles.

Before he even realized he'd moved, he grabbed the jewel and, as if to perfect his outfit, passed it around his neck. The piece of sap swung against his chest, without any temperature of its own, weightless. Against his pale, slightly pinkish skin, the object took on a darker, redder hue. Around Domino's neck, the amber had always seemed brighter, like an incandescent flame compared to the beautiful dark bronze that enveloped his body.

A scream echoed outside. Gus raised his chin distractedly. Through the window he saw nothing at first, then a figure came running toward him. A gray shawl, black braids swaying with each step. It was Belma.

"Dadou! By the faces!" The woman bent down and disappeared from Gus's sight. "No, no, no, don't move," said the woman in an alarmed voice. "Show me."

"The bucket was too heavy," replied a small voice made hoarse by age.

"What bucket?"

"The bucket full of . . . of fish. The handle broke. There's never anyone to fix broken things."

A pause and then a sigh.

"You're bleeding, Dadou."

"But my fish . . . "

"Do you want me to call the Vestige?" asked another voice in the distance.

Gus looked down at his own body. Invisible under Domino's large clothes, bruises swarmed across his skin. On his arms, his legs. Although Beïka hadn't touched him for nearly a week, Gus's face was still marked.

"I'll go get him," said another voice, one that Gus recognized immediately despite his mind numb with memories.

Matta was coming.

Gus took off the tunic and was retrieving his own when three knocks rang out against the door leaf. Having anticipated them didn't spare his heart, and he started. Beïka didn't announce himself before entering, but the knocks against the wood were like a fist crashing against Gus's temple.

He hurriedly tied his clothes, slipping the necklace under his tunic—which had also been a little too big for some time—and joined Matta outside. She didn't have time to announce herself or explain the situation. She looked up at Gus with squinted eyes as he passed her without a glance. He walked around the hut and found Dadou sitting on the floor, blood on her face. She'd lost a shoe in her fall, and Belma, crouching in front of her great-grandmother, didn't seem to care. She was far too concerned about Dadou's condition. A wound hemmed the old nichan's wrinkled forehead.

Without a word, Gus approached and knelt before the village elder. When she noticed his presence, Dadou moved backwards, and the hand she raised in front of her trembled. "What's that?" cried the old woman.

Gus stopped immediately, heavy-hearted. Dadou had known him for years. With Mora and Domino, he'd shared more than one meal with Belma and her great-grandmother. She hadn't spoken to him often, but Dadou had never had such a reaction upon laying eyes on him.

She had not seen him up close for more than three years. Since Mora died, since Belma forbade Domino to approach her family. Besides, the old woman was senile, and her condition had probably worsened since they'd last met, he told himself. Even so . . .

"Dadou, it's Gus," said Belma, stroking the dean's gray hair. "You know him, Dadou. Mora took care of him . . . "

Gus dared a brief glance in the woman's direction. If pronouncing the name of her dead partner was difficult for her, she hid it perfectly.

But her words slipped through Dadou's mind like water on a duck's feathers. "His—his eyes!" the old woman stammered. "It's a monster."

Gus's heart tightened. Dadou looked at him with glassy eyes tarnished by cataracts. Even though Belma held her still, the old woman kept backing away, or at least trying to do so despite the shock inflicted to her head.

"Dadou," Belma repeated.

"Don't let him put his hands on me, Belma. I'm begging you. I did nothing wrong. I didn't want to lose the fish. The bucket was broken."

Words without meaning. That didn't stop Gus from stepping aside when Belma signaled him to get away from Dadou. Behind his back, Matta was still there, discreet but unmistakable.

"Let's go see Muran, all right?" Belma suggested, and the old woman let herself get back on her feet, remaining attentive to Gus's every move.

He thought of going back to hide out of sight. Only Matta paid attention to him, but the Santig'Nell's Eye could be much more intimidating than the attention of a whole crowd. However, Gus found the strength not to run away. He'd done nothing wrong, didn't have to lurk in the shadows, driven by shame of any kind.

He went to the fountain behind his hut. As if nothing had happened, ignoring the ball clogging his throat, he activated the pump and bent down to take a few sips.

"I've thought about your request," said Matta behind his back. She walked closer and leaned against the wall near the water source.

Gus avoided looking up at her. "Forget about it."

"You didn't give me time to answer you the other day."

"I'm not interested."

Could she not leave him alone? The slightest presence in the space around Gus made him nervous and feverish. Even though he knew Matta's intentions weren't malicious, the woman reminded him of what had happened the last time he'd spoken to her. Gus could still feel Beïka's hands on his neck, his wings, his ass . . .

Don't think about it. Not here, he scolded silently.

He bent down and splashed water on his face to cool his burning eyes.

"You seemed interested enough when you came to see me," Matta continued in a neutral tone filled with something Gus couldn't identify.

Fear. Or nervousness, perhaps.

He remained silent. She didn't. "That stubbornness reminds me of someone I knew well." A pause during which Gus looked for the nichan who had been causing him so much trouble lately. "His name was Elidei." Matta seemed to be searching for her words, as if something—an invisible force—was trying to silence her. "I told you and Domino about my role in the Worth of the Santig'Nells, didn't I?"

Gus didn't answer, didn't move. His legs shook, as did his hands. But he remembered Domino's words very well, a seven-year-old Domino bursting with energy, joy, and excitement over all the details the woman shared with them between lessons, as to keep them invested in the task.

"So you are the mother of the Santig children?"

Matta had opened her mouth without saying a word. No doubt she'd considered denying what Domino had just said. But she'd been forced to admit that he'd somehow spoken the truth. After reminding them that once a Santig'Nell became part of the Worth, they became one of the Matrons' children, she'd replied, "I watch over them as a mother would, indeed. Or a mentor."

She used to raise the young Santig'Nells, teaching them to read, write, and count. She was in charge of their education and the development of the gifts offered by the Matrons' Eye. She also taught them the art of combat. This information hadn't fallen on deaf ears. It was for this very reason that Gus had come to see her, asking her to teach him how to defend himself.

As Gus bent to drink more water, Matta silently took a deep breath and continued.

"Elidei wasn't a Santig'Nell. He was the first born of King Manàdei; he was the prince of Netnin. The Sards have a custom in Netnin. When an alliance is formed with another estate or country, the firstborn of their leader is offered to be raised by the future ally. At the time, Manàdei had just concluded an agreement with Sirlha. His people had finally accepted the Matrons' protection after almost eighteen years of conflict. Sards are known for their unwavering pride and obsession with lineage. This agreement was no small victory, and Elidei had only just been born when it was reached. Manàdei offered the Worth to raise his son according to the Sirlhain traditions so that when he returned to Netnin, the prince would be a son of both nations. Elidei would thus become a symbol of peace."

Gus turned his eyes briefly to Matta. She was smaller than he was, and as she said these words, vulnerability showed on her face. A sentiment he wouldn't have associated with Matta until today. Then she noticed the look in Gus's eyes, and he turned away. But he didn't run away when she spoke again.

"Several of my brothers and sisters went to Netnin to retrieve the child. When he was first placed in my arms, he was only two months old. All the Santig'Nells in my care were then entrusted to others. Elidei was to be my priority, as the agreement required. He grew up in the Defense Palace in Laranga."

"Salted Harbor," Gus whispered to himself.

Matta nodded, the muscles of her face softening into a smile. Gus remembered his lessons. He was born in Sirlha. Even when he'd tried not to listen, to detach himself from his homeland, he hadn't missed a crumb of the Santig'Nell speeches. Sirlha, the land of rivers. Laranga, the white capital, also called Salted Harbor by foreigners and islanders because of its salt-covered coastline. Places Gus would never visit unless to seek death. This country had been the Blessers' headquarters for more than twenty-five years.

"You are as stubborn as him," the woman said. A reproach. Gus waited for the anger to rise in him, but his heart remained closed to the feeling. "He was a very gifted and intelligent boy, just like you. He was also a very good fighter. He had to be raised according to Sirlhain customs, so I set out to teach him dagger fighting when he was eleven years old. The boy wouldn't listen. He wanted to fight with spear and staff, like the greatest Sard warriors. The Mother Regent of the Santig'Nell had even given him a beautiful silver dagger to motivate his enthusiasm. Elidei put it away and sulked for weeks. What am I saying? Months. I eventually surrendered.

"The truth is, he wanted to prepare himself for the meeting that was coming up. His father sent a contingent of his best subjects to Laranga to be introduced to the prince, among other things. Elidei, in a duel against one of his cousins whom he was meeting for the first time, proved to be exemplary. His abilities promised him a bright future. But his cousin didn't see things the same way. She more or less openly mocked Elidei's abilities, comparing his technique to that of a rock incapable of producing sparks. Elidei was furious, but he didn't let it bring him down. Oh, no, he didn't. He took the dagger he'd received from the Mother Regent and came to me. He told me that the spear and staff were the weapons of cowards, wielded by warriors who dare not approach their opponents. He was ready to learn how to wield the dagger. He said that under his reign, Netnin would grow stronger."

"He sounds like a boaster," Gus mocked halfway through.

Matta nodded her head before sighing through a smile. "Yes. There was a little bit of that. More importantly, I think he wanted to convince himself that he could run a country that he only knew by name and whose reputation was enough to scare him. The Sards, his own people, were strangers to him. This reminds me of someone else."

Matta's voice had soothed him.

Gus had always loved the stories Domino told him. He'd listened to him for hours, marveling at his best friend's way of speech and imagination, an imagination in which lay more than a scrap of truth.

Matta awoke in Gus the pleasure he had in listening to someone he trusted confide in him. But as she insisted on associating Gus with her story, he tensed up. He didn't want Matta to make a sermon out of her past.

He decided to divert her attention. "Where's Elidei now?"

A silence fell between them, and Matta took another deep breath.

"He's dead. The Blessers killed him. One of our own servants was working with them and made the capture of the palace possible. I couldn't find Elidei in the upper town or at the palace when the attack began. I remained hidden in Laranga for several days after the Blessers took power and destroyed Reason and Hope, the Matrons. I searched relentlessly for a way to get into the palace without getting caught. In vain. With the Matrons gone, the connection between us, between Santig'Nells, was gone as well. I was lost, left in . . . silence." She swallowed, eyes down. "But I kept searching and the city fell into chaos. At the end of that time, several people were hanged at the entrance of the palace, facing the city, then burned. Elidei was among them. He was seventeen."

She fell silent, however, she looked up at Gus. He regretted having asked the question, to have forced her to relive these moments. He could be insolent, but he refused to cause Matta any grief or to let anything write such sadness in her eyes. Both shone more vividly than ever. This Elidei had probably been like a son to her.

Did she witness the killing?

"I just want to help you," Matta said in a soft but firm voice, almost begging.

Gus turned his dark eyes to her. "I don't need help."

"You know that's not true."

"Matta, stop . . . "

"Who gave you all those bruises, Gus?" The language shifted in her mouth, yet the words remained clear to him. After so many years, Sirlhain was still his mother tongue.

Gus looked around, alarmed. "What the fuck is wrong with you?" He wouldn't speak Sirlhain. "You want to get us in trouble?"

"There's no one around."

"Then why talk in this language?"

"So you know I'm on your side. I'll always be on your side, Gus."

"I told you to stop."

"If someone's hurting you, we have to end it. I can do it."

"I didn't ask you to do anything."

"On the contrary. You wanted my help, and I'm willing to offer it."

"I don't want your help. Get the fuck out of my face!"

"I'm your friend," she said as she took a step toward him.

"I'm not Elidei!"

Matta stood still and pursed her lips. "Yes, indeed. You're not Elidei. Unlike him, you may live beyond the age of seventeen if you get the chance."

Seventeen. What a joke.

The truth was, Gus didn't know the month or even the year he was born. Since he was destined from his first breath to die by the Blessers' purification, the woman who'd raised him had never bothered to celebrate his birth. Because Gus and Domino had learned to read and write at the same pace, Matta had concluded that the two boys were the same age. So it was she who had suggested matching Gus's age on Domino's. But Matta didn't know either. No one knew.

Seventeen . . . Maybe Gus was younger or older than his best friend. Being reminded of this gap in his own history knotted his gut.

Matta was a good person; she'd done everything she could to make Gus feel accepted in an environment where neither she nor he belonged. But what was the point? No matter what she said, Gus had stopped believing that things would ever get better. He didn't want to get his hopes up to see them be crushed into dust again.

"You should leave this place," he said, standing as upright as possible.

"Excuse me?"

"Go back to your sisters and brothers Santig'Nell."

"Gus."

"Stop."

"No, Gus. Listen to me. For a long time I thought I was running away from my pain—"

"That's what you're doing. Just go."

"It's true, I was running away. I should have rallied Ponsang with my people. Instead I left behind the ones I cared about. My friends, my wife . . . She will never forgive me—" She took a shaky breath. "But when I met you, I realized the Gods had other plans for me—"

"One last time," he said between his teeth before leaning over to her. "I'm not Elidei, and I don't want to be saved."

Once again, Matta's gaze was imploring. She shook her head, as if about to add more. Gus had no intention of hearing a word more. He turned away from her and walked along the side of his hut to go around it. He didn't watch his steps, had no direction in mind. He just had to get away from her. Matta was probably following him. He didn't look back to check.

Orsa, who was coming from the heart of the village, noticed him and walked right up to him. Gus tensed in spite of himself. The nichan faced him, blocking the way, even bigger than he remembered. Before she opened her mouth to speak, he noticed the freckles on her tattooed cheeks.

"You're relieved of your week's chores starting tomorrow," the clan chief told the boy. "You're coming with us on the hunt."

Gus just stood there gawking for a handful of seconds. He knew this day would come; they'd warned him years and years before.

He had to go with them. Outside. He was going to walk out of the village. He'd done it before, but not like this, not officially. Not when his life depended on it.

"What should I bring?" he asked, emerging from his amazement.

Orsa detailed him up and down in a neutral expression. "Warm clothes for the night . . . and shoes. No bags. You put them on you. " Gus nodded mechanically. "Then rest tonight and be at the gates by dawn. I hope you can go the distance."

WAS THERE any other way out of Surhok than this one? Once out, could Gus slip away from the nichans? If so, which direction should he go? Unlike nichans, the north was a mysterious concept to him. Would it be wiser to hide some food in his clothes so he wouldn't starve to death? The nichans would smell it, get suspicious, and search Gus. What if he couldn't get away? It was unlikely Gus would be left unattended for even a minute. And even if he did manage to get away, they would go after him. They would follow his scent, chase him down like an animal.

Like prey.

Gus turned in his bed. Outside, a cricket had been chanting continuously for hours, refusing to acknowledge the arrival of winter.

The young man was overwhelmed with thoughts. He was aware that his idea of running away was out of reach, yet he kept thinking about it and looking for a loophole to exploit to see it through.

His belly growled, and he lay on his wings, taking a deep breath. He'd tried to eat something today, but after hearing the news from Orsa, he'd felt too nervous and anxious to put anything in his belly.

His mind was in turmoil. His thoughts were, of course,

disordered, but that was enough to keep him awake. He'd swallowed a whole cup of the same soothing herbs he'd offered to Domino more than once after Mora's death. In fact, they'd always kept a sufficient quantity in their hut, furtively restocking at the infirmary when the supplies became too thin to have an acceptable effect. After several hours, the bitter mixture still hadn't worked on him, and Gus knew he'd continue to struggle for some sleep until exhaustion knocked him out.

If I manage to get up and walk straight in the morning, it will be a miracle.

He closed his eyes, trying to chase away the thoughts parasitizing his mind.

The door of his hut slammed open.

Gus reopened his eyes and sat up in one fell swoop.

No! Not again. Not now . . .

Beïka walked into the room, lit by the burning lantern outside, his silhouette standing out in the half-light. Unable to resist his fear, his fatigue making him weak, Gus backed into his bed and almost fell out of it. Before losing his balance, a firm grip seized his collar. The door had remained open. Another silhouette appeared on the threshold. Another man.

Gus didn't have time to recognize him or understand what was happening. Beïka's fist fell on his face, and the world dissolved into a painful, acidic mist.

Out of breath, his nose clogged with blood, the boy felt his body rise, a sharp pain in his forearm and shoulder. The next moment he was lying on his stomach, upside down, an arm as solid as rock passed around his waist. Something was swinging and bumping against his forehead. The necklace, he was still wearing it . . .

The world wavered again. A door slammed gently.

The wind blew across Gus's face, over his bare arms, over his wings. He shivered and shook his head. A little blood came out of his nostrils, but he was still struggling to breathe.

What's he . . . what's he doing? Where is he taking me?

The world wavered around him, as if he were floating in the air, taken from one point to the next. Beïka had probably lifted Gus up and put him back on his shoulder, hence the pressure beneath his ribs.

No! Gus thought again, and he fought off the haze and pain in his skull.

Despite the dizziness, he managed to lift his head and open his eyes. At first, he only discerned the ground moving over him. Now, below, he understood. He recognized the wooden planks that paved the path between the huts, barely revealed by a flickering light. Gus turned his head. Blood rose to his face and put his nerves to the test. He was suddenly so desperate for sleep. If he closed his eyes, he would fall unconscious, but would he ever wake up? He could hear the answer whispered through his marrow.

Another shudder shook him from head to toe, along with a sob that he managed to hold back. The moaning that slipped between his lips was irresistible.

"Wait," whispered a man's voice.

Gus searched for its owner. Before finding him, a piece of cloth was inserted between his lips and teeth.

A gag.

He reacted immediately. He expelled all the air from his lungs and screamed. Only a croak-like complaint rose from the depths of his throat. Without warning, a hand covered Gus's face to silence him, forcing the cloth even deeper into his mouth. The wide palm was enough to cut off the boy's air. He wiggled on his perch, trying to push away the hand that was choking him, but his arms were firmly wedged against his flanks by the arm Beïka used to hold him on his shoulder.

"Hush," the same man calmly said. "Hush, you little wild beast. Look what you made me do. Forcing me to touch you. Only fire can purify this hand now." Gus blinked and shook his head to free his face from the grip clenching his cheeks. To no avail. "Behave yourself and you won't feel any pain."

Tears finally flowed out of Gus's eyes, and his sight cleared in the darkness. At first only the shape of a grease lamp swinging at the end of a metal ring appeared at the edge of his sight.

Nearby, the muffled creaking of a heavy door sliding on its hinges.

The village gates.

Gus opened his eyes wider, the palm of one of his captors still tightly pressed against his mouth. He then saw the face of a man. His sight was troubled, the world turned upside down. The human still recognized the nichan who faced him and who now accompanied Beïka.

Orator Issba.

Beïka and Issba were taking him out of the village.

Gus's blood turned cold.

I'm dead . . .

XXXII

NIGHT AND SILENCE HAD FALLEN ON VISHA SEVERAL HOURS
ago when Domino tiptoed out of the house and climbed up to the
fortress through the sleeping city.

The two guards at the first gate let him in without making a
fuss, as though anyone could invite themselves in, or as if the
young man was expected.

One went to fetch Lienn, who showed up a few minutes later.
Calico was with her, dressed in her armor, her short black hair
messy over her ears. The presence of the second nichan annoyed
Domino. What he had to tell Lienn didn't need to be shared with
anyone else. But Calico kept her gray eyes intensely fixed on him.

"It's late," Lienn said. "Is everything all right?" Unlike Calico,
she didn't seem to have found her way to bed yet. Her complexion
was fresh, her eyes bright.

"I heard my uncle accepted the alliance," Domino said.
"Congratulations."

He couldn't stop the bitterness thickening his mood from
piercing through his voice. This alliance affected him closely. He
should have been invited to the negotiation. But more than

anything else, he would have wanted to be told of Lienn's schemes and marriage plans before his uncle.

"So you know the details?" said the young woman.

"Ero remained vaguer than you can imagine. To believe that he's the one you're going to marry."

"Your uncle wanted to keep this conversation between clan leaders."

"Of course." Domino pinched the bridge of his nose, glanced at Calico standing upright like a post, and sighed. "I'd like to talk to you, in private, if possible."

"I understand. Come with me."

Which he did. Calico, however, followed suit. As they left the vestibule, another nichan left his guardhouse by a door and joined them. Then another. And so on and so forth. As a fifth nichan joined them along a large corridor, Domino halted, his escort and Lienn doing the same.

Behind him, the guards and Calico positioned themselves to fill the entire width of the corridor, blocking the way back.

Domino remained calm, but already anxiety was coming to the fore. "I have the impression that 'in private' doesn't mean the same thing in this region. Is there a problem here?"

Lienn turned around, her face closed, or was it an effect of darkness on her features? "Absolutely not," she said, shaking her head.

"All right. Let me rephrase the question," Domino insisted. "Did I make a mistake coming to see you tonight?"

"On the contrary. I would have come for you myself if you hadn't." He opened his mouth to speak, but she resumed her advance, adding, "I want to help you, but to do so, you have to trust me."

The other nichans followed him closely. None of them touched or pushed him, but their presence alone was like a threat behind his back. His face slightly to the side, Domino kept an eye on his escort. For the time being, the guards' attitude showed only one intention: Domino had no right to turn back and leave. He'd come all the way here and would have to accept what they would give him.

So Domino caught up with Lienn. They climbed stairs less and less decorated. Draughts swept down the nape of Domino's neck. The temperature dropped as they advanced, walking almost in step, quiet. The last corridor they reached was full of matted spiders' webs and dust. The stone floor was crusted with salt. Lienn stopped here and opened the first door on her right. There was no lock, only a rudimentary latch and a beam to block the opening. The young woman entered, and this time a hand led Domino inside. Looking over his shoulder he saw that it was Calico who pushed him slightly, her jaw tight.

Even though his curiosity was growing, Domino began to doubt. If this was a trap, he could already see his doom at the end of the road.

The inside looked unfamiliar. It was a small, arched room carved out of rock. It was neither furnished nor lit, except for the lamps that two of the guards brought with them. Only here and there the remnants of thick rusty nails were embedded in the wall. The floor was littered with bird droppings and feathers. It looked like a cell. But what took Domino's breath away for a moment was the complete absence of a wall at the back of the room and an unsettling view on the emptiness of the dark night. Beyond, invisible at this hour, the sea raged. Its spray had encrusted the stone even more than the smell of birds' excrement.

Lienn stood one step from the precipice and faced the night, her long, blonde hair swept by the furious eastern wind. Domino hesitated to join her. Calico pushed him again.

"Could you stop that?" he said, trying not to let his sudden fear show through. But his heart couldn't be so easily controlled and his pulse drummed in his ears as loudly as the waves bursting below.

He was far enough away from the edge, but knew that whoever would be thrown over that opening would either crash into the sea or into the rocks.

"Calico, leave him alone," Lienn ordered, turning around, and then she laid eyes on Domino. "You're not planning to run away, are you?"

The young man looked back. The nichans were in the way. "I'm a good swimmer, but I doubt I'll make that dive," Domino said, the bitterness rising like bile in the back of his throat. "And I don't feel like I'm going to have a choice if I try to get through the door."

"You'll have it soon. This is not a trap. I promise you that. Come closer."

"I'm fine where I am."

Lienn nodded once. "I'm sure you have questions about the agreement made between your uncle and me."

Your uncle and me.

Domino knew his uncle. He didn't need to be told about the requests he'd made that morning. The Unaan had probably demanded to remain the chief of the Ueto Clan, to command Domino in the battles to come, to choose several of the members of the council that would be born from the merger of the two clans. That sort of thing. Control was all that Ero would always refuse to give up, apart from his children.

Domino didn't care. He had something else in mind. "The marriage, why didn't you tell me about it before you told my uncle?"

"Because you're not the leader of the clan, and it's not your decision to make." That answer froze Domino's blood. Did he really have no say in the matter? "You're not the leader, but you will be," Lienn added.

"That's all very nice, but I'm lost. And apparently, I'm also trapped. If this is a game, maybe I should know the rules first."

"This is not a game, Domino."

"Well that's a relief, because I'm not enjoying myself."

Lienn stepped toward him, a tall figure in the middle of the night. The marks inked in her chin and neck were more striking than ever.

"So here's the truth, as I see it. This alliance means more to me than you can imagine. The man I'm going to marry will be no one's puppet. That man must be my equal, able to think and act on his own free will. He must be a clan leader willing to rule by my side, to fight for my nichans with the same rage that I'll use to protect his. This man will also be the father of my children, and the father of my children must never be at the mercy of an Unaan such as your uncle. That man must be you, Domino."

"And I'm not your equal, nor am I a clan leader."

"Exactly."

He finally understood what she had in mind. He also understood the purpose of this room for such a conversation. The cell was large enough for a good number of guards to surround Domino if he decided to attack. But it was also too small to allow him to transform himself if he wanted to. After all, his handicap could have been a feint, a way to get close to Lienn while making himself look as harmless as a child. Lienn was taking precautions, nothing more natural than that. She had no way of knowing if Domino wasn't as surly as Ero.

"Your uncle is a danger to this alliance," continued Lienn. "He wants to stay in power. Worse yet, he wants to keep you under his control. You, a Liyion, one of the strongest links in our species. Aside from the fact that you won't learn anything about your true nature as long as this man is tied to you, he may jeopardize the most important union our people have known since the Great Evil."

"You want me to leave my clan," Domino guessed, calmer than he would have thought now that the truth had been revealed to him. "You want me to break the blood oath that binds me to him."

"Yes and no."

"Elaborate, please."

"No, because that would take too long. It would take months, maybe more, before your blood was cleared of your uncle's presence."

Indeed. Domino knew that his mother, on leaving the Ueto clan, had long felt the weight of the oath made to her brother pulling her down, making every decision a challenge.

Nichans needed to lead, or be led, whether they lived in clans or in small groups. They felt protected and empowered. Together, they had a purpose and a family. For those who decided to live far from their people, without a leader . . . Domino ignored how these individuals managed to survive. Ako could have created her own little clan and sworn in her sons. She would have only strengthened the bond that already existed between the four of them. But she'd never done it. Domino was too young at the time to ask his mother why. The thought hadn't even crossed his mind.

So he understood what Lienn was getting at. Getting out of Ero's clutches as his mother had done would take too long, if he succeeded at all. Ero would be constantly breathing down his neck, telling him to do this and that, treating him like a child, as he'd always done. Domino dreamed of breaking that bond, of no longer feeling that uneasiness and suffering tearing his guts and heart and bending his spine every time Ero opposed his will.

"Your training needs to start as soon as possible," Lienn said. "This alliance must be announced to my people in the coming days to prepare the village for the changes to come when we welcome yours. So yes, I want you to break your blood oath. You must end it with your uncle tonight."

End it?

For a moment, Domino pictured the worst. Was Lienn planning to go after Ero? And Memek . . .

But his attention moved onto the next of his fears when Lienn added, "Swear me an oath here and now. Break the blood oath that binds you to your uncle."

Domino's breath was taken away and a hot flush of surprise ran down his entire body. "Did I hear right?"

Then the cell door closed and someone barred the door from the outside. The nichans inside lined the walls, ready to react if Domino made the slightest sudden move. If he tried to attack Lienn, her guards would rip his throat open, or would throw him in the ocean.

"If you pledge your allegiance to me, you will be free," she said. "Your uncle will no longer be able to control you. You'll have to pretend to still belong to him until your clan is here, until everyone is safe, but you won't suffer anymore."

"But you'll control me," Domino said in a cold voice. "We met, what? Four days ago? And is it even fair to swear in your future husband? How does that make me your equal?"

"The oath you swear to me will only serve to free you from his grip. Once it's done, you can begin to break your bond with me."

"Of course. You're just gonna let me, right?"

"Unlike him, I won't stop you."

"You spent a few hours with him, and you already know exactly the kind of person he is . . . " He shut his mouth as she took a step in his direction, her face now darkened by something Domino hadn't seen before on her soft features.

"One of his conditions was half of our children."

Domino froze. "What do you mean?"

" 'I want every other of your children to swear the oath to me, to be a Ueto.' These were his words."

Domino licked his lips with his suddenly dry tongue. He recognized the taste of disgust in his mouth. "Did he, now?"

"He considers that it's only fair since he's offering his own pure blood to the alliance."

"Did you accept?"

"What do you think?"

Fury and hate. Domino knew what Lienn felt right now. He felt it too. "I'm going to guess that you refused."

"Over my dead and rotting corpse," Lienn said, a void deeper than the night beyond her silhouette filling her eyes. Her young and soft voice was now threatening. "The first to draw my children's blood will lose their life."

Here's something we both agree on.

This could be a trick, though, he told himself, but the thought was a vain fight against what he already knew. To request the control of his children, potential pure blood. To bargain with their future mother. If the hollow scar at the edge of Domino's eye hadn't been there, he might have doubted Lienn's honesty.

But the scar was there.

"Once you are free," Lienn said, "you can begin to welcome your own protégés. You'll become the leader of your own clan. My equal."

Domino assimilated all this information, struggling to believe what came out of Lienn's mouth. She kept her distance, but he could still feel the determination in her posture.

"You've been thinking about this for a long time," he said.

"Since our first conversation."

"I see. Always a step ahead."

"I know it's a heavy sacrifice to make."

"It's not just my uncle I'd be betraying by doing this. It's my whole clan."

"You are a Liyion, Domino. When you come back to your

people, stronger than ever, they'll understand that it is you they must follow, not your uncle. They'll respect your choice."

Domino laughed despite the tension contracting his muscles and sending unpleasant spasms into his right arm. "You know them even less than you know me."

"True, but your uncle is an easy man to figure out, and I doubt you're the only one in your clan to find his temperament unworthy of a protector."

Another statement Domino could have easily denied. Outside of Mora, no one had ever reacted to Ero's violence. For his clan, Domino was two things: a failure responsible for his brother's death; the boy who had willingly shared his bed with a Vestige for over a decade. Two things worthy of his uncle's punishment. For all Domino knew, his fellow Uetos would kill and die for Ero.

And even if Lienn were right, that didn't change anything. He'd gone on a pilgrimage to change, not to overthrow his Unaan. Yet he wanted this alliance, despite what it would force him to do.

In the span of two months, he'd escaped death by a hair three times. This couldn't happen again. He wanted to control his true nature and protect his people from the approaching threat. Gus, Natso, and Belma. Without the Riskans' help, without his nichan abilities, Domino would be useless. To keep them alive and safe, he was willing to do anything. To marry, to have children with a stranger, to leave Surhok, to fight every individual who would attack his family and threaten the survival of his species.

It wasn't the life he'd dreamed of for him and Gus. In truth, he'd long thought that things would stay as they were, that nothing would separate them, that the two of them would always share the same hut, that they would finish growing up and care for each other. But Domino was different, and that difference demanded sacrifices from him.

This gift from the Gods required constant payment, apparently.

He took several steps in Lienn's direction and then walked around her to look at the sea. In the complete absence of light he saw neither the waves nor even the walls of the fortress. But he heard the tumult of the water and foam bubbling and was completely overwhelmed by its din. In his mind, a void had formed.

"It's funny how everyone seems to have a definite plan for me, but no one ever thought to ask my opinion. Tell me, do I really look as stupid as everyone think I am?"

"Then talk to me," Lienn said in a softer voice. "I'm listening. Tell me what you want."

What I want . . .

He quickly sorted out his thoughts. "No more lies. No more plots behind my back."

"All right."

Domino went on as if he hadn't heard her, still looking at the sea whose surf was denied to his sight. "If we are to raise children together, I want it to be in an honest home."

"All right."

He took a look at her, studying her careful expression. "In case it wasn't clear, I'm talking about you."

"It was clear."

He turned back to the invisible sea. "I'll take responsibility for my betrayal. Anyone who joins me won't know it was your idea. When Ero hears about it, I'll deal with the consequences myself. I'm used to it."

"Why?" Lienn asked.

"You mentioned a puppet. It's a role I don't want," he answered, turning to her, still feeling in his throat the humiliation of being reduced to silence by a couple words from his uncle. "If I accept this plan, which I'm obviously about to do, I won't flee. I'll pay the price if things go wrong. I alone. No matter how hard you pull the strings, there's nothing stopping me from jumping off the edge right now to escape your plans. You want us to be equal, it starts by giving me control of my own life, even if I have to spend the rest of it with you."

They stared at each other for a long time, both swept by the violent night wind. He could barely make out her face in the shadows. He wished he could, if only to get used as fast as possible to the face of his future wife. To know her face well could pass as familiarity.

When Domino remembered the presence of the guards, he licked his lips and sighed. "Anyway, I'm not my uncle, I can admit when I've made a mistake."

"You already consider this a mistake."

"It could become one. I'm not perfect."

"All right."

"I'll need more than that. I still don't know if I can trust you."

"Calico!"

The woman turned her head to her leader and took a step, moving away from the wall against which she was leaning. "Ma'am."

"When Domino has freed himself from the oath that binds him to me, you will give him your allegiance if it suits him. My order is final."

Calico nodded, staring at her chief with serene eyes. "Yes, ma'am. I will."

Then Lienn rested her eyes on Domino. "Calico is my best hunter. She will protect you with her life. I won't go back on that decision. This is a promise."

But Domino knew words meant nothing. It was Gus who had taught him that by proving his friendship to him over and over again through his actions and not with fine words.

"We'll see," he said.

Seconds stretched out, no one spoke. It was time. Maybe it was a trap, maybe it was the worst decision Domino ever made.

Something still told him he could trust Lienn, but nothing was less certain. If he left this room now, he'd never become the nichan he was destined to be. Only Lienn could help him tame who he was. The coming war would crush him and his clan if he refused her offer.

"You will be strong and brave," Mora had told him an eternity earlier. What would Mora have thought of what Domino was about to do?

Lienn took a breath and walked to him.

"Another cut might catch your uncle's attention," she said.

"Yes, he sees everything." She scrutinized him from head to toe. Domino clenched his jaw. Enough of this. "One of the partisans who attacked us hurt my shoulder. You could undo some stitches, draw some blood. The wound is fresh enough. Ero won't notice it." A brief hesitation, then Domino froze, the wind whistling in his ears. "I'm connected to Ero. Will he notice my . . . departure? Will he feel it in his blood?" Domino was suddenly aware of his lack of knowledge on the matter.

"If he truly is the Unaan of a full clan and not just yours—"

"He is."

"How many of you?"

"I'm not sure. Maybe two hundred."

Lienn nodded. "Then you're safe."

"You're sure about that?"

"You'd have to die for him to feel something, but tonight is not the end."

"Good," Domino sighed.

He then untied his shawl, leaving it hanging at his waist, and pushed back the sides of his tunic, revealing his chest and his left arm to the wind swirling into the cell. His skin immediately covered with gooseflesh. Facing him, Lienn turned to Calico who handed her a short knife.

The memory of the sanctuary full of curious nichans came

back to Domino. Ero, gigantic, cutting Mora's skin, then Beïka's, opening the tip of his thumb before joining the wounds, exchanging blood, binding their beings.

Domino rejected this thought as Lienn crossed the few steps that separated them. He knelt down in front of her, before the eyes of the other nichans, still tense and waiting for the slightest sign or change in the air to act. They wouldn't have to.

Lienn cut through the blood-stained threads running through Domino's thick skin. The wound had begun to heal. The blade was soon to reopen it. Domino gritted his teeth, his eyes straight ahead as Lienn spilled his blood. It flowed down his arm, followed the prominent vein curling around his biceps. He didn't blink when Lienn bit her tongue, hard enough to start. Here was a wound that no one would notice.

She slipped two fingers inside her mouth. They came out blood-stained. She pressed those same fingers onto Domino's severed shoulder.

No matter how far they were from Surhok, the words were the same. In truth, the words bore little power compared to the intention itself. "My protection comes at a price," Lienn said. "Swear to obey me, swear to follow me, swear to respect me, and it is yours."

Domino sustained the look in her eyes, forgetting the blood that colored her tattooed lips and chin. "I swear to obey you, I swear to follow you, I swear to respect you, Lienn." He couldn't help but pronounce her name. No title, just her, flesh and bone, like him. A first taste of their promised equality.

The dizziness took him from all sides. A metallic and sweet taste passed between his lips. A nosebleed, nausea, confusion; reactions too strong to be natural. Like the last time, ten years earlier, the oath crept into Domino.

He was about to collapse backwards, straight into the emptiness, when Lienn held him back by his open tunic. Instead of crashing on the reefs, Domino fell face down to the ground, his cheek in the more-or-less dry bird droppings. Hands turned him over on his back and one of them touched his forehead briefly.

"It's done, Domino," said Lienn's voice above him, pressing against the wound in his shoulder with a delicate hand. "You won't regret it, I promise you." Then to someone else. "Jenian, get Melbim for his shoulder. You two, take him to the room near—"

The rest disappeared as Domino lost consciousness. But in his last moments of lucidity, he hoped with all his heart never to regret it.

XXXIII

ONE STEP AT A TIME, BEÏKA CARRIED GUS FARTHER AND farther away from Surhok. Issba led the way, a lamp in each hand breaking through the night's embrace. Tossed from right to left, Gus growled. His gag partially muffled the next of his many complaints. Only the footsteps of the two nichans through the ferns and the forest terrain disturbed the silence. Each trampled branch was a fractured bone, the rolling of rocks like teeth grinding hard enough to become sand. Apart from the golden flames, darkness was absolute, like a trap hiding many more in its depths. The wind rustled the invisible foliage above their heads. Winter walked through Gus's every pore. A thud twisted his eardrums. With each jolt, the pressure of the blood pulsed through his skull.

Tap-tap-tap. The piece of sap still knocked on the top of his forehead. It kept him awake and aware of his new reality.

They're going to kill me. They're going to kill me . . .

It had driven away all of his previous confused thoughts. In Gus, there was no room for anything else but this certainty. Imminent death. Impossible to think, impossible to calm the trashing of his heart. With every step they took away from the village, with every minute that prolonged his torment, he drowned in his own lack of power. Soon he would be released from these dark waters . . .

Gus was going to die.

He flapped his legs, an uncontrolled reaction as his mind and conscience narrowed around this fate. In response, Beïka's arm closed tighter around his waist, bending Gus's ribs. "Stop moving," the nichan said.

The man jerked and repositioned Gus on his shoulder until the human fit the curves of his strong bones and muscles. The force of the movement buried in the human's soft abdomen. As air left his torso, spit rained from his lips, traveling along his jaw.

"Keep control of this thing," Issba said over his shoulder.

"It was your idea, remember? Maybe you should carry the thing."

"We're almost there."

"Where is there?" Beïka asked.

"Far enough away from the village for the others to lose his scent."

"Fuck! We forgot the shovel."

The Orator chuckled. "Vigorous hands like yours will soon get the better of a bit of dirt. Since the abomination is already soiled, his grave doesn't need to be deep."

Adrenaline coursed through Gus's chest.

His grave. Issa had it all planned. In the middle of the immense forest, no one would waste a minute to search for Gus's body. The Orator and Beïka would return to the village without the slightest scruples. Whoever had opened the door for them would let them in quietly. The group would move on from this setback, finding the comfort of their bed, of a good meal, of their peaceful mind that no shame could penetrate. In a few hours, when Orsa realized Gus wasn't ready to hunt, she'd send someone to his hut to fetch him. No one would be found, not in his house, not anywhere . . .

"Here," said Issba. "Yes, it should be far enough."

"Great." Beïka dislodged Gus from his shoulder and threw him to the ground.

The young man crashed without a sound apart from the shocked groan that spurted from his chest. His wings took most of the shock, avoiding the worst to his spine. With his arms finally free, Gus ripped off his gag, soaked in saliva and blood, and took a deep breath. The violent cough that seized him threatened to release his organs through his mouth. Gus clenched his chest and his palm pressed hard against Domino's necklace. Ever harder.

Issba hung his lanterns from low branches and faced him. His face was bathed in darkness, but the flames burning on the surface of the fat outlined the contours of his partially shaved skull, of his bare, square shoulders, and of his hands, which he held in one tight bundle of fingers against his heart.

"Here we are," said the Orator motionlessly. He sighed. "Lift him up."

After a brief, annoyed hesitation, Beïka obeyed. He grabbed Gus by the elbow and lifted him off the ground. He interrupted his gesture, squinted, and his hand fired towards Gus's chest. It seized the necklace, the amber resin disappearing into the nichan's fist. "Hey, that's not yours."

"Don't touch—" Fire erupted in Gus's stomach. The coughing returned, loud and visceral.

Beïka smiled and snatched the jewel from Gus's neck. The worn-out leather sting snapped. "Family heirloom," Beïka said, shoving his loot in his pocket.

Thoughtlessly, having yielded his body to fear and instinct, Gus threw his fist into the nichan's chin. His knuckles met the skin and bone without moving Beïka back even an inch. A ridiculous attack and, in his present state, devoid of any strength.

Before the pain reached his joints, Gus received a punch that immediately sent him back on the humid ferns. His senses swirled, as if in search of a way out of his body. A drilling sound rang in his ears. Pain surged in his cheekbone, invaded his whole face. No more right or left. Blood ran down his face.

Issba uttered an impatient grunt. "Enough of this! We're wasting time. Orsa will be up before dawn, and we must be back before Jaro's watch is over."

"I'm just settling scores with this worthless shit," Beïka defended himself while wiping his chin.

At his feet, Gus clung to the dirt and wet grass. If the situation hadn't been so overwhelming with pain, he would have thought it was a nightmare. He'd been there, he'd faced death before tonight. He'd always known it would come sooner rather than later. Yet, more than ever, he didn't want to die. More than ever, he needed pain to stop.

Domino.

No, he was mad to dare think of him. Domino wouldn't come to save him. No one would come to save him. Gus had asked to be left alone, for good reasons. Now he was.

In the dead silence of the night, Issba cleared his throat. "Get him up and control him. Are you capable of it, or are you as useless as your uncle claims?"

The silence returned, as cold as death itself. Then Beïka bent down and grabbed Gus again, by the neck this time. As he squeezed, he forced the boy to stand on his feet and face him.

"What are you doing?" Issba said, taking a step in their direction.

"You wanted to kill him, yes? Then I'm killing him," Beïka announced.

He held Gus's throat tighter and the boy stopped breathing.

The rope, Gus thought as he tried to breathe, to open his

attacker's fingers. *The rope, it . . . He . . . He's going to kill me. I'm gonna die.*

Issba closed his hand on Beïka's biceps. "You idiot! Stop that at once!"

"What? Changing your mind?"

"I'm trying to save this boy's soul. To clear it of the Corruption. Before the killing, words must be spoken for—"

A scream ripped through the night and Beïka loosened his grip.

After a long silence during which Gus tried to suck in some air, another squeaky scream froze their blood. Beïka opened his hands, and Gus crashed to the ground, too weak to stand on his legs. He coughed and struggled to escape, gesticulating to the best of his ability. For a moment he crawled away from Beïka and Issba. He didn't want to run away like a frightened worm, but for the first time, his survival instincts overcame his resolutions and pride.

I'm not dying. I'm not . . .

"Is it—is it one of them?" asked the Orator, horror in his voice.

"Yes," said Beïka.

Another scream shook the woods, closer. It forced Gus to crawl faster. His hands slipped on the wet vegetation. He fell facedown to the ground, straightened up, and crawled again, searching through his being for the strength to get up.

"We have to run!" Issba said.

"A nichan doesn't run away." On the contrary, Beïka took a step in the screams' direction.

"You fool!"

The next scream froze Gus in place. Suddenly, even the night breeze stopped its whispers. Trembling from head to toe, his breath stuck in his tight chest, Gus made himself as small as possible, his face buried in the plants and rocks. Something was approaching. He could feel it in his flesh, in his veins . . .

As slowly as possible, he turned his head, ordering himself to look over his shoulder. The thing was close—closer than it had been back then, in that cave. Close enough to be revealed by the weak light of the lamps.

This creature didn't look like the one that had chased him and Domino three years earlier. It was entirely gray except for the black splash that hemmed its mouth. It had a small, bald, shiny, chiseled head, resting on narrow, round shoulders. Its long arms hung down beside it, ending in claws on the tips of which the flames of the lanterns glowed.

Bright blue eyes. Shiny veins of the same color mottling its skull and forearms. A dohor.

His face stretched out in terror, Issba grabbed one of the two sources of light. In an instant, he turned on his heels and ran off into the darkness.

Beïka, for his part, faced the tall creature. The nichan had transformed, his skin now black, melting into the night, an aggressive growl flashing between his sharp wide smile.

Dark and huge shapes in the darkness, the dohor and the nichan gauged each other for a moment.

Gus tried to move. Why didn't he move?

Don't just stay here. Move the fuck out of here! Move!

He couldn't.

The dohor then attacked. Beïka parried the first blow by bending down. The claws split the air, whistling an inch from his head. The nichan retaliated with a cross attack. His arm moved faster than the eye could see, flashing the veins protruding from the surface of his arms. His blow missed its target. Not fast enough, not precise enough.

The dohor moved with unsuspected grace. As Beïka attacked again and again, the creature never lost its footing. It swirled, bent, avoided the nichan's hand. For long seconds it did only that and Beïka's attempts remained vain.

Then the dohor struck again. And again. Every time, Beïka stepped back and ducked. Until . . .

The next attack sent blood splattering through the treetops. Nichan blood.

Beïka froze, his throat, chin and lips slit deep. A breach opened in the middle of the tattoo inked in his skin, and more blood spurted out of the wound. The dohor hissed. Then the man lost his balance, and his body fell backward.

It was Beïka's turn to collapse, to crawl. His blood ran out with an endless gurgling sound. He reached out his hand to Gus, who had managed to stand upright. But not to run away.

And then the creature noticed Gus's presence. It took a few steps in his direction, forgetting even the existence of its first prey.

It was approaching, almost twice Gus's height. Closer and closer. Only ten feet to go.

Gus couldn't blink.

Six feet.

Gus struggled to breathe.

Three feet . . .

A sudden discomfort gripped his lungs and heart. In front of him, the creature halted abruptly and took a step back. The pain vanished, as if it never existed. The dohor cocked its head and took another step in the direction of the human.

The same pain tortured Gus again, as if long icy fingers hugged his heart and compressed the raw organ again and again with brutal squeezes, without bothering to match its natural pulse.

His valid wing suddenly cramped. Gus grumbled, hugging his chest with one hand.

The dohor, drooling from every corner of his deformed mouth, did the same. The creature retreated once more and then forced against this ache that they both shared and that kept them far from each other.

More pain.

Gus moaned, nailed to the ground, unable to flee. The dohor bent in two, one of its long-clawed hands scraping the earth, the other reaching out to Gus. Both of them stepped back, cries of agony in their mouths.

A single step in Gus's direction was enough to neutralize them. This proximity put them to the rack.

They were suffering together.

It hurts ... it hurts ... But ...

Whatever that common affliction was, it was the young man's only chance of survival. He had to take it and live. He could use it. There must be a way to survive.

He wouldn't crawl anymore.

A scream escaped him as he wiped his bloodied face and charged the dohor. His discomfort intensified, choking his breath, begging him to stay away from that thing, beating out his eardrums, threatening to stop his heart. He was so close to shitting himself, every organ pushing down, trying to escape the pain. Gus ignored this part of him, this vital impulse, and got as close as he could to his enemy.

The dohor retreated and curled up, its giant stature reduced to a ball of suffering limbs. It belched, held its hollow chest with one vibrant hand, ripped its face open with the other.

Its torment was as agonizing as the one tearing Gus apart from the inside.

Good! Let it die!

It was for the one who would last the longest, the one who would endure the pain. The more intelligent of the two. And unless it killed him first, Gus would hold on.

He pushed again against the pain that pulled him back. He shouted hard enough to break his throat, to crack his dry lips open. He spat, and his blood splashed across the creature's bloated face.

As dark red human blood and whitish dohor's met, the beast whimpered and retreated.

The dohor stumbled against a root and gave up. It turned away from Gus and fled without looking back. Within seconds, the thing had disappeared beyond the rows of trees.

Air finally inflated Gus's chest with burning ease. With tears in his eyes, he wavered on his legs.

If the thing hadn't been around, the young man would have fallen into the dirt and dead leaves. Instead, he remained on his feet. He would stand. Always.

Whistling moans and wet borborygmus at his feet. Holding his throat in one hand, eyes bloodshot, chin and lower lip sliced from bottom to top, Beïka stared at him.

The fucker was bleeding to death.

If Gus didn't do something, if he didn't put his gift to use, Beïka would die. Beïka who had conspired with Issba to kidnap him and bring him here. To kill him.

Far from his people, the nichan had signed his death warrant.

The irony of the situation didn't even snatch a laugh from Gus. He was still in a state of shock, dazed and exhausted, face swollen and dripping with sweat, spit, and blood. The beating, the creature, the drumming of his heart gradually returning to normal . . . In this moment, his world looked like a divine punishment.

But he'd driven the monster away just by standing up to it. And the man who had abused him was dying at his feet.

Gus had never been in such a position of power before.

Ever.

Beïka reached out to him, imploring. The tears in his reddened eyes rolled down his cheeks, mingled with the blood gushing out of his pleading mouth. Gus stepped back, getting out of reach. Two steps were enough. A whimper of agony rose from the body lying on the ground. It wouldn't be long now. Death would come quickly, yet Beïka made one last effort to beg for Gus's mercy. Gus took another step backwards, almost galvanized by the feeling of power growing inside him. The power of life and death.

Then his foot struck something. As he lowered his eyes, spikes of color shone through the darkness. Green and vibrant with life. Bright yellow, almost aggressive to an unprepared eye. And the dark red of blood. Human blood.

Gus's blood.

The young man contemplated the stain for a moment, analyzing with his disoriented mind what lay at his feet.

Knowledge came back to him from the depths of his memory, remnants of stories shared so many years before, of a reality only long-buried men remembered.

As he understood, a faint laugh, barely a breath, slipped between his blood-red lips.

Yellow flowers at the end of thick green stems.

Some fucking flowers . . .

The whole thing seemed to spring up out of the ground where there'd been nothing like it a few minutes earlier. Gus had seen flowers and leaves before. Never that color. Apart from a few rare exceptions, the vegetation since the Great Evil had come in shades of faded black, gray, and brown. Not yellow or green. Colors so rich that they seemed artificial.

And his blood . . .

Gus leaned over and stroked the soft petals with his fingertips. He moved down the stem and then grazed the earth that had been splashed with his blood when Beïka had punched him in the face.

His blood. The plant grew rapidly, its petals and quivering buds still blooming, even in the middle of the night, taking root where the crimson stains fed the soil.

Gus reflexively put his hand to his wounded face. His fingers met the sticky blood clotting around the wound on his cheekbone.

What the fuck? What . . .

He had done this. His blood had done this?

His blood had . . . created life?

This boy is full of the Gods' beauty. This beauty, this Light has been saving lives in this village for more than ten years. Matta's words. Mere beliefs, and yet . . .

Not blood stained by the Corruption. Blood touched by Light. The Light of the Gods.

Light thief. A name sometimes given to Vestiges.

The truth hit him harder than Beïka's fist, even deeper. He was precious. Him. Gus. Not just the Light inside him. He'd healed wounds, saved lives. Now life itself was being born from his blood.

This truth made him tremble, for it came with a realization. He was out of Surhok; Issba had fled; Beïka was no longer a threat. Gus could leave.

He understood that now. He wouldn't go back in that cage.

Not ever again. I don't ever want to see their faces, their houses, hear their voices . . . Domino.

Gus's hand stopped on a flower whose dark heart seemed to scrutinize him like a starry eye.

Domino.

So Gus had seen him for the last time that night, lying next to him, his body still warm and flustered from their passionate embrace. The feel of Domino's lips and hands, of their bare chests pressed against each other had faded.

A memory. A dream. Gus would never bathe in the warmth of Domino's arms again.

There had been no farewells, but perhaps it was for the best.

Gus had to go. He would miss Domino. By the Faces, he missed him so much at this very moment that he could have burst into tears. Domino's voice, his smile, the miracle of his arms and laughter. His presence by his side, the habits and rituals that made their daily life bearable and sometimes . . . beautiful. All that had disappeared, replaced by a bottomless void.

With Domino, Gus had known happiness.

But he wouldn't stay for him. Whatever feelings and memories bound them together, they weren't enough.

Why stay? To become what? To live off Domino, or through him?

Domino was an exceptional person, hope for his people. He had so much to accomplish. The bond that held all nichans together existed between Domino and his people. Their lives were linked. And Gus didn't belong there. A human like him, a Vestige, would never belong with nichans—another truth he'd accepted long ago.

He wouldn't wait for the rest of his life for Domino to need him, for Domino to protect him. Gus deserved better than this life. By lowering his eyes to these flowers, he'd understood this and finally embraced it.

He was going to run away, no matter the risks. He'd never been surer of himself.

He looked away from the colors blooming at his feet and checked behind his back. Beïka's face pointed skyward. He didn't move; his chest didn't rise anymore. Dead.

The air slowly filled with black particles. Soon they would completely cover the nichan's body.

No burying for him. There would appear a spirit.

Gus approached the body and quickly went through its pockets. He found a time-polished silver head, a pair of nam nuts, and a handkerchief. In the other pocket was Domino's necklace. Gus held it with trembling hands.

It reminds me of your eyes, Domino had said. What a foolish dream. Hoping for a better life had led him nowhere. Gus tied the necklace's cords and hung it to his neck. A lesson to remember. To grow up and face reality.

Gus dipped the silver coin in his pocket, tossed the rest away.

Then he looked up at the remaining lantern. The fat wouldn't burn forever. If he wanted to leave he had to do it at once and cover as much distance as possible before daybreak. Tomorrow, the Uetos would notice his absence—and Beïka's—and start the hunt. Gus knew the nose of these men and women. The lead he would make in the coming hours was critical. He also knew how to prevent them from following his scent. Growing up with nichans, he'd learned a thing or two.

He wiped his bloody cheek and nose with the back of his hand. He was barefoot, filled with the cold of the night. It was dark, and there were beasts and dangers in this world that Gus was probably no match for. There was no guarantee that the reaction he'd produced in this dohor would occur in his fellow creatures. But he had to take a chance, even if it led to his downfall.

Freedom sometimes required looking death in the eyes and saying, "At least I fucking tried."

Gus got up, unhooked the lamp and gathered up the rest of his strength and determination. Then he ran off with none other than himself to guide him.

XXXIV

DOMINO WOKE IN A BED HE DIDN'T KNOW, IN THE MIDDLE OF A room he didn't know. Raw beams ran through the ceiling. Hanging from one of them, just above his head, was a string with a shell as large as his palm. The inside of the shell was painted a striking red. The rest of the room consisted of a bench wedged against the wall under the only window there, a hemp rug embroidered with red ribbons, and the bed on which Domino had just spent the night. It was dark and cold. Through the crumpled window panes, the singing of the waves could be heard, like a constant humming.

Lying on his back, the folds of his tunic playing with the bumps of his spine, Domino passed his tongue over his teeth. The taste of blood. Memories of that surreal night jostled against his skull. Lienn's plans, the cell . . . the oath.

He sat up. The shawl usually wrapped around his waist lay at the foot of the bed. His crumpled tunic was open, revealing the long scars hatching the side of his abdomen. Caught between dream and reality, Domino spread his robe farther apart, uncovering his left shoulder. The stitches crisscrossing the surface of his skin were new. The wound itself was swollen but clean. Domino rolled his joint, stretching the flesh and muscle. The pain was minimal, a faint stinging, yet the young man felt the need to measure his breathing.

It's done. Look at that. I betrayed my uncle and my clan . . .

No, not his clan. It was for them, to put all the chances on their side, that he'd consented to this trick.

Apart from a hint of guilt, Domino felt no different. Ten years earlier, when he'd recovered from his fainting after taking Ero's oath, he hadn't felt any different, either. However, today he was connected to a much more powerful nichan than his uncle.

He could still feel Lienn's bloody hand resting on his open shoulder.

Domino pushed back the sheet that kept him warm and closed his tunic before tying his shawl around him and throwing it over his shoulder. Along the way, his other shoulder cramped. A pinch went through the length of his arm, and his fingers went numb. Frozen by a spasm, his hand stilled for a moment.

It's never going to heal, is it? Or is my body punishing me for my mistakes?

A silly thought, he told himself immediately. His shoulder had been damaged in the fall. He was made of flesh and bone and blood. Even if his shoulder's condition failed to improve, the injury was just that: an injury. It was neither a punishment nor a bad omen. Domino repeated it to himself until control of his hand was restored. If he allowed doubt and guilt to gnaw at him today and distract him from his goal, he would achieve nothing and would only lead himself to failure.

He walked out of the room and searched for his way. The corridor that opened up before him was foreign. The fort was huge; he knew only a small section of it. So Domino followed the draughts. Several times he could make out the smell of freshly boiled eggs, but he turned away from them radically when the stench of fish tickled his nostrils. After a few wrong turns, he at last found his way, spotted two guards at a door, and was shown the exit.

Even before he saw its owner, he heard an angry voice that froze his blood.

"What have you done with him?"

Ero was here.

"What do you think we can do to him?" Vevdel.

"Is he here? Is he inside?"

"How could I know? I'm not tracking your nephew, believe it or not. He's free to go wherever he wants. My daughter has given you the freedom to move about Visha as you please, if I remember right."

"So I am going to allow myself to move about your fortress as well."

"Ero, calm down," Domino said.

He crossed the vestibule and arrived at the fort's entrance. Vevdel stood at the gate, a thin, twisted smoking pipe in her hand. Day was breaking outside, and the city already swarmed with brightly awake nichans.

Facing the woman, Ero stood slightly bent, threatening.

He immediately spotted Domino, and his jaw tightened under his beard. "You've been here all night?"

Domino stayed where he was. Putting some distance between him and Ero seemed wise, as if his action from the past night could be read on the lines of his face. "Yes," he said.

"Who allowed you?"

"Myself. I do that sometimes. Choices and things. Who would have thought?"

Ero looked down briefly at Vevdel, who brought her pipe to her mouth, not allowing herself to be disturbed by Domino's presence within the walls of her fortress.

"I suppose you've found him," said the woman, smoke billowing between her lips. "In one piece."

Domino in turn took a look at Vevdel. She and Lienn seemed particularly close. Vevdel was probably aware of what had happened last night but didn't let it show.

Ero walked around the woman and camped in front of his nephew, so close that he wrapped him in shadow, hiding the morning's bluish aura from him. The clan chief opened his mouth to speak but refrained from doing so. Instead, with his lips still half open, he swallowed the air before bending over to sniff Domino.

"You smell like her, like Lienn," Ero said without lowering his voice, not caring one bit about the guards posted at the ends of the room or even about Vevdel behind him. "I smell her. Her scent is all over you."

All inside of me.

Domino repressed a shiver and looked down.

"What have you done?" Ero asked. "Answer me!"

An order. Or was it? In any case, Domino could only assume so, for this time nothing happened to him. No impulse on his will and body. Gone.

Domino almost smiled at the relief filling his chest with unprecedented joy.

Even though part of him was ashamed, the unparalleled relief gave him the confidence he needed to respond. To lie.

"I wanted to know if I could do it," Domino said, looking up.

"Do what?" Ero insisted. "Answer."

Another order, and no reaction in Domino.

"I'm going to have to marry her, have children with her. That's what you've decided without me, isn't it?" said the young man in a low voice, trying to keep their conversation private. "I wanted to make sure I could do it. With her."

He took a quick look at Vevdel over his uncle's shoulder, then looked down, feigning the embarrassment of a young man forced to admit to his uncle—in front of Vevdel—that he'd just spent the night with a woman he barely knew.

"You slept with her?" Ero asked, incredulous in the face of such boldness from his nephew.

Would he doubt it? He'd ordered Domino to speak. So Domino spoke. Ero underestimated his nephew too much to even imagine a betrayal on his part. At least Domino hoped so. He knew he wasn't the best liar.

Without raising his eyes to them, Domino felt the silent guards staring at him. This lie . . . Had he gone too far? To announce in front of them that he'd just had sex with their beloved Unaan . . .

Not the best way to build an honest relationship with my future wife.

"Yes," said Domino, clenching his jaw, daring to look Ero in the eyes.

Ero's eyebrows went to a frown. "You smell of bird crap too. Where did you fuck—"

"I won't go into details, if that's what you're waiting for."

After a long silence, the Unaan chuckled. He burst out laughing and sent a blow to Domino's shoulder. It was the same shoulder that had been used for the oath. Domino didn't flinch at the pain. All that mattered was that Ero believed him.

"What a face you have, boy." The man laughed. "It looks like the mask of shame. As if you've just been trampled on. Not so easy to please a woman without the pheromones of the seasons to help, right?"

He kept laughing in his beard as Domino refused to answer and add to Ero's hilarity. Behind him, Vevdel sighed and turned away from them.

When Ero and Domino left the fort a few moments later, Domino resisted the urge to apologize to Vevdel. He'd fooled his uncle; the lie didn't matter.

He had succeeded. He was free.

Lienn . . .

Or close to it.

THE UETOS LEFT their house before nightfall. Ero, dressed in the Riskan fashion, his chest girdled with black fur, a purple wool tunic falling to his knees, offered his arm to Memek and led her outside. The young woman still couldn't walk unassisted. Her fists clenched, her eyes darkened by black circles, she walked with her head held high, limping with every step.

She, too, had prepared for this historic day. "Once I'm healed, I'll go see if the Riskans have a nice-looking girl in their ranks," Memek had said earlier as her father changed her bandage. Ero had chuckled with a hint of disapproval. "What? We'll be one big clan, soon. Better become friends with them."

"Friends," Domino had laughed, playing with the thick golden rings weighting at the end of his earlobes. He was nervous, there was no denying it.

Memek had flashed him a smile. "I wouldn't be against that kind of friend."

"We have plenty of fine and strong women in Surhok," her father had said.

"Well, thanks to you, I'm related to a lot of them. So no thank you." Domino had laughed and Memek's expression had turned serious, shadowed by the pain. Then she had told her cousin, "Don't fuck this up, Domino. Marry the girl and be a good nichan."

Closing the door, adjusting the collar of his thick blue tunic, Domino stepped behind his uncle and Memek in the main street of Visha.

If no one in the clan had paid any attention to him until now, tonight all the nichans Domino came across glanced at him. The news had been announced the day before. Tonight, things would become official. In Domino's veins, they already were.

As he walked up through the city to the fortress, curious and interested eyes locked on him. Domino felt apprehension and doubt, but also excitement. He could hardly contain it. His whole being was reacting to the approach of his new leader. He hadn't talked to Lienn in days since he'd been sworn in. Tonight, they would both proclaim the Ueto-Riskan alliance treaty.

The young man bowed in greeting to all the nichans he caught staring at him. Most of them, sometimes surprised by this friendliness, returned the same gesture. Although distracted, part of him urging him to quicken his pace, Domino found a way to calm his nerves. He offered a smile to an elderly couple wearing shellfish on their necks, a good evening to the guards who kept the fortress doors open for the crowd.

Most of all, he controlled his breathing. Mora's advice would never cease to be precious to him. Now that he kept a secret that could easily destroy the future of this alliance and everything that bound him to the rest of his family, Domino found the ability to draw strength from it.

No one should control this beast inside me. It only belongs to me. It is mine.

He repeated these words to himself throughout his ascension.

The right doors were opened to lead the way. The others were guarded to deny access to the rest of the fort. Extra skin lanterns shone and hung from the ceilings, casting a warm light on the loud passersby.

As Domino reached his destination, Lienn's aura overwhelmed him before he even realized what room he'd just entered. He looked for her through the lined-up tables and the many lamps hanging from the walls and every beam. A small crowd already gathered around the benches, and a head table at the end of the long room had been set on a platform overseeing the rest of the space. Standing before this table, eyes focused on the entrance, Lienn waited. She noticed Domino and immediately pulled herself away from the nichans conversing with her.

The young woman had tied her fair hair in two intricate braids set with a golden chain and cultured pearls. She had also put a gold ring through her nose that drew even more attention to the tattoos inked on the bottom of her face. Her clothes remained as simple as those the Riskans had given Domino and his, although the purple was a perfect match for the young woman's lighter complexion and ash-blonde hair.

Lienn joined them. Domino smiled at her and found himself relaxing, as if the bond that had recently united them had been stretched too far by staying away from her for several days. He'd never felt this way with Ero, but his uncle wasn't a Liyion.

Although he felt physically more serene, Domino remembered that the sooner he'd be rid of this new oath, the better off he'd be. That Lienn's mere presence had this effect on him was a weakness he found intolerable.

Soon I'll be the only one left in me.

"Welcome," Lienn said as she reached them.

"Riskan Lienn," replied Ero, still supporting Memek with an inflexible arm, then he pointed to the head table. "Is this the table reserved for the clan leaders?"

He wasted no time in politeness. Looking proud, Ero stood there as if he owned the place. He didn't need any details about what was to come. *Nothing could surprise me anymore,* said the jaded look he casted over his host.

Lienn nodded. "My mother waits for you there. Your daughter will naturally sit by your side."

Without thanking her for her consideration, Ero walked away to the platform and the table, guiding Memek.

Domino followed their progression through the room for a

moment and then returned to Lienn. She was staring at him intensely, an impenetrable expression on her face.

"I doubt all your nichans will fit in this room," he said.

"Don't doubt for a moment their determination. They were all invited. They will all come."

"An event that won't happen twice." Domino considered the large room framed by rough stone columns carved here and there with Torb texts. "Even if my marriage wasn't to be announced, I wouldn't want to miss it either."

Lienn smiled. "Your uncle didn't give you too much trouble?"

Domino understood what she had in mind—Vevdel had probably repeated the altercation between her and Ero—and he took it upon himself not to blush. "He smelled your scent on me," he said in a low voice. The hubbub of the conversations and the distance Ero put between them was enough to conceal his words, but Domino preferred not to take any chances.

"You should have taken a bath before running away like a thief."

"A bath wouldn't have made a huge difference. You know that."

"I do. What did you say to him?"

Either Vevdel hadn't told her daughter, or Lienn was testing him for lies. The young woman's question was no order, but Domino refused to lie to her.

He marked a brief hesitation. "I told him we'd spent the night together."

"Spent the night together?"

"Just as we'll do once we're married," Domino said. Facing him, Lienn raised her eyebrows imperceptibly, visibly controlling her reaction. Her mouth shut, slightly tense. "I'm sorry." He was sincere.

He knew so little about Lienn and didn't know her opinion on the matter of such promiscuity before their official union—or even after it. Yes, he knew so little about her and couldn't tell whether he was eager or anxious to change that.

"There's no need to be sorry," said Lienn.

"My uncle was very suspicious. You've marked your territory, after all." This time Lienn really raised her eyebrows and Domino pursed his lips to repress a smile. "Forgive me. I didn't get the time to come up with another excuse as credible as that one."

"It is credible. It's going to happen anyway, right?"

He nodded slightly. "Right."

"Having an intimate relationship with my future husband won't offend anyone."

Domino nodded again and looked away. In that instant, other eyes had appeared in his mind, black and amber eyes whose existence had always been an important part of his life. The nichan swallowed with difficulty. There was still a side of this alliance that he refused to think about for the moment, a part of himself and his hopes that he wasn't yet ready to give up.

"So your uncle is convinced that you shared my bed?"

Domino came out of his musing and laid eyes on Lienn. "I've never seen him so . . . ecstatic. He was overjoyed. He's disgusting." To utter such words without pain left a taste of victory over Domino's tongue.

"And what about you? Did this night of . . . love suit you?" Lienn asked.

She smiled slightly, but barely knowing her, Domino could hardly tell if the young woman was joking or testing him again. So he played the same game, relying on Lienn's shortcomings about him to get himself out of this difficult conversation.

"No regrets so far," he said. "But I'll reserve my final judgement for later. After all, you're still the one in charge."

"Not for long."

To break the oath again, this time without the help of anyone. Lienn.

His betrothed.

He stepped to her side and offered his arm to her, inviting her to join the head table. When Lienn's hand rested on Domino's arm, many voices fell silent and attention shifted to them.

They went up to the stage where Vevdel, Ero, Memek, and another middle-aged nichan waited for them. The others sat down at the tables as the large room filled up again and again, soon leaving no space to move around. Those nichans were there for one reason. It was useless to keep them waiting. The meal would come once all these people were satisfied and gone.

Lienn walked around the table and stood up straight in front of her clan. Vevdel stood as well. Domino and his uncle followed in the next few moments.

The clan leader waited for silence. "On this day, we are preparing for the future," said Lienn. "The Gods have seen and felt our distress. In their infinite Light, they found the strength to thwart the Corruption's schemes. Behind me stands a pure blood, just like me, heir to the power of our ancestors. Ueto Domino." Lienn turned her eyes to Domino and reached out to him. "Come."

Ueto Domino.

A lie. For the last two days, he'd been a Riskan.

Not for long.

Domino complied under the watchful eyes of those who were now his people. He walked past his uncle, not without receiving a slight hug from him on the back, and stopped at Lienn's right. He grasped the hand she held out to him. A long, thin hand. Warm fingers as strong as the jaws of a nichan. For a moment, Domino watched this interlacing of fingers and thought about the last time he'd held someone's hand.

That someone was waiting for him in Surhok, and the urge to lay eyes on him again stole Domino's breath.

He looked up and met Lienn's gaze instead. Although he

couldn't read her, she seemed much more confident and serene than he was. But when she smiled at him, the same smile appeared on Domino's lips.

In one movement, Lienn guided their bound hands toward the crowd. All eyes fell upon this strong and symbolic bond.

"Since the Great Evil, we have struggled, and we have conquered. Today, we are stronger than ever before. This strength will turn into greatness. It will only grow. On this day, the Riskan Clan promises to unite with the Ueto Clan from Surhok. My marriage will be its binding force. Ueto Domino will walk at my side. Our clans will become one. Nichans don't run away." Whispers of assent rose up here and there in the compact crowd. "Our people will even overcome the end of this world." Chin high, Lienn glanced at the crowd, but Domino felt as if she was giving every face the same attention. In this moment, even he couldn't look away from her. "The Gods have blessed me and saved me twice. Now they bless us all. Faces above, bring us the Light!"

Words chanted during the Calling, at the feet of the Prayer Stones. Domino knew them, had shouted them fervently since his earliest childhood. He didn't need to look back to see if Ero and Memek would follow. They would, just as everyone.

"Bring us the Light!" the nichans repeated in unison.

"Bring us the Light," Lienn whispered as if to herself.

"Let it shine on the way," Domino said softly.

Lienn turned her eyes towards him, smiling. She seemed out of breath and, through the storm of hearts beating in front of him, Domino perceived the one of his new Unaan. A clear and steady beat, to which his own heartbeat matched. Part of him wanted to let go of Lienn's hand and break this contact as quickly as possible. Another part begged him to hold on to the nichan, for soon she would be his wife.

"I will fight with all my strength to protect this union," Lienn said to Domino.

Words are worthless. Only actions matter, Domino thought, remembering bitterly the truth he'd learned from his best friend.

Soon the couple was joined by Ero, who grabbed Domino's shoulder with a firm hand. A reminder of two intricate realities.

Ero was in control, or so he thought.

This alliance was born out of a lie.

The cheers of the nichans shook the fortress.

GLOSSARY

Arao: High altitude Holy Land located in the western center of Torbatt.

Artean: Religious book written by the Blessers, following the Great Evil.

Bathia: Multi-purpose plant mainly used for oral hygiene.

Blesser: Sirlhain religious cult created after the Great Evil whose dogma aims to bring back the Gods by destroying the creatures carrying Their light.

Calling: Monthly meeting at the Prayer Stones to praise and thank the Gods for their generosity.

Coroma: Continent composed of Torbatt, Sirlha, Meishua, and Netnin.

The Corruption: Unknown phenomenon that caused the disappearance of the Gods and the alteration of many elements of the world they created.

D'Jersqoh: Country located beyond the southern sea and not included in the Coroman continent.

Dohor: One of the three main dominant species in the world. The dohors are now devoid of intelligence and enslaved to their baser instincts, an effect of the Corruption.

Great Evil: One of the names commonly given to the appearance of Corruption and the simultaneous disappearance of the Gods.

Head (money): Name given to a silver coin (or coin of the highest value) by Torbs. In the country, this denomination applies to any currency, local or foreign.

Kaibalar: A group of mainly dohor (but sometimes human) riders who trained and rode mounts reputed to be indomitable. This order quickly disappeared (all of its dohor Kaibalars tainted and reduced to beasts) as did its mounts, after the Great Evil.

Kesek: Plant with soothing and decongestant properties often consumed in the form of broth or cigar. It is mainly cultivated in hot or subtropical climates.

Kispen crystal: Highly flammable crystal whose fractures are as sharp as razor blades. Kispen's crystal is used among other things as ammunition for flintlock pistols.

Kivhan (or Major): Elected in charge of a Torb village and its council.

Koro: Culmination of a year celebrated by nichans at the summer solstice.

Laranga: Capital of Sirlha

Liyion: Torb contraction of the words "li" "ayi" "yon," meaning "pure blood." Title given to a present-day nichan capable of achieving a complete transformation to their original bestial form.

Matron: Giant crystal deposit having developed its own consciousness. Five of them have been listed in the world. They founded the Santig'Nells Worth to protect the creatures of the Gods. Two of them (Hope and Reason) were destroyed by the Blessers during the siege of Laranga.

Meishuana: Refers to the people and the main language of Meishua.

Myrt: Currency used in Sirlha.

Netnin: Smallest country on the Coroman continent. Located north of Sirlha, it is one of the two countries of origin of nichans (with Torbatt).

Nichan: One of the three main dominant species in the world. Once powerful beasts, the Gods gave them the ability to take human form at will. Since the arrival of the

Corruption, nichans have lost the power to return to their original form.

Nohl: Very large centipede whose nutrient-rich fat is used as fuel, most often for lighting.

Oné: Gold-colored and translucent flesh fruit growing in the warmer regions of Torbatt. Its shape is reminiscent of a human heart and its consumption is said to bring strength and luck.

Op crystal: Rare crystal that sometimes appears on certain burials. It is known to some for its devastating effects on the organism of Vestiges.

Orator: Nichan entirely devoted to the worshipping and memory of the Gods.

Prayer Stones: Monoliths carved by nichans to honor the Gods. It is at the feet of these stones that nichans religious ceremonies take place.

Ponsang: Capital of Meishua.

Riskan: Nichan clan based in the city and fortress of Visha in Torbatt.

Santig'Nell: Humans chosen at a very young age to serve the Matrons.

Sard: Title meaning "the people of the Gods," or "divine people." The inhabitants of the Netnin consider themselves Sards although most other people call them Netninyts.

Seasons (rut): Peak of puberty in a male nichan characterized by a strong desire, a rise in temperature, and the creation of hormones to stimulate desire and pleasure in female nichans. Only sexual intercourse puts an end to the seasons without any risk of physical or even psychological after-effects for the man.

Sirlhain: Refers to the people and the main language of Sirlha.

Spirit: Unknown entity appearing on the location of death of a human or a nichan left unburied. Although their origin is also unknown, their emergence is attributed to the Corruption.

Torb: Refers to the people and the main language of Torbatt.

Tuleear: Refers to the language spoken in the eastern lands adjacent to the Tulleen Sea. It is today the main language of Netnin and north of Sirlha.

Ueto: Nichan clan based in the village of Surhok. Its Unaan is Ueto Ero.

Ukatehontasan: The northernmost large lake in the Osska region.

Unaan: Leader of a nichan clan.

Vestige: Human, animal, or plant developing deformities or gift. The origin of these creatures varies from one people to the next.

ACKNOWLEDGMENTS

I wrote this book alone, but did I? In many ways I was surrounded by a lot of kind souls and kind words (and a messy desk).

First of all a big thank you to my family for their support, especially Laurine, Olivier and Jennifer. Sorry for releasing a book that most of you won't be able to read. You'll have to believe me when I tell you that it's great (or wait for the French version.)

A big thank you to Susan Dennard for all her advice on writing and planning and for supporting me when the art block kicked in. This book wouldn't exist without her dedication and time.

Of course, many thanks to Meredith Spears, Natalia Leigh, and Enchanted Ink Publishing for their work. It's never easy to entrust your baby book to a stranger, yet you made it exciting and simple.

A massive thank you to my Instagram followers! Guys, some of you have been following and supporting me for years, and so many of you were already so excited when I shared the first art of Domino and Gus. Back then I knew these boys would be important to me. Even better, many of you knew it as well and believed in me. Special mention to Meg (after so many years, I'm so happy to still have you around), Kai, Victoria, Richel, Briony, Amelia, Amalie, Ambrine, Cielo, and Joyce for their precious help and kindness.

A thousand thank you to the beta readers of Le Sourire Nichan (because you were all Frenchies). You were so dedicated and helpful, and I'm forever grateful for your help. In your way, you shaped this book.

And Oh My! Thanks to Faecrate for the special edition of The Nichan Smile. You did more than just make my dream come true. Thanks for giving this opportunity to indie authors!

I'm not forgetting you, Heather, you Cheerleader Extraordinaire! We met just when I started to work on this book, and you never stopped being great and positive. Prepare yourself, the next book will hurt (you know me).

And last but not least, thank you, Benjamin, for being here, for being quiet when I need to write, for pushing me to believe in myself when all I do is cry and pout. I love you, and yes, there will be more crying and pouting.

Oh and no thanks to Pimousse because honestly, girl, you only came home for food and pets and... Nah, thanks to you too, kitty cat.